Praise for

THESE IMPOSSIBLE THINGS

A *Today* Show Read With Jenna Book Club Pick

"A fun, witty, sharply observant work…El-Wardany captures perfectly the uncertainty of life in one's mid-twenties… readers will be thinking about Malak, Kees, and Jenna long after they close the book."   —*Library Journal* (starred review)

"The complex characters are well observed and the prose is often moving…Fresh, witty, and insightful, this is an auspicious start."   —*Publishers Weekly*

"Sparkling, incisive debut…While frothy and chatty, with witty dialogue and plenty of weddings and other gatherings that spark interactions among the characters, the book doesn't shy away from more serious issues…This novel is blessed by a light touch and evenhanded treatment of its two generations of characters."   —*Kirkus*

"THESE IMPOSSIBLE THINGS is an addictive portrait of three Muslim friends moving through a pivotal time in womanhood, caught between expectation and possibility, hungry to earn wisdom of their own. Salma El-Wardany deftly reveals searing and poignant truths about the female experience, ones so rarely confronted in fiction. What a gift to be inside this author's mind through the pages of her beautiful and memorable writing."

—Ashley Audrain, *New York Times*
bestselling author of *The Push*

THESE IMPOSSIBLE THINGS

SALMA EL-WARDANY

GRAND
CENTRAL

New York   Boston

Copyright © 2022 by Salma El-Wardany
Reading Group Guide Copyright © 2022 by Salma El-Wardany and
Hachette Book Group, Inc.
Cover design by Shreya Gupta. Cover illustration by Anna Morrison.
Cover copyright © 2023 by Hachette Book Group, Inc.

Grand Central Publishing
Hachette Book Group
1290 Avenue of the Americas, New York, NY 10104
grandcentralpublishing.com
twitter.com/grandcentralpub

First published in 2022 by Trapeze, an imprint of The Orion
Publishing Group Ltd., in the UK.

Originally published in the U.S. in hardcover and ebook by
Grand Central Publishing in June 2022.
First Trade Edition: June 2023

Grand Central Publishing is a division of Hachette Book Group, Inc. The Grand Central Publishing name and logo is a trademark of Hachette Book Group, Inc.

The publisher is not responsible for websites (or their content)
that are not owned by the publisher.

The Hachette Speakers Bureau provides a wide range of authors for speaking events. To find out more, go to hachettespeakersbureau.com or email HachetteSpeakers@hbgusa.com.

Grand Central Publishing books may be purchased in bulk for business, educational, or promotional use. For information, please contact your local bookseller or the Hachette Book Group Special Markets Department at special.markets@hbgusa.com.

Library of Congress Control Number: 2022932277

ISBNs: 9781538709313 (trade pbk.), 9781538709320 (ebook)

Printed in the United States of America

LSC-C

Printing 2, 2024

For my mother, the greatest woman alive.
For my father, for giving me a dad
when I didn't have one.
For Salwa and Tasneem, for lighting up my life.

MALAK

"Do you think Eid sex is a thing? Like birthday sex, but just the Muslim equivalent?"

Malak lifts her head from her books to stare open-mouthed at her friend.

Jenna is lying on her stomach, elbows up, chin resting on her hands, with a look on her face that suggests the question is a serious one.

"Surely Muslims can have birthday sex too," Malak replies.

"That's not what I mean," says Jenna, with an air of exaggerated patience.

Malak is saved from having to say anything as Kees, who has given up studying and is lying next to Jenna, attempting to have a nap, snaps, "Well, she obviously doesn't know what you mean, Jenna, because that's a fucking ridiculous question."

Jenna's only response is to roll her eyes before turning back to Malak. "You do know what I mean. For example, what do you and Jacob do on Eid day? It's a day of celebration and he's always really involved."

Before Malak can answer, Kees interrupts again, snorting with laughter. "Yeah, and by celebration they mean go to the mosque, pray, and eat food with your family, not gag on the end of your boyfriend's dick."

"Oh Jesus, give it a rest," says Malak, finally intervening by throwing her empty water bottle at Kees. "She's not asking you. Go back to sleep."

Kees mutters something not designed to be heard and lays her head back down, the sun resting perfectly on her face.

Malak turns to Jenna, who's waiting patiently for her answer. "Babe, you haven't even had sex yet. Eid isn't for ages and, not that I like to point out the obvious, you're not even with anyone. Unless there's something you want to tell us?"

Kees opens one eye, lifts her arm off her face, and tilts her head up off the grass in interest.

"Obviously not," replies Jenna. "I'm just wondering."

"About what?" asks Jacob, who has just arrived, throwing his bag down onto the grass before peeling off his jacket and immediately lying down to rest his head on Malak's lap.

Kees groans and lies back down.

"Whether Eid sex is a thing," replies Jenna.

"Of course it is; Malak and I have had sex on Eid loads of times."

Jenna sits up in indignation. "Ha! You see, it *is* a thing."

Malak sighs. "He's not even Muslim, Jenna."

"And you're a virgin," says Jacob, frowning in confusion.

"Yes, thank you both for pointing out the obvious," replies Jenna, elaborately gesturing with her hands for what, Malak imagines, is dramatic effect.

"Well, if you will ask stupid questions…" murmurs Kees.

The sparring swirls around Malak and she pauses to watch Jenna and Kees. Wonders if this is how mothers feel when they stare at their children: frustrated but flooded with love.

The last to join their group is Harry, Kees's boyfriend, who bends to kiss Kees on the lips the way you do when no one is watching—softly and with a slight pause—before turning to

Jacob. "What happened? I was waiting outside the library for you."

Jacob sits up with a guilty look on his face. "I'm sorry, mate, I meant to message you to say I'd just meet you here. I came out of the library and saw you chatting to some of your rugby friends and didn't want to disturb you."

Harry narrows his eyes. "You just didn't want to talk to the lads, did you?"

Jacob grins and lies back down. "Absolutely not. Sorry, mate."

"What were you all talking about anyway?" Harry asks, moving the conversation along, satisfied with the answer he'd known he'd get.

"Well," replies Jacob, "Jenna wants to know if Eid sex is a thing."

"Have we ever had it, Keesy?" Harry asks, looking at her.

"It's not a thing, Harry," sighs Kees. "Plus, when have I ever even seen you on Eid? I'm always captive to the human samosa-making chain my mum insists on every year."

"Shall we make it a thing this year?" he asks.

"I'd like to direct your attention back to the samosas, Harry."

"Well, I could come and help make them. Your mum would love me," he replies with a grin.

They all laugh and he looks slightly hurt before muttering that he'd like to try. He lies down next to Kees, who works her fingers through his hair with one hand while she reaches for his hand with the other.

Jenna's phone pings loudly, breaking the sudden silence. Her face lights up and Malak smiles.

"Jenna," she says, "who are you messaging?"

"Ahhh, I thought you'd never ask."

They turn their attention to Jenna, which is how she prefers things. She doesn't need the afternoon sun on her to shine.

3

Malak knows women who hate hanging out with their friends' partners, but, for Jenna, it's two extra pairs of eyes and a willing audience for performances she has been putting on her entire life. Ever since she marched up to Malak and Kees, huddled in the corner of the playground of weekend Islamic school, and suggested faking sickness to get them all out of class, they had been watching her. Even at seven years old, Jenna was exceptional. As she had cried in pain, hysterically insisting she needed Malak and Kees by her side while she waited for her parents, effectively getting them all out of class, she had cemented the three of them as inseparable. Even life decisions, like what university they would attend, had been made as a group, ensuring that their small circle never broke. The boyfriends that had arrived were merely fourth and fifth wheels to Jenna, as well as extra people to practice on.

"So, he's called Mo and I met him online, obviously," begins Jenna, seamlessly slipping into her performance.

"Let me guess," interrupts Kees, "he's a doctor?"

"Not yet," replies Jenna, "but he will be when he graduates. Anyway, shut up. I'm studying to be a doctor."

"That's your first problem," snorts Kees.

"Kees. I'm trying to tell you about the man who could, potentially, maybe, perhaps, be the love of my life, not to mention the sixth and final addition to this group."

Before Kees can respond, Malak interrupts. "Ignore her, Jenna. Continue."

Jenna tilts her head in gracious acknowledgment, every movement a calculated flair, and continues. "He's six three. Dark features. Very beautiful. He's got a jawline that makes you want to lick his face for days. Big hands. You know how I feel about big hands!"

They all nod.

"He's toned and muscled, but not beefy, which is good. Clearly looks after himself and eats well. Oh and impeccable fashion sense! Not a scruffy white sneaker in sight." With a raised eyebrow she looks across at Harry's and Jacob's sneakers, which are white and covered in marks.

Jacob rolls his eyes in unison with Harry.

"Other than his clean shoes and lickable face, does he have any other qualities perhaps?" asks Malak. She has more patience for Jenna's love life than Kees does. Maybe it is the way Jenna so firmly believes that she'll get what she wants in the end. It gives her hope about her own situation with Jacob.

"Well, I only met him yesterday, so I haven't really had time to find out."

"Wait a second," says Kees, interrupting again. "Weren't you supposed to be going on a date with Saleh yesterday? I thought he was still the front runner?"

"Ah!" says Jenna. "Well, I was running late for our date and he got annoyed and left. I thought he was joking but I turned up and he'd actually really left. How rude is that? Mo was around and so I messaged him to come down instead because I'd matched with him earlier that day and I didn't want to waste a full face of makeup or my outfit."

Malak groans. She knows where this conversation is going. Kees has sat up and is staring at her friend.

"How late were you, Jenna?"

With a raised eyebrow and a shrug that shows no remorse, she says, "Two hours."

The boys howl with laughter and she grins at them. If ever there are two people Jenna can count on to be a diligent audience, it is Harry and Jacob.

Kees, with her regimental appreciation for efficiency, and having been on the receiving end of Jenna's bad timekeeping, isn't laughing. "Why are you incapable of comprehending the basic principles of time, Jenna?" she asks.

"I wasn't even that late," argues Jenna.

"No, you weren't. At that point, you'd just failed to show."

"It goes against nature for me to be on time," wails Jenna as she picks up the bag of grapes that sits with the pile of snacks in the middle of their circle and begins stress-eating.

"How does that make sense?" asks Kees.

"Well, I'm Arab, aren't I? We have a genetic inability to arrive at any one place at the given hour. Even though we do try, it's actually physically impossible because we're going against biology."

"Excuse me?" scoffs Kees.

"Yes, babe," sighs Jenna with exaggerated patience as she passes the grapes to Jacob to free her hands up to make her point. "Look, each Arab country has varying degrees of lateness, and the Palestinians are some of the very worst. If you're from Syria, you might only be an hour late to any given event. Seeing as Turkey is half in Europe, they have quite a good grasp of time and are never more than half an hour late. If you're from Sudan, you're bound to be at least three hours late, and as you get to Egypt it gets practically impossible because to them time isn't a real thing, just an illusion. They'll turn up four hours late and consider that punctual. Because Palestine shares a border with Egypt, all that lateness just rubs off on us, so we too are always late. So actually, me being two hours late is technically early, so I honestly don't know what his problem was."

Kees stares at her in disbelief, questioning both Jenna's thinking and her own choices which have led her to be friends with someone who would employ that kind of logic.

"That's the stupidest thing I've ever heard. Malak, can you talk to her?"

Malak has been desperately trying to control her laughter but also to stay on the sidelines of this argument. Jenna, in full actor mode, is mostly entertaining because it annoys Kees so much. Diplomatically she says, "But you're half-British, Jenna."

"So?"

"So, according to your geographical allocations of lateness awarded to each country, your British efficiency should count for something. Seeing as the English are always early, the British and Palestinian should just cancel each other out and technically you should be bang on time to everything."

Kees shoots her a skeptical look.

"Ahhh, I'm afraid it doesn't work like that," sighs Jenna mournfully, flopping onto the grass next to Harry. "The Arab gene is dominant and so it overrules the British desire in me to be on time. Truly it does. I've tried over the years but alas, it's out of my hands. You can't fight the genetics God gave you."

"But your mum is English," laughs Malak. "*They* are the genetics God gave you."

"I know," Jenna adds, "but after seven years in Palestine, all the Arab ways seeped into her, like osmosis, and now she's barely on time to anything."

"You're an idiot," says Kees.

Jenna is unfazed.

"But Saleh is Jordanian," says Malak, adamantly trying to work to Jenna's logic. "They share a border with Palestine, so how come he didn't understand the genetics theory and wait for you?"

"I know," exclaims Jenna, leaning up on her elbows in indignation. "That's what I thought, but that's what assimilation will do to you. He's a traitor to his kind and if he wants to play the colonizers game, that's on his shoulders."

Even Kees grins at this as Malak continues to egg her on.

"Again, one side of your family is British. Doesn't that make you the colonizer?"

"And yet here I am. I'm basically the entire resistance at this point."

"Not up for dating a British boy, then? Look at Harry and Jacob. They're way better than some of the weirdos you've made us meet."

Jacob reaches for Malak's hand and kisses it lovingly. "I'm sure that was intended as a compliment, baby, but you really should work on that."

Harry nods in agreement. "We're not royalty, but I think it's fair to say we're a little higher up the chain than some of Jenna's dating misfits."

Malak waves them both quiet. "Oh, shut up. Jenna knows what I mean."

"I do." Jenna nods. "But if there's any way you think I'm ending up like you guys, you're mad."

"Hey!" laughs Jacob. "Harry and I aren't that bad."

Jenna reaches for Jacob's hand, giving it a quick squeeze, her face suddenly serious. "You're two of the best men I know—my favorite, in fact—but you're still not Muslim and you're still white, and no matter how great you are, it won't make you less white and more Muslim, and I see the way it splits the four of you in half. I see the way you all love each other and it still doesn't make a difference. You love in secrets and whispers and in made-up university trips just so Kees and Malak can spend a weekend with your family. Then they go home to parents who don't even know your name. So yes, you're the best of men, but I won't condemn myself to fall in love with someone I can never be with. My mum would kill me if I brought home a non-Muslim."

8

And just like that the laughter disappears, the boys sink back against the women they love, their hands reaching to fill the spaces words can't.

The silence lasts a minute before Malak quizzes, "But your mum wasn't Muslim when your dad brought her home, surely she'd understand better than most?"

Jenna rolls her eyes and shrugs. "Osmosis, babe."

Kees, who no longer wants to think about being in love with someone you can't bring home, leans up and says, "I'd like to remind you, Jenna, that you once went out with a man named Mohanned and all your friends called him Mohammed because they couldn't grasp the difference, and who wouldn't look you in the eye because he thought it was disrespectful, and then proceeded to wear gloves every time you went on a date just in case your hands touched and he went to hell. So you don't have that great a deal either, babe. You spent that whole relationship feeling like a leper and staring at the top of his head while he stared at your shoes. Hardly a recipe for romance."

Their laughter split the air and, in a heartbeat, lightness was back. It's always easier to laugh about things than to cry about them.

The afternoon stretched out ahead of them and the heat made Malak drowsy. It was a cruel paradox to be bent in study during the summer months. She had gotten used to long summers and no responsibility during their undergrad years, but graduation had come and the prospect of leaving while Jenna completed a longer course and Kees stayed on for grad school was more than she could stomach. And so she clung on to the halls of academia in the form of a Masters, ensuring that their circle remained unbroken for one more year. Sometimes she recognized that they were all existing in a perfect moment and, eventually, it would have to end. Other times, it felt like it would always be this way.

This was one of those times. Bodies sprawl across the grass. Laughing away fears too big to talk about. Jenna's theatrics making them feel okay about the things they weren't actually okay about. With summer unfolding before Malak, the heat hazing her vision into dreams, everything seemed so possible. The smell of happiness clung to everything. The precipice and threat of change, of responsibility and full-time jobs, was too many tomorrows away to think about today. She yawns and feels her eyelids meet, her body sliding down to join Jacob's on the grass. Kees continues to argue with Jenna, practicing to be the lawyer she is training to become. A handful of blossom drifts over their heads while weathermen report on record-high temperatures. The city has never looked better and the university buildings that sprawl across every corner shine white in the sun, their spires resting across a perfect sky. In the suburbs, a woman stares at the view while rocking a newborn baby who has finally stopped crying and believes, for the first time, that she can do this. Two streets away in a bakery a couple of strangers meet for the first time; later they will tell their friends that maybe you can fall in love at first sight. Students work from corner tables in coffee shops, each one believing that the rest of their life is just about to start. Mo takes his latte from the barista and smiles at his phone. He feels more like himself than he has in a long time. Four blocks away Saleh stares at the woman he'll marry one day and is ecstatically happy that his date didn't show up last night. A cleaner gazes out the window at the group of friends on the grass and is excited he's saved enough money to fly his children to him. The breeze slowly makes its way through everyone and they all believe in utopia, at least for a moment. Malak smiles to hear the bickering around her and hope is full and round in her mouth. She can almost taste its sweetness, which is why, later that night, when Jacob leaves her and utopia becomes a mere philosophy to be scoffed at, it sends a jolt through her so sharp that, for an instant, she could swear her teeth shattered.

BILQUIS

Kees goes home for the weekend and tries to pull the sins out from between her teeth before she gets there. Tries to be the fever dream her parents had imagined when they sat in their village on their wedding night and England was just a story Grandma used to tell between mango stones and pumpkin seeds.

She has her grandmother's hands. Big and weathered, and no matter how much cream she smooths into her lifelines, her life doesn't get any softer. The women in this family are made of hard things.

She walks the forty-five-minute journey home instead of taking the bus because she needs time to find the version of herself that will please her mother the most. The one that will keep the family whole and bright-eyed, free of any shame that could cloud them over. The version of an eldest daughter that will keep the family chin high above their chest.

Her long hair swings with the wind and is freer than she feels. Her brown skin still smells like the almond oil Umee used to rub into it, even though at least two blood moons have passed since she last sat at her mother's feet and Kees feels harder than she used to. It's also getting increasingly difficult to find the right version of herself to bring home.

She manages to find the correct one somewhere between the park and the laundromat around the corner from her childhood home. The Kees that got stuck in time, somewhere between the ages of eleven and sixteen. They were probably the years she was exactly, wholly, and totally everything her parents wanted her to be. Diligent. Studious. Ambitious. Serious.

She is still those things, but other sides of herself have crept in over time. Rebellious. Loving. In love. Sexual. Things that you don't talk about around the dinner table or even within the four walls of a home that has wrapped itself in silence.

Some people are careless with words. Use them often and recklessly. Throw them around as if they'll never run out. In this family, words were the last grains of rice at the bottom of the bag. The scraping out of the butter dish. They were just like the pennies her parents carefully and covertly collected every month in the hope that they would eventually turn into a bigger pile of money that could save them all. Kees didn't know if the words they were saving would ever come out, and how maybe, if they had used them more often, they wouldn't need saving in the first place.

In this house, things were said differently. There was a mug of tea that was always waiting for her father. It said, here, I love you. The family meals that were always on the table said, here, we care about you. To ask how you were was to complain that you'd been in the bathroom too long. To say I love you was to shout that you didn't look both ways when crossing the road. Love came under the guise of anger and rough voices, which didn't make it less loving, it just held a different shape.

Kees turns her key in the lock and steps through the front door just as her father steps out of the sitting room to greet her. His armchair is perfectly positioned to watch both the latest drama coming out of Pakistan on the television, and the gate to their home. He's watched all his children come up that garden path as they were growing up and knows exactly how long each one takes from street to door.

"Beta, how was the journey?" he asks, as she bows her head for his hand to rest briefly on top. With her books tucked under one arm, she leans in and puts her other arm around her father in an awkward hug. He never likes it. Always breaks away as soon as possible but she does it anyway.

"It was fine, Abaji. The first train was canceled, as usual."

"They need to put someone better in charge of running the country and maybe the trains would be on time."

"I agree," she replies, laughing. "I think you should run for prime minister in the next election. I'll be your campaign manager."

Her mother walks out of the kitchen and catches the last sentence while catching her daughter in a hug. "Bilquis, stop filling your father's head with politics. It's bad enough he goes to the council meetings every month. You'll be getting him to run off to Westminster soon and then where will the family be, huh?"

Before Kees can answer she catches her sister's eye, who is walking down the stairs to greet her, and they both roll their eyes behind their mother's back.

"In a better position with more money, Umee. That's where we'll be if Abaji works in government," interjects Saba, who pulls Kees to her in a hug.

"Are you ready? She's about to go off on one," whispers Saba, giggling in her ear as she squeezes her.

Before anyone can answer, Kees's younger brother opens the front door, hitting their father on the back, which earns him a swat around the head from their mother. "Hakim, be careful with your father. Why are you always stomping around like a buffalo? You'll kill him and then he'll never be prime minister, heh." She marches off to the kitchen muttering about politics and how it always ruins the dinner.

Kees laughs at the confused look on her brother's face.

"Are we talking about Abaji going into politics again?" asks Hakim.

"Of course we are," replies Saba. "Kees is home, what else would we be talking about?"

"Hey, I didn't even start this," laughs Kees, "Abaji brought it up."

"Give it a rest," groans Hakim while mouthing a swear word over their father's head.

Itasham knows his son too well and automatically turns to clip him over his head. "Don't swear, Hakim."

Kees laughs and pulls her brother into a hug. "When did my little brother get so tall? Stop growing up so fast."

Hakim groans again and pulls himself quickly out of her embrace, but not before squeezing her hand and grinning in a way that says he's glad she's home. It's been six months since she's been back, which isn't that long, but it's too long, given that she only lives an hour away, and the familiar guilt begins to take its place in her stomach.

Saba reaches over and gives him a third clip around the head, just because their father is standing in the middle of them all and it's one of the few opportunities she has to do it without getting a harder punch back from her younger brother; Saba is one to always take an opportunity when she sees it. In typical fashion, Hakim shouts for their mother, which earns him another hit from all three of them, who tell him to stop being a mummy's boy. A further yelp from Hakim sends their mother charging into the corridor to deploy orders, reminding them that at this rate no one will eat if they don't make themselves useful.

The prospect of not getting fed within the next half an hour is a sobering one and they all rush to help. Hakim gets each person's drink preference out of the garage without having to ask what anyone wants. Saba pulls plates from cupboards. Her father begins to clear a space on the floor and Kees smiles. In the moments between her father's aspirations, her mother's scolding, and the teasing of siblings, Kees wonders how a person is expected to choose between family and love. As if the two things were mutually exclusive. As if they weren't born of each other and part of the same breath. She begins to think about Harry but before she has time to feel heavy, her father is at her arm, guiding her into the kitchen and asking her opinion on the latest speech from the Labor Party conference and what's the insider gossip.

"Abaji, you know I just joined online. I don't have direct access to the MPs and I definitely don't have time to attend the actual conferences."

As usual, her mother insists that Kees makes the roti when she's home and although she never says it, she's glad. She washes her hands, rolls up her sleeves, and begins rolling out the dough between her palms. She's been doing this since she was ten, when she begged to be allowed to make the roti for the family, standing up on a stool as her mother taught her how to roll the perfect circle, slap it between her hands, and then put it on the flat pan to cook before throwing it on the open flame to puff up. This is a dance she's been doing all her life.

In these light balls of dough is a heavy tradition of women who have come before her. Each young girl craning her neck around her mother's quick movements and flashing gold bangles as they learned how to make the family bread. Her mother once stood just like this with her mother and her mother before her, and in the passing down of something so simple, Kees has always found great comfort. She likes to think that somehow, even in the smallest of everyday tasks, she is connected to tribes of women who have all kneaded dough and silently folded love into their families.

It's also the time reserved for Kees and her mother to chat about the day. Saba has never been interested in making roti and Hakim was never asked, and so the half hour before dinner is their time.

She makes the roti now without thought. It has long since become muscle memory, each turn of the bread stamped into her ligaments so that even when she forgets, even when she's tired, the bread is still made perfectly round.

Her mother takes her chin in her hand and turns it to face her. "Beta, you look tired and skinny. Why aren't you eating?"

Kees laughs at her mother's sternness and wonders why anyone in this family can't just say, "I'm worried about you."

"I'm eating so much, Umee. All I do is study, which means lots of revision breaks, which means snacks."

"Snacks, eh? I'll make some proper food this weekend for you to take back."

Her mother makes this statement as if she had planned to let her daughter go back to university without a bag full of curries ready to be frozen.

"Okay, Umee, that would be nice." There is no point in telling her mother not to go to the effort, because she'll always go to the effort. Plus, she'd be stupid to try to refuse her mother's cooking. It's better than the beans on toast she's been eating recently.

They all eat together, food laid out on a cloth on the floor, and talk about the things that mean something but also nothing. Who's getting married and what happened at the mosque. As usual, as soon as the meal is over, Kees's mother packs curry into old margarine tubs, wraps roti in tinfoil, and sends Hakim with the food parcel to the next-door neighbor, Mrs. Carson.

The house is quiet as Kees sits on the bed in her childhood room, staring fondly at the Bollywood posters on the wall. They're the dreams of a different life when she and Saba used to practice the dance routines from the films and reenact scenes in the garden.

She makes sure the door is closed before calling Harry. He picks up on the second ring.

"Hey, baby," he says, a weariness in his tone. She's back home and that's often the same thing as going back in time. The rules of your adult life, the days and nights spent away from your mother's hip, suddenly fade and you're somehow reattached to her, as if you never left. Sometimes that's a comforting thought but mostly it's suffocating and sad. Like time will never move on for you.

"Do you think they'll get back together?" she asks.

She's already asked him this question numerous times over the last few weeks and knows there is no good in asking it again but still can't help it and here, back in the family home surrounded by her family, it feels even more urgent.

He knows that this question isn't really about Malak and Jacob. It's about him and Kees and whether they'll make it. She's asking if he'll accept her enough and if she'll compromise enough and if, against all the odds, they can love each other.

He gives her the only answer he can and says he doesn't know. Because he doesn't. And in moments like these, there isn't much else to say.

She can hear Saba running up the stairs and so she quickly ends the call, throwing her phone across the bed like a thief caught stealing.

Her sister runs into the room and jumps on the bed next to Kees.

"So, can I tell you something?"

"I've got a feeling you're going to anyway," Kees replies, grumpily. "And why are you sitting on top of me? You have no concept of personal space."

"I'm in love," blurts out Saba, ignoring her older sister's reprimands.

Kees stares at her, mouth swinging slightly open, and replies stupidly, "How can you be in love?"

Saba rolls her eyes. "Well, you see, we're not all heartless, cold, and devoid of emotion like you."

Kees bites her tongue and wonders, not for the first time, if she's kept her boyfriend hidden too well. Created such a false persona of disinterest and disdain for love in the hope that no one in the family would ever ask her, and now she's taken it too far. She never had the romantic outpourings or the urgent hunger for love that has followed her sister around her entire life, but she thinks cold and heartless is a stretch too far.

Now isn't the time to prove her baby sister wrong, however, and so she settles for playfully hitting her. "But what do you mean 'in love'? Do you even have a boyfriend? You're nineteen. You're too young."

This last comment earns her a withering look from Saba, who loftily explains, "Kees, I've been in and out of love my whole life. This is not new."

Kees snorts sarcastically at the idea but, thinking about it, she thinks Saba is probably right. It started when Saba declared her undying love for Shahrukh Khan when she was ten and, ever since then, there has always been someone—the latest Bollywood star, the boy from Quran class, their cousin from

Pakistan, one of the neighbor's sons...Saba fell in and out of love quicker than the seasons changed and she enjoyed every minute of it. If there was ever anyone ready to be in love, it probably was her.

Attempting to be a rational and supportive sister, Kees picks up her mug of tea, sips on it quietly, and becomes determined to say the right thing.

"Okay, so how did you meet?"

"The matchmaker introduced us. I told Mum and Dad I wanted to marry a few months ago and I've been meeting people ever since."

Kees's attempt at being supportive flees as quickly as it came and she chokes on the tea, screeching, "The matchmaker?"

Hakim sticks his head around the door. "Guess you've told her, then." He grins at Saba.

Kees curses the thin walls of their tiny house, offers a prayer up to God for having given her the good sense to move out to university, and tells Hakim to get lost.

"Are you crazy? You can meet someone naturally without all that. You're beautiful and young and have loads of time. It's not like you don't have options."

"Yes, but I want to meet someone from the right family."

"What the hell is the 'right' family, Saba?"

"Someone who's Muslim and Pakistani and good and kind and who our parents approve of. I'm ready, Kees. I'm not like you. I don't care about politics or being a lawyer."

"Who said you had to be a lawyer, Saba? You can have any career you want."

"I'm not really interested in a career. I want to have babies and kiss their fat little feet and feed up the people I love."

"You can't even make roti and you've never learned to cook. What are you going to feed them?"

Her sister looks hurt. Kees reaches for her hand to squeeze an apology but Saba snatches it away.

"It doesn't matter. Umee says there's enough time to learn and she'll teach me. By the time babies come I'll know all the dishes."

"And what about before you have children?" Kees replies angrily. "When it's just you and him and you don't have a career. You're going to just sit at home and wait for him while learning to cook dhal?"

"Of course not. I'll finish university."

"And then what?"

Saba blushes. "I'll probably be pregnant by then."

Their mother's shout for Kees to come downstairs interrupts her before she can say anything else.

Walking into the sitting room, Kees turns to her father and says, "This is why you wanted me to come home this weekend, isn't it?"

"Yes, Beta," he replies. "The rishta is coming tomorrow and we want the family to meet everyone. But we also wanted to check if you're okay with Saba getting married before you."

Her mother snorts in disdain and Kees thinks this is where she got it from.

"Leh! Of course she's okay with it. She has her head in charities and politics all the time. She even has a book in her hand now. She doesn't even think of these things."

Kees thinks bitterly that now is not the time to prove her mother wrong by telling her she thinks about whether she'll be able to marry the man she loves most of the time.

"Beta?" asks her father. "It would be good to know what you think. We've always trusted your opinion."

★

Some evenings demand you walk through them. You can't get on a bus or in a car because then you'll miss it. Miss the exact moment the changing summer sky turns from blue to pink to black.

Kees walks home from the station even though her bags are heavy and even though she's weighed down by the margarine tubs of curries her mother has neatly packed up ready for her freezer. She shifts the bag again and keeps walking, chin slightly tilted up as if ready to receive a blessing.

Her sister is getting married and life is changing. She wants to make it stop. To stop the sky from turning, the summer from ending, and her sister from leaving the small, cramped home they all grew up in, to live in a far bigger house with a new family and new ways of doing things. She's young, she should like change, but she never has.

She twists the key in the lock and pushes open the door, already knowing that Harry will be inside. He has his own flat but he also has a key to her small studio and prefers to spend the nights here where there are no noisy flatmates to bump into in the kitchen in the morning. When she first moved into her own space, she told him that they couldn't spend every night together. It would weigh on her too heavily but it's funny how quickly you can reconcile your conscience when you're in love. Now she never says anything. She'd prefer to have him here than not and tonight she's glad he is.

He's lying on the sofa watching a documentary and as she walks into the room, he swings himself up, grabs her bags, and takes her in his arms.

He quickly scans her face and says, "You're sad. What's wrong?"

"I'm not going to make a very good lawyer if my face is that easy to read," she replies.

"Well, it's just me and I don't plan ever to be on your opposing counsel," he says.

"Saba is getting married," she says, leaning her forehead on his chest.

He doesn't say anything and she's glad. He just picks her up, takes her to the sofa, and begins to undress her gently. Each piece of clothing he peels off he replaces with kisses until she is naked and on top of him and the evening is blowing through the open windows and the city is alive beneath them and weddings and in-laws don't matter anymore because dusk is always the best time to believe in magic.

Later, as their mingled sweat plasters them to each other and their breathing has slowed, Kees feels a hot tear slide down her face and although she doesn't feel like crying, she knows there are too many emotions on the inside and whether she likes it or not they will come out of her any way they can. You can't stuff so much sadness into a body and think it can be contained. Like water running to the sea, it will always find its level.

"Everything always happens for a reason, doesn't it?" she asks Harry, her words muffled against his chest.

"Yes, it does," he murmurs into her hair.

"So, there *has* to be a reason God brought us together."

"Well, maybe we're just made for each other," replies Harry.

"Well, if we're made for each other, making me Muslim and you Catholic is what, exactly? His idea of a joke?" she asks bitterly.

"Hey, hey, come here," says Harry, swinging himself up and taking Kees with him.

He places her legs on each side of him so she's wrapped around his body. Lifting her chin and pushing the hair back from her face, he looks into her eyes and she knows they're full of anger, because it's easier than worry.

"You and I *were* made for one another," he says. "We believe in the same God, Bilquis. We're not praying to different people; he hears us both. We just choose to worship him in different ways. And it's not easy, but if the hardest thing for us is that you're going to the mosque while I'm going to church, then I reckon we're pretty damn lucky. Because that's nothing. Yes, your parents and family and the entire community won't like it, and there's plenty of people on my side who will hate it too. The Catholics don't exactly have a reputation for tolerance. But you'll come to church with me on Sunday and I'll come to the mosque with you on Friday and, eventually, all the bullshit and the arguments against us will just fall away. And in fifty years, some young kids from two different worlds are going to be sitting just like this, madly in love and wondering how on earth they'll ever tell their parents, and one of them will say, 'Yeah, but look at Bilquis and Harry, they did it and no one even cares now and look how happy they are.' The drama always quiets down eventually and when it does, I'm still going to be here with you."

As he finishes talking, she feels the salt sliding down her face and instead of saying anything back she kisses him hard on the mouth. At this point, what good are words? And she doesn't know what to say anyway. She doesn't even know if her tears are for him, for herself, or for her family. What Kees does know is that somewhere along the way, no matter what decision she makes, somebody's heart is going to crack.

MALAK

The morning arrives, halting and jarring to her eyes, and, for the first time in her life, Malak curses the sun. The pale autumn light isn't strong but it's bright enough to make her wince. She can hear the house is already awake and she feels like she's late for a day that doesn't care if she's there or not. She's learned how to hate the morning over these last few months. She despises how it brings another day that doesn't have him in it.

As has become her routine, she stumbles to the bathroom, washes, and returns to sit in her bedroom on her mat, back pressed against the cold radiator with the Quran in her hand. She's been doing this for weeks and the lifeless green book hasn't brought the peace she thought it would. Staring at black letters that she knows only from memory and endless hours in Islamic school, she reads the Quran every morning, looking for answers in a language she doesn't speak.

Today feels harder than yesterday. Like she's spent the night being run over by a truck and now has to knit her bones back together to go about the day. She knows they'll break again in her sleep tonight so doesn't know why she bothers.

She completes her morning prayer. Bends down and touches forehead to mat. Submits to God and wonders where the fuck he is and why he isn't making this easier. If you leave one man for another, it's supposed to feel better than this. There is a part of her that knows it doesn't work like that but she's angry anyway. Furious that life hasn't unfolded for her, that the birds aren't singing and worship isn't flowing through her veins. She's going through the motions and trying to give her whole heart to her faith but it's hard to give something that you're not entirely sure is yours to give.

The familiar stinging flutters behind her closed eyelids and she rises from prostration, trying to drag her mind back to the words she should be saying. It is in the middle of declaring there is only one God and the Prophet Muhammad is his servant and messenger that her tears begin to fall. She isn't sure if they're tears of anger because, for all the times she's bowed down these last few weeks, the creeping sensation that it might not be worth it is still there. Maybe she's just sad and misses Jacob. Maybe it isn't about God after all.

The night it ended didn't happen the way she thought it would. The sky wasn't filled with thunder. No one cried. No one screamed. No one fought. It was a conversation that could have been had over dinner, the summer evening as amicable as they were.

He suggested it, she ended it, and although the breakup was mutual, it was an unexpected specter, slipping quietly unnoticed through the door. The evening had pushed away the day and they had sat in his bedroom, limbs entwined, watching reruns of a show she couldn't remember the name of now.

When she'd asked him why he'd brought it up in that moment, he had said, "It's just hard."

She agreed. "It's always been hard."

"I know," he replied. He looked unsure of himself. As if he'd just lost sight of her in the crowd and was wondering how it had happened. "It hurts to love you this much and know it doesn't end well for us," he said. But he was wrong about that. They had ended many things together and done it so well. Ended days in each other's arms. Ended each other's sentences. They'd celebrated the end of three whole years together. They'd ended arguments with laughter and ended tears with kisses. No. They definitely knew how to end things.

She got up then, kissed him goodbye, and took a taxi over to Kees's house. She couldn't go home as she'd already told her mum that she was staying the night with Kees and heartbreak still had to abide by the rules and logistics of secrecy.

Kees had barely said anything. She'd told Harry to sleep on the sofa and had brought her into bed with her. Cuddled her as all the tears Malak had held in began to soak through the bedsheets. That was the night she thought she would never stop crying. Kees didn't say a word. Just cried with her, knowing that some sadness is too big to squash into sentences, and Malak was thankful. They both knew that in the morning they would all have to go back to pretending so now was the time to howl.

With her forehead pressed to the mat, leaves blowing against the window and empty days stretching in front of her, Malak feels hollow. She shakes her head, finishes her prayer, and stands up. Another prayer down. Still no closer to God.

She's spent time in the mosque. Volunteered at a soup kitchen. Helped her mother around the house. Picked her father up from work. Given herself to causes bigger than a broken heart, but most days she still finds herself wrapped up in a duvet staring at old pictures of herself and Jacob, or staring at the wall. The life she is living feels stale. The only times she's managed to feel better were when Kees came and got into bed with her, laptop balanced on cushions, relentlessly studying while

Malak, on her phone, idly zoomed in and out over different countries on the map, wondering what it would be like to exist in another place. Or when Jenna dragged her to the spa because in Jenna's mind there wasn't anything that money couldn't buy that wouldn't eventually make you feel better. Malak mostly felt alive when they were both beside her, teasing each other, but the minute they left she felt herself floating and unanchored, once more scrolling across the tiny globe in her phone.

Walking into the kitchen, she finds the scene that is always there: her father brooding over the newspaper, Nile TV on in the background, while her mother talks on the phone to one of her friends. She can never understand how they are always on the phone. Didn't any of them have work or jobs to do? Her older brother, Samir, is ironing a shirt while stopping every few seconds to reply to messages on his phone. She can tell from the stupid look on his face that he is messaging Elizabeth and, for a second, she hates him. Hates that he is with her and doesn't have to ever break up with her if he doesn't want to. Hates even more that their parents know about her and occasionally invite her over for dinner.

"Elizabeth, like the queen," her father had said when he first met her, and everyone had laughed, including Malak. Except now it didn't seem so funny anymore.

Samir looks up and smiles sympathetically at her, which means her eyes are puffier and redder than normal or else he wouldn't have noticed. She feels guilty for feeling angry toward him.

"*Sabah el kheir, Baba*. What's going on in Cairo?"

Her father shakes his head dramatically, sighing and shaking the paper out. "Habibti, it's not good. Our country is going to shit. Whalahi, if it comes to a revolution, I'll go back and fight.

28

Masr oum el dounia. We're the mother of the world. We need to set an example."

She shares a glance with Samir and they both roll their eyes. Their overweight, far-too-comfortable, secretly-in-love-with-England father isn't going back to fight in any revolution, but as an Egyptian, he was morally and politically obliged to be dramatically over the top about everything.

Samir looks over at her and says, "Yo, sis, come and help me with my tie outside."

She shoots him a withering look and before she can tell him to get lost, her father says, "Go help your brother, ya bint."

She snatches the tie from Samir's hand and walks to the stairs where she stands one step up from him and begins to wrap it around his neck, wondering if she can get away with strangling him with it.

He grabs it back out of her hand. "Get off me, you idiot. I don't really need help."

"Well, why the hell did you ask, then?"

"You look like shit."

She begins to brush past him, but he grabs her arm and drags her into the living room, closing the door so their parents won't hear.

"Malak, I'm serious. Your eyes are so puffy it looks like you're in the middle of an allergic reaction, you're wearing sweatpants for the fourth week in a row, and it looks like you haven't tasted food in about a year. You're a mess and, honestly, it's disgusting."

She wishes she had strangled him when she had the chance.

"Well, excuse me for not looking good enough for your standards but I don't care," she snaps. "And what's it to you anyway. You're too busy out there with your girlfriend, who, can I remind you, you don't have to break up with. So spare me the lecture about pulling myself together and getting over my broken heart when yours is beating just fine."

"You could have stayed with him," he says. He doesn't mean it though. They both know it is an empty thing to say. "Look, I get that you're hurting, but you're going to have to do a better job of hiding it from Mama and Baba. They've started asking me if you're depressed and whether they should force you to go to therapy."

She grabs her brother by the shoulder and drags him further away from the door. "Don't you dare tell them I need therapy. I swear to God I'll tell them all about the time you flew to Paris with Elizabeth and told them it was a work trip."

"Fuck's sake, Malak, get off me and calm down. I'm not going to say anything. I told them you were just stressed with the end of your Masters. But you need to start showing them some signs of improvement because they're ready to stage an intervention and if you think we can't all hear you crying at night, you're stupider than I thought. We live in a council house, Malak. The walls aren't that thick."

She looks down at her feet and doesn't know if the tears flooding her eyes are embarrassment or shame.

"Look," says her brother, his voice softening as he pulls her into a hug, "I've got your back, don't worry, but maybe just think about leaving the house a little and showering a bit more, okay?"

She laughs in between tears and nods.

"And stop wearing sweatpants, it really is disgusting."

She shoves him away from her, looking down at her sweat-pants that are currently covered in ramen stains and something else she doesn't feel entirely confident naming. Running her hands through matted hair, she concedes he might have a point.

"Me and Liz are going out with some mates tonight. I know

you're on a whole no-drinking, read-the-Quran-all-the-time, trying-to-be-a-good-Muslim thing or whatever, but why don't you come out with us? Just for a bit. It will be good to get out of the house and Liz is dying to see you. She says you're not returning her calls or texts."

Rubbing her nose across the sleeve of her sweater, Malak is about to say no when she catches her brother looking at her with disgust and wonders when she became someone who wipes their nose on their clothes. At that moment, seeing herself through her brother's eyes trumps the heartbreak. "Okay, I'll come. Just promise you won't try to cheer me up."

"I swear."

Her mother has finally got off the phone and has begun screeching that Samir is going to be late for work, so they both walk back to the kitchen.

She stands, leaning in the doorway, watching her mother fuss over her prodigal son, her father paying no attention to anyone as usual, and the news reporter in the background discussing the political tensions in Mubarak's government. The streets of downtown Cairo flash across the screen and although the news isn't good, she slips her phone out of her pocket and opens the map once more. Her fingers hover over Egypt and she zooms in along the coastline. Remembers the one summer they spent with her cousins at the beach. How they ate fresh fish caught on her uncle's boat and how every day felt like it lasted the entire season. She rereads the out-of-the-blue message her cousin in Cairo has sent her. Egypt might be politically tense but she is hardly relaxed in England and maybe God did have something to say to her after all.

MALAK

The thing with weddings is, they're never really about the bride and groom. They're an opportunity to show the rest of the world what you have, what you're about to have, and what they can no longer have. They're not even about young people. Weddings are for the aunties and uncles who do their curtain-peeking out in the open. Who sit and comment on who looks well, who isn't doing so well, and whose children really would be an ideal match. They're for the grandmas and grandads bent over walking sticks swapping notes on how things used to be. It's for the long-time married couples, tired of their routine and each other, who need to attend a wedding to remember why they did it all in the first place. Above all, it's for the parents of the bride and groom. A triumphant parade of their offspring to help validate their parenting skills. It's an opportunity to say, look, I didn't fuck them up completely!

Malak wonders if she's now classified as a fuck-up as she watches Saba and her fiancé, Amer, sit surrounded by aunties and uncles who are intent on feeding them their body weight in jalebi. Is it her mum's or her dad's fault, or is it just her? She watches Saba laugh and squeeze Amer's hand and the way he looks at her makes her hate everyone, but mostly herself.

She wants to believe in what she's looking at. Tries to rear-range her face so she's just a loving friend of the family smiling in happiness for the soon-to-be-bride, but her teeth are pressed together harder than they should be.

She doesn't feel Kees come to stand beside her until she real-izes she's squeezing her hand.

"Thanks for coming," says Kees.

"Don't be silly. I wouldn't miss your sister's engagement, plus, I'm here for you. I know how difficult this is."

"If only—"

"I know," says Malak quickly, reaching out to squeeze her friend's hand in return. "I know."

She can feel the familiar lump in her throat. The stinging in her eyes that comes along with any reference to the man she's left behind. "Where's Jenna anyway?" she asks quickly, changing the subject. There are times to cry with your girlfriends and the middle of an engagement party isn't one of them.

"Late as usual," says Kees. "Honestly, I don't know how she functions in life."

"Well, speak of the devil and she will appear. Here she comes and only an hour late," says Malak, who has just spied her weav-ing her way through the crowd toward them.

Kees watches Jenna approach. "She looks beautiful."

"When doesn't she?"

A pale pink gown of soft silk is wrapped tightly around her body, a long train billowing out after her as she walks toward them. Her hair, wrapped up in a hijab, unconventionally in a bandanna style, supports a huge pink-and-white lily that wraps around the bun at the nape of her neck, and somehow elegantly hangs across her ear.

If Malak had wrapped her hair up in a scarf and stuck a droop-ing flower in it, the entire effect would have looked ridiculous, but on Jenna it's breathtaking. Jenna is the woman that other women gape at before looking at online makeup tutorials. With huge almond-shaped brown eyes and perfectly symmetrical features, Jenna has a face that makes her look beautiful, no matter what she does to it. Malak always wants to tell the women who stare at Jenna in the streets and in bathroom mirrors that they might as well give up. That there is no lengthening mascara, vitamin C serum, or outfit they can buy to look like a woman who likes what she sees when she stares at herself in the mirror.

As Jenna reaches them, Malak kisses her twice on the cheek and says, "You're only an hour late. Are you feeling okay?"

"I'm drunk," Jenna giggles, while turning to kiss Kees, who is looking at her like all her nightmares have come true.

"Oh my God, Malak, she's drunk," hisses Kees.

Malak closes her eyes for a brief moment. This night was going to be harder than she had, at first, thought.

Turning to Jenna she says brightly, "Babe, what's going on?"

Jenna is giggling over something that isn't apparent to either Malak or Kees.

"Nothing. What's going on with you?"

Malak stifles a sigh. "Oh, nothing much. Just chilling. How come you're drunk, babes?" she asks casually.

"Ohhh, well, I was studying with Lewis and we went for a drink afterward and I really only had a couple, but I forgot that I hadn't eaten today."

"Mmmm hmmm," murmurs Malak.

"Here, don't worry, I've got some. Lewis gave me his flask," says Jenna, pulling out a silver canister from her clutch bag before Kees snatches it off her and gives it to Malak for safekeeping. Jenna immediately grabs it back from Malak.

"Jenna, why in Christ's name have you brought alcohol to my sister's engagement party?" chokes Kees.

"Excuse me," says a suddenly indignant Jenna. "Are not most of the Muslim community here?"

"This is my point," hisses Kees.

"Exactly," says Jenna. "You know they're all going to be trying to get us married to their deadbeat sons. Anyway, calm down. It's vodka, so you can't even smell it. Practically drank a bottle of mouthwash on the way and I haven't stopped chewing gum all evening. It will be totally fine. Look," she says, breathing into Kees's face while Kees looks like she wants to strangle her.

The music suddenly stops and the athen rings out across the crowd, bringing with it a hush in conversation as everyone starts scrambling for headscarves and prayer mats.

"Fuck, I need to go help Mum," mutters Kees.

"Babe, you really shouldn't swear when the athen is going off," says Jenna, shaking her head.

Incredulously Kees turns to stare at her friend. "You're holding a hip flask of vodka, Jenna."

"Oh well, yes. Yes, I am," she concedes, nodding drowsily toward Kees, who looks like she is teetering on the edge of a mental breakdown.

Malak stifles a grin for the first time that evening and says, "Go, it's fine; I'll stay with Jenna."

Jenna begins to float toward the prayer lines and Kees, looking instantly panicked, grabs the back of her dress, hissing, "Jenna, you're drunk; you can't pray to God now."

"Trust me," says Jenna, patting Kees's arm with a faraway look in her eyes. "This is when I need him the most." She walks away from them to stand shoulder to shoulder with the other women who were getting ready to pray at the back of the room.

"God help us all, she's going to be the death of me," says Kees.

Malak laughs. "Don't worry about it, Kees. I'll keep her out of trouble. She goes home drunk all the time and if she can get past her parents, then she'll be fine tonight. I'll keep an eye on her. Now go help your mum; she's calling you."

Aunty Abida had been gesturing wildly in Kees's direction since the call to prayer had gone off.

"Just keep her away from Saba's in-laws, please," murmurs Kees.

"I will, don't worry. Give me your dupata so I can join the prayer."

She takes the emerald-green scarf around Kees's neck and pushes her toward her mother before quickly wrapping it around her hair, kicking off her shoes, and jumping in line next to Jenna, who is happily swaying on the spot with her eyes closed. Malak hopes people will take it as extreme devotion as opposed to unbalanced drunkenness.

Malak's prayers are more regular than they've been in years, yet she feels further away from God than she's ever been. As the imam recites the first words to start the prayer, she lifts her hands up and gives in to it, hoping to feel the familiar sensation that used to settle on her when she prayed. A gentle wave would go through her and while she wouldn't exactly call it peace, it felt like a kind of softness. Especially when praying in congregation. When everyone raised their voices to say "ameen" in unison was the exact moment she felt less alone in the world. As if her body knew that there was a better way to live. She hasn't found that softness lately, and is annoyed that her prayers feel hollow and empty. That her love for her faith has fled when she needs it the most.

As she turns first to her right and then to her left to end her prayers, she hears Jenna strike up a conversation with the aunty on the other side of her and immediately makes up an excuse to haul her away.

"Sweetheart, I think we really should limit how many conversations you have tonight."

As Jenna hiccups, she replies, "You know, you might be right."

"We need to get some food and water into you to sober you up."

"Oh, do I have to?" Jenna wails. "That will make this far less bearable."

"Yeah, I hear you. I'm not going to lie, I'd really love to be drunk right now."

"Oh yeah, how is your no-drinking policy going? You're really getting your bismillah on these days, huh?"

"Yeah, it's not going that well, to be honest," replies Malak, steering Jenna through aunties and uncles. "These days I just want to get drunk all the time but I'm afraid if I do, I might never stop."

"Well, breakups will do that to you," says Jenna, hiccupping again.

They are about to turn into the room where food is being served when they bump into Aunty Najma, who envelopes them both in a hug before they can change direction.

"Ohh no," says Jenna.

An offended Aunty Najma looks at Jenna who, after a sharp nudge from Malak, says, "Sorry, I just stepped on my dress. How are you, Aunty? You look beautiful tonight."

Malak lets out a small sigh as a mollified Aunty Najma laughs shrilly and begins batting off Jenna's compliments with a kind of gusto that should only be reserved for the stage, before asking the inevitable question: "When are you two girls getting married?"

Malak avoids looking at Jenna, whose body is already tensing next to her. In perfect unison, they deliver the appropriate answer they learned as soon as puberty hit.

"Inshallah, Aunty, inshallah."

"Inshallah, inshallah" is whispered by every woman standing within earshot, a fervent prayer that God will bless their girls with suitable, successful, and, above all, Muslim husbands.

"You haven't found one yet, then?" presses Aunty Najma, who was never satisfied with a generic response.

Malak loves these women who have been a part of her life since birth. But they are also the women who told her off, sent her on errands, and who had spoken to her mother when she'd done something wrong, so they stirred up an equal measure of dread. If it takes a village to raise a child, that village comes without boundaries, and dealing with un-boundaried aunties was hard enough, but doing it with a drunk Jenna on her arm was testing Malak's patience in new ways.

"No, Aunty," she replies, through a half-smile.

"Even at university? You've got to be always looking or you'll miss your chance. In the car park, at the bus stop, in lines; you need to be constantly looking. In the supermarket, even try the post office."

Malak feels, rather than sees, Jenna's jaw hang loose. She feels the tension rise in her own shoulders as a passing aunty who, as if able to smell the questions like a lion hunting its prey, stops to join in, saying, "Sometimes even in the lift. I know someone who found one in the lift; are you keeping your eyes open in the lift?"

Aunty Najma nods serenely as if the prospect of finding a suitable husband while you are on your way to the twelfth floor is completely reasonable.

"I don't normally close my eyes in the lift," Malak says, smiling. Years of respect for her elders kept her tongue between her teeth but she doesn't know how long it will last.

"How about in the park? There're lots of men there, I've seen them. Or the airport. Nothing to do in the airport but look for one; it's the perfect place."

Before Malak has the chance to open her mouth, a third aunty joins in. The pack is gathering.

Jenna has begun to sway on the spot and Malak prays she will keep her mouth shut. "I promise you, Aunties, I haven't found a husband yet. As soon as I do, I'll let you know. Also, I'm not sure I should be looking for one in the car park. Anyone I find there probably wouldn't be suitable."

It is a thin stab at humor; however, the comment is received with earnest protestations that as long as you were vigilant you might find the man of your dreams anywhere.

They are saved by Kees, who, at that moment, bursts into the group talking about how she needs Malak and Jenna to help serve the food. Kees receives the usual round of smiles and blessings that are always showered upon her. Ever serious, always diligent, Kees can do no wrong when it comes to the elders.

Malak wonders how far their blessings would reach if she were to tell them that, every night, Kees slid into bed with a man who then slid into her, and a white man at that.

Kees leads them both away from the aunties to where two plates piled high with food are waiting.

"What happened to getting her to a quiet spot?" asks Kees, with a raised eyebrow.

"Aunty Najma is what happened," replies Malak, sourly. "She was interrogating me about my love life and obviously half the Muslim Umah had to join in because, God forbid, we're anything but married."

"You know I had your back," says Jenna, picking up her dinner plate.

Malak shoots her a withering look, which Jenna happily ignores.

"If I have to have one more conversation about why I'm not married I'm going to lose my shit. I don't know what's wrong with these women. I even got told I should look for a husband in the lift."

Jenna laughs loudly, bits of rice flying from her mouth, a chicken leg in one hand and her plate precariously balanced in the other while Kees shakes her head in disgust.

"How anyone as beautiful as you can eat like such a pig is truly beyond me, Jenna."

"Get off my dick, Kees," is the muffled response through a mouthful of chicken.

"What the hell does she think happens in lifts," continues Malak, "and also, how long does she think I spend in them? It's not as if I sit riding them up and down all day long in the hope that Mr. Darcy will get on at the eleventh floor."

"Even if he did," interrupts Jenna, "he wouldn't be Muslim, so you'd still be unmarried."

They both ignore her and Malak continues. "And why are they all under the impression that I'm secretly hiding a husband from everyone?"

Jenna points her half-chewed chicken leg at Malak and interrupts again, "Well, that's one good thing about you and Jacob breaking up. At least you don't have to hide him anymore. Kees is still working harder than the CIA to keep Harry secret, so silver linings and all that."

"For fuck's sake, Jenna," snaps Malak, "you really are a prick sometimes."

She walks out of the church hall and into the dark, wishing she'd never come tonight and wondering why a broken heart isn't enough to hospitalize you and excuse you from all events.

You cannot crack open a chest and expect people not to notice. Hearts break loudly. Ringing like 3 a.m. sirens. Everyone in the area hears it, but they know there's nothing they can do and since they can't help, they lower their eyes and keep walking. When the thunder claps and the sirens pass and the wind howls, not many people choose to stand and stare at the storm. To be brokenhearted also means you become a selfish thing.

Malak sighs, leans her head back against the pillar of the bandstand, and lets the cool evening air run over her. She knows it was selfish to leave Kees with a drunken Jenna, but the hall was too hot, and the night had already wound its way around her too many times. Her tongue too heavy. Her shoulders too high.

Everything is hilarious and endearing when you're in love. The aunties pushing for your wedding while your drunken friend sways on your shoulder is a story you'll laugh about over breakfast, but when you're tired and the sadness is an ache in the small of your back that you cannot ease no matter how much you stretch, all the funny things become bricks weighing you down.

The music from the hall floats out across the church gardens to reach Malak where she sits and she pulls her green dress high above her thighs to cool down, not caring if anyone sees. None of the elders will find her here and fuck them if they do. It is dark and she is sitting in the middle of a deserted church garden surrounded by bushes. If God had a problem with her showing this much leg, he could take it up with her another day and she will tell the trembling aunties that.

She hears a rustle of bushes and footsteps approaching and Kees and Jenna emerge to find her in their old hiding place. As girls they would come here to escape Arabic lessons, chores, and all manner of disapproving aunties. She had assumed that by this age there would be no need for hiding behind bushes from the elders, but apparently some things didn't change.

Jenna is carrying two plates of food while Kees is balancing a bottle of Coke under her arm and glasses in her hands.

"I'm sorry, babe," says Jenna, handing her a plate and leaning in to kiss her forehead. "You're right, I was being a prick. I didn't mean that about you and Jacob."

The familiar tears that now come with his name pool in her eyes and she squeezes Jenna's hand. "I know."

Kees hands her a glass and begins to pour the Coke while Jenna, hitching her dress up around her hips, sits behind Malak so she can lean against her.

With one arm around her chest, Jenna says, "It will get better."

Kees nods. "It will."

Malak scoffs. "When?"

No one says anything.

"You got any vodka left in that flask, Jenna?" asks Malak.

"What do you take me for, of course I have. Here."

"I thought you were in a no-drinking period," says Kees, with a raised eyebrow.

"I was. But it turns out I don't give a fuck right now. Fill me up, Jenna."

"M'lady," Jenna says, pouring the vodka into her outstretched glass of Coke. "Are you sure you don't want to join us, Kees?"

"Oh yeah," snorts Kees. "I haven't drunk my whole life but now, in the middle of my baby sister's engagement party, surrounded by literally every aunty we've ever known, and our mothers, that's the time I'm going to start."

Jenna shrugs. "Just asking."

Malak takes a gulp and as the sharp alcohol hits the back of her throat she laughs bitterly. "It's funny, isn't it? I've talked to God more over the last few weeks than I have in my whole life. I've followed the rules in ways I never used to. Bent my spine five times a day in prayer, stayed sober, and definitely haven't had sex, and yet I've never felt further away from him. But, all the times we've gone out and I've drunk and ended up at the bottom of a bottle, I swear I've seen God. Felt him right there in my chest. Or even naked in bed with Jacob. And here, in a churchyard surrounded by Muslims, following the rules like they always told us to, he's nowhere to be found."

"I think that might be the breakup and missing Jacob," says Kees quietly.

"Well, how does that make sense?" Malak replies, sitting up, feeling annoyed. "I might as well have stayed with him, if that's the case."

"Maybe you should have," Kees says, shrugging.

A sudden silence hits Malak as the music in the distance fades behind her ringing ears. She feels nauseous.

"What?" she replies quietly.

"Yeah, what are you talking about, babes?" interjects Jenna. "I thought I was the drunk one."

"I'm just saying," says Kees. "Is it worth it?"

Malak snorts in disdain and wonders if everyone has lost their minds tonight and maybe something is in the air. Maybe it's midsummer. Maybe it's just the moon. Something has to be in retrograde for her friend to be asking such stupid questions. She detangles herself from Jenna's embrace.

"Look at your sister, Kees. Look at the way the aunties are all smiling at her like all their dreams just came true. Look at the way our entire community has stopped what they're doing to honor and love her and celebrate with her. Who's going to celebrate us? Who's going to feed us sweets and wrap flowers around our hands and pour the blessings over us if we stay with men who aren't Muslim? You know they have to be Muslim. It's the one cardinal rule. Bring anyone home as long as he's Muslim. He could be a drug dealer with five kids from five different marriages but as long as he knows what words to say when the call to prayer goes off, then we can bring him home. Bring your sinners, bring your bad boys, bring the men who have done fuck all with their lives and are living at home with mothers who still buy their clothes for them, and as long as they're Muslim, then here, have our daughters. It's pathetic."

"So why do you care?" Kees says. She shrugs, ever practical, ever solution-oriented.

Malak looks down and sees the splashes of tears turn her dress into spots of dark green before she feels them run down her face and says quietly, "Because I want the sweets and the flowers wrapped around my hands. I want to be covered in blessings. I want to feel the weight of my people behind me when I take my husband's hands. I want my mum and dad smiling from the corner, secretly pleased because their daughter's wedding went better than Aunty Najma's daughter's wedding. I want the aunties to think I've never had sex and to sit with me the night before putting oil in my hair and henna on my hands and making jokes about what the wedding night will be like. I don't want to get married in secret and embarrassment. I want my love to lift my father's head, not hang it in shame. I want my mum to brag about the wedding all year. If I stay with Jacob, I don't get any of that. My parents will never accept him, and you think this lot dancing around your sister will?"

"But that only exists as long as we buy into it," says Kees. "How are we ever supposed to change it if we keep doing it the way it's always been done, the way the elders want it?"

Malak laughs even though it isn't funny. "Oh please, Kees," she replies. "This isn't one of your causes. Activism won't help now."

The dig straightens Kees's shoulders, she lifts her chin and with a flash in her green eyes she replies, "Activism is the only way we change our activity and your reluctance to do anything at all doesn't change shit."

"Oh, so this is my fault now?" says Malak. She can feel her irritation turn to anger.

"I didn't say that," replies Kees. "But you're just accepting it because you can't see a way out. You haven't even tried. You could have told your mum about Jacob."

"Oh, you mean the same way you've told your mum about Harry?" she replies.

"That's different."

"How? How is that different, Kees?" she asks.

"I haven't broken his heart, that's how," snaps Kees.

Jenna puts down the flask and starts to stand up, saying, "Ladies, why don't we go and get some dessert?"

"Shut up, Jenna," they say in unison.

Always eager to avoid conflict, Jenna quietly sits back down and takes another sip of the vodka, silently thanking Lewis for making her bring it tonight.

"*I've* broken his heart?" Malak asks. She can hear her voice rising to an uncomfortably shrill tone. "Is this how you see it? I'm the wicked witch?"

Kees sighs. "Don't be dramatic."

"I think now is as good a time as any to be dramatic, to be honest," Malak says coldly.

"You just didn't have to do it, Malak. Why now?"

"We're graduating next week," she says, angrily. "University is over for us, Kees. Jenna has a year left but we're done. You've already got a job in the city after graduation and it's time to grow up. How long did you think this could all last? It's over. This dream ends the minute our degrees do. You'll come to your senses soon enough and end it with Harry because you know there's no other way. You're being stupid letting it drag on this long."

She knows that calling Kees stupid is the quickest way to hurt her, but there under the moon and her unrelenting sadness, the alcohol sitting warm in her stomach after so long, and with the urge to wail constantly trying to claw its way out of her throat, she no longer cares for her friend's feelings. Which is exactly why heartbreak is such a selfish thing. It makes you self-centered even if you weren't previously. Gives you license to throw caution to the wind and not in the good, reckless way by skydiving or asking to be kissed. You throw away care and effort and other people's emotions because you're so weighed down by your own and you no longer have space to hold anything else. You say things you don't truly mean. In this state, Malak carries on, "It's going to end, Kees. Do the right thing and end it now. You two don't have any kind of future together."

The air has gone quiet. Nothing moves. As if the breeze senses that these women are disagreeing and knows the only thing to do is to leave. Malak's words hang above them and Jenna tries to swallow the lump in her throat. Kees's face is rigid with anger as the unspeakable thing they promised not to say to one another appears between them like a slow tear. Every time Kees had ever asked, "Do you think we'll…" Malak had always hushed her, saying, "Don't even say it," and vice versa. The word "breakup" had never been admitted into

46

their whispered fears, their drunkest moments, or their tear-streaked sobs when love made them cry, and yet here it was, suddenly spat into life. For the smallest of seconds Malak considers the cruelty of what she has just said, but the moment passes in one quick breath and all that is left in her is white-hot anger that Kees, the smartest of them all, can't see what a fool she is being.

Kees takes a step back.

Jenna doesn't dare move.

"You always think you're right, Malak, but it's going to break your heart when you realize how wrong you were. You've cut yourself up into these tiny pieces for those aunties and uncles sitting in that hall behind us and for what? So someone can smile at you on the one day of the year they turn up at your wedding? So they can whisper 'What a good girl' to your mother when you're not even there? You've broken your heart and left a good man for a community that doesn't give a shit about you. Sure, they'll put flowers in your hands and paint henna on your palms but when the plates are cleared and the music has stopped, who's going to be standing next to you? They're not going to be there the other three hundred and sixty-four days of the year but sure, all for this one day you'll live by their rules."

As she speaks, Kees's voice gets colder, taking any of the night's warmth with her, and she sees Jenna wrap her arms around herself to keep warm.

"And you know what, Malak," hisses Kees, "whoever you end up with, whichever Arab man your parents and all the aunties and uncles think is amazing, is the man you have to sleep with every night and come home to. They're not going to be there day in and day out helping you make a marriage work. They don't have to lie next to him. They don't have to wake up to him. *You* have to do those things. You have to make it work when it's not working and fix it when it's broken because they sure as hell won't step in. For all their talk about a village, where the fuck are they when you need them?"

Kees's voice rises and she cannot tell if it's in panic or anger. She cannot tell if she is righteous or wounded. Something slips away from her and her spine feels softer, which makes her grit her teeth and resolve to be, as usual, the stronger person out of the two of them. She judges Malak for her weakness and there, in that moment, she finds her mark for all the things she has never said before, not even to herself.

"And here's something they never tell you: they won't love you more for it. Malak Abdel-Aziz, always needing to be loved by everyone. Always everyone's darling. Too afraid to say no to anyone and so busy trying to please everyone around you just so you can be liked. Now you've broken your own heart and turned yourself inside out and how does it feel? How does it feel knowing they don't give a shit because how can they like you more when they'll never know what you gave up in the first place? When you're alone at night thinking about all you did to keep them happy and how they didn't even blink, ask yourself, are you fucking happy now?"

"Go to hell, Kees," Malak says, turning around and walking as quickly as she can away from her, the anger spilling from her lips. As she walks toward the gates of the churchyard, she hears Kees shout, "I will, but at least I'll be with the person I love."

JENNA

"You think you are better and more fortunate than I; in full health and strength: you are sorry for me. Very soon that will be altered. I shall be sorry for *you*. I shall be incomparably beyond and above you all." With a half-sob, Jenna lets the tears roll down her face, standing up and into the light, only to then fall with the perfect assurance that she will be caught. Ola catches her and immediately sweeps her into his arms and brings his lips down to hers in a kiss that is half passion, half art.

"Cut!" yells Sarah. The room lights flick on and the rest of the cast clap. "Beautifully done, Jenna," says Sarah. "Are you sure I can't persuade you to abandon your doctor dreams and take to the stage permanently?"

Jenna gives a mock bow while brushing away the tears that had stopped the minute the scene ended. "Absolutely not, but you can keep casting me as the lead," she says with a smile.

"I'll think about it. Might give it to someone else next term."

Jenna laughs with the confidence of knowing she's had the lead in almost every play during her years at university. She knows she's better than most, the best here, and she supposes she should be more humble about it, but the limelight and the praise are far too tempting, so she just grins and says, "Okay, darling, sure."

Sarah rolls her eyes. "Ola, amazing work from you too; your Heathcliff is getting better every day. All right, everyone, we're wrapping up for the night. See you all tomorrow."

Jenna turns to Ola and asks, "Are you walking to the car park?"

They leave together and begin their walk through campus.

The night air is sharp and a constant breeze lifts Jenna's hair. She pulls her jacket tighter around her, already sick of the fading light. Change is coming. She can feel a coldness in the air that she doesn't entirely attribute to a new season. She hears Ola talking and tries to work her way back into their conversation.

"...so I just think it was really smart of them to show progression, you know?"

"What's that?" she asks.

He turns toward her, shaking his head. "Are you even listening to anything I'm saying?"

"Yes, of course I am," she laughs. "Sometimes I just get distracted by how gorgeous you are and forget to pay attention."

He raises an eyebrow. "Do those lines ever work on the men you charm?"

"You tell me." She grins.

"Yeah, unfortunately, they kinda do," he laughs. "I really should make a point about reverse sexism here. If I'd said that I would be in serious trouble."

She laughs and loops her arm through his. "True, but I can say it because the power structures don't support me, so really your argument would be redundant."

"I'm a Black man, Jenna. The power structures don't support me either."

"Ahhh well, you're still a man though. You have dick privilege."

He looks at her with a glint in his eye. "Yeah, and that's never stopped you enjoying the privilege of my dick."

"Well, when I'm on my knees it's questionable as to who's the privileged one."

"Don't kid yourself, Jenna. You're never on your knees. You always sit and make me stand."

"Well, consider it my way of redressing the power balance. I'm deeply against women being on their knees in front of a man in any capacity. We've knelt for decades and so I'm ending it."

"You're going to single-handedly end sexism by refusing to kneel down while giving me head?"

She shrugs. "Well, change comes in the everyday."

"Are you suggesting giving me a blowjob every day? Because that's the kind of activism I can really get behind."

"I'm sure you could," she replies, sarcastically.

As they cross the square patch of grass in front of the student union, she hears someone screech her name and turns to see Sofia from her course waving at her from the middle of a group of people and pint glasses.

"Do you know everyone in this university?" asks Ola, looking at her out of the corner of his eye.

She half laughs. "Of course not."

"I don't know, Jenna. Every time I walk anywhere with you, someone always stops you or says hi. Without fail."

She shrugs and wonders why it bothers him.

"I just like talking to people. Don't you think people are interesting?"

He shrugs and the light of a nearby street lamp falls across his face. He really is gorgeous, with the highest cheekbones she's ever seen in a man and something about them makes her fingers ache to touch his face.

"I think people are fascinating. I could watch them all day. Talk to them all night. Figure out why they do the things they do."

They continue walking, the campus getting quieter as they approach the car park. Students are either drinking in warmer bars and pubs or trying to fit one more body on a single bed in cramped student accommodation. She's always grateful that she didn't move out of home for university. The thought of a single bed and shared bathrooms makes her shudder.

"People do things for the same reasons. Power. Greed. Desire," Ola replies.

She rolls her eyes. "For someone in the drama society you're annoyingly pragmatic."

When they reach her car, a small cream Mini, she asks, "Want to sit inside for a bit?"

With his hands stuffed into his pockets, he nods. They both knew this was how it would end the minute she asked if he was walking this way. She doesn't always ask, but nights like this, when she feels like she's done well on stage, are always the ones when she wants to sit in the car with him.

They get in and don't say anything. In the darkness, he leans over to kiss her and she reaches up her hands to touch his face.

She sighs into his mouth in happiness, his weight on her like a comforting blanket in the cold. She feels his heat slowly seep into her body, smiles and kisses him harder.

With a practiced hand he reaches over and pulls the lever so that her seat leans all the way back.

His hands are familiar with her body and he knows where to touch her and how to stroke her skin. He is one of those rare men who understand that you cannot rush a woman's body. That everything is timing. He knows how to wait and how to slow his breathing so his heart rate slows, and his hands slow so that everything becomes longer and nothing is rushed or fumbled. By the time he has finished stroking her skin, her hips are pushing their way into his hands, impatient and greedy.

He brings his lips back to hers so that at the exact moment he sinks his fingertips inside her, he catches her moan in his mouth. Hearing her moan into his mouth is one of his favorite feelings but he doesn't really know why. Doesn't know why swallowing the sighs of a beautiful woman feels like collecting butterflies.

Jenna feels his fingers flutter inside her; she hears a distant student getting into a car nearby. Another passes dangerously close to the car, chatting to a friend. None of these things bothers her in the slightest. This car park is called "The Quick" among students for a reason.

Ola had made sure she was comfortable and as he kisses her and his fingers find their way in and out of her, she wraps her hands around the back of his head and pulls his tongue deeper into her mouth. They stay locked like this until Ola swallows her final scream of pleasure with another smile.

She puts her arm behind her head and looks at him, smiling. Notices his jeans bulging behind the belt and buttons that want to break free and smiles again. It always pleases her when she hasn't touched or done anything to the men who have worked so hard to make her come. Some people would say it was selfish, but Kees called it closing the gender orgasm gap and that has always stuck with her. Plus, when she feels like it, she puts in the work. Tonight, she just doesn't.

"I have to go."

He nods. "Text me when you get home."

"You know I won't."

"I know," he says, climbing out of the car. "Drive safely."

She has already buttoned up her jeans by the time he leaves the car and has switched the engine on.

She beeps goodbye and drives out of the car park, a warm throb happily pulsing between her legs. A productive day.

Later that evening on the sofa, half watching a film with her parents, her fingers muscle memory their way to the group chat to tell the girls about her latest orgasm with Ola. The last message pops up, Malak asking Jenna what time she was arriving at the engagement party, and she is reminded that this chat is silent and unused now. Over the last two months it has become an abandoned building, years of conversation fading into memories and old messages that she scrolls through on the nights she really misses them, which is most nights. Having orgasms and not being able to tell your girlfriends made the orgasms less enjoyable. A lot of things had become less enjoyable.

She swipes instead to the notifications from Mo that always flash across her screen. He is persistent. Even after their initial date when she didn't message back. Even when she only replies with an emoji. He always finds something to say. She replies mostly when she's bored or has nothing else to do. Her first real date with Mo was unremarkable. She kept the conversation flowing because she's always been good at that. Jenna knows how to shine a light on someone so they feel like they're the only person in the room. She suspects this is why men always end up liking her. She makes them feel good and that's enough for most men. On their date Mo was respectful and nice and all the things a Jordanian boy should be: polite, held open doors, insisted on paying, didn't try to kiss her or make a move. She didn't try to touch him. She never does with the Muslim men. Knows there is a line you don't cross with them, not if you want to marry one, anyway.

54

He sent flowers the next day and Jenna liked the gesture so she forgave any lack of spark and continued to message him. Potential is everything.

Her parents lean over and share a kiss and she catches it out of the corner of her eye. When she was a child, her parents' tactility and overly romantic attitude toward one another was something to roll her eyes at; now that she was an adult, it was something to be admired and to aim for. But as someone who missed her friends and kissed boys in the hope that they would fill the gaps left behind, it was something that made her feel empty. She wants to message the girls again, but doesn't. Neither Kees nor Malak have talked to each other since that night and she no longer understands how the three of them work or what the point of a group is if it's split in half.

Instead, she replies to Mo to tell him she's free this weekend to meet. He messages back in the same minute telling her to leave it all up to him.

She throws her phone away from her and picks up another slice of cake before she can think about why she's meeting him. She already knows there's no chemistry. Knew this from the second date when she wished she was anywhere else but on a date with him. The girls would have laughed and told her to get rid of him and to stop wasting her time. But they aren't around, and she hasn't told anyone about the second date. She feels annoyed and doesn't know why and so now she's agreed to this third date and she doesn't know why she's done that either.

It's funny, the things you do when the women in your life are suddenly absent.

MALAK

She dreams she's drowning in a red sea and when she wakes there's a pool of blood between her thighs, the familiar ache settling at the small of her spine.

She can hear the house slowly groaning its Sunday song around her and she pulls the sheets off the bed as she leaves it. She walks into the kitchen with the bloody bundle and drops it on the floor by the machine, next in line for the wash. Her brother briefly looks up from his turkey and bacon sandwich.

"A rough one this time, eh?"

"When isn't it?"

She pulls a plate from the cupboard and sits down next to Samir to eat. Sunday brunch has been observed in their house since she was a child. A tradition started by her mother, who wanted at least one part of the week to be sacred and un-touchable. A point when the entire family came together to sit, eat, and talk. Over the years, as they started university and jobs, they rarely missed a Sunday, and the foresight of this tra-dition became apparent to her. That her mother was smart for knowing they'd all get busy and start to show up less. She knew family time needed to be nurtured or else it wouldn't happen. On days like today, Malak is thankful for her mother's insis-tence. At least here something is constant and familiar. She and

Samir had always shown up, even if they were hungover or still a little drunk from the night before, even when they stayed out and didn't make it to their own beds on Saturday night, they always found themselves crawling home on Sunday morning like worshipers to church.

Pulling a pancake onto her plate, she takes her first mouthful just as her father reaches up to caress his wife's neck and suddenly the lump in her throat is bigger and she chokes down a half sob. It takes only her mother's worried frown and her father reaching out his hand to her to break open her tears and she bends her head over her arms and sobs into the table.

Samir is murmuring to her in what he hopes are sympathetic words while her mother strokes her back and her father holds her hand, all of them holding vigil with her while she cries into pancakes that are now inedible. As she begins to breathe again through long, drawn-out gasps and sniffs, she considers telling her parents that her heart hurts and she doesn't know how she'll love anyone else again, but she doesn't. There is something in her that knows it's not only heartbreak splitting her open. That something has been growing roots in her for years and her broken heart is breaking open the thing that kept all her wants stuffed quietly inside. She cannot stop running her fingers over maps and the desire to be more Egyptian than English is swallowing her. She knows her family laughs at her bad Arabic while her friends think she's bilingual. They get starry-eyed when she mentions her heritage but then again, everyone fantasizes about Egypt. Even her parents spin tales of the glory days and you can't listen without wanting to live it. Most people had Cinderella for bedtime stories but she had stories of Umm Kulthum and how even the president would come to watch when she sang. All Malak's life, Egypt has sat just past her fingertips and she is tired of the wanting. She has had enough of yearning for something that is supposed to be yours but never quite feels like something you belong to. When she first visited the place her parents call home, as a twelve-year-old kid, it was easy enough to believe that she too could claim it for her own. But she's old enough now to know that it takes more to make a home. Her mother had told her that in Egypt they have a saying: those who drink from the waters of the Nile will always return to it and she wonders if it's true. If myth and genetics are calling her back and if, when she was with a white man on her arm who couldn't say "assalamualaikum" without sounding like he had stones in his mouth, she could never answer that call. But now heartbreak has broken the banks and everything is split wide open and all the longing of her life has come out to play.

"*Hayati, ya rohy*, what's wrong?" asks her mother. "Is your pain that bad?"

Before she can say anything, her father interrupts.

"Of course it's not her period. She's been sad for weeks. Tell me what Baba can do for you, habibti. Samir, put the kettle on, your sister needs tea."

Samir doesn't try to argue that the tea won't fix everything but silently gets up to make a pot for the family.

Between sobs and sips of the tea, Malak explains that she's restless. Doesn't know who she is. What she's supposed to do. Her mother says it's just because university is over and everyone feels like this, but she insists it's more than that. Samir agrees with her because he didn't have a mental breakdown when he was finishing university, which earns him a kick from their father, but a gentle one because Samir's comment makes her laugh and they are all glad of anything that cracks a smile across her face.

Her mother suggests some time out. Samir recommends a spa day. Her father pleads his case for a family holiday and Malak softly drops moving to Cairo onto the breakfast table, the idea occurring to her at the same time that it spills out of her mouth. Loss has made her brave. Her thumb twitches to open the map on her phone once more. She mentions better Arabic and more time with the family and her parents' faces light up.

Her mother says it will do her good to have some time at home between studying and getting a job. Points out that her daughter has spent too much time bent over a desk and that she needs fresh air. Her father scoffs and says she won't get it in Cairo, but if that's where her heart is calling, then he couldn't be happier.

"You're a daughter of the desert, hayati," he says. "Egypt will always call you home."

Samir scoffs and says that his father has done a good job of not picking up the phone for that particular call all these years, which earns him a harder kick.

Rubbing his shin, he says, "I, for one, love the idea of you living in Cairo for a while. You can get a nice pad and me and Elizabeth can come visit. Make sure you have a spare bedroom, yeah?"

"I don't want to move there for your convenience, Samir," she replies shaking her head. "It's just, I dunno, maybe it's not the right thing?" She bites her nails while thinking; it's a new habit she's developed in the last few months.

"Well, just think about it," says Samir. "It is a good idea to take some time before getting a full-time job because this nine-to-five life is a joke. I wish I'd done it."

"Bezupt!" exclaims their father. "Think about it but let's make tea first."

Samir rolls his eyes and turns to the kettle once more. Malak looks up at her mother, fingertips still in her mouth.

"Mama?"

"Of course it's a good idea; you can live with my sister, your Aunty Hala. And you never know who you might meet out there."

Her brother and father groan and her mother begins to make her a new plate of pancakes with a small smile on her face.

"Mama, I'm just going to think about it, that's all."

"Yes, habibti," her mother says, placing the plate in front of her, "just think about it."

Brunch lurches back into motion. Everyone continues to voice their opinion between mouthfuls, and the possibility of something new, something answered, brings Malak's appetite rushing back to her in a way it hasn't for weeks.

Yes, she will think about it.

Everything happens quickly after brunch. The days seem to speed up and the slow march to winter doesn't feel as bad. Malak attends her graduation ceremony, for the second time, for her Masters, and with a whispered prayer of thanks that she and Kees are part of different departments so they don't have to see each other. She hasn't spoken to her since that night two months ago and neither of them has tried to get in contact with the other. Jenna texts her congratulations on the day and she replies. But she hasn't seen her much either. None of them are sure how their friendship exists outside of the three of them. It's easier to ignore things instead of considering what it means to not be talking to the woman she's spoken to every day for most of her life. She thinks she should see Jenna but she's already learning how to be without Jacob in her life, without university lectures to go to, and she doesn't have any space left in her body to try to learn how to be just the two of them. Confining their relationship to texts and the odd meme that only requires a "lol" is all she can manage for now.

She talks to cousins in Cairo who tell her that they want nothing more than to have her there. She googles expat jobs. Researches apartments, even, though her family begs for her presence in their home. She joins an online group for young Brits living in the city. Somewhere between saved bookmarks and Google searches of the Red Sea, she stops thinking about it and decides to do it. When she books her one-way flight, the muscles in her neck unwind and she sleeps for eleven hours that night. She cries less.

She starts her packing only a few days before she's due to fly. It doesn't feel important and she's not worried. Once upon a time, she'd try to take everything with her, but now she doesn't know what the point is. There is so much from her old life that she has lost, so why bother carrying the memories of it into her new one? It won't bring the people back. She divides her life into boxes: keep, pack, toss. She does it quickly and with little thought.

The only time she hesitates is when she picks up a frame of herself, Jenna, and Kees. The picture was taken on Jenna's bed at one of their many sleepovers. Kees was holding the camera while Malak's head rested in her lap and Jenna's head on hers. They're all laughing in the frame and Malak remembers the moment as vividly as if it were in front of her.

They were, as usual, discussing the probability of Harry and Jacob converting to Islam and Jenna, with the enthusiasm and bright-eyed view she always employed, had said: "Look, I think maybe this is just how we do our Jihad these days. Imagine how many of us will get to heaven if we convert men to Islam. We'll basically be saints."

Kees snorted in disbelief. "Considering we're having sex with these men before marriage, I think that might cancel out our sainthood."

"Not necessarily," said Malak. "Redemption has to count for something." She nudged Jenna, who was drinking white wine out of a thermos. "Pass the drink, please."

Jenna screwed the top back on and threw the bottle across the bed to Malak. "Exactly, redemption is where it all evens out," she said.

"Jenna, you can't throw wine," said Malak, "it will go funny."

"Darling, we're drinking wine out of a thermos; I think it's already gone funny."

Kees sipped her coffee and laughed at her friends. "I don't drink and even I know that drinking wine out of a thermos is gross."

Malak shrugged. "Needs must, my friend, needs must."

Kees wanted to debate the exact pressing need that drove her friends to drink wine at a sleepover, but thought better of it and said, "How does redemption help exactly, Jenna?"

"Well, the Catholics do it all the time. Commit a sin, confess, and then there's redemption and everyone is fine."

"Exactly," said Malak, with a grin. "So we can have as much sex as we like, get them hooked on how good the sex is, then convert them, power of the pussy and all, and then repent our earlier sins of having sex outside of marriage and voila."

"But we're not Catholic," argued Kees.

"Oh please," interrupted Jenna. "It's all the same God. If he's forgiving Catholics, he's definitely forgiving Muslims."

"So why haven't you had sex yet, then, Jenna?" asked Kees, always ready to tear a hole through any of Jenna's arguments. "If God is so forgiving?"

Jenna shrugged. "God might be forgiving but Arab men aren't."

Kees and Malak both groaned and Jenna held up her hand. "Don't even start. That isn't the topic of discussion tonight. It's how you two are going to marry your men."

They groaned again.

Malak flopped her head down onto Kees's lap in a state of dejection and Jenna curled straight up on Malak's lap, never wanting to be left out of the inner circle.

"Look," she continued. "I know a friend of a friend who was going out with a white atheist and he converted to Islam for her. And not even for show. Like genuinely, actually believed in it all and so converted, and now they're engaged."

"That's beautiful," sighed Malak.

"That's bullshit," exclaimed Kees. "There's no way he did it just for himself."

Malak threw her hands up in despair. "Kees once again ruining the magic. He could have found God."

"What he did find is some pussy and a woman he loved," replied Kees. "How interested was he in Islam before she came along? Obviously not much if his atheist ass is adamant that God doesn't exist and then suddenly, poof, he's found him?"

"Miracles do happen, Kees."

"Yeah, well, it would have to be a miracle for an atheist to suddenly become a staunch Muslim."

"Well, he said he would never have done it just for her," said Jenna, "that it had to be true for him."

"Can't argue with that, Keesy baby," said Malak, providing unhelpful ad-libs.

"Of course you can," yelped Kees. "He has to say that, doesn't he? To salvage his pride and reconcile how he's done this massive thing for her. It's literally the oldest trick in the book. Take an idea a woman has and pass it off as your own."

They all burst out laughing and that was the moment they had taken the picture, while there was still the shine of wiped tears of laughter on their face.

As Malak stares at the picture frame in her hands and pulls herself out of the memory, she picks up her phone and texts Jenna before she can change her mind. She tells her that her flight is in two days and maybe they can meet at The Diner tomorrow night to say bye.

Jenna is tactful enough not to make a big deal out of the fact that she's just been told that one of her best friends is leaving the country indefinitely and Malak loves her for that.

They arrange the time as formally as acquaintances would, using the word "babe" every few sentences to make it sound as if everything is normal.

Something feels tight in Malak's chest. Ever since she ended things with Jacob she's felt funny. Like he'd pulled out all her bones and she'd tried to put them back together but hasn't got all the pieces in the right place. She's almost used to it now so she shrugs it away and returns to her packing, folding her life and the last few years neatly away. Deciding what to bring, what doesn't make the cut, and who she's going to be.

MALAK

Her phone flashes beside her as she tries to sleep, Jacob's name swimming into vision.

"I'm outside. Can you come out?"

Her whole body shakes as she sits on the side of her bed clutching her arms to her side. Prays that her parents don't wake up as she stumbles into the sweatpants she'd set aside for the plane tomorrow morning.

They haven't spoken since they broke up that night. There was nothing left to say, so why is he outside her house now?

She slips her hoodie over her head and creeps down the stairs and out of the house.

She stands at the gate looking down an empty street when a message flashes up: *Round the corner. Didn't want to wait too close to the house just in case.*

She thinks she loves him all over again in that moment.

She turns at the end of the street to see him leaning against a car looking anxious.

"Hi," she says, walking up to him.

"Hi," he replies.

They laugh nervously at each other, at the formality of those tiny words.

"I borrowed Oli's car. Can you come back to mine for a bit? I know you're leaving in the morning."

"Who told you?"

"Jenna."

She laughs. "Of course she did."

She would have said no, that it was too risky, she could be caught out of bed in the middle of the night by her parents, but the way he looked when he mentioned her leaving made her spine feel soft, so she nods instead.

"Of course."

They get in the car and drive the twenty minutes to his student house.

"Oli didn't mind you taking his car?" she asks.

"Why would he?"

"Because he hates me now."

"Don't worry about Oli."

They creep into the house and past Oli's bedroom, up into the attic to Jacob's room. It looks the same, which feels strange to Malak because everything is different now and she doesn't understand how big things can happen with so little to show for it.

"Do you want a cup of tea?" he asks.

She nods at him. "Always."

As she looks properly around the room, she notices that the picture frames with her in them are gone. The only thing left is a small picture keyring on his bedside table. It's the image of them sitting outside the Louvre in Paris. Him in his light-blue sweater, the one that makes his shoulders look big, and her face leaning against his, foreheads resting softly together like hands in prayer. You can tell she took the picture because there's more of Jacob in it. Their smiles are easy and gentle, not the bare teeth of big grins or the fake laugh of picture taking, just the small smiles of two people who know something no one else does.

He hands her a mug of tea in her favorite mug, as if nothing has changed.

"You missed one," she says, nodding toward the keyring.

"Don't be mad," he replies. "Oli said it was probably for the best and would help me move on. I've put them all in a drawer for now but I couldn't bear to hide this one. Had to leave something."

"I'm not mad," she says, sitting down next to him on the edge of the bed. "And he's probably right."

She doesn't say that seeing her removed from his room feels like they just broke up all over again. Knows that she doesn't have a right to be upset about it when there were never pictures of him in her bedroom to begin with. That he had always been hidden, and not for the first time she curses her absolute lack of courage to tell her parents about him.

They say nothing, sipping tea, legs touching, shoulders leaning against one another.

Eventually, he turns to her and says, "So you're really doing it, then?"

"Yes." She nods.

"I'm glad."

The worst thing is, she knows he means it.

"You've wanted this for so long," he continues. "You always told me you'd go back to Egypt to live one day and now you're actually doing it. You wanted to so badly, but I wasn't sure if you ever would. I'm proud of you, Malak."

She doesn't know if it's his sincerity or his maturity in wishing her well that starts the tears rolling down her face.

He reaches up and wipes the tears from her cheeks. "Don't, Malak."

The tears fall faster.

"It's going to be amazing. You're about to go on the most exciting adventure."

The sob she's been biting down bubbles out of her and the tension that has become a constant presence in her shoulders breaks against his chest.

He takes the mug out of her hand while wrapping an arm around her. Murmurs comforting words she doesn't quite hear and strokes her hair, trying to soothe her.

If he were to ask her why she's crying, she wouldn't have an answer. At least not one that would fit into words.

She wipes her nose on the back of her sleeve in a way you can only do with someone you trust. She turns her wet face up to him in a question and he answers by bringing his lips down to hers.

They've always been this way. Talking to each other without saying anything. As Jacob peels off her sweater and unties her sweatpants, she feels him saying, you are loved. Have been loved. Will continue to be loved. And it makes her cry harder while reaching out her own hands to pull him into her in a way that says, I love you too, and I don't know if I'll ever stop, and I'm sorry that it's not enough to stay.

They lie still afterward and as she listens to his heartbeat, feeling it running through her whole body, she knows that nothing has changed. That in the morning she will get on a plane to Egypt, a country she's known only through her parents' longing and brief summer holidays, and leave behind the home she actually knows. She will trade family and friends and a great love, an epic love, for a fantasy and a myth about the Nile her mother told her when she was a kid. The madness of it almost makes her laugh. But the constant restlessness that resides somewhere in her ribcage has been growing for too long now and so she keeps her face still and is resigned to leaving.

"What will you do?" she asks him, leaning up to look at him.

He shrugs his shoulders nonchalantly. "Dunno. Be a responsible adult. Contribute to society. We're all supposed to get jobs now, aren't we, although I don't know what job you're supposed to get with a Masters in Eastern Philosophy. Maybe I'll run away and join the circus. I think I'd be good at that."

She stands and starts gathering her clothes from around the bed. The sky will soon be getting light and she needs to get back into her bed before it does.

"Harry told me that you and Kees aren't talking," he says, and for a minute she freezes, wondering how it hasn't occurred to her that the boys would still talk to each other.

"I didn't realize you guys were talking," she replies.

He raises an eyebrow at her. "Are we supposed to end our friendship just because you've ended yours with Kees?"

"Oh please," she scoffs. "Since when were you and Harry friends?"

"We've always got on."

"There's a difference between getting on and being friends, Jacob." She pulls on her sweatpants harder than intended, suddenly annoyed at the idea of their friendship.

"I don't know if men differentiate that line as much," he says, leaning back on his arm and staring at her.

"Well, men are stupid," she snaps.

"Maybe," he replies. "But we had dinner last week."

She stops and stares at him. "Where?" she demands, as if prodding at the details will make the reality of it fall away.

"At his place. He cooked and we watched a film."

"What did he cook?"

"Beef Wellington."

"I thought you hated rich people's food?"

"Well, if you think about it, a beef Wellington is just a bigger version of a corned beef pasty."

Malak grunts in disbelief. "You're a sell-out."

Jacob rolls his eyes. "A beef Wellington and a movie hardly make me a sell-out."

"Well, what film did you watch?" asks Malak.

He rolls his eyes again. "Will this determine how much of a sell-out I am?"

"Well, that depends," she snaps back. "If you watched an indie film with subtitles, then yes, yes it would."

"*Lord of the Rings*," he replies.

"*Two Towers*?"

"It's the best one," he answers.

She nods. "It really is."

She continues getting dressed, sitting on the edge of the bed to put her socks on.

"How is she?"

"She looked pretty exhausted." He knows that this is the question she wanted to ask straight away and this is what she's really snappy about, and because he loves her, he offers the information willingly, granting her the kindness of not having to probe. "She's shadowing at the law firm before the job starts officially and by the sounds of it, the hours are pretty long. Harry says he barely sees her. Even on weekends she's in the office prepping. You know what Kees is like."

"Classic overachiever," Malak says, nodding.

"She misses you."

Malak catches her breath. "Did she say that?"

"Not to me," says Jacob. "Harry says she does though. He did also say she's still pretty pissed off at you. Apparently, you said some things."

She nods and doesn't know what to do with her body. Jacob slides over, a leg on either side of her, and wraps himself around her. She thinks that a person who can still hold you together when you've broken them apart must love you a terrible amount.

"You guys will figure it out," he murmurs into her back. "Just give it time."

She shrugs. "Now isn't the time."

"It's always the time to make up with someone when you've hurt their feelings, Malak."

"Well, she hurt my feelings too." She knows how petulant she sounds and sighs.

"I know," he replies. "I know."

They sit like this for a minute, him wrapped naked around her, ready to hold on to her forever, and her dressed and ready to leave, glancing at the clock on the wall. With him like this she suddenly realizes she's still more excited about leaving than staying and she feels less sad. A hardness settles in her stomach and she is resolute. In that moment she has the all-encompassing satisfaction of feeling like she is doing the right thing. She smiles to herself and, one hand still on his, she swipes the app open on her phone to call a taxi. Jacob doesn't notice, still lost in a moment he thinks they're both having.

Finally, she squeezes his hand and says, "My taxi is outside."

He jolts and says, "Don't be stupid, I'll drive you."

"No." She is firm. Turns around to face him. "Please stay in bed. It's late. And I want to say bye to you here. We've had so many beautiful moments in this room. I don't want to kiss you around the corner from my house and worry we'll be seen. I don't want that to be the last thing between us."

He stares at her and she is suddenly lost at sea again. She wants to pull him to the shore and tell him it's going to be all right, but she's already running through the list of things she needs for tomorrow morning. She has left the room already, even though she's still on the edge of the bed staring at him.

"Look after yourself, Jacob."

He nods and says nothing, just looks slightly sick and she can feel his desperate sadness seep into the bed and across to her.

She puts her hand on the back of his neck and pulls his lips to hers. Tastes the salt on her tongue and knows that she isn't the one crying.

She gets up and walks to the door. With her hand on the light switch she looks back.

"Can I get you anything before you sleep?"

He shakes his head. "No, thanks."

They stare at each other. He lies down and pulls the duvet up around his chin and settles into the position he always falls asleep in, still looking at her.

She flicks the switch off and leaves them both in darkness. She doesn't want to be the one to look away and knows that he won't either.

"Goodnight, Jacob."

"Goodnight, Malak."

JENNA

They both know how to take pleasure from everything around them. They have always been this way. She wonders if this is why they've been best friends for so many years. Both bold and fearless, perhaps this is what drew them to one another initially. She'd met Lewis at a teenage house party, some friend of a friend of their friends, and against a rough brick wall they'd stamped their lips on each other and just like that, a friendship had been born.

They'd spent the night learning what a body could do when stroked in the right way. The things that were possible in the guest room of your friend's parents' house. The first man to ever kneel before her and put his lips to her had been Lewis. Trapped between youth and a longing to be something more, he had shown her what it was supposed to feel like and how a tongue inside of you could feel like sinking into a hot bath. She'd relayed these details while walking home the next morning with Kees and Malak, both of whom had yet to experience this newfound pleasure, which she described as the most delicious thing she'd ever done. Up until this moment they had been more interested in days at the beach together and dissecting plotlines in their favorite series. But biology and the sting of desire had begun to prickle across their skin, starting with Jenna.

In later years, when the botched fumbling of drunken men hadn't gone as well, she'd always thanked Lewis for showing her how it was supposed to be. She imagined this did great things for his ego. Their experimenting with one another had ended within a year of meeting. Lewis already knew what sex felt like and wasn't prepared to miss out on this new, wild thrill he'd discovered. Because she, like him, understood the importance of pleasure but was adamant to hold on to her virginity, they decided they inevitably couldn't be together and so comfortably settled into a very familiar friendship. There was never a question of not being in each other's lives, no petty lovers' quarrel, and they never "broke up" as such. They just stopped slipping off together at house parties or in the club. Once you've let a man lay his head between your thighs you can either be with him, never talk to him again, or become best friends. At seventeen, when life was easier and everyone was too happy and young to be jealous, they had chosen friendship.

Jenna had stayed at home for university and Lewis had left for Liverpool the minute their A-level results had landed on the doorstep. Despite the distance, they continued the way they had always been, and every holiday found him back home knocking on her parents' front door to see her, but also sneaking into the kitchen and being fed by her mother. Her father begrudgingly accepted Jenna's friendship with a boy, if only because his wife assured him that Jenna would never marry a white, non-Muslim.

Lewis had finished his three years with zero desire for further education, happily taking his degree in one hand and crippling student loans in the other, something he was incredibly nonchalant about, and was living back home until he found a job. As far as Jenna could tell, he'd spent most of the summer sleeping around, enjoying himself, and doing anything but look for a job, while attempting to entice her away from her studies at every available moment.

Jenna laughs as another rose lands on her head. Lewis is sitting opposite her ruining the bunch that Mo had given her earlier in the day by aiming them at her as she tries to study.

"I should never have let you into the library. I could have made you wait outside in the cold, you know? The sooner you let me finish the sooner we can go to dinner."

"I don't want dinner, I want a drink," replies Lewis, throwing another flower at her.

"Same thing. Liquid dinner. And stop ruining my flowers."

"Who gave them to you?"

"Mo."

Lewis groans. "Mo is an idiot."

"You say that about everyone I date," says Jenna, barely lifting her head from the pages she is trying to work through.

"That's because they're all idiots, Jenna. And especially Mo, based on what you've said about him, so what does that tell you?"

"That you're a moron, Lewis; that's what it tells me."

He leans across the table, squinting at Jenna through a petal held up to his eye. "Considering you're waiting until your wedding night to have sex, I think that's a bit rich. Jenna, I hate to be the one to piss on your parade here, but you're essentially a virgin whore."

She swings her book at him and the satisfying thud of six hundred pages of medical text connecting with his head makes her smile.

"Jesus, woman," says Lewis, rubbing his head and sitting back.

"I thought you didn't believe in him."

He rolls his eyes. "It's a figure of speech."

"No, it isn't; he's a religious figure who you cannot call upon if you refuse to acknowledge his existence. And don't call me a whore. Plus, a virgin whore is oxymoronic, Lewis."

"Which sums you up perfectly, Jenna. I've never known a woman to get so much dick without ever actually having sex."

Reaching over to retrieve her book, she asks, "Why do you even care? I have fun. By medical standards, I'm virginal and no one gets hurt. What does it matter if it's penetrative or not?"

"You're riding on a technicality there, Jenna."

"Anyway, even if I did lose my virginity, you wouldn't like the person I lost it with."

"No, probably not." He nods. It's the only thing they've agreed on all evening so he drops the subject, looking up at her, his face suddenly transformed into a boyish grin. "Can we go and get a drink now?"

Jenna laughs and nods, the rest of the night given up to the enjoyment that comes easily to them.

They've always been full of the quick happiness that comes from people who believe they deserve it. Between cocktails and pool games they knock back shots and move on to a different bar where the lights are lower and the drinks more elaborate. Between bars they give each other piggyback rides, simply because it seems like a good idea. They flirt with strangers. They are perfect wingmen for each other. Jenna chats to the women, a compliment here, a shared glance of understanding naturally passing between them, and a gentle suggestion that her friend thinks she's beautiful. Often, all it takes is a suggestion. Lewis talks easily to women. Doesn't get tongue-tied, and most of the time that is enough.

He never has to sell Jenna. His job is to persuade the scared and intimidated men to approach her, although, most of the

time, he'll look up to find her already in the middle of a conversation with a man who looks like God smiled down on him
that night.

They collect numbers and kisses in corners, sometimes fumbles in bathroom stalls, but they always depart together, leaving
the people they were chatting to feeling like the lights have
suddenly been turned off.

Jenna notices two missed calls on her phone from Mo and
wonders why people call again when the phone isn't picked up
the first time. Two missed calls is just impatience. It says, "How
could you not have picked up? I'm waiting." She shakes her
head and slips her phone back into her bag. Jenna has never let
anyone rush her. She's already told her parents she's in an emergency rehearsal that's running late and they're the only people
who need to be appeased. Anyone else gets very little consider-
ation. She has always been good at staying in the moment.

The night winds around them both and she's glad that Lewis
is back home. Malak is in Egypt and Kees has started her new
job and may as well be an ocean away. Since the night of the
engagement party, their friendship has taken on a different
form. Twisted itself into something she doesn't recognize. Her
mother says it's just because Jenna is the last one left at university and when she leaves and their lives take on the same
rhythm again, they'll be back the way they were. She knows
this isn't true. That whatever unraveled that night has become
too disjointed to recognize. In all the difficult things they have
spoken about over the years, and all the hard truths that have
been delivered, mainly from Kees, there was never that much
on the line. But with love in the mix and life choices to be
made, everyone was holding on to someone else's heart. There
was too much to lose. She shakes the girls out of her head and
returns to the night. A dance remix of "Jolene" suddenly blasts

out of the speakers and Jenna and Lewis both jump up at the same time to sway together, a song they have spent years danc-ing to, a song reminiscent of an easier time. Their night ends in the kebab shop as it always does, the food soaking up some of the alcohol lining her stomach. The shop is almost empty. It's 10:45 and it's too early to be in a kebab shop for most, but she has lectures and studying tomorrow and parents who have never allowed her to crawl home during the early hours of the morning. The only person allowed to do that is her father as he returns from late-night surgeries and emergency calls.

Lewis rubs his eyes and sighs. "We're getting too old for this, Jenna."

She giggles into her chips and leans over to steal a slice of his pizza. "Speak for yourself, old man."

He grumbles about her always stealing his food and why she doesn't just order her own in the first place. She replies with her usual answer that she doesn't want pizza. It's the same conversa-tion they've been having for years.

It's 11:30 by the time she creeps through the front door. She knows how to act tired enough so that any mishaps will be blamed on exhaustion as opposed to intoxication. She knows the distance you have to keep so the alcohol isn't smelled, and she always has a travel bottle of mouthwash in her bag for the taxi ride home anyway. There is a drunk line she knows not to cross when she's staying at home.

She doesn't meet her parents in the hallway tonight and slips into bed easily, bringing her makeup remover wipes and a big glass of water with her. She flicks through her phone and sees Mo is online. Remembers that she needs to reply to his calls but scrolls past his name anyway. She sighs, thumbs back to the chat with Mo because she knows it's the right thing to do.

She thinks he might be the type of man she has imagined in a thousand daydreams so can't understand her reluctance to go on more dates with him. She's been avoiding his requests, conveniently hiding behind the pressures of studying and their impending debut into the world of full-time work. She had managed successfully until one day he had turned up outside the library and insisted she take a study break because everyone had to eat.

She wasn't sure if it was the way he demanded, or his absolute refusal to take no for an answer, but something in the authority in his words made her smile and meant that if she concentrated hard enough, the hint of something fluttered, for just a moment, in her stomach.

"It's a bit cold for a picnic, isn't it?" she had said when she met him outside the library, pulling her coat more tightly around her as she walked up to him.

"A little," he replied, "but I have blankets, a flask of mint tea, and the sun is shining, so I thought we should take advantage."

She noticed that he had a wicker basket over his arm and she hid her smile, resisting the temptation to tease him about being old-fashioned. A man who turned up with picnic blankets and romantic notions should never be teased. Some things needed to be cultivated, not culled.

He was immaculately dressed, as he always was, and it was one of the things she really liked about him. He was clean-shaven and his dark hair was cut short. The deep forest-green Hugo Boss sweater he was wearing fit perfectly along his shoulders. He understood sizes and how things were supposed to fit, unlike the majority of men on this campus who employed an "it will do" attitude to their appearance. Watching men who were poorly dressed made her insides curl.

"You had me at blankets," she laughed.

They walked ten minutes down to the River Cam, past the green where everyone always sat, until they found a spot where the hum of thousands of students vibrating off sandstone buildings slowly faded away. They talked about dull things like medicine and exams and she nodded when she was supposed to and was happy to let him talk.

As he was talking, he took a packet of tissues from his pocket and within the small breaks of his speech he discreetly turned away from her to blow his nose, before turning back and pocketing the tissues. She smiled and did him the courtesy of looking the opposite way, as if admiring the sky or the tops of the trees until she was sure he was finished, then turned back once more as if she hadn't seen a thing.

"We're taught to treat patients like body parts," he continued, "just something that needs solving, so we're always looking at the part, not the person. We rarely bring it all together. But if you take the time to have the conversation, the more you find out about a person's life, then the easier it is to diagnose them. To find out what really hurts, because sometimes the thing that's hurting them the most is not the thing they point at, you know?"

He caught Jenna staring at him open-mouthed and his shoulders dropped a little.

"You think it's stupid? I don't know, I just think it helps." He shrugged and kept his eyes forward until Jenna interrupted, touching his arm to turn him toward her again.

"No, I don't, not at all. I think that makes total sense, actually. My dad is just about best friends with all of his patients and he seems to be a good doctor."

Mo laughed. "A good doctor might be an understatement."

She nodded and laughed, watching him from the corner of her eye as he carried on talking about the patient he once made friends with.

She made the right sounds at the right places to encourage him to continue as they spread the picnic blanket on the ground and he began to take out items. With rays of sunlight coming though the weeping willow and summer still lingering in the air, and a man opposite her talking about human connection, she smiled to herself and thought, *yes, yes, this could just be it.*

For the next hour Mo fussed over her, piled her with blankets to make sure she was warm, and ensured that every bit of food was within arm's reach. He kept her plastic cup filled with sparkling elderflower and although at times she had wished it was vodka, she leaned in toward him a little more than she had done before.

For the rest of the afternoon he had spoken about medical journals, her father's work, and who in their year was going to fail, and although she found it dull, the glimpse she had gotten of the man she thought he just might be had kept her asking and leaning in for more.

But moments like that didn't come often and earlier today when they had gone for a walk and he had turned up with a bunch of roses, he had remained a stubbornly closed book, despite her best efforts, and she wondered why she was trying.

Jenna flicks open Mo's message and thanks him again for the beautiful flowers while realizing she left them in one of the bars. She types that she's been revising late in the library, hence not picking up her phone. Once again, exhaustion saves her as she pleads tiredness, ending any possibility of conversation before it has even begun. He replies straight away anyway. Tells her how much he admires her work ethic and how it inspires him. Tells her goodnight, and leaves a string of kisses at the end of the message that says, "I'm here to stay."

Jenna stares at the message before rolling over. She always sleeps well, regardless of who sends her kisses at night.

The next day she has forgotten about him again. She slips into the sisters' room in the mosque, the way she has done every Thursday night, and takes her place in the circle of women reading the Quran. She feels a homecoming of sorts.

Her mother has saved her usual spot next to her and she quietly squeezes Jenna's hand in greeting, passing her the Quran she likes best. For a moment Jenna looks at the spaces next to Malak's and Kees's mothers, sees them taken by other women, and misses her friends so sharply that she feels a sudden pain lace across her chest and catch the breath in her throat. She wants to message them and say it wasn't supposed to be like this, but she picks up her Quran and begins to follow along to the recitation, resting her back against the wall and breathing deeply. The little green-and-gold book in her hands feels like an anchor, and with every turn of the page something washes over her that feels like stillness. Aunty Nourhan is reading and she wonders, as she always does, what it would sound like to hear her sing. When they were younger, she, Malak, and Kees would beg Aunty Nourhan to sing because her voice was so beautiful, but she never would. Said she didn't like to draw attention to herself and the gift of her voice was saved for the words of God.

As she recites, Jenna thinks that perhaps if she sounded like that she would save it all for God too, because what else could possibly matter when you sounded like all the angels had come to rest in your chest? The Quran floats through Jenna and up into the room, dripping down the walls, hanging off the ceiling. At some point, the light outside the windows changes but no one notices. Later, when they leave the building, they will comment that the stars are brighter tonight and they won't know if that's true or if they themselves are brighter. They sit, bodies folded around each other, women young and old who have gathered from different countries, all following the same lines of curled Arabic letters, bodies swaying ever so slightly as the word of God vibrates from a woman's throat so beautifully that at one point or another, it brings them all to tears.

BILQUIS

She has picked up her father's habit of checking doors to see if they're locked. She pushes against the wood, once, twice, and for a third time. Harry says nothing, just walks past her as she does it. He's learned not to say anything, and if it gives her peace of mind he's content to leave her to check as many doors and windows as she wants.

He has more patience for it than Kees's mother, who berates her husband for his stubborn mind, but Kees thinks it's something to do with living in this country. If closed doors are all that's offered, you learn to push against them, even when you know they don't move.

Maybe she's overthinking it. She always overthinks it. Finally, she climbs into bed with Harry, who is already half asleep.

"My brain hurts," she says, not expecting a response from him. She doesn't hear his mumbled reply before she's already asleep.

For once she doesn't hear the alarm and is woken at 5 a.m. by Harry mumbling that it's time for Fajar prayer, and from somewhere deep in her slumber she smiles.

"I'm going, I'm going."

She stumbles into the bathroom and lets the water run hot before splashing it over her and washing for prayers. She silently thanks God that the morning prayers are so short.

She rolls out the mat in the corner of their small bedroom and prays in the only space left free. Everything else is taken up with a wardrobe or a chest of drawers or something else to hold their life's possessions in. As she stands from the last prayer, she hits her back on the corner of the bed and groans loudly. She turns to see Harry's eyes glowing at her through a blue dawn.

He lifts the corner of the duvet. "Quick, back in, you can sleep for another hour."

"Why are you awake?" she asks. "Go back to sleep, baby."

"Well, apart from you thudding around and banging into everything…"

"Oh God, I know. Sorry."

He grabs her by the waist as she climbs into bed and kisses the back of her head. "Keesy, this place is too small for us. We can't keep living like this."

She sighs. "I know."

She doesn't tell him that he could stay at his apartment. She has given up pretending that they don't spend every night together and doesn't want to imagine it anymore.

The alarm screeches them both out of bed an hour later and they fall over each other as they get ready in a studio flat that is only supposed to fit one small person, let alone two adults with busy schedules.

She laughs as Harry falls over her bag, which she had left in the middle of the floor, and as he spins round to look at her with a piece of toast in his hand and his tie halfway down his chest, he says, "Kees, this isn't funny. I'm going to break my neck one of these days."

She sobers up quickly and says the prayer that her mother always used to say to ward off the evil eye. "That isn't funny, Harry, you shouldn't joke about that."

He kisses her and holds her face in his hand for a moment.

"Have a good day, Ms. Lawyer."

"You too, Mr. Lawyer," she laughs. They call goodbye to one another and she runs out the door three minutes after him to be swept up into the city. She smiles, remembering how much they longed for the day they would be lawyers and now that it's here she feels a happiness she can barely name.

Her entire life has been taken over with her new job at a law firm that works with refugees, asylum seekers, and marginalized groups and she is happy to give her life over to their causes. Her law firm offers legal aid and representation where normally there would be no hope or ability to afford help, and the long hours and awful pay are made up for in the faces of her clients who come to her scared, but if she is really lucky, and if one of the gods are shining down on her, they leave smiling. She's still too new at the job to know that a charity-based law firm assisting immigrants, ethnic minorities, and poor people is a losing side and she hasn't lost enough cases to be jaded yet. The senior partners noted this, smiling over their coffee breaks that they now actually took because the years had taught them that grabbing a coffee on the go and forgoing lunch breaks didn't make you a hero but a martyr to a cause they'd learned wasn't worth dying for. They slept well enough, knowing that the work they did was the heroic thing and the outcome didn't change that.

Kees hasn't seen her parents in months but they're so proud of her they don't complain. Her mum sends curries in the mail even though she tells her it isn't safe and she shouldn't do it. John, at the apartment concierge desk, comments on how great they smell and she always sends food down to him. Every time her parents have come to visit he has offered up the storage room on the fifth floor to hide Harry's things and never mentions it or questions either of them about it, and for that she loves him.

Thinks she'll always send him curries as long as she can, even though it feels a little bit like buying his silence.

Despite telling her mother to stop with the food, she's thankful. She doubts she and Harry would eat anything but cheese on toast without them because that is all they have the energy for these days.

Saba's wedding is creeping up and, as always, she feels guilty for not being around. Saba sends her pictures of outfits and bangles and asks for her opinion. She scurries to the bathroom and looks before replying her preference and running back into the conference room in her pencil skirt and silk blouse to pick up more case files. She thinks of the people she is trying to help when she feels the guilt creep in, and knows that Saba understands that she's doing something good here. It's not as if she's neglecting her sisterly duties to defend rich white men in corporate litigation, but ethnic minorities, their own people.

Her mother has made her promise she will be home the night before the wedding and her father is proud of her and right now, this is enough.

She thinks of Malak in Egypt and still can't bring herself to talk to her even though instinctively she reaches for her phone and slides open their messages when something funny happens. She often thinks about what Malak said, that she and Harry were biding their time and that soon it will all be over, and although she would never say it out loud, she worries that it's true. She is still furious with Malak for giving up on Jacob. Feels sorry for him when she sees him with Harry, looking worn out. She always gives him an extra-long hug and as if he knows what she is trying to say, always mutters, "Yeah, I'm fine, honestly."

She wants to strangle Malak in those moments and then the longing to talk to her friend disappears.

She rarely speaks to Jenna either; she has been lost to the

world in a haze of medical exams. She and Harry promised to see her final university play and it's the only arrangement they've made. They are all scattered to the dreams they have spent four long years planning.

Kees has the uncomfortable thought that Jenna isn't okay and the quiet coming from her end of the phone line isn't just due to exams and rehearsals. Jenna's silence has always been a red flag because when loud people go quiet, they are either desperately sad or doing something they shouldn't be doing, but without Malak to step in with her, she dismisses it.

Kees's clothes are beginning to hang off her, creating spaces between the fabric and her skin that didn't used to be there, so she knows how schedules can change a person.

She is becoming busy, swallowed into the city's commute and coffee run and the late-night suppers with colleagues. Her days have a routine she shares with the rest of the capital who rise with her to make the rent they need, and save the money for the holidays they need even more, and when she groans her way into bed each night she feels fulfilled.

She is happy, apart from the moments she feels like she's going to die of sadness because she doesn't know what to do about Harry and her friends living lives that don't have her in it.

It is mid-November when Harry reminds her they have dinner with his parents that evening. She is looking forward to seeing them. Always enjoys the way time seems to pause when she's in the DuVaughn house and for a little while everything seems less serious, which is the opposite feeling to her own family home where life feels heavier.

Vivian opens the door to them in a flurry of kisses, comments about how cold it's getting and how the damn leaves are forever cluttering up the driveway and how she must talk to the gardener about it.

"Nathaniel," she calls, "your son is here; do come and say hello."

She holds Kees by the shoulders and shakes her head. "Have either of you eaten in the last three months at all? Bilquis, you look exquisite but we need to feed you."

Kees laughs and hugs her, wondering if it's a mother's trait to always use a full name. "It's lovely to see you; it's been too long."

"Far too long. Nathaniel, for God's sake," Vivian calls again.

"Yes, yes, I'm here. What's going on?" He emerges from the corridor smiling and kisses her mouth. Kees looks away to give them privacy and Harry laughs at her, the way he always does when she blushes at public affection.

"Your son," says Vivian.

He turns to Harry and pulls him into a hug. "Why does she always say 'your son' like I don't know you're mine?"

Harry laughs and wraps his arms around his father, who kisses him on the cheek. "Maybe she's just trying to reassure you, Dad. You always had questions about that good-looking postman she used to fancy."

"And you know what a little flirt your mother is. Who knows whose son you are?" replies Nathaniel, his arm still around Harry's neck. Their resemblance is so striking you could never doubt Harry's parentage.

They all enjoy the joke and Kees feels mortified to her very toes at even the joke of an affair and wonders if she'll ever get used to this family. For a moment she considers her father coming home and joking about his wife and the postman and she feels momentarily sick. Shakes her head quickly and thinks that rich white people are, in fact, crazy and all her previous assumptions about them are true. She deliberately avoids acknowledging to herself that she is in love with a rich white man.

"Can I get you a drink, son? Your mum's just cracked open a good bottle of red," says Nathaniel, already pulling a wineglass off the shelf.

"Not tonight, Dad, I'm driving," Harry replies, adamantly not looking at Kees.

"Oh, what a shame," says Vivian. "Kees, I know you don't drink, so I've got some lovely sparkling grape that's apparently supposed to taste like wine but has zero alcohol in it. Would you like a glass?"

Kees smiles and thanks her, ignoring the fact that most non-alcoholic wines still have 0.06 percent of alcohol. She catches Harry about to say something, but she quickly shakes her head and silences him. God would have to forgive her tonight, and anyway, family is one of the biggest tenets of their faith. He would understand.

"I'll have a glass too, Mum," says Harry.

"Are you sure? You can leave your car here and get a taxi back so you and I can go in on this bottle." His father looks at him expectantly and Harry shakes his head.

"No, Dad, honestly, I'm fine. I've got a big day in the office tomorrow; I need a clear head."

"Exactly," interrupts Vivian, taking the bottle out of her husband's hand. "You could do with taking a leaf out of your son's book."

Nathaniel looks across at Kees and rolls his eyes and she laughs with him. It's the least she can do, seeing as she has taken away the joy of drinking with his son.

Harry doesn't view it like that, says he gave up alcohol and pork on his own, because he wanted to, but she knows that if it wasn't for her he never would have done those things and it is another piece of guilt she carries around with her.

It is midway through dinner when Nathaniel clears his throat and looks pointedly at his wife. Kees, who notices everything, tenses.

Harry is oblivious to the shift at the table and continues eating until he looks up and sees his parents watching him, and Kees watching his parents.

"What's up?"

"Well," says Nathaniel, clearing his throat again, "your mother and I have found a new property we're thinking of buying."

"That's great, Dad," replies Harry and he looks genuinely happy for his parents and Kees loves him for being the kindest man on the planet.

"Well, the thing is, it's in East London."

"You're moving East?" asks Harry. "Why? You hate East."

Vivian shudders delicately. "I really do."

"No, son, can you imagine your mother in East London? Don't be daft. We're thinking of buying it for you and Kees."

She's aware that her mouth is hanging open and Harry hasn't said anything.

Nathaniel takes the silence as encouragement. "We know you're not really staying at your apartment because Kees's is closer to both your offices and that place can't be comfortable for two of you."

He hurriedly turns to Kees and puts his hand on her arm. "Not that your place isn't lovely, you understand; we were just thinking you might like a bit of space."

"It really is a lovely little flat," interrupts Vivian, smiling at Kees.

"But you're both moving on with life and you've got great jobs. We know the housing market is a bastard these days. We thought it might be a nice little first place for you both. It's three bedrooms, has a garden, which is a miracle these days in London." Nathaniel laughs and expects them all to join in.

No one does. Kees is thinking about the word "little," and then "three bedrooms," and wonders again how wildly different their worlds are. She thinks that should they ever see her family home they might finally understand what "little" meant.

"Could also be a great place to start a family," he finishes.

Kees feels her neck snap toward him and hears Harry say, "Dad, no one is starting a family just yet."

"Well, of course not," exclaims Vivian, looking equally shocked. "You'd have to be married first."

For the first time, Kees feels like their worlds have taken a small step toward each other as she's silently as shocked as Vivian at the suggestion of babies before marriage.

"I'm not pregnant," she blurts out, stupidly.

Harry sighs and puts his hand on his mother's arm. Vivian is looking horrified. They might be liberal Catholics but no son of hers would be fathering a child without honoring the mother by marrying her. The very suggestion is enough to drain the color from her face.

"Well, of course you're not," she stutters. "What would Father Bastian say? God forbid."

The mention of the family's priest tells Kees just how shaken Vivian is and she thinks that maybe her own mother would get on with Vivian after all. But she has the feeling that this conversation is sliding away from her and by the look on Nathaniel's face, it isn't going the way he expected it to.

Harry, who can always be relied on to bring logic to any proceeding, interrupts. "Okay, let's all just take a breath. No one is having any children right now so that doesn't need discussing. We're a long way from that point. Regarding the flat, Dad, Mum, this is incredibly generous of you."

Nathaniel clears his throat again, relieved that the conversation is back where it should be. "Don't be silly, son. We bought your three brothers a flat when they graduated, and we want to do the same for you. What else are we going to spend our money on?"

Kees has numerous responses to this but doesn't think Nathaniel and Vivian DuVaughn would appreciate her breakdown of how they could distribute their wealth to help those who actually need it because, if truth be told, their four perfectly capable white sons with high-paying jobs and private educations didn't.

Harry has gone around the table to hug his father and as they all embrace and kiss, he thanks them and she can tell he means it.

"Isn't this wonderful, Kees?" he asks her, smiling.

"I'm really happy for you, Harry, congratulations."

He laughs and kisses her on the head. "Not me, silly, us. It's for both of us."

"No, it's not."

She feels as if she's just turned the lights off as the smiles drop from the three perfectly symmetrical faces that turn to stare at her.

She tries to make her voice less cutting but doesn't quite manage it.

"This is your parents' gift to you, it's nothing to do with me."

"Oh darling," interrupts Vivian. "Of course it is. Your name won't be on the papers, of course, but we wouldn't dream of you paying rent or a penny toward it, and since you'll be living there with Harry, we want to buy a place that you like as well. We thought we could all go and view the flat on the weekend before we make an offer."

"It's really not about rent," Kees says, smiling back. "I wouldn't move in with Harry before we were married and my family certainly wouldn't be happy with that, nor would I."

They blink at her. There is a moment where the frame freezes and nobody moves. They are suspended around this large oak dining table, sitting on the edge of saying things aloud that could shatter the illusion Kees has spent years building. A beat. Two beats. Then everyone says something at once.

"But you live together now," says Vivian.

"Can I get anyone a drink?" asks Nathaniel.

"Let's discuss it later," says Harry.

Kees looks at them all and feels sorry for tilting their smiles to frowns but also annoyed that they've made so many assumptions without asking her.

"There's nothing to discuss. It's important that I'm married before I officially move in with anyone. That's just how it works in my culture."

Now that she's mentioned the C-word everyone bustles and says something over each other until the consensus is that no one will say anything anymore and dinner continues, haltingly, despite the tension rising off everyone's shoulders and necks.

It never fails to amaze her that the real C-word for white people is culture and once it's mentioned people compete to show their respect for it or their knowledge of it. She knew the effect it would have before she used it, and had she been feeling kinder or if she'd had more grace today, she probably wouldn't have.

Despite her irritation at their assumptions, Kees remains in awe at the way Vivian, one of the most skilled diplomats she's ever met, expertly steers the conversation away from awkwardness. All traces of the previous conversation are swept away and Vivian is warm and open and loving, and if she feels any annoyance that her son's girlfriend has made the family dinner uncomfortable by refusing a flat they want to buy for her to live in, she shows no sign of it. She asks Kees for help with something. Reassures her husband. Offers help to her son. Squeezes Kees's shoulder in a way that says you are wanted, and it occurs to Kees that she doesn't possess a grace like this and doesn't know if she'll ever be able to learn it. Nothing more is mentioned of the flat. It's as if it never happened. Even she almost forgets it during post-dinner board games and the feeling of being surrounded by people who genuinely love you.

The car ride home is quiet. They listen to music and she strokes the back of Harry's head and says nothing. She can feel his thoughts vibrating beneath her palm, and like the lawyer he is he will think through every argument, every scenario, and every possible outcome before bringing anything to the stand. He is meticulous and thorough and doesn't believe in fast think-ing. He has always maintained that it creates sloppy decisions and she knows he'll be a better lawyer for it, even if sometimes she wishes he would snap to conclusions quicker.

She has become someone who watches the clock constantly. If they get home in the next ten minutes and she's in bed in the next half an hour, she'll get six, maybe six and a half, hours' sleep before she needs to wake up.

By the time she's taken off her makeup, prayed, and gotten into her pajamas, it's six hours and a quarter, if she can get to sleep straight away. She walks into the bedroom to see Harry kneeling by the bed, head bowed in prayer, and she smiles. Thinks he must be the only person left on earth who kneels by the bed to pray before getting into it and wonders if she pulled him out of a Dickens novel and into her life.

He lifts his head to see her and holds out his hand and she joins him by his side, bows her head, and talks to God for the sixth time that day, wondering if they're praying for the same thing.

He says "Amen," and she says "Ameen," before they both climb into bed.

She's about to turn the light off when he says her name and climbs on top of her.

"Hello, you," she says, looking into his eyes, trying to understand what he's feeling.

"Hello," he replies.

He doesn't say anything else but peels off her pajamas, kissing her everywhere, and she wonders what he's trying to say. She gives up trying to work it out and gives in to the only person who's ever touched her like this.

An hour later, as they lie breathless, passing a glass of water back and forth between them, she looks at the clock.

Five hours, if she sleeps now.

She switches off the light and lies against Harry's body in the same way she does every night, wondering if she could live without this. She falls asleep picturing a life without him in it and wakes to his kisses on her neck. The clock flashing beneath her hazy eyes tells her she's been asleep for an hour and she's about to ask him why he's still awake when she feels him slide down the bed and between her thighs and suddenly she too is awake and the sleep is gone; her eyes are bright and the silence of their bedroom is taken over only by a steady murmur that hums out of her and she stops watching the clock.

He wakes her up twice more in the night; each time he is hungrier than the last. They say nothing, just reach with hands and mouths and pull at skin in a new kind of language where each point seems more urgent than the next. It never occurs to her that she could refuse him and get the sleep she needs.

By the time her alarm goes off, she feels her body before she wakes to her mind. A thud of satisfaction is sitting in the pit of her stomach, tiredly savoring the aches and stings that come from a man roaming across a woman's body all night long. The morning always brings the pain that pleasure erased the night before.

She hears Harry walk into the room and finally opens her eyes as he slides a hot-water bottle wrapped in a towel between her thighs and places a mug of coffee on the bedside table.

The imaginary world in her head in which this man doesn't exist is hazier and harder to form today.

"Stay in bed and drink your coffee. You need to rest," says Harry.

"I'll be late for work."

He shakes his head and kisses her forehead before turning to leave. "I'll drop you off."

"But then you'll be late for work."

"I've taken the morning off, it's fine."

She knows him well enough not to say anything, that he's still not ready to talk, and she knows that somewhere he is embarrassed that his world is one where parents offer their children three-bedroom flats over dinner. She also knows him well enough to know that mornings off are not something he takes and even though he comes from a world where the money is easy and life is gentle, he's not one to ever take advantage of it, so the conversation last night with his parents must have shaken him more than she's giving him credit for.

So she says nothing. Kees yawns her way through the morning, occasionally sliding open her phone to stare at the group chat that sits quietly like an abandoned house, before closing her phone again.

She supposes not everything needs to be discussed and de-liberated with friends, even if that happens to be whether or not you should break up with the boyfriend you're wildly in love with for the family you haven't seen in weeks, just to stay on the right side of the gossips at the local mosque. Not that she cares about them, but her mother does. Her mother really does.

MALAK

You can never call Cairo quiet, but in the morning, at 5:30, when the day has just cracked itself open across the city, it is not busy and "not busy" is the closest Cairo will ever get to quiet.

Malak has learned this in the few months she's been here and although she has never been an early riser, Cairo has changed her. She sleeps less and laughs more. Her wide-open smile has become the most noticeable feature on her face.

A morning mist hovers over the Nile as the last of the coolness clings to its banks. The dirty green railings of Zamelek match the cloudy water that flows past, and dust is everywhere, even here by the side of the river where a rush of water cannot wash it away. Her aunties have spent a lifetime trying to wash away the city dust from balconies and floors and children's faces and have yet to succeed for longer than an afternoon. She often wonders if this is why her aunties are such strong women. Scrubbing constantly at something that never comes fully clean would give you a steely backbone.

Cars move past quietly and both those things are a miracle in themselves. Cars rarely move faster than a slow crawl and they're never quiet. She didn't know an entire language could be kept in a car horn until she arrived. "Congratulations on your marriage," "I'm passing you on the left," "I'm so happy I want to share it with you," "Your mother was a whore," "It's been a long day," "How you doing?" When she drives around the city with Haytham, the one cousin she has found a real friend in, the kind of friend you can swear with and spit in front of and tell secrets to, she reaches over and beeps the car horn for no reason and the answering horns around her make her throw her head back and laugh.

Africa has a certain sound to it and the constant hum and trill of car horns becomes a soundtrack you stop noticing eventually. She'd realized that every country has a sound. In England, it was the polite chorus of apologies that rose like a choir in neat harmonies, but here, it was the yells of strangers who didn't believe in the idea of strangers, so, really, you could say anything to anyone at any time.

Climbing through the gap in the railings to sit on her favorite crumbling piece of wall, her feet dangling over the Nile, Malak considers how everything is different here as she pulls out her sandwich. The round bread squashed full of tamaya and salad, the tahini dripping out the sides, has become her favorite way to step into a new day. She gets it from the same place every morning and they recognize her now, shouting greetings and practicing their English on her while she practices her Arabic on them and they all understand maybe five words in total, but it's enough conversation for the morning.

A fluka floats past her and the old man at its helm shouts something she doesn't understand. Her Arabic is still dismal and the lessons she is taking with a tutor mostly reveal that she lacks any real skill with languages, but she has learned how Egyptians say things, so what she lacks in understanding she makes up for in understanding tone. She knows the old man was telling her to be careful and she nods and waves back in acknowledgment. He seems appeased and, judging by the grin that is forcing its way through the gaps in his teeth, he makes a joke in return, so she laughs. It is the right answer and he laughs with her and continues floating past. She marvels at the way you could have an entire conversation with another human without speaking the same language.

Finishing her sandwich, she stands and starts her morning walk to work through Zamalek. She walks mainly on the road because sidewalks don't really exist in Cairo. It was easier to walk in the wide-open street and if a car wanted to pass it would always beep and let you know. By the time she arrives at the school, the sun is high and the heat covers her like a comforting arm around her shoulders. She doesn't know how she lived without this.

She is now a teacher, having never wanted to be one, but there isn't much use for history degrees in a country whose history predated anything she'd learned about in the halls of marble institutions that didn't recognize Africa's significance and so hadn't bothered with the continent. Her Arabic isn't good enough to work in business here. Nobody has the time to translate every single word of the team meeting to her, so after spending her first month drifting through the city, her cousin Akram had a friend of a friend who worked in an international school and they were always looking for native speakers. She was, after all, highly educated, and by a British university at that. Her position was gained and held mostly by her perfect British accent, but this was Egypt after all, and life was different here.

She has a light schedule and as long as she is there for morning assembly and her classes are done, the day is hers. She gets into her car and drives to the local members' club to spend the afternoon lying by the pool, watching her skin change color as she bakes, the sun pulling who she really is out from beneath her bones every day. Her university weight has fallen off her like baby fat, her hair is turning lighter, as her almost-black locks burn a chocolate brown and everything about Malak Abdel-Aziz hums and pulses beneath what she considers to be her own Egyptian sun.

If her afternoons are slow, her evenings are fast. This is the part she loves the most: when night comes and the heat has fallen off the day and everybody spills out of their houses to meet and talk. To sit in the restaurant-filled plazas as fountains splash and shisha boys run around replacing hot coals and keeping a haze of fruity tobacco smoke above them all. To float down the Nile on a fluka wrapped in fluorescent lights blasting the latest Amr Diab song from speakers tied to the boat in a way that, in England, would be tacky but here is a bubbling joy. To drive through the city to find the best sweet shop. To sit on the balcony with her aunties sipping tea and eating supper. Supper has turned into her favorite meal because it means there is still so much of the night to come. Her aunties stuff egg sandwiches and her favorite kunafa into her hand with cups of mint tea that are always refilled, and while they may shout at her to scrub harder while cleaning or to stop lying in the sun, here is where they claimed her. They asked about her parents every time, talking about how much they missed them and telling Malak stories about them that she stored away to tell Samir.

When finally she refuses another plate of sweets for the sixth time, and has practiced her Arabic enough, she leaves her aunties on the balcony, their cries for her to come again soon floating after her in the air, and the night is suddenly hers. She drives home to pick up Nylah and Rayan, her new flatmates who have become her friends and who are helping her forget how much she misses the women she's left behind. By this point, Nylah will already have made a plan. Found the best club they should go to. A party that's happening. A new restaurant that's opened up which they can all afford because here on expat salaries she lives a life that is not possible in England, where every penny counts for so much. Here she has found herself suddenly with money. Not rich, but rich enough to not check the price tags when she buys new outfits. She has an apartment that is beautiful and pays a sum every month that is laughable in London. A car she pays a monthly rental on. Bills that are so comparatively small she barely notices them. Just hands over the two hundred Egyptian pounds that convert to pennies in English pounds and doesn't think about it ever again. A cleaner who comes to the flat once a week means she hasn't changed her own bedsheets for months now. She fills her tank with ninety Egyptian pounds and spends the same amount on a Caesar salad in her favorite restaurant. The drinks are the real expense when they go out to the clubs, but when the money is spare in her pocket, she doesn't think about it. There are always men around to buy them drinks and in this new life which feels like a holiday, she always chats to the men who want to buy her a drink. The guilt comes with the hangover the next morning and she remembers her promise not to drink and how her mornings used to start bent over the Quran searching for answers, but the guilt lessens every day. She has traded her white boy in for God, so, surely, he can allow her a good time in the evening? She has given enough.

One weekend, as she had been groaning on the living-room floor, wondering what she drank last night, Nylah had asked her if maybe they should go to the mosque.

"You want to take some pictures?" she asks.

Nylah had taken the pillow she was leaning on and thrown it at her head in a way that made her regret every drink she'd ever had.

"No, you idiot. I mean to pray. I've been feeling like a bad Muslim lately. We've done a lot of drinking and not much praying. If only they were both as much fun," she sighed.

They had agreed then that more praying would happen, and although that hadn't strictly happened at home, they had maintained going to the mosque every Friday for Juma prayers and that was, as far as this household was concerned, a big enough step in the right direction for now.

She had met Nylah and Rayan at an expat event in the second week she had arrived. She'd hated everyone there and had escaped after ten minutes. As she was leaving, she found them both sitting on the wall complaining about the event and by the time her car was brought around they'd agreed to go to dinner. A month later, since she was already suffocating in her aunty's house, sharing a room with her two cousins, while the third sister, Eman, bunked in with their mother, the offer of their spare bedroom was heaven sent. Nylah and Rayan were half-Italian, half-Libyan sisters who came from a family of six and, at one point or other, each child was sent to Egypt for a year to learn the language fluently and attend daily lessons with the teacher who had taught all the children to speak Arabic, or at least had tried. The sisters came from what Malak called Jenna's lot, and when Jenna, in one of the brief calls they'd had, asked her what that was supposed to mean, she had replied, "You know, the rich Arab crowd." She's aware that her circles are unrecognizable to the ones she formed in England. She occasionally pulls out a picture of the three of them lying on the grass in the park one summer, each body touching to form a connected ring. She clutches the picture tighter than she means to. She always stuffs it back behind the sweaters. The thought of having it up in her room for Nylah and Rayan to see and ask questions about is more than she can stomach, but she won't pack it away. It needs to belong somewhere, even if that place is out of sight but within reach.

She is stubbornly moving forward, every step in this new life taking her closer and closer toward the woman she has always imagined herself to be. She has become a person with roots. Someone who finally understands the love of a country. She is a happier person.

So when Malak finally meets him, finally places her hand in his as they shake and introduce themselves, and he says, "Hi, I'm Ali," she feels like all the steps she's ever taken have been leading her to this very moment. And here, in the courtyard of one of the most famous mosques in the world and, in her opinion, one of the most beautiful, she feels like she's arrived. There is the distinct feeling that suddenly she has pulled up at a platform, reached the last stop on the route, stepped out of the car, and this journey has been God sent because how else could she be here, in the land of her ancestors, underneath the minarets, palm to palm with a man who's so beautiful she is suddenly lost for words?

He takes it for shyness and thinks it makes her more beautiful.

"We probably shouldn't be shaking hands in a mosque," he laughs. "The religious police will be after us." His eyes twinkle and at that moment, somewhere in the back of her mind, Jacob silently floats out of her subconscious and starts to make his way back over the ocean.

She laughs back. "I can already see the old uncles shooting disapproving glances so you're probably right. You're from England?"

"Yes," he replies. "London. Born and bred. But Egyptian originally. I'm sure you know the story?"

"Yes," she replies. "Except born here. Mum and Dad moved straight after."

"Better life, better opportunities, right?" He laughs as he says this, and she feels like she's sitting in the middle of a shared joke that nobody else in the entire world could possibly understand.

"Exactly," she agrees. "Until you're not going to mosque enough and then suddenly..."

"It's the worst country in the world," he finishes.

They both laugh, grinning stupidly at each other.

"Well, we're both here so I reckon we didn't do too badly after all." He leans in as he says this, and Malak is pulled further into something that exists only between them.

"I guess so."

"I've seen you coming here for a few weeks. You come with your friend, right?" he asks.

"Yeah," she replies. "She forgot her shoes in the sisters' area, I'm just waiting for her."

"I'm glad. It gave me the chance to talk to you."

She grins up at him. "Are you telling me you were too scared while she was here?"

He laughs. "You're cheeky. I like that."

She suddenly feels inordinately pleased and passes it off in a shrug that she hopes is nonchalant.

"I guess you must be new to the city if you've just started coming here?" He is smiling at her and her breath catches.

"Oh no, I've been here quite a few months now, but we were going to a different mosque. We thought we'd try a new one and I think this one's the best, so it's worth the drive." She is surprised at how quickly the lie floats off her tongue, but then again, they are in a country that believes in worship and modesty so the lies always sit close to the surface.

"I agree. I've never seen anything so beautiful," he says, without blinking or breaking his stare, and she smiles again, not quite sure why she just lied about going to the mosque but feeling glad she did, rewarded by that look on his face.

"Well, my friend is waiting for me outside so I'd better go," he says, pulling his phone out of his pocket. "Put your number in and I'll message you. Just in case you ever need a tour guide or someone to show you the best shisha spots. We Brit-Egyptians have got to stick together."

She taps her number into his phone and hands it back and a breath later he's gone. She watches his back and feels like something important and big just happened in one small conversation. Nylah arrives next to her.

"God, I love a man in a tight white T-shirt," Nylah says, looping her arm through Malak's.

"Right. Did you see his body? Jesus," Malak replies.

"Of course I did. Why do you think I waited and kept my distance?"

Malak turns and kisses Nylah on the cheek. "This is why I love you. What a wing-woman."

"I know." Nylah nods. "I was scared for a second you wouldn't swap numbers and honestly I would have killed you."

"Well, he took mine," Malak replies.

"Yes, but did you see the way he was looking at you? He'll call."

"The things I would do to that man. How beautiful is he?" Malak asks, although she doesn't need an answer.

"Babe, I hope you do many, many things to that man, for both of us," says Nylah. "One of us needs to get laid."

"Seif still holding out on you, then?" Malak asks sympathetically.

"Yes," groans Nylah. They start walking across the courtyard, their long black abayas trailing on the marble behind them. "He's forever taking me out for dinners and every time he drops me off at home he does nothing but kiss me and while the kissing is great, he could at least slide a hand down my pants or something."

"You also could just ask him up to our apartment," replies Malak.

"Yeah, I did think of it, but the rules are different here and we can't be too blatant about it."

"True." Malak nods in agreement. If Ali did text, she was going to have to learn to play a completely different game. "We just need to orchestrate an excuse for him to be already in the apartment. Oh, why don't we have a party?"

"For what reason?" asks Nylah.

"Who needs a reason to have a party?"

"Hmm. In England, no one. But here I think we need one to make it more legit. We don't want the bawab's family to think we're whores.

"He sees us going out to the club most weekends," laughs Malak. "He already thinks we're whores."

"Excellent point," Nylah says, nodding.

They bend down to slip on sandals at the entrance to the mosque, smiling at the doorman and calling "Assalamualaikum" in unison.

He smiles back with all of his teeth and calls "Nawartoona"—you've lit us up—after them and they both agree that of all the doormen they've come across, he is their favorite and they must ask his name next Friday.

BILQUIS

The offices of Thellem Aid are impressive from the outside and a dump on the inside. Apart from the conference room, which is decked in inexpensive furniture and expensive-smelling candles. It's the only room that doesn't smell of freshly printed paper and ink. Everywhere else is covered in dossiers, reports, contracts, and case folders. When she had walked in here on her first day, Kees had made a sarcastic joke about literal paper trails that nobody had laughed at but Addy, which firmly decided who her friends here would be.

Now, months into the job, she finds the smell comforting and doesn't notice the paper anymore.

Addy places a coffee in front of her and then perches on the desk, on top of the case files she's reading, and she sighs.

Adnan is Pakistani and by day insists on being called Addy because it is just easier for everyone to pronounce, while occasionally by night he becomes a drag queen named Nana who performs eighties classics, but mostly just Madonna hits.

"Can you please get the fuck off my notes," says Kees, looking at him in a way that withers most people in the office, but Addy merely leans to one side, lifting his ass and winking at her. "Get it, gurl."

She shakes her head and snatches her notes out from under him.

"Grumpy today, aren't we?" he says.

"I said please, didn't I?"

"True," he agrees. "And that's practically upbeat for you. Why are we always the first ones in?"

She doesn't look up. "Because we're brown."

"Second excellent point." He nods, opening her drawer and rooting around for the breakfast bars he knows she keeps in there.

"When are you going to bring your own food in, instead of stealing mine?" she asks him.

"Bitch, I have my own food. Trust me, your supermarket-value breakfast bars are nothing to rave about." He finds them and pulls two out of the box, throwing one at Kees and leaning back to unwrap his.

She looks disparagingly up at him with a raised eyebrow.

"I just thought," he continues, "that we could have breakfast together, but since we both work like dogs, this is the closest we'll get, and also so that you can tell me what went down at your in-laws the other night? You've been particularly cunty these last few days."

"They're not my in-laws, Addy," she replies.

"I love how that's the bit you take umbrage with," he laughs.

"Yeah, well, precision matters."

"They're the parents of the man you've been in a committed relationship with for four years; fuck precision, they're practically your in-laws."

"Have I really been that cunty?" she asks.

Addy half barks, half laughs. "Steven actually trembled when you were talking to him the other day."

She throws her hands up and gives up making notes. "Yes, but come on, Steven! He fundamentally lacks backbone."

"Yes, darling, we know; that's why he works in admin. But I'm telling you, as your best friend."

"You're not my best friend," she interrupts.

"Objection! You see. This is what I mean," he replies. "Best friend within these walls and don't you dare try to even contest that."

"I'll allow the point. Continue," she says, nodding.

"You're snappy and while everyone here already thinks you're an ice queen, there has been an extra wind-chill factor these last few days and I want to know why."

She experiences one of her rare moments when she wonders if she should rein it in and try to drop more honey from her tongue than salt, trying to remember that she is a professional now. The ties from university and childhood, where everyone knows you for who you really are and doesn't mind the sting because of years of loving history, have fallen away.

"Harry's parents want to buy 'us,' but really him, a three-bedroom flat. They wanted us to go and view it with them to see if we liked it before they put in an offer. They told us over dinner that night."

"Ooooh, tricky," says Addy, shaking his head.

"Exactly," she says. "What the actual fuck am I going to do?"

"What has Harry said? By the way, have I told you how beautiful he is?"

"Every single day."

"I know, I know, but the point bears repeating. You get to go home to Adonis every night."

She laughs for the first time that morning. "You have plenty of Adonises in your bed."

"True." He nods. "So?"

"He hasn't said anything. We haven't talked about it yet," she replies.

"Are you hoping that if you don't say anything it will just quietly fade away?" he asks her.

"Yeah, a little bit."

He smiles while nodding at her understandingly. "Yeah, I used to do that too. Turns out that no matter how much you ignore it, it doesn't go away."

It's her turn to look at him with sympathy. "No, I'm sure it doesn't."

"So," he says, looking at her, "it's time to make a call, kid."

"And yet, I'm still trying to figure out a way to work this so I don't have to and everything can just continue the way it always has."

"I know." He squeezes her arm. "Honestly, it's times like these I'm so glad my parents died and I never had to make this decision."

"Addy!"

"Don't look at me like that," he says. "I know it sounds awful but I'm honestly glad because having to look my mum in the eye and tell her I liked boys and also was secretly dressing up in her saris would, honest to God, have killed her and I'm just glad I wasn't responsible for putting her in her grave."

"You still had your aunty, though," says Kees.

"Yes, but I hated her and left home the minute I could and never went back, so really, I don't give a fuck what she knows or doesn't. She wasn't even worth coming out to."

She has heard about Addy's aunty on staff nights out when he was drunk and crying on her shoulder in the bathroom and she knows enough about her to say nothing now.

"Having a family you actually like and want to be close with, and having to make this choice, that's impossible. I can't imagine that. I'm sorry, love."

She quickly blinks to stop any tears pooling in her eyes. She will never cry in any office.

People have started coming in and the morning is beginning to grind into motion.

Addy throws his wrapper on her desk and stands.

"Well, we'll discuss later. I need to go and find my idiot associate and hope he hasn't ruined my case files."

She laughs and is grateful for his jokes. "I thought you were going to fire him?"

"Honestly, I'm this close. If he doesn't start getting in before me, I'm going to lose my shit."

"Addy, you get into the office at six a.m."

"Well, then, he should get in at five."

He squeezes her shoulder as he leaves and she watches as the junior interns scuttle out of his way.

She is thankful for a job that requires long hours and all of her head space. There is no time in the day to worry about what to do or to try to decode Harry's silence. She has always trusted his timings and doesn't feel like stopping that practice now. When she had met him, he had been the only person she would stop and listen to. He was the opposite of what she imagined a lawyer to be: quiet, still, happy to sit on the sidelines, and in his quietness she had wanted to know more. She would watch him debate in their seminars, see his raised hand in lecture halls, and she would stop and turn her head slightly in his direction to catch every word. She was vaguely aware that most people turned to hear what she had to say, but, for the first time, she had been interested in the thoughts that emanated from another person.

She knows there is no point in rushing Harry. As a lawyer, she has learned that sitting in somebody's silence is an opportunity because most people are uncomfortable with them and if you were questioning a witness, all you had to do was wait.

Eventually, they said something because they couldn't bear the discomfort.

Her day doesn't finish until 10 p.m. Harry has already texted her that he's out to dinner with a friend. She eats another sandwich from the board meeting that has been left to dry in the kitchen before bending back over files, searching for loopholes and missed information that will get a nineteen-year-old Bangladeshi boy out of prison and back with his family. Though his family now thinks he's done something wrong, so she doesn't even know if he'll have a place to go to. One problem at a time.

Once she makes it home, she doesn't climb into bed as she should, but on a whim pulls her book of Rumi theology off the shelf and sits down to find the chapter on faith. It occurs to her that if she can find loopholes in the law, a solid concrete of legislation, then she can find loopholes in a faith which has been mostly open to interpretation as opposed to absolute conviction. The scholars could barely agree on anything, let alone the big topics. Someone, somewhere, must have written something about marriage and how she as a Muslim woman might be able to hold on to her faith, her heart, and her family.

She pulls the Quran off the shelf and cross-references it with a book on Bukhari that she'd bought in a fit of elevated devotion.

By the time Harry slips in the front door at midnight she is asleep on the sofa, a trail of books between the shelf and her fingers, which hang, fallen from the pages she was reading at the time. She remotely registers him picking her up and carrying her to bed but doesn't fully wake because she feels safe and there is no need to.

The following morning, Kees wakes to a warm mug of coffee and a note from Harry saying he's already left for early meetings and that he loves her. She smiles and thanks God.

She's making her second mug in the kitchen at work when Addy joins her and says, "So, any answers on what to do about your gorgeous boyfriend?"

"No," she replies. "I was asleep by the time he came home and he'd left by the time I woke."

Addy shudders delicately. "Gross. Sounds like a middle-aged marriage where the sex has dried up."

She indicates for him to pass the milk. "I don't think you need to worry about our sex life."

"Oh, want to tell me all about it?"

"Absolutely not."

"For someone so outspoken, you really do have a weird attitude to sex."

"Not everything has to be discussed, Addy, especially not in the fucking office kitchen."

"Fine, let's talk about how your boyfriend's family wants to buy you both a big flat to live in rent-free."

Emily Fortridge, who has been hovering nervously around the kettle, pitches herself into the conversation.

"Oh, you're buying a property, Kees? Congratulations."

Kees tries to keep the irritation out of her voice as she feels Addy tense behind her. They have spent many hours detailing Emily Fortridge's extensive flaws and interrupting conversations is high on the list.

"No, I'm not; my boyfriend's parents are buying one for him."

"Oh right. So, you're moving in there with him?" she asks.

"No."

She looks offended and Kees wonders why people seem affronted by something that is entirely none of their business.

Emily gives a nervous laugh. "Why ever not?"

"Because I'm Muslim, Emily, and we don't live with people before marriage." It is getting harder to hide her impatience.

She laughs, loudly this time, saying, "But you live together now."

"Not really, no," she growls in reply, shooting a glance at Addy, who is staring intently at Emily's face with his arms crossed.

"But doesn't he stay at yours every night?" she asks.

"What's your point, Emily?"

"Well..." She pauses. "He lives with you." Her laughter has been replaced by a confused look.

"Not officially, he doesn't, and I wouldn't officially move in with him before we were married."

"Well, that's a little hypocritical, isn't it?" she asks.

Kees stares at Emily and, for a brief second, considers throwing her mug of coffee all over her before refraining.

"I mean, no offense," Emily continues, "but you live together, share a bed together, but you still won't say you're living together because of some technical religious law so you'll pretend instead. It's just a little two-faced, isn't it?"

Kees reconsiders throwing her coffee.

"It's complicated," she replies.

"Well," says Emily, "why don't you get married?"

Addy snorts, finally unfrozen from gaping at Emily, but offers nothing further.

"Because," replies Kees, breathing in deeply and hoping to stifle the overwhelming feeling of being washed out to sea, "he's not Muslim."

Emily looks blankly at her. "So?"

"So, I can't marry someone who isn't Muslim, Emily. It's against our religion."

"Well, then, break up with him," she says easily.

Addy finally interjects. "Surely love counts for something, Emily?" he says. "I know we don't really believe in such things here in this institute of law and logic, but I'm sure even your cold heart can comprehend it."

Another loud laugh bursts from Emily's throat and under Addy's seniority there is a forced softer note to her voice as she leans over to pat Kees's arm. "Well, of course, of course. And if you love him, you have to just break all the rules, I suppose. Isn't that love, after all?"

Kees squints at her and wonders if Emily Fortridge has ever had to work for anything in her life, or if it's simply been passed from parent to child in a long line of ease and "as long as you're happy" protestations.

"My parents would disagree," she replies.

"Oh, darling," sighs Emily, smiling and patting her arm again in a way that makes Kees recoil. "Parents are always such a storm in the beginning, but they get over it. They just want you to be happy. Trust me, Kees, they'll be fine with it in the end. When I told my parents I was becoming a vegan my dad went on and on. He's a hunting man, you know. Really wasn't happy. But now he's totally fine with it because he knows it makes me happy. Your parents will be exactly the same."

She gives Kees one last smile and, with a satisfied air, like she's just got someone out of a jail sentence, walks out of the kitchen, a bottle of oat milk tucked under her arm.

Kees stares at Addy. "Did she just…?"

He nods. "Compare the love of your life, who you can't actually be with because your entire family will disown you, to being a vegan? Yes. Yes, she did."

"White people," they say in exactly the same tone, and Kees feels less alone. Or less like a traitor.

"We need to stop loitering in the kitchen because this is what happens," says Kees.

"Agreed. See you later," he replies and they both leave the kitchen to sit back at opposite sides of the office.

Her phone rings as she sits down and reception tells her someone by the name of Jacob is downstairs waiting for her. Quickly she scans her calendar, wonders if she's missed an appointment with a client, but can't see anything, so she swings on her suit jacket and walks downstairs.

When she sees Malak's ex-boyfriend, Jacob, standing there, her heart suddenly leaves her body and she stands motionless. In the lobby of her office, he is so out of context she feels like the world is spinning, and she stares at him before she reminds her feet to move. She stops again as the thought that something has happened to Harry laces its way through her and she reaches out for a wall that isn't there. It takes her longer to make her feet move toward him a second time.

By the time she reaches him she has stuffed her trembling hands into her trouser pockets and in a panic asks, "Is Harry okay? What's happened?"

"Oh my God, he's absolutely fine, Kees, please don't worry. You look terrified," he replies.

Her heart thuds back into her chest and her fear is replaced with anger.

"Well, what else am I supposed to think when you turn up at my work in the middle of a fucking Tuesday afternoon, Jacob?" she hisses through her relief.

He shuffles in his shoes, the rubber soles squeaking on the tiles, and she notices that he's wearing the same scruffy white sneakers he had throughout their university days. "I just wanted to talk to you about something. Could we grab some lunch?"

She stares at him, still too shaky to wonder what he could possibly want to talk about. "And you couldn't fucking call?" she asks.

"I don't have your number anymore, Kees," he replies, look-ing hurt.

"Well, how did you even find out this is where I worked?"

"I looked it up on LinkedIn."

She laughs. "And you couldn't send a message on there?"

Suddenly he looks tired, and she notices that he has bags under his eyes. He looks like shit.

"It was painful enough just trying to figure that site out, let alone messaging you on it. Look, I just want to talk, okay, and preferably not over the Internet."

"I can't do lunch, Jacob," she replies. "It's the middle of the workday, for Christ's sake. Come back at seven-thirty and we can go for a drink."

He nods. "Just don't tell Harry, okay?" And he's left the build-ing before she remembers to ask what he wants to talk about or why she shouldn't tell her boyfriend.

She spends the rest of the day running through every possible thing Jacob might want to discuss, her mind spiraling out of control.

By the time she meets Jacob in the lobby after work, her stomach is a gnarled knot of nerves and a rising panic has settled somewhere in her chest, just beneath her throat, and has made eating impossible since lunch.

They say very little as Kees walks them to the nearest bar, which is, in fact, a pub she's never been in, but she can't walk any farther because she cannot stand another minute.

"I'll grab us some drinks if you want to look for some-where to sit," says Jacob, nodding through to a room that looks quieter.

She nods back and takes his backpack, which he holds out to her, and finds the only table left, which happens to be beneath a bookshelf stuffed full of fake books, for whatever reason it is that people put fake books on shelves, perhaps to give the appearance of a country pub.

Jacob places a pint of Coke in front of her and then places his own pint down, which she notices he's already taken a big gulp of.

"I figured life hadn't completely turned upside down and you'd taken up drinking, so I settled on a Coke," he says.

She grunts. "A safe bet." She looks him up and down as he takes another sip. "You look awful."

He splutters over the rim of his glass before wiping stray beer off his chin with the back of his hand. "You know it's always a real pleasure talking to you, Kees."

She raises an eyebrow and ignores his comment. "What's going on? I assume you don't have a job yet, seeing as you're dressed like an eighteen-year-old freshman."

He leans back and grins for the first time. "Well, technically, I am a freshman. I've started another course."

"Jesus, Jacob, how many degrees are you trying to get?"

"As many as it takes to keep me out of an office job and the slow death of boredom."

"Oh, grow up."

"No, thanks. If you and Harry are anything to go by, it looks like shit."

Kees laughs. "So what, you're going to be an eternal student?"

"No, I'm doing a training course. I'll be a teacher next year and then I can work wherever I want. There're plenty of jobs for teachers."

Kees cocks her head to the side and frowns. "Since when did you want to be a teacher?"

He shrugs, leaning on the back legs of his chair, his faded jeans scuffed at the bottom, swinging at an angle. "I dunno if I do, but I thought I may as well try. Every day is different; I can do it anywhere in the world and plus, I'm good with kids. I've had plenty of training, at any rate."

She nods her head, for the first time acknowledging that he has a point. "I suppose five younger siblings will do that."

"Yeah." He laughs. "I was always helping someone out with homework when my mum had to work late shifts so I'm pretty sure I've been through the whole curriculum already."

He carries on talking about his family until Kees realizes she hasn't been listening and interrupts him gently. "Jacob, as nice as it is to catch up with you, what is so important that you had to turn up to my work like you're on some covert mission?"

He looks at her, opens his mouth a few times, starts to say something, and then stops.

"Yes?" she asks impatiently.

He looks as if he's in pain and then finally blurts out, "Harry's going to ask you to marry him."

She can feel her mouth hanging open as she stares at her friend's ex-boyfriend who is sitting opposite her telling her that her own boyfriend is going to propose. She is silent, can't seem to react. Jacob offers nothing else. He sips his pint and she stares at him until she feels the numbness receding and the first thing she feels is her stomach. The gaping hole of her stomach and how she hasn't eaten anything today because breakfast was derailed and she had to work through lunch.

"I need to eat something," she finally says, and Jacob raises his eyebrow.

"That's your response?"

"Oh, shut up and do something useful and pass me that menu off the other table."

He does as she asks and wisely offers nothing further while she scans the menu and calls a waitress over before ordering fish and chips because it's one of the only things on the menu that doesn't involve pork.

"How do you know?" she asks him.

"Because he told me," he replies patiently.

"Why would he tell you?"

"Because we're friends, and that's what friends do."

Kees snorted again. "Since when were you and Harry friends?"

"Why does everyone have such an issue with this?"

"Hanging out when your girlfriends were together doesn't make a friendship, Jacob."

He laughs into his pint. "You know, Malak said exactly the same thing the night before she left."

Kees doesn't say she was right, but the comparison hangs in the air and beneath her irritation she recognizes how much she misses her friend.

"Misery really does love company," he continues, "so I guess Harry and I have gotten closer."

Her hand tightens around her glass. "And what does Harry have to be miserable about?"

"Well, he's in a relationship with a woman he loves who has spent the last four and a half years refusing to tell her parents that he exists. That's pretty miserable, Kees."

She opens her mouth and is about to laugh, but Jacob holds up his hand and silences her.

"No, don't even say anything, Kees, because I know what's going to come out of your mouth. Some sarcastic comment about white boys and our privilege and how we don't have anything to worry about because we have families that will love us no matter what we do. I've heard it all, if not from you, then from Malak, who I was with for four years, remember, so don't think I haven't been well versed in this speech. I get it."

Kees opens her mouth to respond but Jacob waves her down.

"Kees, do me a favor and pipe down. Please, God, don't start one of your lectures, okay? I didn't come here to have an argument with you about privilege. I've got it, I know, although to differing degrees in comparison to some."

He shoots a pointed look at Kees and she knows he's making a comment about Harry's family and their wealth. She says nothing and lets him continue.

"But just because we have, it doesn't mean we're immune to any other feeling. We still get to be sad and miserable about things and wanting to build a life with someone who keeps you hidden is brutal. And we can't say anything to you guys about it because it's harder for you, but it's heartbreaking, actually." He laughs bitterly and the sound is jarring for Kees because all she's ever known of this man is his jokes and his placidness.

"You know, my mum would occasionally tell me to be careful," he continues. "She said that a woman who won't take you home to meet her mum is one who doesn't ever want you to meet them. And I, of course, argued to the death that this situation was different, and Malak and I used to laugh about it. Talk about how my mum just wasn't 'woke' and didn't understand the complexities of culture, but now I think maybe my mum was right all along. Malak never had any intention of taking me home and I'm an idiot for staying so long."

"Jacob," she sighs, "you know that's not true." Her instinct is always to protect Malak, even if she does think she's been an idiot. "She loved you very much."

"I know," he replies rubbing his eyes and rubbing the traces of tears shining through. "That's probably the worst thing about it. I know just how much she loved me. But that's not what I wanted to talk to you about. I wanted to tell you that Harry is going to ask you to marry him and you need to get your shit together so that when he does, you give him the right answer."

She feels her stomach ache at the mention of Harry and marriage and thankfully, in that moment, the waitress arrives with her food. It is perhaps the most unappetizing thing she has ever seen. A green slush of peas slopped to one side, lukewarm chips that have stood beneath the light too long, and a long piece of cod that has too much batter on it and a lonely slice of lemon, but she digs into it and starts eating energetically.

"Does he know you're here telling me this?" she asks between bites.

"Of course not. That's why I said don't tell him, and, seriously, do not tell him I came here, Kees."

"Why are you telling me, then, Jacob? If you claim to be his mate, then surely you shouldn't be here ruining his surprise. I'm pretty sure the rules of friendship are that you have loyalty to that friend."

He laughs at her. "I'm pretty sure you're in no position to lecture me on friendship and loyalty, Kees."

She stops eating and gives him a cold look. "Don't push it. Leave me and Malak out of this."

He holds up his hands. "Fine, fine. Too far. But me and Harry being friends is the very reason I'm here."

"Explain," she snaps. She has now given up on the knife and fork and is tearing into bits of fish with her hands. She is always more comfortable eating with her hands. The food tastes better.

"If he asks you to marry him, what's your answer going to be?"

She stares at him and says nothing.

"Exactly," he continues. "Most people who have been in relationships for this many years, and who love each other as much as you and Harry so clearly do, don't even have to pause to think about it. But you girls do because there's culture and religion and the added problem of falling in love with white men."

"I can't fucking magic away my religion and ethnicity, Jacob," she interrupts. "We don't have that privilege."

He sighs at her pointed *we*.

"I know that, Kees." He looks suddenly tired, as if her anger has washed him out. "You can't do any of those things. But you can make a choice, and that's all there is. Malak made her choice, and now you're going to have to make yours, and I don't want you to make the wrong one. I don't want you to do what she's done because it's not worth it. I never knew I could feel this much pain."

Kees feels bad for snapping at him and reaches out to squeeze his hand.

"You really miss her, don't you?"

He forces out half a laugh that doesn't reach his eyes.

"No. I don't miss her. Missing doesn't cut it. I don't know what life looks like without her, Kees. I have to reconfigure my whole future and make it work without the one person I wanted to build a life with. I'm going to have to fall in love with other people while still knowing I love her. Do you know how fucking cruel that is?"

"But time will pass, Jacob and—"

"No," he interrupts. "It won't fade, Kees. It will just change places. Move to somewhere else in my body, somewhere I keep hidden from the next person to step into my life. And hopefully, on the really good days, I'll forget about it for a little while. We're soul mates, Kees. I will love her forever and she will love me forever. She just doesn't know it."

"But how can you be so sure of that?" Kees might not have spoken to Malak but she isn't blind. She still sees her pictures, mainly because she searches Malak's name on different social media sites, and if they were anything to go by, Malak is having the time of her life. There is a glow emanating from her in every picture that Kees hasn't seen in years and no longer under-stands.

"Because I know her, Kees," he replies. "I know her better than I know anyone else on this planet. I know every expression on her face and most of the time I know what she's thinking by the way she holds her shoulders. I know she wants to be with a Muslim man, one she can bring home to her family because she doesn't know how to disappoint them. And what's fucked up is, I would have converted for her. I told her that. I would have done whatever she needed but she always said she couldn't be held responsible for me changing my life and she would know it was all a lie anyway. Because she doesn't actually want the Muslim man, does she, Kees?"

Kees stares back at him and says nothing.

"She wants everything that *comes* with the Muslim man. The culture, the family, the traditions," he leans forward toward Kees, "and how the hell was I ever going to give her that?"

He laughs bitterly and leans back, breaking the air between them. He picks up his pint, taking another long gulp. "Can you imagine me introducing my agnostic family and five siblings to her parents?" He shrugs. "So even if I had converted, I wouldn't have been able to give her that because that's what's at the heart of it, that's what she wanted. And the funny thing is, this life she's now living is the real lie. Sure, it's part of her, but it's not all of her. And one day, she's going to remember that, and she's going to remember the way we were, and she'll realize she didn't make the right choice."

At that very moment, somewhere across an ocean, Malak feels a sharp pain run up her right arm and shoot across her chest. The first thing she thinks of is Jacob as she stumbles backward, falling out of step with her friends who are walking through Tahrir Square, the lights of Cairo whirling around them and everyone laughing at a joke Ali is telling. She is surrounded by everything she has ever wanted, so she cannot imagine why Jacob's name is on her tongue.

But thousands of miles away in a very English pub Kees blinks quickly and once more reaches out her hand to squeeze Jacob's.

"And if that happens, won't you forgive her? If you love her the way you say you do," she asks.

He nods. "Of course I would. Eventually. But I don't know when she'll come back. It could be a year, it could be ten. And life doesn't wait. It just keeps moving and it will move me with it whether I like it or not."

The look on Jacob's face as he says this is one Kees will never forget, nor will she forget the cold feeling that came over her as she watched Jacob resign himself to a life lived without the one person he wanted to spend it with, and the thought of Malak one day coming back to find him in a reality that has no room for her makes Kees feel nauseous.

She feels sick for the next few days just imagining it. Every time she remembers Jacob sitting opposite her, hollow, as if someone had scooped out his insides, she feels a coldness settle on her. She is suddenly aware that time is moving faster than she gave it credit for and the reality is that there are very few moments in life where real choices are made because, for the most part, we're all swept along and most things happen to us. The idea of not having as many choices as she thought she did is one of the most uncomfortable sensations Bilquis Saeed has ever felt.

She spends the rest of the week feeling sick. By Thursday she throws up in the bathroom at work, and on Friday she doesn't bother eating because it only makes the sensation worse. The only time her stomach stops churning is on Saturday when Harry drives her out to the country for the weekend, and although the drive makes her nauseous, when they arrive at the most beautiful country lodge she has ever seen, her stomach stops threatening to throw up. It only stops completely when Harry leads her to their room, a huge suite that opens onto winter gardens that twinkle with fairy lights and the flickering flames of the candles that are placed on every possible floor space and surface, and there in the middle of a thousand pinpricks of light he proposes, and without letting him finish his speech, without pausing, Kees says yes, and only then does her stomach finally settle and for the first time in days, she doesn't feel sick.

As Harry slides the ring onto her finger and kisses her long and deep, she thinks of Jacob's face, gaunt from not eating, and the dark circles under his eyes which drag his features down, and the sadness that has settled somewhere in the base of his throat that she isn't entirely sure will disappear, and, God forgive her for thinking of another man while her new fiancé kisses her, but she sends up a prayer of thanks for Jacob. Stubborn as she is, even she can admit that perhaps she is kissing the man she has now decided to marry because of another man's misery. That was the day she learned that the way a heart breaks can change the course of a life.

MALAK

Ali notices everything about her. She expects him to notice the big stuff but it's the little things he mentions that always surprise her. The color of her toenails the day they drove to the beach. What top she was wearing when they went to brunch last month. The way she had her hair when they went galloping from pyramid to pyramid one weekend.

When she'd mentioned this to him, he had replied, "I notice everything about you, how could I not?" She thinks that she has won whatever lottery deals out unobservant husbands to wives who then complain when their husband doesn't notice their new haircut.

They're sitting in the gardens of one of the hotels that is nestled on the banks of the Nile, the river softly running just below their feet, the constant hum of seventeen million inhabitants somehow fading into the background as they scrape the final remnants of dinner off their plates.

"Do you want to come with me tomorrow to visit my grandma?" he asks.

She looks up at him in surprise. "Are you sure?"

"Of course, why wouldn't I be?"

She takes his hand, which he's reached out across the table.

"Well, we've only been dating for a month and a half. It's soon, you know."

He laughs and lifts her palm to his lips. "I know how I feel about you. It's not soon for me, but if you're not comfortable, then maybe you can meet her another time, there's no rush. Whatever you want, hayati."

Her breath catches in her throat. Her Arabic isn't great but she's always known that hayati, my life, is used only in the most tender, most loving situations and she feels caught in a layer of happiness she didn't know existed.

She shakes her head. "Don't be silly, I'd love to meet her."

They smile stupidly at each other and break their hands apart as the waiter arrives to clear their plates. Malak leans back in her chair and watches as Ali laughs with the waiter in perfect Arabic. She wants to learn the language more quickly now, just so she can understand his every word, because never has she been more interested in hearing what one human has to say as she is with Ali.

"What were you guys laughing about?" she asks as the waiter walks away balancing their plates above his head.

He leans over to take her hand again. "He was just telling me how the waiters all have second and third jobs to ensure they make enough money for their families."

She frowns. "And that's funny because…?"

He laughs at her confusion, gently bringing the tips of her fingers to his lips before answering. "Well, that isn't funny, of course, but you know what Egyptians are like. They always find the humor somewhere."

"I'm not sure there's any humor to be found in poverty," she replies.

"No," he agrees, "but their lives are unimaginable to us. We're all Egyptian but our Egypt is different from theirs. We grew up in England with a welfare state and a healthcare system that is one of the best in the world."

She snorts in laughter. "It's not that great." She has many opinions about government cuts and the disappearance of the welfare state.

"It's incredible, Malak," he says, leaning toward her, elbows resting on the table, one hand still holding hers. "Look around you. We're in North Africa and although all the upper-class Egyptians don't want to admit it, this country is still developing. The infrastructure barely holds this city together, the justice system is up for sale if you've got enough money; there's nothing you can't buy your way out of in this country. The political system is a case of who you know, and our country has seriously questionable dealings with other world leaders. And if anyone gets sick or has an accident, you either have enough money to pay your way to health or you'd better hope the herbs from the village aunty will ease your pain, and the likelihood is they won't. Aromatherapy can only get you so far. It's a shit show here. In comparison to that, our healthcare system is the most beautiful thing I've ever seen."

"I suppose," says Malak. Before she can say anything else, he carries on, his eyes shining with a fervor that makes her smile, although she's not entirely sure what he's so excited about.

"So why do you love being here so much?" she asks.

Ali leans back in his chair and laughs, one hand gesturing to the Nile behind him. "*Haya de Masr,*" he replies.

"What does that mean?" she asks.

"Literally, it translates as 'This is Egypt.' But it means this is just the way it is. It's an acceptance. It's got love rolled into it because everyone who says it really means, 'Yeah, it's a mess here and nothing works, but it's our mess and we love it.' *Haya de Masr.* This is Egypt."

He grins across at her and his excitement seeps into her. She asks more questions about the political setup of this country she now calls home because she's interested, but also because she never wants him to stop talking in these hurried monologues, a fever for the country he loves burning off of him. Malak has often wished she could climb into his brain and spend the day among his theories and philosophies. She is used to being one of the smartest in the room. She's used to other people looking at her for answers but now she looks to him and can feel her brain bending in new and unimaginable ways. It is addictive, and when he reaches to push a strand of hair back off her face mid-sentence, or when he stops mid-debate to cup her face and leave a trail of kisses over her forehead before continuing to tell her why the country needs to change, she feels like a woman who finally knows who she is and where she belongs.

"Why are you smiling?" he asks, pausing for a moment and reaching for her hand once again.

"I just think you're going to make an amazing professor. When do you hear about your PhD application?"

"Not for another couple of months," he replies. "Do you really think so?"

She knows what he's asking and she smiles and squeezes his hand. "Are you kidding? You were made to be a professor. Your students are going to be obsessed with you."

"Nah, they'll think I'm old and boring."

She raises an eyebrow and leans to the left, surveying him up and down from his designer shoes to the rippling muscles that she can see beneath his shirt, to the silver watch gleaming off his wrist and the perfectly threaded beard line along his jaw. "Uh huh, sure," she replies.

He laughs and says nothing else.

"You know, all the women in your lectures will have massive crushes on you."

He laughs harder. "Don't be silly."

"I'm not, I'm deadly serious. They will message about you in their group chats and share your staff picture around all their mates. It's what my friends and I would do."

He leans back in toward her, eyes suddenly serious, and curls his hand around the back of her neck, bringing her a little closer to him.

"Maybe they will," he says, "but every night I will come home to you and think that I'm the luckiest bastard to walk this earth."

She feels her stomach drop and the world becomes a softer place.

JENNA

"I've met her, Jenna" is Lewis's only response to her greeting as she kisses him hello before easing into the car.

"Met who?"

"*Her*. The one. The woman of my dreams. The person I thought didn't exist."

He springs into action and starts the car, pulling away to drive to the pub they always start their night at. It's only when they're sitting opposite each other, drinks in hand, that Jenna finally asks, "Well, who is she?"

"She's amazing," replies Lewis. "Wildly hot. I met her on a gaming forum. She's called Zee, she's French Moroccan, and possibly the most beautiful woman who's ever talked to me."

"Zee?"

"Well, her full name is Aziza, but no one calls her that," he replies.

She raises an eyebrow. "I bet her parents call her that."

"Fine," he sighs. "No one but her parents call her that."

"Is she Muslim?" asks Jenna.

He pauses, takes another sip of his pint. "Yes."

She doesn't say anything, but she gives him the look she has always reserved just for him, normally when he asks her to set him up with one of her friends.

"She's not Muslim in the same way you are," he says, leaning back, one arm slung over the back of the chair.

"What's that supposed to mean?"

"It means she doesn't really believe it or practice it. She's definitely not holding on to her virginity until her wedding night," he remarks, shaking his head.

"Lewis," she moans, "just because she's fucking you doesn't mean she no longer believes in her religion anymore. The two are not mutually exclusive and although you like to think you're some kind of god, you are, in fact, not an adequate replacement."

He leans forward. "Why do you always have to bust my balls, Jenna?"

"Someone needs to," she exclaims, irritated. "Didn't you meet her on a gaming forum?"

"What's your point here, Jenna?" he asks.

"Zee is probably called Dave and is actually a fifty-year-old bloke from Leeds who never grew up and likes playing *Super Mario* online."

"Well," he replies with a grin, "that's where you're wrong. She lives in Liverpool and I've met her. And she's hotter in real life. No sign of a beard."

"Are you mental? You went to Liverpool to meet a stranger off the Internet?" She's staring at her friend like he's just slipped out of his own skin. "Why didn't you tell me?"

Lewis rolls his eyes. "Because if I was getting catfished, I didn't want an audience, Jenna."

"You could have been murdered," she hisses back.

"Okay, let's try and keep your dramatics in the realm of the possible," he replies, evenly.

"People are murdered every day, especially idiots who travel across the country to meet bloody strangers off the Internet without telling anyone where they're going. Especially off an online gaming forum. That's exactly where murderers go for their prey."

"Okay, first," replies Lewis, "I don't know what you've got against gamers, and second, who the hell wants to kidnap a skinny git like me? They'd end up giving me back. Now can we please come back to reality so I can tell you about her?" he asks, leaning forward and taking her hand.

She snatches it back and picks up her drink, rolling her eyes at him, and says, "If you must, let's hear all about her."

And so he tells her every little detail: from the way she looks, what she does, how many siblings she has, and how Lewis, *her* Lewis, has never felt like this before.

Jenna asks questions, listens, and smiles a little at the way his face lights up and agrees that she too has never seen him like this before. He talks about her all night, which is the most time he's spent on any woman in a long time, and Jenna wonders what magic Aziza possesses. She feels jealousy gently take a seat in a quiet corner of her stomach.

She doesn't want Lewis, but she is acutely aware that she has subtly been moved to the outer circle, and feels a longing to return home. She leans forward and grabs his arm to pause his monologue and says, "I'm so happy for you, babe. Mainly happy that she isn't a serial killer, but honestly, I'm ecstatic for you. But if she hurts you, I'll kill her."

Lewis grins at her and replies, "I should bloody hope so."

She squeezes his hand and feels a warm glow in her belly for him. She loves him a lot at that moment.

He looks at his watch and says, "Actually, I can't stay out late tonight, I've got a FaceTime date with Zee."

"Oh my God, of course. In fact, I told Sarah to join us tonight and she's on her way now, about five minutes out."

"Sarah? The one from your drama club who you occasionally hook up with?" asks Lewis.

"That's the one," she replies.

"Are you hooking up with her tonight?"

"We're friends too, you know, so sometimes we do like to just hang out. Not everything is about sex, Lewis."

They stare at each other for a second before they both laugh.

"Are you sure you're going to be okay? I can wait," he says, already swinging on his jacket, which she has shoved into his hand.

"Don't be silly, I'm fine. Get out of here, and tell your new girlfriend I said hi."

She can't help but grin at the stupid look that comes over his face when she says girlfriend, and she waves him away. She looks down at his half-finished pint in surprise; she's never known him to leave a drink and, once more, the eerie feeling of being on the outside drifts over her.

She pulls out her phone and texts Ola and Sarah at the same time to find out if they're free. She'd lied about Sarah turning up because she couldn't bear to be the reason he stayed.

Ola doesn't reply and Sarah messages back that she's on a date with someone and is everything okay? Jenna doesn't bother to reply and so instead texts Mo, who she knows will be available to her, and, as predicted, he agrees to pick her up. The minute she sends her location she regrets it, the urge to be at home flooding her so suddenly she calls a cab. She forgets to message him, throwing her phone in her bag, suddenly sick of it all. She pulls out her headscarf and wraps it back on in the cab ride home, just to pull it off again once she walks through the front door and into the living room to find her parents exactly where she had left them.

"Darling, you're home already?" asks her mother.

"They didn't need me in rehearsals after all so I thought I'd come back and take you up on that offer of a movie."

Both her parents beam up at her and she smiles, seeing them wrapped up together on the sofa yet still so delighted to have her back; she has always sat so firmly in the heart of their adoration.

"Any movie you want, habibti," says her father.

"Can we watch *The Notebook*?" she replies.

"Of course we can. Did I tell you about the time me and my brothers built a house?" he replies, and both Jenna and her mother laugh and groan together.

"Go get your pajamas on and I'll make you a cup of tea. I've got some atayef as well for dessert," says her mother, kissing her as she walks past. "I'm glad you're back."

Jenna feels a lump forming in her throat and buries her face in her mother's neck, wishing she could tell her mother she feels like she's losing everyone she's ever loved, but some things are too big to say out loud.

"Me too, Mama, me too."

She leaves her bag and phone in the corridor and, once in her pajamas, pulls her favorite blanket from the basket by the sofa and curls into her favorite corner, happy to be spoiled by parents who are glad to have her home on a Saturday night.

It's only when she picks up her phone the next morning that Jenna sees seven missed calls from Mo, who had called to say he was waiting in the car outside the pub, ready to pick her up.

Jenna is twenty-two years old. She has the highest grades in her year, and everyone says she's brilliant. Her father is famous, and his work is referenced by her professors in lectures who look across the hall and smile at her as if they are sharing an in-joke. She has played the lead in every play the theater society has ever put on and people regularly tell her that her performances bring them to tears. She is known by most people on campus because of all the things Jenna Khatieb excels at; making people feel seen is the thing she does best of all. She is rich because her father believes his only daughter should get everything she wants, which is something she has never challenged. She wears a hijab, for the most part, and unlike most people, it makes her look more beautiful and the aunties with daughters who refuse to cover their hair smile at Jenna, wishing their daughters were more like her. They use Jenna as an example of how beautiful you can look in a hijab but their daughters know better and shake their heads in refusals that will not budge. Jenna is friends with everyone because she loves to talk and is genuinely curious about their lives. But Jenna Khatieb is lonely in a way that makes her feel like she's ninety-two and standing in a large marble hall all alone.

She read a theory once that loneliness resides in the same part of the brain as physical pain and although the medical professionals laughed and quickly disregarded the notion, she thinks it might be the most accurate thing she's ever read.

She's been in pain for months and thinks it started around the time of Kees's sister's engagement party, but, lately, it has become unbearable. Like most body parts that ache, you can distract or sedate it, and so she busies herself with classes, studying, rehearsals, and an obsessive desire to be around other people, just so she doesn't have to think about how alone she is.

Lewis becoming a couple started it off and then suddenly everyone around her is walking in twos. Sarah has a girlfriend and is now out of bounds. Ola has started seeing somebody but says he hopes they can still be friends. Malak is in a different country while Kees may as well be on another continent for all she sees of her. The group chat is like a badly healed bone and every day it remains unused is like built-up tissue that becomes harder and harder to break down. Most nights she considers messaging to tell them both to cut it out, that enough is enough and everyone has to talk to each other, but the prospect of silence stills her fingers. Her mother and father remain in a world of their own and the space around her grows wider and wider.

She imagines people feel like this when somebody dies, except this is worse because no one has died. There is no finality to it. You couldn't grieve people who were busy falling in love because what kind of person did that make you? But the sudden absence of those people from her life feels a lot like grief and she resents not being able to cry at funerals for the people she has lost. So, she goes to lectures and does the work that always needs to be done. She goes to the mosque with her parents and prays for God to deliver her from the drudgery of loneliness. She feels better when in rehearsals and every eye is on her, but the lights eventually come on and people couple up to walk home and she feels like the only person left in the world.

Even Mo isn't replying to her messages and, seeing as she has stood him up, she doesn't blame him. She's annoyed at herself for not appreciating his affection and attention when she had it. She'd thought he'd be like all the others and wait around for her but, apparently, he has more self-respect. It makes her like him so much more.

Her schedule is full, but she is surrounded by emptiness. A vast stretch of nothing and every rom-com she watches and love story she reads, and every couple in the street that leans over to touch one another, stretches her empty horizon a little further. She considers calling someone to tell them she's lonely but all the people she would normally tell are in a relationship and the only thing worse than loneliness is the sympathy of someone who's not. If you're going to be lonely and miserable, it has to be with someone who is equally so. She had messaged Malak, hoping to exploit her broken heart, but Malak had blurted out that she'd met someone, and in all honesty sounded happier than Jenna had ever heard her, so Jenna didn't tell her that she felt so alone that sometimes she asked Siri a question just to hear someone talk back to her while she lay in bed.

She spends hours making up her face and trying on new outfits before smearing off the makeup and throwing the clothes into the corner of her room. She has forgotten that you can dress up for someone other than a lover. She spends too long scrolling through relationship blogs and watching celebrity couples online who have perfect relationships, and while she knows that it's not true and you shouldn't believe everything you read, she wants to buy into this particular dream so she cashes it all in. Puts all her time and money on red 2, but her number is never called.

She messages old lovers whose faces light up when they see her name, but after a few messages she remembers why they are old lovers. Some of them entertain her for longer than a day, sometimes stretching across an entire week as she wonders why she didn't give this one a chance, perhaps she has grown and changed and is ready for something real. She thinks this until she meets up with them again and suddenly the reason she stopped talking to them floods back. That annoying habit that hasn't gone. The stupid sentences that still make her roll her eyes.

She reads empowering articles online about single women who are conquering the world and listens to a lot of Destiny's Child but by the time she crawls into bed and stares up at the dark ceiling in her king-size bed she is lonely again.

The evenings are long these days, which gives her plenty of time for swiping through apps. Sometimes the dates are just a means to an end; a way to get a bit of pleasure for the night. She ends up in their flats and tells them she isn't prepared to sleep with them on a first date, but they could do some stuff and so she gets what she needs. Mostly they are too entranced with her to care and happy enough that they had her attention. Some try to persuade her otherwise, promising to not think any differently of her for having sex on a first date. She will always smile and agree but firmly insist she isn't that type of woman, and although they are disappointed, something swells in them and they are secretly glad that women like this do exist after all. They make plans in their head for the next five dates and tell themselves that Jenna is worth waiting for, but by the time morning comes, she is gone and never replies to their messages again.

She often thinks about deleting the apps because they are a waste of time, but she needs a distraction and since every single one of her friends is falling in love, they stay for now.

She only deletes them the night she meets Mark; the gentlest, kindest man she's ever met until, back at his flat, when she says stop three times and he doesn't say anything, but quickly slides inside of her and, in her wide-open shock, slams his hips into her one, two, three times before he grunts out his quick groan of pleasure and rolls off her saying, "Sorry, I just couldn't stop; you're irresistible." He laughs then and throws the tissue box onto her stomach and with a wide grin that makes her think of the devil says, "I assume a girl like you is on the pill?"

MALAK

She didn't know that stars could be this bright or the desert could be this cold in the middle of the night, or that you could physically feel like you were falling through the air when you were falling in love with another human. She didn't know any of these things, but they all came to her in a sudden rush when she was staring up at the constellations in the middle of the Siwa Desert, Ali's arms wrapped around her and nothing but their tent and the flames of their campfire breaking up the horizon for miles.

"I didn't know I could be this happy," she sighs. "Did you?"

"No," he replies. "But I knew something good was coming."

"Really?" she asks, tilting her head slightly to one side as he kisses her neck.

"Yes. I remember sitting on my balcony a few months ago with my morning coffee, and for the first time in months, I felt at peace. Felt like I was destined for something, or that something incredible was about to happen. And then I saw you, Kookie, and you were what I'd been missing."

She smiles and kisses his arm, holding on to him a little tighter, drawing him a little closer. If she could find a way to slip inside his skin, she would.

It is the most perfect moment she's ever been in. "I didn't know. I had no idea you were coming, that life could be this sweet."

"Alhamdulillah," he adds and she replies, "Alhamdulillah."

The thrill of being able to thank God with the man you're sleeping with delights her every time it happens. When she stays up late at night talking to Nylah and Rayan about every detail of this new and unexpected love, she always mentions this particular thing. Tells them that finally she understands the importance of shared faith and how God can create something holy between two people because falling in love with Ali has been the most divine experience of her life. It has been worship; approached with the same intensity and fever of religion, the rewards almost transcendental.

Malak is used to God tearing things apart. Countries. Treaties. Relationships. But here on the hot streets of Cairo, in marble mosques that outshine the churches of England, God has pulled the world into a perfect pattern that keeps them both at the heart of it, and believing that God has brought you together is perhaps the most powerful aphrodisiac she has ever taken.

And because he is God-sent, she hasn't slowed or paused or hesitated but has thrown herself fully into every moment since they clasped hands in a mosque courtyard months ago.

If she is being honest, she doesn't think she could slow down even if she wanted to. She is constantly falling into moments and laughter like a drunk, even though she hasn't touched alcohol since they met. On their first date, he had spent ten minutes discussing the evils of alcohol before asking her if she drank and as he stared at her like an answered prayer, she'd found her head moving back and forth in a firm no. Everything in life is exciting now because there is nothing more thrilling than meeting the man of your dreams. She doesn't feel guilty when she says this out loud because in the days when she'd spent a lot of time in the mosque with her mum, or when the entire extended family would come over for dinner and the house was full of aunties in headscarves and uncles who stopped the conversation to call the athen, and everyone would bend their knees for God, even though she was in love with Jacob at the time, she did dream about a man like Ali. A man who could sit down with the uncles and her father and join the conversation, instead of standing awkwardly on the outside asking, "What does that mean?" A man who could be the one to call the athen. Growing up, she had watched her father lead their family in prayer, and often the congregation in the mosque, and every time it happened, she stood a little taller, proud that it was her father's voice guiding them to God. She dreamed that one day her husband might do the same.

There had been one moment early on, in their desperation to find out everything about one another, when they had raced over their pasts in their haste to bring themselves into the present, and Malak had tripped and made a mistake, which, when she thinks about it, still makes her feel a little sick.

They had been lying in bed together, smiling like idiots at each other, the way newly in love people do, Ali tracing a line from cheek to hip, and somewhere in the middle of their conversation about sex, she had asked, "How many women have you been with?"

She wasn't jealous the way some women were and the thought of searching for his exes hadn't crossed her mind; she just wanted to know everything about him. Given that Jacob had been such a significant part of who she was today, logically it stood to reason that the women who had come before her would be to Ali what Jacob was to her.

He had answered easily and without hesitation. "Seven."

She had nodded and smiled, asked a few more questions and felt like the door to who he was had opened a little more, and she had drawn herself closer to him and kissed him and felt the deep comfort of melting into another human.

Later that evening he asked the same question of her, the light in his eye shining as usual, and, for some reason, she hesitated; she didn't want to spoil the story and so she formed the lie and said, "Just one, my ex who I lost my virginity to. The guy I told you about."

The idea that she was virginal was too much of a stretch to squash into a lie.

Ali nodded and leaned over, kissing her with such softness and tenderness that she didn't know how to bear it.

"I'm going to look after you, Kookie," he said.

She had swallowed and felt terrible, kissing him back before he rose to shower.

In the time it had taken him to shower and walk back into the bedroom, laughing, complaining of hunger and how she had tired him out, Malak had decided she couldn't live with a lie between them.

"Ali," she said.

"What's up, baby?" he replied, walking to hold her face and kiss her on the nose.

"I lied. Just now."

He had stared at her, still holding her face. "Okay."

"I've actually been with four men."

He dropped his hands then, backing away to sit on the edge of the desk, nodding and crossing his arms. "Okay."

"I did lose my virginity to my ex, but we broke up for a while before we got back together, and in that period, I was just so sad, and obviously it didn't mean anything, but there were others."

"So why did you lie?" he asks.

She shrugs. "Honestly, I don't know."

The air around them had turned colder and something in his eye had shifted. His shoulders had changed and in a rush, she felt sick and in danger of losing something rare and precious.

Malak had heard about men like this. The ones who liked to believe that they were the first to settle here. The ones who could conveniently ignore how the women who brought them to the edge of their greatest pleasures knew how to do it. Men like that told themselves that it was in fact because of them, they brought it out of the women opposite them, and they were showing them a whole new world.

Kees and Jenna had called this the Aladdin complex and they all laughed whenever they had come across men like this, mercilessly pulling them apart.

But here, opposite a man she cared too much about, she could barely swallow down the rising need to vomit and she could feel the sweat pooling in her palms.

"I hate that you lied," he said.

"I know. I'm so sorry."

He didn't say anything, so she said it again.

"I'm sorry."

She had meant it. She felt stupid for telling him when just moments ago everything had been perfect and now she had ruined it and for no good reason. She had destroyed his peace of mind and also made herself a liar in his eyes. She didn't know what it was to hate yourself until that moment.

She expected him to leave, but, instead, he had kissed her on the top of her head and said, "Come on, let's go and eat, we're both hungry," and she thought that might have been worse than him leaving completely.

She had done everything that night to make him look at her the way he had earlier in the day, but she could see that the light in his eyes had changed.

The next day she started to bring it up again, to repeat the apologies, when he held up a finger to her lips and said, "Don't. Let's not talk about it anymore. I love you, Kookie."

She had cried then, sobbing heavily into his chest, and he held her and stroked her hair and murmured that it was okay and that he forgave her. Hearing him say that made her cry more, which made him say it again and they stayed like that for forty minutes, her tears soaking his T-shirt and his forgiveness raining down on her.

Thinking about that night still makes her uneasy and it isn't until years later that she'll be able to say why that exact memory makes her feel like she's about to throw herself off the roof of a building, but, for now, she tucks it away and reminds herself that since that night everything has been perfect.

BILQUIS

"Oh my God, what's wrong?" Kees says.

The living room is the same as it always is; furniture in place, frames and Quran on the mantelpiece along with Great-grandad's walking stick behind it, and the TV remotes wrapped in plastic wrap, placed next to each other on the coffee table, but her mother is doubled over on the sofa crying into her dupatta and from the way her shoulders are shaking, Kees feels her stomach lurch into her chest.

"She's looking at baby pictures of me," laughs Saba, who takes Kees's bags off her. Hakim stands behind Saba grinning and shaking his head.

She lets out an exhale and, as her breathing returns to normal, smells the family scent and is homesick while standing in the sitting room she grew up in.

"Umee, don't cry." Kees sits down and puts her arm around her mother, rocking back and forth with her sobs and smiling up at her laughing siblings.

"The wedding isn't for another couple of weeks and she's getting married, not dying."

The mention of anyone dying is enough to still the sobs and her mother reaches up to slap at her arm. "Hay hay, God forbid. Why are you talking about death?"

"Umee, I wasn't, I'm just saying—"

"Well, don't, it's bad Nazar. Chalo, we have to make samosas, come."

She slaps Kees on the back and hits Hakim on the arm as she passes, telling him to go and help in the garden, pulling herself together the way she always does, by pulling her children into order, murmuring prayers under her breath to ward off the evil eye, and fulfilling her role as a mother, which has been the greatest accomplishment of her life. As she walks into the kitchen and out of sight, she smiles, feeling the fullness that only having all the people she loves most in the world back under one roof can bring.

When Kees had told them she wanted to move out for university, Abida had refused, feeling shame sear through her at the thought of her unmarried daughter living outside the family home, especially when the university was only an hour away. She pictured shocked faces when she went to the masjid and didn't know if she could bear the questions, knowing that other daughters were going to the local polytechnic university to ensure they stayed within ten minutes of the family home.

But Abida and Itasham had made a promise to each other on their wedding night: whatever decisions had to be made, they would always make them together and the other person had to support the decision, even if they didn't agree. For their thirty-five years of marriage, it had worked. So when Kees wanted to go and Itasham had pleaded with his wife, saying that their daughter couldn't become the prime minister if she didn't go to one of the best universities in the world and spend all her time studying, she had seen the look in his eye and knew she had to agree and, once more, they had presented a united front. She saw the logic of it, but she always felt a part of her family was missing when her eldest was gone.

As they hear their mother begin to bang pans about in the kitchen, Kees stares at Saba and Hakim in disbelief.

"Is she always like this?"

"Every day, fam," says Hakim.

Saba nods in agreement. "She blows hot and cold and you never know which way she's going to go."

"But…" Kees pauses momentarily, looking for words that won't hurt Saba. "You're only getting married," she finally says, at a loss.

Thankfully Saba laughs. "Try telling her that. She keeps talking about the first one in the family."

"Well, it was never going to be you, was it?" laughs Hakim, hands in his pockets, grinning with the pleasure of sparring with the older sister he has yet to outdo.

"Hakim, you're not too old to get punched," she replies, before turning to Saba. "What's Dad been like?"

"In the garden mostly. He says he's trying to get the flower beds in shape for the wedding."

"But you're getting married in the Hilton, what the hell have our flower beds got to do with it?" she quizzes.

Saba tilts her head as if Kees has just asked an unbelievably stupid question. "Well, guests will be coming over to congratulate Mum and Dad. He wants the place to look good."

Kees feels frustrated already. "Are they sitting in the garden?"

Saba and Hakim sigh in unison.

"You've been around white people too much," says Saba. "Of course they're not in the garden, it's too cold, but you know how they are about the house."

The suggestion that her thinking is influenced by white people is irritating to her, mostly because her sister might be right. "Saba, just because you're getting married doesn't mean I won't punch you either. I just think this is all a little unnecessary; don't you think?"

Saba laughs and throws her arm around her shoulders. "Ahh, there's our sister, hopeless romantic and all-round softie."

Kees frowns and shrugs her off, but Saba is, as she has always been, persistent and insists on kissing her until they both fall on the sofa and Hakim suddenly jumps on top of them both and their screams bring both their parents running into the room. Their mother picks up a pillow and laughingly hits Hakim with it in her attempt to get him off his sisters and their father watches them all, arms crossed, laughing deeply in a way that reminds them all of when they were children.

The next day is Saturday and although Kees has planned on doing some work in bed in the morning, her mother has other ideas and the day becomes something entirely different. She drives the family car from sweet shop to caterers to dressmakers. Goes to three different jewelry stores to discuss churiya and earrings. Cooks mince and peas and then sits on the floor in the kitchen with Saba and their mother stuffing hundreds of small parcels of pastry, ready to be frozen and taken out when guests arrive. She agrees to be the guinea pig for the Mendi and lets one hand and one foot be painted in flora patterns and sits with it drying for hours, trying to use the time to read case files but Saba insists on trying on every outfit her in-laws have sent so Kees can offer her opinion and give judgment. She stands for measurements her mother takes and flicks through endless magazines with Saba to pick the outfit she will have made up for the wedding and all the events that go along with it, which are just as important in a Pakistani wedding. She climbs up into the attic with Hakim to search around for dusty boxes of old Eid decorations that will now serve as wedding decorations and begins sticking the silver stars they made as children on the corridor ceiling. She helps her father string fairy lights around the garden and then helps him order more online. She rolls roti for the family dinner and offers to take food round to Mrs. Carson, who comments that she's lost weight and she should come home to check on her parents more often. By the time she sits down that night, case file in hand and a cup of tea that Hakim has, by some miracle, made her, she falls asleep on the sofa before the files are opened and the tea drunk.

On Sunday morning, she doesn't even bother to take the files out of her bag and when her mother says she is going to go into town with everyone so Kees can get her work done, she tells her it's okay. She cannot give them much when she is working in London or contribute to this wedding the way she really should, but now that she is here she can give them this small bit of her time, even if it means she will be working nights all next week. Coming home has done what it always manages to do: bring her a great sense of comfort with an equal measure of guilt.

She spends the rest of the afternoon sitting at the dining table with Saba, cutting and sticking together paper chains, following the strict wedding color chart Saba has stuck to the wall as a reference point for the family.

She peers up at Saba, who is concentrating on cutting straight lines, tongue sticking out between her teeth the way it used to when she was a baby, and she suddenly feels desperate to apologize.

"I'm sorry I haven't been around much." She leans over and squeezes her sister's hand, pausing her cutting.

Saba looks surprised and squeezes her hand back before continuing. "You don't have to apologize. You're going to be there for the wedding, aren't you?"

"Of course I am!"

"Well, exactly," Saba continues. "That's all that matters."

They continue stringing the paper chains together in silence, the *Kal Ho Naa Ho* soundtrack playing in the background because Saba maintains it was the greatest love story to ever come out of Bollywood.

Without slowing her cutting, Saba says, "But why haven't you been around?"

Kees pauses and looks up but Saba doesn't meet her eyes. It occurs to her that she must be some kind of monster to be jealous of her sister's happiness. If she thinks about it, it isn't jealousy, but rather the knowledge that this will never happen for her. That if her mother is bent over her dupatta crying, it's going to be for a completely different reason.

Instead, she says, "Work is just crazy, and because it's still pretty new, it's hard to get away. The job was also really hard to get and I don't want to mess it up."

Saba nods. "I figured it was that."

Her father drops her off at the train station to catch the last train back to London and their conversations are filled with politics and government and the laws that he thinks Kees should change. She listens and nods, not bothering to tell him that it doesn't work like that and she's not really into policy law; she just likes hearing him talk to her about it.

Before she gets out of the car, he asks her, as he has always done since she was fifteen years old, "Are you keeping up your prayers?"

"Yes, Abaji," she replies. "Every day."

"Mashallah," he says, lifting his hand to place it on the crown of her head in a blessing and as a way of saying goodbye.

As she begins to walk away, he winds the window down and calls her back.

"Yes, Abaji," she says, sticking her head into the window.

He passes a ten-pound note to her. "Here, get yourself a cup of tea for the journey back."

She smiles. "It doesn't cost ten pounds for a cup of tea, Abaji. Give me two pounds fifty and save the rest for Saba's wedding."

She is worried about how they're paying for this and already feels bad for not being able to give some money to contribute. She has the distant thought that she needs to get out of the charity sector.

He tuts. "I can spoil both my daughters if I want to. Take it."

She doesn't argue with him, just takes the money and tells him she loves him, although he doesn't say it back. He just waits in the car park until she gets on the train, and then waits until the train pulls out of the station and watches it speed off, waiting five more minutes, just in case there are problems or his daughter doesn't get on the train. He wants to be there if she needs him, although Kees has never needed anyone.

He still waits, leaving the station exactly five minutes after the last train has pulled away.

JENNA

The house has never looked so good and Jenna takes a rare moment to appreciate how many hours her mother spends creating a home that could, at any moment, be photographed for a magazine. Everything is casually beautiful, but behind each carelessly flung throw are hours of preparation and research, color palettes and sample boards, and the intense focus of a woman who refuses to be idle.

Her mother booked the cleaners twice this week, which is how Jenna knows how seriously she is taking this dinner.

Tonight, the log fire is full and blazing and candles flicker on most surfaces in the house. Each room has one or more vases packed full of fresh roses, lilies, camellias, sweet pea, and any other stem that is currently in season. Even the dining table has a single deep-red calla lily next to each plate and she smiles at her mother's attention to detail.

The air is full of the heavy musk of the candles and the closer you get to the kitchen the smell changes into the six-course meal that has been a week in the making. She had tried to persuade her mother that a bowl of rice and some chicken would have done the trick, but she has insisted on hors d'oeuvres and appetizers and now the four of them are sitting around the dining table laughing, everyone looking beautiful in the candlelight.

"So, Mohammed," her mother smiles, "tell us how you two met."

"Aunty, you can just call me Mo, everyone does," he replies, politely.

"And you can stop calling me Aunty and just call me Evie."

He shakes his head, laughing but adamant. "Absolutely not. My mother would disown me."

Her mother smiles at him again, pleased. "Well, then we're agreed. If you're sticking to Aunty, I'll stick to Mohammed."

He smiles and bows his head in her direction. "In that case, I concede; you win, Aunty."

Her father smiles over at her mother, leaning over to pick up her hand and kiss it. "I wouldn't bother arguing with my wife, Mohammed; she's always right."

"Of course, Uncle."

"I don't know why the youth of today insist on shortening everything anyway, including your names. It's like you're all in such a hurry to erase yourself," he says, standing to begin carving the leg of lamb that is sitting center stage in the middle of the table. "A good long name builds good character. Mohammed, Abdelrahman, Fatima, Zariyah. These are good names. Instead, you all go around calling each other Zo or Mo or Ri or whatever stupid abbreviation you've come up with."

They all laugh as with each sentence he waves the carving knife to emphasize his point.

"Baba, you called me Jenna," she interrupts. "It's hardly a long name."

"I wanted to call you Ruqayya but your mother wouldn't let me."

She mouths "thank you" to her mother and her father shakes his head.

"Your mother said that you were our piece of heaven and so we should call you Jenna, which is the only reason I agreed, because she was, as usual, right."

"So, back to my question," says her mother, looking pointedly at Mo, and Jenna laughs and indicates for him to tell the story, leaning back to watch the scene. She can almost bet that what will follow is her father telling the story of how he met her mother, and how he swears to this day that, although she was on stage and couldn't see the audience because of the lights, their eyes had met across the theater and it had been love at first sight.

She watches Mo explain Tinder and for a moment feels something slipping away from her, but the minute her father launches into his tale she forgets that feeling.

For the first time in her life, she watches as her parents tell their love story and laugh and joke and talk to a man she is dating, whose lips have touched hers, and tectonic plates shift. Something moves closer and she feels a form of contentment settle, so she smiles.

She is glad that Mo agreed to date again after she had stood him up, not that it had been easy to persuade him. Initially, he had ignored her messages and only when she had found his class schedule and waited for him after his lecture did he agree to talk to her. Sometimes a grand gesture was necessary. She had spun a story about feeling suddenly sick and how her leaving had nothing to do with him, combined with pressures of the final year and family expectations. Over the following weeks, after she messaged more than he did and always first, he warmed up and began to trust her again and, gently, they resumed where they had left off.

Jenna has a vague memory of telling him that she wasn't ready before, but she was now, and as she said that, she believed it.

After three more months of dates she suggested he come home for dinner to meet her parents.

They had seen each other nearly every day over those months; going for long walks, either back to the river or through one of the parks and, slowly, he unfolded himself to her. It was still a laborious process; at times, just when she thought she was wrong about him, he would say something interesting or insightful or creative and she would be shocked back into falling for him. He was a lesson in patience. A reminder that first impressions don't last. That not everything needs to bubble on the surface. He was also the only time she didn't feel lonely and that counted for a lot.

As she listened more than she spoke, she found out how close he was with his family, how his three brothers were his best friends, and how they all, still, went shopping with their mother every Saturday morning. She had laughed upon hearing that, asking, "What if you want to go to brunch with your friends or you've had a late night?"

He had shrugged and looked at her as if she was slightly dim. "It doesn't matter if I'm tired. My mother is always more tired than us and my friends can always rearrange the time. She is my mother."

He said it with reverence shining from his eyes and once upon a time Jenna would have messaged the group so that Kees could make a sarcastic comment about men and their mothers, but she too was tired and found it endearing. With every realization she had pulled out of him, she liked him more, but it wasn't until he told her about the women he'd previously dated and how he'd decided to no longer be physically intimate with anyone before marriage that she decided to commit to him.

"It just doesn't morally feel right," he had told her. "I was young and stupid the few times it happened, and it just made me feel bare inside, you know?"

He said it with a shrug as if not expecting Jenna to understand what it feels like to give someone your insides and lie next to them empty, hollowed out with nothing but drying sweat on your chest to show for it, and she had nodded and smiled and a light had come on in the corner of her eyes.

"If it makes you feel like that, I think you've made the right decision," she replied. They smiled at each other across the car, London disappearing behind them as he drove her back from the high tower restaurant they'd had their Friday-night date in. He didn't once ask if she had ever been physical with anyone and that made her like him even more. She didn't offer the information. Didn't tell him that sometimes you could feel vacant, but most of the time she felt like she was being worshipped and the feeling of a man making his way across her body had often taken her up to the face of God. She didn't tell him that if she could do it all again, she would and the regrets had never come home to roost for her the same way his had.

At least, they never used to. Life has been different recently and she has become a different creature, and beside Mo her transformation is complete. The slate wiped clean. Nothing exists before, only an open road ahead. He is romance and absolution rolled into one delicious man.

The reality, that he is a man and things are different for him, hangs between them delicately, neither of them willing to break it by interrogating it or looking too closely. If she is honest with herself, she would have argued that point once upon a time, but now she lets things go and it feels nice.

As she watches her mother and father smile at Mo as he tells their story, she can almost feel her two worlds slowly and gradually roll toward one another like iron doors that haven't been used in a long time, metal creaking forward to join together in a satisfying thud, and a wave of relief washes over her. She leans even further back in her chair to watch the scene. Mo is charming and effortlessly at ease with her parents. There is none of the awkwardness that normally hangs from young men morphing into adulthood and he speaks to her parents easily. He hangs a compliment over her mother's shoulders and does it in Arabic, which makes it all the sweeter. The English language isn't built for sweetness the way Arabic is, and as the compliment rests on his lips, her mother looks to her father for the translation and her father beams with happiness.

Meanwhile, Jenna watches the faces light up around the table and feels the satisfaction she gets at seeing a perfect scene acted out in the theater. Everyone is perfectly on cue and although she doesn't really know if this man is remarkable, having the man she is dating break bread with her parents while they all talk about love feels remarkable. For now, something swells inside her chest and she thinks that, finally, she is happy. She thinks this is enough.

After the dinner, Jenna calls Lewis.

"So how did it go?" he asks, not bothering to say hello.

"Perfectly. Everyone was perfect."

"And what do they think about him?"

She shrugs. "They think he's nice and ticks lots of boxes. They like him but my dad feels a bit funny about the fact that we met online. Says he doesn't know who his family is or what stock he comes from. Honestly, I thought we'd stopped referring to people as if we're breeding horses."

"Yeah, unless you're rich, Jenna, which you are, and seeing as you're also Daddy's little girl, the breeding metaphors are going to continue, so you'd better get used to it. Anyway, what else?" he asks after a minute of silence has passed.

"Nothing else."

"Don't insult my intelligence. What else?"

She shrugs again and then sighs. "I don't know; I just thought they'd be more impressed, you know?"

"Well, I did tell you he's an idiot, so what did you expect?"

"All right, I'm going."

"No, no, don't go; come on, you know I'm just messing."

"Except you're not, Lewis. You've maintained your position since you met him for all of five minutes three months ago, and I can't be bothered with you criticizing my love life tonight."

His voice softens and she hears him sigh down the line.

"Jenna, as far as I'm concerned, no one is going to be good enough for you, ever."

She doesn't say anything for a second before asking, "How's Aziza?"

"Zee," he corrects her. "She's good, she's actually with me. She came down for the weekend."

"Oh, I should let you go, then; I know you guys don't have much time together."

"She's gone to make a cup of tea; I have a few minutes before she's back. Jenna..."

"Yes?"

"We need to talk about that night."

Her stomach clenches.

"We really don't."

"Jenna!"

"What, Lewis? There is literally nothing to say about it. It happened. I was an idiot. It's done. I've moved on."

162

"But that's exactly what I'm trying to tell you; you weren't an idiot."

She interrupts before he can say anything else.

"I hear Aziza's back. Enjoy your evening and tell her I said hi. And stop worrying. Honestly, I'm fine."

She hangs up the phone without waiting for his response and throws it onto her bed, as far away from herself as possible.

"That night" is the only way they refer to what happened with Mark.

She won't refer to it as the night she lost her virginity because she tells herself it wasn't real. That it didn't happen. Although it was real enough for her to ask Lewis to drive her to the pharmacy so she could get the morning-after pill.

She thinks about that night like she's viewing someone else's story, peeping through a window and witnessing something she shouldn't be looking at. The memory is clouded and foggy around the edges, even though it's only been three months. She can recall the clearest details from her childhood with such sharp clarity that being unable to remember every detail from three months ago helps her believe it happened to someone else.

She watches Mark laugh at her for lying in the same position he left her in when he went into the shower, saying, "Come on, silly billy, I've got work in the morning so I need an early night." She watches someone who looks like her apologize and say, "Of course, I'm so sorry, let me get my stuff together." She watches as he calls her a cab and walks her out of the flat, stopping in the corridor when they bump into his flatmate, a man called James who has a bright, warm face and shakes her hand like he means it. Says, "Lovely to meet you," and Mark mentions that he's just called her a cab and James replies, "Absolute gent, this one."

She watches as she smiles and waves to James, turns to Mark, and says, "He seems nice," and Mark agrees. Says life is too short to surround yourself with dickheads and you have to be positive. She sees herself nod and thinks, *yes, positive, positive.* At the door, he drops a light kiss on her lips, smiles with his whole mouth, and says, "It was lovely meeting you, Jenna," and she, to her dismay, nods back and responds, "Yes, lovely, take care."

She has replayed this movie every night, and every night, the hardest bit is the moment she nods and agrees politely that the entire evening has been delightful. Jenna knows that if she was ever raped, she would call the police and scream and shout, so she keeps watching and looking back at "That Night" and it's so easy to think it's someone else. Easy to disassociate herself from the woman who looks so much like her, who nods instead of screams and says "How lovely" instead of "Fuck you."

At least, that's what she feels in her sharpest moments of clarity when the day has been good and she's felt more strong than soft; but those days are few and far between so she can't stop calling herself an idiot for being drunk, for getting into that situation, for not saying more when she had the chance. She's so disgusted at herself she can barely stand to look in the mirror, and there's nothing that Jenna likes more than to stare at herself in the mirror.

She is also annoyed that, on that night, she ended up on Lewis's doorstep and burst into tears in his confused father's face. He backed away from her like she had something contagious, shouting for Lewis that his friend was here.

Once Lewis had taken her into his bedroom, she had, as if with no control, blurted out that she'd had sex and, for a brief moment, the last one that would be perfect between them,

Lewis laughed and congratulated her and told her not to cry because any man who truly loved her wouldn't give a damn.

But then she hadn't been able to stop crying and Lewis had stopped laughing and when she'd said that she hadn't meant to, and hadn't wanted to, and had tried to say no, Lewis had turned gray, picked up his phone, and started dialing the police until Jenna screamed so much that he hung up and his parents both ran into the room.

Upon seeing a sobbing woman and Lewis looking guilty, both parents had turned to him and while his mother asked him what he was doing to make this poor woman scream like that, his dad had already thumped him on the back asking what he had done to her.

Jenna, seeing that Lewis was about to lose the thin hold of his patience, had hastily stepped in and explained that she was just a little upset and Lewis had done nothing wrong.

That night she made Lewis promise not to tell anyone. That she wasn't ready, and this was something she needed to deal with in her own time and, really, what could he say? There are some things that a person can't be pushed on and Lewis, recognizing this, said nothing more. Just that he would kill him when Jenna was ready to give him a name and address.

Because she couldn't bear the thought of sleeping alone, she texted her parents to say she was staying at a friend's house and curled up beside Lewis, who didn't loosen his hold on her all night, his arms around her as they talked about the house parties they used to go to when they were kids and how much fun they had been. They looked up old friends on Facebook and laughed at old pictures, remarking at who was working where and which couples had stayed together and who was married. It was an exercise in nostalgia because she couldn't bear to be in her adulthood.

She deleted the apps and canceled the social plans she'd made for that week. Told friends that actually she had too much studying but, really, she was done with alcohol and didn't want to be in environments where she'd have to explain why she wasn't drinking.

When she looks back, she barely remembers laughing with Lewis or him holding her. She mostly remembers how that was the night she decided to get her shit together and stop being so irresponsible, because that's all it was. Her recklessness had finally gotten her into a situation she couldn't undo and the consequences of her actions had settled into a dull ache at the bottom of her spine.

That was also the night she sent Mo a text asking if they could give it another go.

MALAK

When Malak was a child, her father would tell her stories about Cairo and her mother would sing Umm Kulthum songs to her as she fell asleep. Between tales of a wide-awake city under the lights of seventeen million people, and the haunting lyrics of a woman who always seems to have lost something or someone, Malak built a city in her mind that was half fantasy, half hope.

Since moving here, she has learned how right her parents were. At night Cairo's citizens make for the streets, and when they congregate on side streets or in squares, they speak about longing; passing stories with dishes of food, remembering the Nasser years, or the years before that, or any year other than the one they are in. A country with so much longing should sink to its knees, weighed down by its own desire, but Cairo is a place that feeds on it, becoming rich with memories that are everywhere. The thing that truly saves Egyptians is their ability to laugh. How could you enjoy the life you stood in if you didn't understand how the past had scraped itself together to get you there? And if you couldn't laugh at what had happened, you might as well stop living. They manage to twist the cruelest of circumstances into the funniest jokes and all across the city laughter always comes first.

Malak thinks this is exactly what her parents meant when they said to live in Cairo was to be alive. And on the banks of the Nile in a restaurant covered in fairy lights that blink down on them, Nylah and Rayan laughing at Ali's jokes, all of them talking, the things they hoped for felt possible.

Ali winks at Malak and it's another light shining down among the thousands dangling above her head.

"Karim just texted me; he said he's going to join us shortly, if that's cool?" says Nylah, putting her phone down.

"Of course," exclaims Ali. "Malak told me you're dating. Tell me all about him, how did you meet?"

Nylah laughs in delight and pitches forward, leaning closer to Ali as she begins recounting her story, and Malak thinks that the smartest thing any man can do to win over his girlfriend's friends is to ask them about the men they are dating.

After she had initially introduced Ali to Nylah and Rayan, the four of them had all started hanging out more. Some weekends, Ali would bring his friends Bassam and Omar with him and a comfortable group of six, anchored by Malak and Ali, had formed. Every time she saw him laughing with her girlfriends it felt like falling in love all over again, or maybe just falling deeper in love. Love feels more solid when there are other people to witness it.

Ali is sociable and confident. Easily guides a conversation and is happy to submerge himself in Nylah's and Rayan's lives. When Malak had thanked him for the attention he gave them, Ali had whispered in her ear that everything he did was for her. Everything that passes between them feels exquisite and it makes her wonder if she's actually ever really been in love before.

"Guys, Karim says he's got us a booth at Zola's downtown. Shall we go there instead? Ali, you can still get shisha there," says Nylah, all of them standing to leave the table.

"Oh, I love Zola's," says Rayan.

"I'm down," says Malak, smiling.

Ali agrees with the consensus and if his shoulders drop, Malak doesn't notice.

After half an hour of traffic, Ali driving and occasionally shouting at other drivers, they arrive at Zola's, a bar that has re-created old-world Egyptian glamour with a modern twist. As a result it has become the watering hole for every expat living in the country who wants to experience Egypt without really dealing with Egypt.

The drinks are imported and expensive and the Egyptians there are either behind the bar or rich.

Malak excuses herself to go to the bathroom and smiles at herself in the mirror. She feels good.

As she walks out, leaving a tip for the woman who sits by the door with a roll of tissue ready to tear off for customers to dry their hands, she finds Ali waiting for her outside the door.

"Hey, you." She smiles at him.

"Look, I'm going to go," he replies, his face blank.

"What?"

"I'm going to go home. I don't want to stay."

She scans his face to see what's wrong, but he doesn't blink or change expressions and she has never seen him like this. She gestures to the stairs and walks out with him where they can hear the sound of traffic and other people, away from the thumping music.

"What's going on? Are you okay?" she asks, worriedly looking in her purse for the car keys his outstretched hand is waiting for.

"I just don't like these spaces, Malak," he replies.

"Well, we can go somewhere else, baby."

"No, no; I don't want to drag people away and Nylah is having a good time with Karim. I don't want to break that up."

"Well, then, I'll come with you," she replies, already starting to walk with him, but his hand stops her.

"No, then you'll be leaving Rayan. Honestly, just go back in and have a good time with your friends."

"But why aren't you staying?" she asks. "I don't understand."

"I just don't like those places, Malak. I don't drink, and I don't want to be in those environments."

"I know you don't drink but you told me you used to go out clubbing."

"*Used to.* I don't anymore and they make me feel tense."

"Tense?" she repeats, still searching his face for clues.

"I saw three men look at you in a way I didn't like, and I just don't want to be around that or have to do something I don't want to."

She laughs and puts her hand on his shoulder, stroking his arm soothingly. "Oh, don't be silly, that's no reason to leave."

He shrugs her arm off and doesn't smile back.

"It's funny for you because you won't be the one forced to do something."

Malak thinks the notion that he would have to do anything at all is what's funny here, but she doesn't say that.

"I hate it when men look at you like that, Malak," he continues. "It's so disrespectful to you, hounding you like you're a piece of meat. It makes me so angry and I don't want to be in that position and then ruin the night for everyone."

"Well, then, let me come with you at least. We'll go for a walk or go and get some ice cream."

"I don't want ice cream. I'm tired and I have lots of work to do."

"But I thought I was staying at your place tonight?" she asks him, suddenly feeling that she has misjudged this situation and isn't sure what's happening anymore.

"Baby, I need some rest and you should be with your friends. Go, have fun. Honestly, I'm fine. I'll call you tomorrow."

He kisses her on the forehead, careful not to touch lips while the valet boys are watching, but before he leaves he tilts her chin and looks into her eyes and says, "Honestly, I'm fine," in a way that Malak knows is not fine, and the creeping sensation that she's fucked up returns.

"Where's Ali?" asks Rayan as Malak sits back in the club, still feeling the urge to ask someone else to translate what just happened because she's sure she missed something.

"He's gone home; he doesn't feel great. I don't think this is his scene," she replies.

Rayan laughs. "I thought this would be exactly his scene."

"What do you mean?" asks Malak.

"He's wearing a Rolex, has tighter T-shirts than me, and is drenched in cologne. He's flashy and so is this place; it just seems like a good fit."

Malak is annoyed at Rayan's comments but isn't entirely sure why because when she thinks about it, she should be more annoyed at Ali for leaving the way he did.

"He's actually quite religious and doesn't drink, so he doesn't want to be in a place that serves alcohol," she replies.

"Where's Ali?" asks Nylah, who has turned back to their conversation now that Karim has gone to the bar.

"He's gone to pray," replies Rayan, laughing.

"What?" Nylah looks confused.

Malak scowls at Rayan. "He's gone home; he's not really into the clubbing thing."

"God, that's a shame. What are you going to do?" asks Nylah.

"What do you mean?" She wonders if every conversation she has tonight will be equally confusing.

"Well, you love it," says Nylah.

"I don't love it," she replies.

"Uh, yeah you do," chips in Rayan.

"I like going out for a drink and a dance, yeah, but I can take it or leave it," Malak remarks. She stands up once more and announces she's going to the bathroom because it's the quickest way to end the conversation.

Rayan and Nylah don't say anything more the rest of the night and Malak doesn't dance the way she normally does when they're all out together. She sits most of them out, begrudgingly getting on the dance floor when Nylah pulls her up or she is caught standing.

Malak is a problem solver and all she wants to do is pick up the phone and call Ali to fix whatever has suddenly bubbled up between them. She checks her phone too many times until the battery eventually begins to fade. Replays the conversations they've had and tries to remember if he'd previously told her that he didn't go clubbing anymore. All she can remember are his stories from when he lived in Dubai and worked for a property recruitment firm that meant clubbing was part of the job and happened on a nightly basis. He's never drunk, but he never seemed to have a problem being in these places and it was one of the things she had fallen for. A Muslim man who was down to party; a killer combination.

Eventually, the night ends and she barely talks on the way home, but since Nylah and Rayan are in the sleepy drunk phase, she doesn't have to. The night has been inconceivably boring, and she wonders if this is what Kees always felt when she was the only sober one on their nights out. She feels a pang when she thinks of Kees and suddenly feels an uncontrollable desire to call her. Instead, she calls Ali the minute she walks through the door. It's 4 a.m. but he still picks up the phone and doesn't sound like he's been asleep.

"Hey," she says softly. "Did I wake you?"

"No. I can't sleep," he replies curtly.

She feels her stomach tense. For most of the night, she has imagined that he wants nothing to do with her.

"How are you feeling?" she asks.

"Fine."

"I'm sorry about tonight," she says.

Her imaginings had involved a mutual apology for leaving her and her friends midway through the evening, but he doesn't say anything and there is no give, so instead she gives more and fills the uncomfortable silence.

"I didn't know you felt like that."

"Of course I feel like that, Malak! You know how much I care about you and I hate to see you in a place like that with alcohol everywhere and no respect shown to the women."

She hears him take a deep breath down the phone line.

"I can't look after you in those environments, Kookie."

She wants to tell him that he doesn't need to look after her, that she's fine, but there's also a tenderness in his voice that she doesn't want him to take away, so she says nothing.

"There are some women who are happy to be stared at," he continues. "They'll go out in low necklines and revealing dresses and wait for men who are no better than animals to pick them up and disrespect them, but you're not like that, are you, habibti?"

She spurts out, "Obviously not," because whatever image he has in his head seems to disgust him and she doesn't want to be it.

"Exactly. And those environments are where women and men like that go and you're too precious to be there, hayati."

She feels warm. "Hayati?" she questions, but mostly just to hear him say it again.

"Of course. You're my life. Hayati. Don't you know that already?"

She sinks to the floor, her back against the wall, still in a dress that she now thinks is a little too revealing. She makes a mental note to ask Nylah if she wants it.

"Yeah, I know," she mumbles. "Honestly, I really am sorry about tonight. It won't happen again. You won't ever have to worry about that again, okay?"

"Okay, habibti."

She nods.

"I'm going to try and get some rest," he says, and she nods again.

"Okay. I'm sorry, truly."

"Okay," he repeats. "Goodnight, baby."

She lies on the hard floorboards and her breathing returns to normal. She feels like she's just dodged being thrown off a train she wants to ride forever and thanks God. She promises to do an extra prayer tonight.

When she had fallen in love with Jacob, it had been a slow and controlled thing, a gentle yawning awake as you realize that the person beside you, whom you've been laughing with all this time, is someone you want to spend infinite days with. But there had been nothing slow about falling for Ali. She had known immediately, craved him instantly, and on the nights she has lain awake with Ali by her side and studied his face by the light coming in through the windows, she has pinched herself to make sure she wasn't dreaming; the small bruise in the morning is a comforting reminder that it's all real.

She remembers years ago sitting at the wedding of a woman they had all grown up with, Nora Hussein, and Malak had turned to the girls and said, "She looks happy," and Jenna, in her usual sarcastic tone, had snorted back and said, "Well, she's won the game, hasn't she? Of course, she's happy."

"The game is bullshit," Kees had replied, to which Malak had said, "Of course it is, but we're all still playing it, aren't we?"

To win the game you had to end up with a Muslim man, but he had to be the right kind. One who wasn't too strict or too devout. He had to be able to go out and have some drinks with you, but still understand the importance of going to the mosque and attending family gatherings that involved group prayer and everyone constantly saying, "Inshallah." He had to be free from cultural hang-ups involving women staying at home, but still want a family and some traditional structures. He had to be experienced, because no one wanted a virgin for a husband, and he had to appreciate that you wouldn't be a virgin. It was a delicate balancing act between rebellion and religion and catching that ever-elusive middle ground was almost impossible. Some girls dreamed of Prince Charming and a white wedding, but for Malak it was this. Oh, and the white wedding. A holy grail.

That was the game and my God did they all want to win.

Malak always remembered that in that moment she had wanted what Nora Hussein had more than anything. She had wanted every single bit of it.

The idea that Ali was all the things they had wished, hoped, and fought for, that this man actually existed, was what kept the lies slipping out of her mouth, like when he asked her if she'd ever drunk before and she had easily and completely said no, erasing years of memories and committing those around her to the same lies she told.

It was worth it. She knew it was worth it in the grand scheme of things, so she lied and continued to fall quickly and deeply and everything was a fast beating heart and all the things she had ever wanted remained just around the next corner.

Eventually she peels herself off the floorboards and slips out of the dress, throwing it to be washed and given to someone who will use it now that she will never wear it again. Malak then joins Nylah and Rayan, who are each lounging on the sofa eating snacks they've gathered from the kitchen and smoking a joint, passing the stub back and forth between them, sucking out the last of the weed burning to their fingers.

Nylah doesn't look up. "You want some?"

Malak shakes her head. "No, thanks."

"You good?" asks Nylah, briefly lifting her head to glance at her.

"Yeah, all is good. I just got off the phone with him."

"And?"

"Nothing. He just said he's not down for those environments and that's his choice, I guess. Have to respect that."

"For sure, for sure." Nylah nods. "If a man tried to make us go into clubs when we didn't want to, it would be war," she says, and they all agree.

"Can you imagine?" pipes up Rayan, too relaxed to offer anything else.

They all shake their heads and Nylah and Rayan don't ask difficult questions or shine a light on anything uncomfortable. They murmur her thoughts back to her. They do what women do exceptionally well, which is to avoid pointing out to another woman that the man she loves might be a bit of a prick.

Because they don't hear the pillow talk, feel the kisses, or see the vulnerable parts of him, and all they have to go on is the way he left the club without saying goodbye and how their friend is suddenly and always unavailable to them, and they know better than to point out the awkward bits. They know you have to turn a blind eye when a woman is in love because it's already too late. They do her the great service of looking in other directions and together they gently take tiny red flags and fold them away, placing them somewhere out of reach, where they'll be easily forgotten.

So when Nylah asks if she's still going to go clubbing and Malak, as nonchalantly as possible, shrugs and says she was getting pretty fed up with it all and she feels like she's outgrowing it anyway, they all nod and say things like, "Yeah, me too," and, "We're getting too old for it," and, "It's not as fun as it used to be."

Malak goes to sleep remembering how she said to Ali, "You won't have to worry about it ever again," and breathes a sigh of relief that another problem has been solved, another barrier removed. She thinks about Nora Hussein as she falls asleep, a soft smile hanging off the edge of her lips.

BILQUIS

It is the fifteenth morning Kees has woken up before dawn and instead of rolling out of bed to catch the morning prayer, she rolls over and stares at the wall instead. She clenches and unclenches her legs, then her hands, stomach, shoulders, and back, holding each movement for ten seconds. She does this because she has spent the last nine years getting out of bed for morning prayers and the muscle memory etched into her body requires her to do something with her stagnant limbs that are aching to bend.

Every day since she agreed to marry Harry she pushes down a feeling she cannot name and walks away from her prayer mat. Harry asked her what was wrong, and she replied that she feels angry at God these days and doesn't feel like talking to him. He doesn't say anything else, just places her Quran on the bedside table next to her, even though she returns it to the shelf every day. It is the first time she hasn't kept her prayers and five times in a day she wonders what to do with her body instead.

A rising shame is stealing its way across her. The shame that has been staved off since the moment she whispered "yes" to Harry's hands on her body has come home to roost. Like an addict who has fallen off the wagon, she can think of nothing other than the red-hot feeling of sin, which she thinks must leave a mark on everything she touches. She puts the Quran back on the shelf every day with a scarf wrapped around her hands so she never physically touches it, afraid that it might dissolve into ash at her very fingertips. She stares at the notifications on her phone that remind her to pray and bites her lip so hard while the athen goes off that a widening cut is formed. It doesn't occur to her to switch the notifications off and stop bleeding from a mouth that no longer speaks to God. She thinks about hell more in these two weeks than she has ever done and googles "the punishments of nar" when she is alone in the office late at night, compiling a list of actions that result in immediate banishment to hell. Thoughts of hell go hand in hand with death and while driving in taxis or on trains she imagines them crashing, and in those moments she makes sure her seatbelt is on as tight as it can get or that she is sitting next to an emergency exit. She isn't ready to go to hell yet. The word fornication has buzzed too many times in front of her and when Harry reaches for her she complains of tiredness or cramps or any number of things that can ease a woman out of a man's arms without it being about him. She makes sure it is always about her, and she mumbles an apology and accepts whatever remedy—a hot-water bottle, some tea, painkillers—that he offers, scrolling through damnations while he sleeps, or plugging in her earphones to listen to sheikhs on YouTube condemn everyone.

Every time she catches sight of her engagement ring she is reminded that Harry is no longer a secret that can be hidden in university halls and at the back of the library. He has moved from theory to practical and the practicalities of bringing a non-believer into her world go hand in hand with all the sin she's ever accumulated. The idea of redemption is a faraway concept that sits beyond her eye line like a lifeboat she cannot reach.

She doesn't know how to lift her eyes up or talk to him when the shame and the wrongdoing is ringing in her head and so she clenches her muscles and finds some small task to do five times a day that keeps her hands busy. So far, the cupboards in her apartment have been steadily cleaned out, windows scrubbed, piles of clothes for the charity shop sorted, and her to-do list has gotten shorter and shorter each day.

Today, however, her baby sister is getting married.

The bedroom door cracks open and their mother bounds in playing the Quran off the mini speaker Hakim bought her for an Eid present, a cup of milky tea in hand.

She feels Saba stir and groan beside her. Saba had insisted on sleeping in Kees's bed last night, despite it being a single that barely contains one person, and even though their beds were only separated by a small bedside table with a shared lamp on it, she had said she wanted to spend her last night as a single woman with her sister because they would never get the chance to do it again. Although Kees was tempted to once more remind Saba that she was only getting married and this kind of hysteria was impractical and completely illogical, she had instead just lifted the duvet for her sister to scramble in beside her.

Her mother places the tea on the bedside table, slapping Kees's hand away when she tries to reach for it.

"It's for the bride."

"You couldn't just pour some of that into two mugs, Umee?" she mumbles, nudging Saba in the ribs. "Your tea is here."

Saba giggles as their mother sits on the edge of the small bed, the dent in the mattress rolling them all more tightly together, limbs intertwined.

Her mother places her hand on Saba's head and starts reciting the Quran to keep the evil eye away today and to bless her daughter with a prosperous and happy marriage.

"Umee, you're sitting on my leg," Kees grunts.

Her mother continues, and so Kees untangles herself from them all and makes for the shower because something is rising in her throat and she doesn't want to cry on the morning of her baby sister's wedding.

By the time she is out of the shower, it's 5:30 a.m. and the house has woken like an irritable beast, already roaring. Her mother is shouting for Hakim to get up. The hair and makeup ladies have arrived and set up their tools. Her father is on the ladder, sent to the attic to bring down the suitcases of gifts for the groom's family that have been wrapped and packed for months now. Saba's bridesmaids have arrived, four squealing twenty-year-olds who can barely fit their excitement into the house, and her mother is in the kitchen making breakfast for everyone. The day has barely started and everything, and everyone in it, is already alive and bright-eyed because a wedding is a reason to be happy at 6 a.m.

That's the last moment Kees has to pause and even think about guilt before the wedding takes over everything and she finds herself soaked in happiness, sitting at the heart of her sister's joy, except for the moments she is so sad she wants to lie down on the floor and cry.

Her grandmother has arrived with her two aunties and six cousins. Her latest cousin, and the newest addition to the family, Hina, a laughing eleven-month-old baby who enjoyed being in anybody's arms so long as she wasn't put down, spends at least two hours plastered to Kees's hip before she could convince her that someone else's arms would be equally enjoyable. The husbands and male cousins are ushered into one room, only to be barked out of it and given tasks. There is a problem with the caterers' oven and so Mamo Fahad is ordered to drive for a gas replacement. Meanwhile, Mamo Imran goes to pick up the flowers from the florist before handing them over to his wife to pin on everyone's lapels. Women are shouted for when their turn comes up, rotating as quickly as possible between two frazzled makeup and hair artists who haven't counted on quite so many commands from aunties who, although they have never put on makeup in their lives and really don't know what any particular bottle does, demand that they want some of it on their face and ask for their gray hairs to be hidden beneath perfectly placed dupattas.

Kees's makeup takes slightly longer on Shelly, the makeup artist's, insistence that the maid of honor—even though Kees has explained that in Pakistani culture they don't have a maid of honor—had to look her best. Shelly had looked horrified and said, "Well, you are the bride's only sister, aren't you?" and when Kees had nodded Shelly had seemed somewhat mollified.

Eventually, once she is free from their clutches, begrudgingly admitting that her face and hair look amazing, the yellow flowers that Siobhan has plaited through an elaborate up-do going perfectly with her yellow sari, Kees knocks on her bedroom door, having long been banished from it by the overweight Pakistani woman called Rabia who has been hired to work exclusively on Saba, spending five hours on her makeup, hair, jewelry, and the excruciating task of placing her bindi and dupatta so perfectly that it looks like it has just fallen gracefully in place when, in reality, Saba is bound by so many pins, grips, sprays, and setting powders that she can barely twist her head to see who has walked through the door.

Against everything Kees has promised, she feels her eyes well up the minute Saba looks at her. Saba gets teary in return until they both fan their eyes and say, "No tears, no tears," in a desperate attempt not to ruin many hours of work.

"I just wanted to see how you were doing and if you need anything. Umee is panicking about time and Dad said the cars will be arriving shortly."

"I'm fine. I think we're almost done, right?"

Rabia nods, her mouth full of pins to make adjustments to the red lenga so thick with embroidery it weighs more than Saba.

"Okay, I'll let Mum know."

As Kees is about to leave, Saba calls out, "Didi," using the honorific of big sister and she takes a deep breath before she turns to look at her.

"Do I look okay?" she asks, nervously wringing her hands together, and it occurs to Kees for the first time that even though Saba wanted this, Saba is still scared. She is still a young woman about to leave behind everything she has known to step into the arms of a man she has never been with.

Kees wants to take Saba into her arms and tell her that it will be okay. That her new husband will be gentle, and she'll find some of the greatest pleasures of her life in bed with that man.

But these are things she cannot say because she isn't married and finally she understands why the elder sister should get married first. So she can tell Saba how it will go and what she should expect because she's pretty sure her mother hasn't done it. The thought that she has failed, not only her parents but now her younger sister, uncurls itself in her belly and she wonders how she'll manage to disappoint or fail Hakim because it seems like she's on track to complete the whole family.

"You look incredible, Saba. He's not going to know what's hit him."

Saba beams up at her. "Can you tell Umee I'm ready?"

"Of course." She quickly stumbles out of the room with her head down before her tears can set Saba off, walking into

Hakim, who has managed to avoid receiving more jobs from their mother.

"Hey, can you find Mum? Saba wants her," Kees says, pulling her sari up to start the precarious walk downstairs.

He nods and then shouts, "You okay?" and she waves him away, muttering, "Don't be stupid, of course I am," and he doesn't see Kees rushing to the garage—the only place left without people—and bursting into tears because she will never have this day and because the shame has turned so hot it has become a white liquid thing running through her.

Eventually, she tears open a packet of paper towels from the bulk pack of twenty-four that her father insists on buying and wipes her face as best she can, before sheepishly finding Shelly and Siobhan again. Although they're packing up their bags, she asks them to fix the mascara running down her face and pad over the blush she's ruined.

Shelly and Siobhan, who love nothing more than a wedding, sympathetically coo at her face, ushering her back into their chair and telling her not to worry because at each other's weddings they had cried like babies.

"I didn't use waterproof mascara on you," pipes Shelly, bent back over her face, her wrists flicking quickly to brush away any sign of emotion. "I had you down as the one who wouldn't need it."

Siobhan shakes her head knowingly, handing palettes of blush over to Shelly with the precision of a surgeon in an operating theater. "It's always the tough ones that cry the most."

Watching Saba get married is beautiful and terrible in the same breath. The happiness Kees feels brings tears to her eyes so regularly that even she's surprised. It must be different when it's your own family. She's never cried at a wedding, even once commenting that the way everyone does so at the end of

Pakistani weddings is merely performative. However, there's no performance in the sobs that take over her body as she clings to her sister before Saba gets into the car to drive to her new home, only letting go when her father murmurs, "*Chalo, Beta, chalo.*" Later on, when the aunties sit with their feet in bowls of hot water complaining about the agony of kitten heels, they will talk about how hard Kees took it and how difficult it must be to see your younger sister get married before you do.

The agony Kees feels is the realization of how much she wants her family around her when her time comes and the knowledge that it won't happen. Malak's face always swims into her head when she thinks this but stubbornly she pushes it away. She keeps looking across the banquet hall to see her mother's beaming smile and her father's quiet pride and, every time, her shoulders droop a little further down until she has to scoop up her sari for fear of it falling off altogether, and only then does she snap her shoulders back and remind herself that it isn't about her. That she would have to be a truly terrible person to let anything take away from her sister's moment.

And so, she runs around after the bride, makes sure her grandma has everything she needs, slows children down from running into table legs, and scoops up the occasional baby to kiss and cuddle. Her mother is constantly surrounded by a swarm of congratulations and mashallahs from various relatives and, apart from occasionally checking that she is actually eating, she leaves her mother to glow over her daughter, who sits on the podium, beaming down at them all, occasionally wiggling her fingers in a wave to friends from university. All four of them are sitting on a table together commenting on how delicious the food is and how bright everyone's outfits look.

At one point, Saba had called Kees over and asked her to check in on her white friends to make sure they were okay and to see that Rachel, who was a vegetarian, had something to eat.

Kees had gone to the kitchens and asked for an extra dish of tandoori potatoes and some coriander chutney and personally taken it over to Rachel, who, so far, had been nibbling on the sliced tomatoes that came with the lamb samosas.

"I'm so sorry, Rachel, the servers didn't know you were vegetarian."

They had all congratulated Kees on her sister's marriage, commented on how incredible her sari was and how they didn't know how she didn't trip over it because, if it was them in it, they would be flat on the floor by now. They exchanged the kind of warmth that strangers, tied by someone they all love, are prone to do.

Kees manages to slip away to the bathroom and snaps a selfie to send to Harry, who has demanded pictures of her outfit and her, once she is all made up.

He responds with how beautiful she looks, the way he always does, and follows it up by telling her how much he loves her and how he can't wait to marry her.

They don't acknowledge that they don't know what their wedding will look like or who will be there or that her engagement ring is burning a hole in her purse, ready to be put on once she gets on the train to go back to London tomorrow.

She loses count of the times someone tells her that it's her turn now and wonders why people rush to get to the next wedding before this one is even over, as if they're afraid love will run out or has an expiration date.

She is in Aunty Naseem's grasp when Jenna rushes up and saves her by claiming that her mother wants her and quickly pulls her out into the corridor.

She hasn't seen Jenna in months, and she pulls her into her chest so hard she can feel the embroidery on her top digging into her skin.

"You came," she says, holding Jenna at arm's length. Jenna, as usual, looks breathtaking. "How are you always this beautiful?" and she pulls her back into her chest.

Jenna laughs and squeezes her back just as hard, neither of them mentioning their friend who isn't here, but should be. "Of course I came. My mother's been talking about this wedding for weeks and there was no way I wasn't going to be here, for you at least."

Kees swallows back more tears, everything she wants to say stuck in her throat.

"Hey, hey." Jenna pulls her further off to the side. "Is everything okay?"

She nods, still not able to speak, and stares up at the ceiling until the threat of tears has passed and she coughs out a laugh.

"I'm fine, just so happy for her and it's bloody emotional seeing your baby sister get married."

"Of course it is," Jenna murmurs, stroking her arm and looking at her in a way that suggests she knows it's not just about that.

"Harry proposed," Kees blurts out, after looking over her shoulder to make sure no one is around.

Jenna shrieks and then also looks over her shoulder. "What did you say?"

Kees grins. "I said yes."

"Oh babes, congratulations. Where's the ring? Is it massive?"

She laughs and silently thanks Jenna for going straight to joy before stopping at tragedy.

"It's Harry. You know what he's like," she replies.

Jenna nods. "Only the best."

"It's pretty perfect, as far as engagement rings go," Kees says and she grins.

"You have to send me a picture," Jenna insists.

"I will, I promise."

"I have news too. I'm officially and totally in a relationship."

"What! In that case, *you* have to send *me* a picture," replies Kees.

They both laugh and squeeze each other's hands.

"Muslim, right?" asks Kees.

Jenna smiles and nods. "Standard. You know me, totally boring."

Kees is reminded of how much tact Jenna actually has and that she has never given her enough credit for it.

Sakina, a skinny, quiet girl who favors her mother's company instead of other children, nervously approaches Kees, tugging on her sari to tell her that her mother needs her.

Kees pulls Jenna into a hug that is still too hard, but Jenna doesn't complain. There is so much they each want to say and no time to say it in.

"I've got to go," says Kees regretfully, looking into Jenna's face and wishing she could stay to tease her or laugh with her or hold on to some small part of who they all used to be. "But text me, please. I'm dying to hear all about this guy."

Jenna laughs, her perfectly white teeth gleaming across her face. "I will, I will, and text me too. I want to know all about the proposal and how he did it."

She whispers the word "proposal" and they promise to send each other messages, and in that moment they mean it completely.

Kees only sees Jenna across the hall one more time before realizing, at the end of the day, that Jenna must have left and not had a chance to say goodbye.

With her mascara washed down her face and smeared off hastily in the bathroom, Kees packs up the candles and holders that Saba had spent hours designing and crafting, just in case she wants them as wedding mementoes. Her father directs the caterers and her mother is already at home with aunties, bagging up leftover wedding food to be distributed to friends, family, and the community, especially to all those who weren't able to attend the wedding because it is, as her mother says, a blessing to have a child married.

Eventually, they are all sitting together at home, her mother finally tasting the wedding cake, Hakim eating his fourth plate of food, her two aunties upstairs putting the children to bed, and her father bringing down blankets and pillows, everyone commenting on how well the wedding went, how beautiful Saba looked, and how so many people had already said that it was one of the most beautiful weddings they'd ever been to.

Kees has never seen her mother so happy and the guilt has never felt so hot.

Her father begins to roll out the sofa bed, her mother's eyes are half closed, heavy-lidded with happiness, when Aunty Bushra walks back into the room, setting herself heavily into the armchair, patting her arm as she walks past.

"Bilquis, you have to be next, huna? You can't let Hakim get married before you."

Hakim shudders and goes back to his phone, bent over the video of him and his cousins stealing the groom's shoe, which he is convinced is the funniest thing he's ever seen and, if edited right, will go viral.

She smiles and replies, "Inshallah, popo," and hopes the usual answer will be enough. It's not.

"Inshallah, yes, of course," she continues, "but you have to do a little more than pray, huna. Tell her, Abida."

Her mother's eyes are fully closed, and she is swinging her short legs that don't quite reach the floor slowly side to side. "She's married already, Bushra, to her career. I've given up with her. She doesn't care about love. She's going to be a famous lawyer and buy a big house and we'll all live together in that. She can help look after her sister's children."

Years later, Kees still won't be able to say whether it was the look that Aunty Bushra shot her—her expression insinuating that it was probably for the best because marriage prospects might be a bit far-fetched—or her mother so quickly painting an entire life that didn't factor in any of Kees's own decisions, or the idea of spending the rest of her life looking after Saba's children that made her snap; or whether it was just the wedding and jealousy at its very best. That was the reason she least wanted to acknowledge because she hated the idea that she was envious of her sister's happiness.

But whatever it was, she looks up at Aunty Bushra now and, as calmly as if she was asking her if she'd like another cup of tea, she replies, "Actually I've met someone and he has asked me to marry him. And I've said yes."

Whatever it was, she later admitted that it wasn't the best way to do it. Maybe, if she hadn't spent the whole day either crying or holding back tears, she might have broken the news more tactfully, but as it happened in the end, this was how the chips fell. And once she has let the words tumble out of her mouth, she allows herself to be swept up in her mother's shrieks and her father's smile—believing in that one sugary moment that maybe it is going to be okay. And although her mother is slapping her arm for not telling them and Aunty Bushra is running live commentary on girls these days and their secrets, everyone is still smiling and on the crest of her parents' love is the wild, unimaginable fantasy in which her mother hugs her and her father rests his hand on the crown of her head, and even Aunty Bushra is silenced by the size of the ring she whips out of her bag to show them.

But in the very next second—when Kees can no longer avoid answering the questions that are being fired at her, and she can't hold back that, actually, the man she has just declared she will marry is white and Catholic and not going to convert—she quickly and effectively wipes every smile from the room and, as she looks into her mother's eyes, she cannot for the life of her remember if her mother has ever actually smiled at her before.

JENNA

She hasn't told people about her relationship, which is surprising because she has always imagined it would be big news. A Facebook update. A picture on Instagram of her new boyfriend kissing her cheek while she laughs straight to camera, or a purposefully poignant tweet about relationships and work. A group message. Something that signals she is new and different. She knows they look incredible together, but still, no one in her wider circle knows about them.

Perhaps that's what has made it easier for Jenna to change. Throughout their relationship, she has learned what Mo does and doesn't like and has bent accordingly. Not that he applies pressure or insists. He makes gentle comments, seemingly off-hand and random, and Jenna is happy to comply, all in the name of pleasing your partner. The way his face lights up makes her happy, anyway.

"It's not that you don't look good, but I just selfishly want you all to myself," he told her one afternoon, and so she had stopped wearing tight jeans. She stopped wearing jeans altogether, given that most of them were too tight because Jenna had always been proud of her backside, which she had squatted to get and didn't mind the world knowing just how hard she had worked for it.

Later on, he had sent her such a tender message, earnestly hoping he hadn't overstepped the mark, and she felt better than she had in a long time. She felt wanted, and that's all she ever really wants from life. Someone who burns for her and can't sleep without talking to her. Someone who reaches for their phone, even before stretching fully awake, to say good morning to her and, although Mo is calm and measured and wild bursts of passion are not, and will never be, his nature, he is thoughtful and consistent, and sometimes that's as good as wild passion. She wakes up to his message every morning and he is the last person on her phone every night. It makes her feel like she has a place in this world.

She invited him to one of her play rehearsals because she wants him to know how good she is, and she wants to share the parts of her life that she loves. She asked Sarah not to re-hearse the kissing scenes that night because, although she hasn't talked to him about it, a slow certainty uncurls in her belly and the growing feeling that he won't be okay with it settles. Despite those precautions, she could tell from the way his jaw kept clenching that he wasn't comfortable with any of it. The next week, she told Sarah she was pulling out due to workload. She didn't tell Mo, but the next time he asked if she needed a ride to rehearsals, she shrugged like it was no big deal and told him she had quit. That she needed to focus on her exams and becoming a doctor. He had beamed at her with pride then and she felt full of purpose. That was a good night. There were no nightmares that night.

If she stopped long enough to think about it, she could admit that she did these things for him, but she is also aware that she has been doing things for her mother and father her entire life anyway. She doesn't want to wear a headscarf anymore; whipping it off at every possible occasion and stuffing it into whatever glove compartment or handbag is next to her, but she still does it because it means something to her mother.

She has always known that drama club would come to an end once she graduated and ending it a few months earlier wasn't going to kill anyone. She wasn't that excited about it anyway and Sarah had constantly been asking her to put a little more energy into her performance. She'd lost the heart for it. It felt fair to give the part to someone who wanted the chance.

One evening, as they walk through the town on a study break, stopping on a bench by the river to watch swans sail pass, Mo nonchalantly asks about her friendship with Lewis.

"How long have you been friends for?" he asks, stroking her cheek, seemingly more engaged in her face than anything else.

"Oh, since we were sixteen; we go way back," she replies, smiling at the memory of their first meeting.

"Your best friend, huh?"

She nods. "One of. Obviously, Kees and Malak too."

"You don't talk about them as much as you talk about Lewis." His finger traces her jawline to her earlobe.

She lifts her chin to give him more space. "Well, Malak is living in a different country right now and Kees has started a job in London so it's hard when we're not all in the same place." Her chest tightens every time she says this.

"Lewis is still around, at least until he gets a job, although since he spends most of his time driving to Liverpool to see his girlfriend, I can't see that happening any time soon."

Mo has moved on to stroking her hand and he picks it up now to kiss her fingertips.

"Just out of curiosity, has anything ever happened romantically between you guys?"

He asks the question so casually that it is clear he cares an awful lot about the answer. Later, Jenna remembers that "out of curiosity" at the start of a sentence really means, "out of something I can't stop thinking about." She is more cautious in the future.

She barks out a laugh. "No, don't be silly. We're just friends."

He sighs into her palms, which he kisses again. She doesn't see the smile or the way it slides off his face when she says, "Obviously, we've kissed. But who didn't snog their mates when they were sixteen, let's be honest."

He sits up, looking confused. "I never kissed my friends."

"Really?" She cocks her head to one side.

"Yes, really."

"What about spin the bottle? At house parties?"

"What?" It is his turn to tilt his head to one side, looking at her through narrowed eyes and questioning brows.

"You know, the game where you all sit in a circle and spin a bottle, and whoever it points at, you have to snog?" She shrugs and looks back out to the river. "It's just a game."

"That sounds disgusting, Jenna," he replies. "All those germs."

She laughs, remembering she's talking to a soon-to-be doctor who takes it so seriously.

"Oh, it's fine. Sometimes we didn't use tongues. It sounds worse than it was."

"So, you have been together, then?" he asks again.

"Well, no," she pauses, frowning, "we've never been together or been a couple. We just kissed."

She has the foresight to leave out the part where Lewis had lifted her too-short mini skirt, her juvenile attempt at becoming a woman, and, using just his tongue, had blown her world wide open. Technically it was a kiss, of sorts.

Mo has dropped her palms and pulled away from her, leaving a small gap between them on the bench where previously there had been none, his shoulders curled up in defense.

"Do you want to be with him?" he asks.

She laughs loudly. "If I wanted to, I would have been years ago."

It's the wrong thing to say. He shifts further away from her and crosses his arms. She thinks he's trying to look annoyed but, given the context, she thinks he looks like a spoiled brat. It hasn't occurred to her that anyone would be bothered by Lewis, or that anyone could meet him and not realize immediately that the two of them are not suited for one another in any way.

She laughs again but it's still the wrong response. He gets up and starts walking and she quickly gathers her bag and trots after him in heeled boots that are not made for running.

"Hey, hey, what's going on? Where are you going?" She pulls on his arm, forcing him to stop and turn to look at her.

"Do you know what I did when we became official?" he asks her.

She shakes her head and gestures toward another bench, but he ignores her, which is a testament to how upset he is. He takes etiquette and chivalry very seriously.

"I went through my Facebook and deleted all my female contacts I've ever dated."

She stares at him, puzzled. "Why would you do that?"

"Because of you, Jenna." He steps toward her and cups her face in his hand. "Because I never want a woman to comment on a picture or post and you to have any questions about any other woman."

"But I don't have any questions," she replies.

"I don't want you to ever think you're not the only one in my life," he continues, talking over her. "There's just you, Jenna. I'm not talking to anyone else."

She shifts from foot to foot, knowing they've had this conversation before when they decided to be official, and she's unsure why they're having it again.

"I know that." She stares blankly at him. It was one of those moments she needed Malak and Kees and the comfort of figuring things out in the group chat because she honestly couldn't fathom what his point was.

"You're friends with a man whose lips have been on yours, Jenna." He says this in the same tone he uses to talk to his six-year-old niece when she doesn't understand something. "Do you not think he is waiting for the day it happens again?"

She throws her head back this time when she laughs, and his hands fall off her face. The idea that Lewis is waiting, secretly hoping for something to happen between them, is one of the only times she's truly found anything funny since "that night."

Years ago, she had ended up staying at his house one evening and they had spent hours watching movies and eating junk food. In the morning they had come down for breakfast and his mother, in a rare display of flippancy, had joked and asked when the two of them would get together and they had both shuddered.

"What!" she had exclaimed, slipping into her shoes as she got ready to leave for work. "You two are adorable together."

"Mum, if Jenna was lying naked in front of me, I'd step over her and keep walking," he had replied, to which his mother had swung her handbag at him and told him not to be rude.

"Jenna is a beautiful woman."

"Thanks, Lisa," Jenna had said, smiling smugly.

"Jenna is the most beautiful woman I will probably ever see," Lewis had interrupted. "But being in a relationship with her would make me want to end my life."

His mother had tutted about her impossible son and left, leaving them both to laugh over the idea that two people as different as they were could ever live happily together.

It is, and has been, one of the only things they've ever managed to agree on.

Now she looks at Mo and says, "I can guarantee you, Lewis is not secretly hoping we end up together."

"He doesn't like me," Mo replies.

"Of course he likes you."

"You told me he didn't."

"I did?"

"Yes, Jenna, you did." He frowns.

"Okay, well, dislike is a strong word. He just doesn't know you, that's all. And he's an idiot, so who cares?" she shrugs.

"He doesn't like me because he wants to be with you," he interrupts.

Why is he being like this? she thinks and sighs. She thinks it must be an Arab-man thing because the rare times she has heard her parents argue, it is always about her mum's cousin Jimmy, who stares at her too much, or the guy in the supermarket who didn't lower his gaze, or some other man her father was convinced was trying to steal his wife from him.

She holds on to his shoulders and makes him look her in the eye. "He doesn't want to be with me. I cannot stress this enough. It's the most absurd suggestion ever."

She doesn't know why he can't see how stupid this is.

"It just makes me uncomfortable. I don't trust him. I know what men are like."

Something acidic curls up in her stomach. *I bet I know more than you.*

The thought drains any remaining laughter out of her and she walks back to the bench and slumps down on it. He follows and picks up her hands once more, looking deeply into her eyes as if he's trying to communicate something else.

"I love you, Jenna."

She looks at him. It is the first time love has been mentioned. She hasn't considered love but now with the word strung up between them, bright and untouched, it seems appealing and right.

"I love you and I hate the idea of anyone else touching you. It makes me feel physically sick. And I know this guy is your friend, but I don't trust him. I don't trust anyone with you but me." He lifts his hand and returns to stroking her cheek, a soft finger trailing its way across her perfectly made-up face. "Do you understand?"

She thinks she does. Does some quick calculations in her head. Lewis has a girlfriend and is around less. She is with someone now and is around less. He's spending most of his time in Liverpool and they both know he's looking for jobs there. It's only a matter of time before he moves. Life is moving on. She will be a doctor soon and who will then have time for movies until 3 a.m.? She has the deeply uncomfortable feeling that this is what it means to be an adult, that to play that role you have to be willing to accept change.

She looks up at him and his pleading face.

"Don't you love me, too?" he asks desperately, and her heart crashes into her ribs. He is vulnerable and afraid, having thrown his heart up into the air for her to catch it, and she loves him for it, so she catches it and kisses him lightly on the lips.

"Of course I love you."

Something is agreed but unspoken at that moment. He suggests they keep walking and so they do.

It never occurs to Jenna to lie to the boyfriend she has always dreamed of having. She will message Lewis later.

BILQUIS

The problem with family is that you can love them completely while despising their every move.

Kees has always believed family was code for excusing the mistakes and actions of people you could keep close without having to interrogate your own moral code. Like when Mamo Imran brought home a blond-haired toddler and called him son, everyone had spoken about blood and how their collective blood now ran in the veins of a little boy who didn't speak Punjabi but that it wasn't his fault and he shouldn't be punished. Her mother had hated her brother then but loved his son more than anyone else, and when Mamo had asked them all to arrange a match with their fourth cousin twice removed from the same village as Grandma back in Pakistan, they had loved him for being traditional and adhering to his parents' wishes. Then, they spoke about what a good son he was and how Islamic the arrangements had been. While peeling okra one evening, Kees had casually remarked that surely it was a little too late for him to be respecting anyone's wishes since he'd got a woman pregnant, refused to marry her, and then had the luxury of someone else sorting out his marriage for him without having to lift a finger, all while expecting his new wife, who was significantly younger than he was, to take on the role of stepmother to his fair-skinned child who would finally have to learn Punjabi if he ever wanted to talk to her.

Her mother had snatched the basket of okra off her, not before landing a slap across her arm, telling her that blood mattered and just because Kees had started going to the debating club at school, it did not mean she could talk to her parents, or about her elders, like they were her friends, and how she was too young to understand everything that was going on.

Blood matters. Blood matters. Blood matters.

Blood doesn't matter anymore.

No one mentions the importance of family. Childhood nostalgia evaporates.

In a tiny council house, the silence widens the spaces between them until they are all standing on separate islands, thousands of miles apart, and as no one speaks, it forms a hard shell that gets more difficult to break. Everyone stands frozen for an hour, rooted to their places as if playing a game of sleeping lions that no one wants to lose. Later, when Kees tells the story, she always emphasizes this point; how no one moved for an hour and how they had done the impossible and managed to stop time. In reality, it is a minute, maybe two, which proves to her that it doesn't take that long for hearts to break.

Eventually, Aunty Bushra displays a tact that no one thought her capable of—absolving her in Kees's eyes of every past sin she has committed—and says she will take Hakim up to bed because it's getting late.

Hakim, who at the age of fifteen doesn't need to be taken to bed, but who will do anything in that moment to get as far away from his three family members with their coal eyes, nods and walks through the door his aunty holds open for him. She gently closes it behind her, praying for a miracle.

Her father eases himself onto the edge of the sofa and Kees is painfully aware that he is getting old.

"You've accepted his proposal?" he asks.

She nods and sees her mother sway.

"Then you must tell him and his family that you cannot marry him and return any rishta they have given you. Do you need the money to do so?"

She wants to ask him, with what money? She had noticed the letters detailing the bank loan stuffed in her father's corner of the sitting room and in that moment had hated Saba for putting the family through this wedding.

Instead, she says, "There isn't any rishta, there's nothing to return."

Her mother's lip curls up in disgust and if she hadn't already made up her mind about these people who were trying to steal her daughter from her, she did then.

"Good. So you must apologize and return the ring to him. You cannot marry this man, Beta." Her father doesn't break his gaze, staring into his daughter's eyes the same way he had when trying to impart some wisdom to her when she was a child and wanted an answer for everything.

"Why not?" she asks.

"Beta. He's not Muslim. There is no way."

"But I love him," she replies.

It is at that moment that her mother breaks her silence. Throwing her head back, she laughs and laughs. She laughs so hard the tears stream out of her eyes and it is the only time Kees sees her mother lift the corner of her dupatta to wipe away tears for her firstborn.

"Love. LOVE. What has love got to do with anything?"

The next fifty minutes last for the rest of her life as her mother strips the paint off the walls with the things she tells her daughter. Once a week Kees will bring up her mother in her therapist's office and some sentence or shred of what she hurled at Kees that day will find its way into the conversation or sobbed into the box of tissues placed within arm's reach. It's not that words can't be taken back or apologies blanketed over wounds, but rather that some blood doesn't clot, no matter how thick.

Her father cannot stem or slow his wife and eventually stops trying, his head hanging in his hands, still perched on the edge of the sofa. Kees stays standing. Her mother barely pauses for breath. Somewhere, someone dies. Hakim lies, wide-eyed, thinking that the video isn't so funny after all. Saba slips into a white silk nightgown she has saved all of her money to buy and stands trembling in front of her new husband. Aunty Bushra's tears are the first to fall. Somewhere, someone is born. Harry sleeps deeply. Vivian whispers her biggest fear and asks Nathaniel if he thinks their son will become a "Moslem." Jenna prays for the first time in a year. The light begins to change as the moon rises higher. Her mother only stops when the final sentence, the one she has been building up to, is hurled like smashed plates across the room to land on top of Kees. "If you marry this boy, you will not be permitted back in this house ever again." Parts of her spine come away. Her father wipes the tears that have been streaming down his face and he follows his wife up to bed.

The train's air conditioning is broken and stuck on freezing. People in suits and jeans huddle down in jackets, sinking further into their seats and asking for tea or coffee as the trolley makes its way through the carriage. The conductor announces again how sorry he is for the inconvenience caused.

Her ring is back on her left hand, its reflection shining off the glass. The woman sitting opposite, with whom Kees shares a table, leans in. "Congratulations, it's a stunning ring." She smiles as if they're sharing a secret.

"Thank you." Kees smiles back in return.

"I make jewelry. I have a boutique shop in Yorkshire, but I come to London for meetings with the wholesalers."

Kees keeps smiling. "Then you know your jewelry."

"I certainly do." The woman nods. "Well enough to know how remarkable that piece is. You're a very lucky lady."

Kees smiles again, lips sealed tightly to one another. She wonders why men don't have something that identifies them as lucky, and then remembers that they do; the woman is the thing men look at while nodding to one another saying, "You're a lucky bloke."

She had risen early to get the first train home, creeping down the stairs to find her parents awake in the kitchen, a pan of tea between them and her mother's hand nestled in her father's hard palm. She hadn't slept and had spent the night writing a twelve-page letter to her mother, which she hoped was the most convincing argument of her career.

"Umee," she'd said, placing the letter by her mother's elbow, "this is for you."

Her mother hadn't even looked at her; she'd just picked up the letter and, as hope had flared in Kees's chest, walked to the cooker, clicked on the gas, and lit the corner of it on fire, eventually letting it drop into the sink once the flames started licking her fingers. She had then sat back down, picked up her mug, and taken a long sip.

There was nothing left to say after that. Her father didn't offer to drive her to the station. He didn't wait five minutes after the train left or offer her a ten-pound note for a cup of tea for the journey.

He just sat, opening his palm and waiting for his wife to once more rest her hand in his.

As Kees steps through the front door of her flat, expecting everything to have changed because her life has, she finds Harry at home, sitting on the floor bent over the coffee table surrounded by papers.

"What are you doing here?" she asks stupidly, blinking as the morning rises through the kitchen window and straight into her eyes, lighting up just how much shit is cluttered around the place and how it really is too small for them.

She hasn't told Harry that her parents know of his existence. That she has just broken something unfixable. That he is the reason she is suddenly orphaned. She desperately thinks that as long as she doesn't say it out loud, it might not be true after all.

He raises both his eyebrows and leans elbows back against the seat of the sofa. Something in the way he does it makes her want to pick up the ornate china vase by the door, which his mother gave her as a Christmas present one year and which she hates but doesn't want to hurt Harry's feelings by giving it away, and hurl it at his head.

"I do live here," he replies. He makes no move to stand up and greet her and so she doesn't cross the room to him either.

She lets her bags drop, not bothering to put them to the side, and picks up the pile of mail so she'll have something to do with her hands that have begun to tremble.

"I meant why are you not at work?" she says impatiently.

"Well, what are you doing here?" he asks in return. "I thought you weren't getting back until the afternoon."

She glares at him. "We're answering questions with questions now? Is that what we're doing?"

He knows how much she hates it when he does that and she is convinced he's done it specifically to irritate her.

He sighs. "No, that's not what we're doing. I decided to work from home today. Why didn't you tell me you were getting an earlier train? I told you I would pick you up."

She walks into the kitchen, which may as well be in the living room because the damn flat is so small, and begins rooting around for some bread. She hasn't eaten since breakfast at 6 a.m. yesterday, when her mother had forced her to eat some paratha and chutney.

"I didn't want to be picked up," she says. She continues rummaging in the cupboards, making toast, and searching for where he's put the peanut butter. The flat is always tidier when she's not there and it only adds to her annoyance. She pulls out things from the shelf and leaves them scattered across countertops.

Finally, Harry stands up and takes the three steps to the kitchen. "Why don't you sit down and I'll make you some breakfast."

"I don't want you to make me breakfast, Harry."

"You don't want to be picked up. You don't want me to make you breakfast. Is there anything you want from me?"

She looks at him coolly and shrugs. "No, thank you."

He shoots her a quizzical look, narrowing his eyes as if to ask, "What's happening here?" and she looks down, trying to twist open the jar of peanut butter, ignoring his look.

"Do you want me to open that for you?" he asks, holding out his hand.

"Harry, are you serious right now?" She slams the jar down and the glass hitting marble makes a cracking sound. "I'm fine. I don't need any help. Go do your work."

He doesn't move as she pops the toast up and begins to butter it with more force than it needs, smearing butter and tearing holes in the bread that hasn't been left in the toaster long enough.

He watches her and she thinks she might scream.

Harry doesn't move, just leans against the counter and stares at her until she looks at him with a face that she already knows has "What the fuck are you looking at?" written all over it.

He stands up straight and crosses his arms over his broad chest and it makes him look suddenly bulkier than he is. His forehead is creased in a frown but he has a determined set to his jaw that she has seen only a few times. "I thought we should talk."

"About what, Harry?"

She pauses and waits for him to say something.

"About us."

She pauses for a second before picking the jar back up, grabbing a tea towel from the wall to help pry the lid off.

"What, you want to break up with me now?"

"Kees, wait, what are you talking about?"

"No, why don't you just go for it. Go right ahead, Harry."

"Jesus, Kees, I just said we should talk. No one is talking about breaking up." He snatches the tea towel from her hand, angrily. "Would you stop for a minute."

She snatches it back from his hands. "No. I'm hungry."

He runs his hands through his hair before resting his elbows on the countertop and cradling his head in his palms. He takes a deep breath before he looks up tiredly at her and says, "I just want to talk to you, Keesy."

"What the hell is there to talk about, Harry?"

"Well, how about the fact that you haven't replied to a single one of my messages or calls since yesterday? Or that you've barely talked to me the entire time you've been away? Or that you won't let me touch you, and every time I come close to you, you flinch or tell me you don't feel well? Or that you haven't prayed in weeks? Or that you won't leave your Quran out? Or the fact that you've been avoiding coming home."

She opens her mouth to say something, but he interrupts. "No, Kees. There's working late and then there's just not coming home. So how about we talk about any one of those things, because every time I try to start a conversation with you, you snap my head off."

He delivers his speech and there is nothing irrational or unfair in what he says.

"I know you've been insanely stressed with Saba's wedding and I figured it would be a difficult time for you, so I didn't say anything and I've been patient, but you've walked back in here all snarly and exactly the same and so ..." He trails off and looks at her helplessly. "Baby, what's going on?"

A man should never mention how patient he's been, and her lip curls up in disdain. *Just be fucking patient and shut up*, she thinks. *Don't tell me how patient you've been because that's exactly the opposite of it.* She picks up the jar and squeezes all her energy into trying to twist the lid off.

"Kees," Harry says, "are you going to talk to me or—"

She feels something click inside her chest, a small pop, an echoing of her mother's last sentence to her, and she throws the jar across the small kitchen to shatter on the cabinet, peanut butter slowly dripping down the drawers.

"Or what, Harry?"

"What the hell, Kees?" he asks, his face twisting in confusion at the woman standing opposite him.

"No, no, or what, Harry?" she snarls. "What's the end of that sentence? You'll leave me?" She picks up her plate and scrapes the toast into the bin, banging the plate into the sink. There's no point in having dry toast. "I don't have sex with you for a couple of weeks and suddenly you have a problem."

"Don't be ridiculous, Kees," he sighs, exasperated. "It's not about that. And why did you throw that jar?"

"Isn't it? Because this sounds like it's about the fact that I've said no to you and won't put out. Which, by the way, is the first time in three and a half years," she shouts.

"Why are you shouting, Kees?" Harry says, palms upturned as if an answer will fall into them. "That's not what I was saying at all."

She feels a fit of lost anger licking at her heels and walks out of the kitchen, brushing past Harry, whose sad face is quite frankly pathetic and makes her want to start throwing everything.

"I'm shouting because it's bullshit that I say no to you once, after three and a half years of fucking you, and suddenly it's an issue. And bear in mind I didn't even want to have sex in the first place. I told you I was waiting until marriage."

"You're being ridiculous," he says quietly.

"Oh, that's funny," she snaps, "because it sounds like you're pissed off that you haven't got laid and don't you think that's fucking ridiculous?"

He is looking at his feet, and after a minute has passed, the air filled with her heavy breathing and the occasional drip of peanut butter as it makes its way down the kitchen, he looks up at her and says, "I would have waited. I told you we didn't have to have sex."

Her accusation is, she knows, unfair, but she is past what is fair. Doesn't care that she had wanted to have sex with him just as much and they had decided together. Her anger only has room for what feels right, and at this moment her fingers twitch to pull their matchstick life down around them.

"Well, it's too late for that, Harry," she barks.

She moves piles of books around the room, shifting objects from one surface to another to give her arms something to do.

He sits on the arm of the sofa. "I can't believe that's the only bit you took from everything I said." Harry has never been a fan of confrontation, which is why she thinks it odd that he became a lawyer. If Kees has tried to have fights, Harry has done everything possible to avoid them, refusing to raise his voice or get angry with her. He is not a man to fill a room with his voice.

"I don't give a shit if you don't want to have sex, Kees," he continues. "But you barely let me kiss you hello, you don't even cuddle or touch me, and I'm sorry, but that does bother me. You spend any time in bed so far on the other side. I may as well sleep alone."

"I'm not here just for your pleasure or to soothe you as you fall asleep, you know." Another stack of books gets banged to the other side of the room. "I do have other purposes in life."

Harry looks at her like she's grown a second head but she feels too far along in this fight to back out now.

"And why the fuck do you care if I'm praying or not? I thought you'd be happy." She snorts a laugh out. "Your parents would be ecstatic to hear I've stopped praying. At least they wouldn't have a daughter-in-law who sneaks off to the utility room five times a day to—what was it they said?—kiss the ground."

"That's not fair, Kees," he says quietly.

"I don't give a shit about what's fair, Harry," she screams. "What the hell is fair anyway? We're lawyers. We don't do fair. The fact is, your parents are petrified I'm going to convert you into a big-bearded, dress-wearing Muslim. I can see it all over your mother's face. She's probably donated an obscene amount of money to the church and asked them to pray for you because throw money at the problem and that will sort it, right?"

"Be that as it may, Kees," he replies in a strained tone, teeth gritted half in despair, half in frustration, "we're not talking about my parents, we're talking about you and why you're not praying."

"Because I don't feel like it."

She looks at him to see what he has to say and as he takes a step toward her, she takes one back, shaking her head.

"Why don't you feel like it, Kees?"

She twists her face and shrugs. "Just."

"It's making you upset, baby," he replies.

"Oh, so now you're going to presume to tell me how I feel?"

He sighs. "It's pretty obvious that you don't feel great. Come to church with me tonight. There's an evening service my parents are going to."

The reality that Harry has parents he can go places with punches her in the stomach. "Oh, so first you're annoyed that you're not getting enough sex, which, by the way, both our religions condemn, and now you want me to come to church."

She laughs and imagines it's the same cruel laugh her mother barked out last night, the pitch perfectly matching in tone. Like mother like daughter.

"Do you want to fuck or do you want to pray, Harry? Make up your goddamn mind."

She throws the files she's holding onto the sofa, papers fluttering down like the first snow.

"I want to have a reasonable conversation with you, without you coming out with, quite frankly, stupid statements." He doesn't shout, but it is the closest he's ever come to shouting and she can see the anger in his eyes that comes from not being able to help her.

"I want to know what's wrong without being accused of ulterior motives. If you want to rage and smash stuff up, then go for it, Kees. I'm not doing it, and don't have any desire to wreck our apartment, but don't stand there and try to make out that I've only ever been in this for the sex because it's quite frankly demeaning to us both."

She spins around to face him. "And did it ever occur to you that I don't feel like talking right now? That not everything has to be on your time? That just because you've always gotten everything you want out of life doesn't mean that applies to me?"

"Oh, here we go," he sighs. "I was wondering when this would come back to me and my privilege."

She shoots him a scathing glance. "Now is not the time to be cavalier."

He forces a laugh out. "I wasn't, I was being serious. Because this is what you always come back to. My privilege."

"Well, you have it," she snaps.

"I know that, Kees," he exclaims. "But it doesn't mean I don't also have feelings. Or can't be upset by things. It's not an invisibility shield."

"Actually, that's exactly what it is."

"You know what, I'm not getting into an argument with you about this. We're not doing it," he says, standing up and pulling his sneakers on.

"Oh, so now you're done?"

"No, I'm just going for a run because the conversation has gotten plain ludicrous right now."

"Well, how convenient for you. As soon as it's on a subject that makes you uncomfortable you get to leave."

He kicks off his sneakers and they land on the other side of the room. "Fine, I'll stay, you want to talk about white privilege, then go ahead, Kees. What is it that you want to say, that we haven't heard before, because I'm all ears."

She shakes her head and stares at him. Feels the ring around her finger twist, the diamond knocking against her little finger. Her hand feels heavier. Everything in her body is heavier.

She picks up his sneakers and throws them at the ground back at his feet. "Go for your damn run, Harry. I need some space."

She hears him call her name as she walks into the bathroom and, for the first time since she moved in, locks the door.

She is still in there, the water running as hot as it will go, when he gets back an hour later. She floats in the tub, adding hot water every time she feels cold, staring up at the low ceiling, and thinks how all the roofs seem to be falling.

Eventually, her body covered in red patches and wrinkled, she drags herself out of the bath feeling heavier than before. She wonders if she's still engaged and her chest aches. It has been aching for so long now she barely notices it, but now the pain has gotten stronger. She isn't sure how you can be so close to a person and then be standing on opposite sides of the world.

She places the engagement ring on her jewelry table—it's the first time she hasn't worn it when they've been together—and climbs into bed with the towel still wrapped around her head. It's only noon, and she doesn't get out of bed for the rest of the day.

She goes into the kitchen to make some tea and sees Harry lying on the sofa watching reruns.

"I thought you were going to church?" she says, her back to the sofa.

She hears him shrug. "Didn't feel like it in the end."

She says nothing else, just gets back into bed with her tea and falls asleep.

She wakes up cold and uncomfortable in the middle of the night and feels Harry sleeping on the other side of the bed, and the previous day and all the days before it, especially the one just before, slam back into her head and she feels the throb of a migraine approaching.

She catches her first tear and she just puts her sleeve in her mouth to stop from making a noise and curls up on Harry's back. If her sobs and the gentle shaking of their bed wakes him, he gives no sign and doesn't turn over to pull her to him.

By the time she wakes up, he has gone to work and so she drags herself into a cold morning to do the same. She leaves her engagement ring on the stand and makes her way into work, her finger bare. It is the first thing Addy notices when she walks into the office and he gasps and grabs her hand.

It's the first thing Harry notices when he gets back from work before her. After staring at the ring lying on the naked wood for ten minutes with a bunch of her favorite flowers in his arms, he gently lays them down so that when Kees eventually comes home to an empty flat, the bouquet is waiting for her, next to the engagement ring she purposefully didn't put on that morning.

MALAK

Malak has moved in with him, although that is not the story she tells her family. Nylah and Rayan will cover for her and since she is duty-bound to visit her aunties in Cairo, never the other way around, she doesn't worry about family turning up on the doorstep. Living with him is too blissful to worry about the details.

It is in September when they have their first big fight, three weeks and four days after their first small fight; as if there has been a loosening of the seams, a stretching of the fabric. In the petty falling out and making up again, they have learned how to break apart but come back together. That it can be done. Malak has learned that if she apologizes enough, is gentle and helpless enough, she can bring him back round to softness. Ali has learned that she won't leave.

It is late but they are not tired. Cairo still screams outside the window—a woman calling her husband, boys kicking a deflated football in the dirt, the shout of bewebs to one another as they talk through the gaps in their teeth from apartment buildings. She is scrolling through conversations, laughing down at her phone; he is watching the news, occasionally shouting at the TV, but mostly engaging in furious debates on Twitter.

Twitter is where all of Ali's observations come home to rest; a flurry of opinions and retorts that always tie in with the political situation in Egypt, the failing party politics of England, or the observations of a man who has once worked for cash and now works for the people; an enlightened reformist who turns big ideas into 140 characters, sounding infinitely more poignant than those who cannot condense a point. She often scrolls through his Twitter when he isn't there or is taking a shower, walking down the corridor of his brain, a secret thrill at being privy to his thoughts, even though 4,367 other people are also watching. He never retweets ordinary things or contributes to the viral tweets that almost everyone finds funny. He tweets the kinds of things Kees would be interested in discussing. One day, as Ali was telling her about the class he was teaching at the British Council, she nearly said, "I can't wait for you to meet Kees; you'll really get on," but then remembered that he might never meet Kees. The thought made her stomach turn with a longing so sharp she couldn't breathe for a moment.

He always retweets people with "Dr." in their handle or bio. Or a researcher. Or journalists specializing in writing about the Middle East. He has never, not once, and she knows because one time she scrolled back to his very first tweet—*New here and interested in talking to anyone carrying out post-colonial research with a Middle Eastern focus #MyFirstTweet*—posted something about his day, the salad he ate for lunch, or the new sneakers he has bought. She looks for signs of herself; a happy tweet after a weekend together, a comment on the importance of partnership, but finds nothing. There are no traces of her here. She had once asked why he didn't mention that he had a partner and he had kissed her firmly on the mouth and said that their relationship was private. That, one day, people would know his name. How he was going to be famous in his field and so protecting his privacy started now. "I never want to put you at risk, Kookie," he had said, holding her a little more tightly than he normally did. "Most of the problems with celebrity relationships is that they are played out in public and that's half of the damage."

She liked the idea that he was going to be known. It was like opening a new door and realizing that there were more possible ways for a life to go than the two or three she had previously imagined. That maybe she wouldn't just marry a Muslim man and have children, happily prioritizing family over work. It was her first taste of ambition, her new aspirations beginning to blur into focus with Ali by her side. The feeling was exhilarating.

His Twitter doesn't bother her anyway. He falls asleep with her, he doesn't need to tweet about her too. Sometimes, after they've spent a particularly romantic evening together, she will later check his feed when he's brushing his teeth or praying his final prayer, realizing that somewhere in the middle of that evening, maybe when she went to the bathroom or he went to collect the car, he has tweeted a string of opinions on the latest football scores, the socio-economic makeup of Cairo, or the benefits system in England, and it makes her feel empty inside.

Lately, he is always grabbing his phone, occasionally reaching over to excitedly clutch her leg and tell her that Egyptians are fed up and something has to change. The program he is watching now keeps flashing up the president's face so she assumes they're talking politics. Her Arabic is still dismal and she's halfway through her latest fantasy novel and so hasn't been prioritizing her lessons the way her teacher insists she should, but small mentions of the police force and the army, words she does know, keep catching her ear.

It's at that moment he looks up, arms leaning forward on his knees, and turns to look at her, saying, "You know, I can't believe you messaged your ex."

She is so caught off guard that for a moment the only sound she hears is the din of the traffic, convinced that she's imagining things, but the way he's looking at her tells her she's not.

Last week had been Jacob's birthday and since they hadn't broken up badly, and since the last time she saw him he had been wrapped around her, both of them still bound by love and affection, and since she had very openly asked Ali if he minded whether she messaged him or not and he had looked up from his phone and shrugged, she had drawn the natural conclusion that it was okay.

She had asked him because she felt dishonest messaging her ex without saying anything; in the silence, it becomes a lie, but in the open, it becomes a passing comment, like, "I picked up some milk on the way home," "I've put a load of washing on," "I messaged my ex just to be polite." And it was politeness. He had messaged her in May to say happy birthday and he hoped she was enjoying Egypt, careful not to invite further conversation. She had done the same, replying: *Thank you, having an amazing time, hope you're well x.*

She didn't want to look petty by not messaging him when it was his birthday and, after all, she didn't have anything bad to say about Jacob. So, she had sent a two-lined message over Facebook: *Happy Birthday, Jakey Boy. I hope the day is amazing and you and the family are well x.* She means it. She hopes he is happy and cared for, that his family, with whom she had spent some of the most blissful times, are doing well.

Jacob hadn't crossed her mind since then, until Ali, leaning toward her with something beginning to cloud his vision, stated his disbelief.

"But you said you were fine with it," she replies, her phone suddenly frozen in her hand.

The room feels still; she has stopped hearing the sound of the TV or the traffic outside, which she knows can't be right because the traffic outside never stops. The look in his eyes is one she has never seen before. He sits pitched forward, as if waiting for a gunshot at a race, staring at her with eyes that are unmoving.

And then, like a crack of lightning, all the sound comes back into the room as he hurls his phone across the room to smash against the wall, splintered bits of plastic flying across the ornate rug.

"Of course I'm not fine with it, Malak," he shouts. "Why the fuck do you think I would be fine with it?"

She has sometimes heard her parents arguing. Her mother's worry and her father's tiredness clashing to cause an argument over something worth fighting about: the bills, how they were going to afford to fix the car, or whether there was enough lamb in the freezer to invite guests over. But she has never faced a man's anger. It is the first time she learns what it is like to drown at sea and still live.

She has no time to catch her breath because he shouts again, this time dangerously close to screaming, "Why would I be okay with my girlfriend talking to her ex?"

"But I wasn't talking to him."

"I'm sorry," he interrupts, "did you, or did you not, message him?"

She stares at him like he is someone she used to know.

"Well, answer the question, Malak. Did you, or did you not, message him?"

"Well, yes, but only—"

"So, then you did talk to him," he says, cutting her off and beginning to pace to different corners of the room. "Because the last time I checked, to message someone you have to talk to them. So you talked to your ex."

She stands. It doesn't feel right to sit down while he is pacing.

"Yes, but it wasn't like we were having a conversation, it was just a quick message to say happy birthday," she stammers.

"Don't argue semantics with me, Malak, it's beneath you," he snaps back.

She feels like she's risen above her body and is watching the scene. She wants to laugh back and ask, "But didn't you just argue semantics with me?" but his eyes look like the hellfire she imagined as a girl when stories from Aunty Hala, the Quran teacher, had her screaming in the night for her mother, so she says nothing.

Another crack. "How could you do it?" he roars, throwing a book across the room. "How could you do it to me?"

She can feel the tears begin to leak out of her eyes but isn't sure why she is crying. "But, baby, I never would have done it if you had a problem with it." She takes a step toward him. "If you didn't want me to, you should have said and I never, ever would have messaged."

He takes a step away from her. "If you had used your fucking brain, you wouldn't even have asked me that question in the first place. Tell me which man you know who would be happy for their girlfriend to message her ex-boyfriend, and on top of that to tell him about it?"

She cannot understand his words and logic. Everything is too jumbled for an answer, so she doesn't try to interrupt and slow him down.

"Which man do you know, Malak? WHICH ONE?"

He has taken three quick steps toward her and she can feel the spit of his anger on her cheek.

She opens her mouth and pauses. She wants to tell him that all her friends' boyfriends don't mind that they message their exes happy birthday, and congratulations, and commiserations when someone dies. She can suddenly remember which friends are good friends with their ex-boyfriends and their current partners have never blinked. Abiola Baron from her course is still friends with Aren, despite now being engaged to John Pritchard. Damion Tashik from the athletics society was the best man at his ex-boyfriend Jack's wedding and his husband, Niki, had loved it. Aya Latif is best friends with Jonathan, even though she is with Suliman now.

Although he is breathing heavily over her, waiting for an answer, she doesn't want to be yelled at again, so she mentions none of these men. She has just learned that mentioning another man will not end well.

She just shrugs and sniffs, wipes away another tear, and tentatively puts her hands on his arms.

"Baby, I never meant to upset you."

She has stepped too close, too early. He raises his arms to shake her off him.

"I'm not upset, Malak," he screams. "I'm disrespected. You have no fucking regard for me."

He turns his back to her and resumes his pacing, never picking up the shattered phone, just stepping on the plastic, crunching it further into the rug and into smaller pieces that they won't be able to find later.

"I would never dream of making a fool out of you like that, Malak," he shouts. More books crash onto the floor. The newsreader continues to talk on the television and Malak still picks out the odd words she recognizes, noting that it's a strange time to practice her Arabic. She feels oddly detached from what's happening, unable to connect the dots and understand how he had gone from his Twitter timeline to this unfathomable rage.

"Do you think I don't have exes?" he asks, spinning to face her, his features contorted in rage. "I've got exes, Malak. Plenty of them. But I told all of them that it wasn't appropriate to continue conversing with them the minute I met you. THE VERY MINUTE." His shouts bounce off the walls. "Because I thought you were worthy of my respect."

She finds a small bit of something inside of her that could be anger. "And you don't think I am worthy anymore?" She can feel her voice rising alongside the panic in her throat. "I wouldn't have bothered if it meant that much to you," she says.

"THEN WHY DID YOU DO IT?" he screams and she finally screams back.

"BECAUSE YOU TOLD ME TO."

"Who the fuck are you shouting at, Malak?" His own voice pitched as high as hers. He turns around and with the force of his anger and the frustrations she cannot pin down, he kicks the marble table leg three times, each time shouting, "My fault, my fault, my fault."

He turns around to face her and she no longer recognizes him. He has become a gargoyle of pain and frustration and even in her wretched state, she has the fleeting, faraway thought that men kicking inanimate objects is one of life's more pathetic sights.

"You're now blaming me," he heaves, his chest racing up and down with the efforts of kicking something that won't fight back.

He takes the four steps into the center of the living room where she is standing, trembling, and his face is so close to hers, the way it is just before he kisses her. She can see the sweat trickling down his temple, the pores on his face opening under the heat, smell his cologne, heightened by his sweat, and for the briefest of moments, one that she wishes to pause, she thinks *this is it*, he will come back into himself and be the man she has fallen in love with.

The newsreader is now interviewing someone from the American University in Cairo. She recognizes the word for university. The string of car horns signaling a wedding pass by and light up the neighborhood. Her heartbeat rings in her ears, or maybe it's his. Her phone pings a notification through. His eyes cloud over. A vein in his neck, one she has never noticed before, draws her eye. She feels his breath wash over her and then hears what he has shouted: "WHORE."

"You're a whore, Malak. For being with this man in the first place. For giving yourself away like that. And then you go around messaging the same man. It's disgusting."

A coldness has settled into him. An ice creeps down from his face until his whole body is covered in it. If she looks hard enough, she can almost see the icicles drop from his eyes. Her face is hot and wet, but she cannot remember crying. She shouts back, "Well, then, why are you with me if you think that of me?" and she screams it, partly because she's so frustrated, she doesn't know how else to get through to him, but partly because you cannot stand in the eye of the storm and talk in whispers.

"I DON'T KNOW. I DON'T KNOW HOW SOME-ONE LIKE YOU CAN BE THE MOTHER OF MY CHILDREN. After I've shown you respect and love and kind-ness. After I've worked so hard to make sure you're always safe and picked you up from places. I INTRODUCED YOU TO MY FRIENDS. And all I ask is a modicum of the respect I've shown you. An ounce of love and affection. And you're sitting here, in the house my grandfather built, messaging your fucking ex and screaming at me about the respect I owe you. You're disgusting, Malak. I never thought you could be like this and look how wrong I am. Always proved wrong."

He picks up his keys and walks out of the apartment, slamming the door behind him, and she sinks to her knees, the storm now within her.

After her sobs have dried up and he still hasn't returned, she moves through the room picking up the fragments of his phone, placing them all neatly on the dining table for when he returns. Perhaps he can fix it somehow. The shattered screen is flashing nervously, the back almost disintegrating in her hands.

She wants to phone him and beg him to come back. To not leave it like this, a whole world between them. She doesn't pick up her phone again. There is nothing to say to anyone. She walks through the empty apartment, shell-shocked. She doesn't know where he is, when he will come back, or whether he will. She doesn't know how long to wait or whether she is single or not.

She sits shivering on the sofa, looking at the door every time she hears a sound, hoping he will walk back in. She can explain things better. Tell him how Jacob is a forgotten relic from another lifetime, one that never needs digging up. She picks up her phone only to delete Jacob from her Facebook, unfriending him and severing the ties. She deletes his number from her phone, not that he would know. She finds the folder of images that save the happiest moments of her relationship with him and, without thinking, deletes them in one quick stroke. She removes all traces of him from her phone and, in doing so, her life. If someone didn't exist in your phone, they could barely be credited with being in your life at all.

Although her eyes droop and she begins to fall asleep, she cannot bear the thought of crawling into their bed alone.

She is scared he will come back and find her asleep in bed, as if she doesn't care.

So she stays, curled up on the sofa, leaning on her arm that begins to lose feeling, and guards the door. Even when her leg becomes numb and her neck begins to stiffen, she stays curled in the same position, paying a penance of sorts. Eventually, she loses all feeling in her right leg and still she stays, falling asleep like a half-strangled cat, awkward and uncomfortable, but determined and resolute.

She wakes up at 6 a.m., the TV still flickering the same news station, the cars still beeping, the man on the corner still selling his bread and life unceremoniously continuing. At some point in the night, she must have stretched out because she wakes flat on her back, her head leaning against the arm of the sofa, her legs full of feeling. She quickly stands up but already knows he hasn't come back. She would have heard it.

The thought of going to work, of acting normal when everything is terrible, is unbearable to her. She texts her colleague, Edlin, and asks her to cover. Calls the headmaster and pleads sickness. Tells him she's so ill she cannot move and, in a way, it isn't a lie.

All that day she is bruised, easing herself into chairs and wincing when she gets out of them. It's as if her whole body has been beaten and perhaps this is what they meant when they said words have power. Or that looks could kill. Some part of herself has died in the night. It's nothing that she can see, but she feels it. She puts her phone on airplane mode because she wants to be unreachable. She has nothing to say to herself, let alone anyone else. She feels less alive than she used to.

She tries to remember what she said and then what he said but it all muddles into one blur of improbable events. *Did that really happen?* is something she asks herself at least a hundred times. She can almost believe that it didn't until she sees the dent his phone made in the wall.

The only task she does that day is to go through her Facebook deleting all the boys she's ever flirted with, liked, joked with, or who could have liked her. There are plenty of men on her Facebook, friends and friends of friends and sometimes just the guys you meet at house parties and never see again, but somehow forge a conversation over messenger with because they always kindly respond to her posts with compliments or encouragements. She deletes all these men. She cannot have him see her Facebook and believe that what he said about her is true. She has to make him see that she loves one man. Slept with a few that meant so little they weren't worth counting. That what she and Jacob had wasn't wrong or sinful, but rather it was just love, and first love. That she is naive at this. But that she is willing and desperate to learn.

Late in the afternoon, she hears the key turn in the door, and his voice laughing in jest with the doorman who happens to be walking past. She wonders how he has any lightness when she has been anchored to the bottom of the ocean all day.

The first thing she notices is his limp, as he hobbles through the threshold, staring at her with his hands in his pockets. It registers how hard he must have kicked the table for him to be limping like that.

They stare at each other and she doesn't know what to say so settles for, "Hi."

She wonders if he hears because he doesn't say anything for a minute, and then he says, "Hey," before telling her he's going to take a shower.

She nods quickly.

"Can I get you anything? Some tea? Painkillers?"

He shakes his head and looks down at the ground. "No, thank you."

She watches him limp down the corridor and takes heart in the fact that he said, "thank you." That he didn't walk in and tell her to get out. That maybe it's not all over after all.

She bites her nails. Sits down and then stands up again. Opens the fridge and closes it again. Puts some dishes away. Does anything to keep her hands busy. Anything that will give her some kind of purpose.

As the light begins to fade, he walks back into the sitting room, droplets of water still dripping from his hair, his sweatpants and a tank top on, ready to settle down for the evening. He sits on the coffee table opposite her and takes her hands in his, and before he has opened his mouth, she is crying and it feels like the city is crumbling around her.

"No, no, no, ya Kookie, please don't cry. I'm sorry, really I am," he says.

She sobs harder in a way that makes her believe that now, in this very instance, her heart is breaking for the first time and everything leading up to this has merely been a dress rehearsal.

He pulls her forward to stand with him, and then they're back on the sofa but this time she is on his lap. It only makes her cry harder.

He kisses her forehead. Murmurs apologies. Says he didn't mean any of it. That he saw red when he thought of her messaging another man and how he might lose her. He speaks of how wonderful she is. That he is lucky and they are both blessed. That they have been brought together by God and how they can never forget that. He strokes her back. Thanks her for tidying the apartment. Asks if she went to work. Wipes away her tears. Kisses her fingertips. Offers her a tissue. Repeats, "Enough, enough." Kisses her mouth. Gets her a glass of water. Pulls her back into him. Cradles her on his lap as if she is a child. Asks how he could have been so mean to his baby. She just cries a little harder and he almost cries with her. "No, no, no, no, no. Habibti. Hayati. Elbi. Ya asal. My darling. My love. Baby. I only have one of you."

They are wrapped in salty tears and kisses. Gently touching one another. Rubbing away the pain that no one can see. Believing tomorrow will be better. Whispering love gently, ever so gently, into broken bodies. He carries her to bed despite his limp. Makes love to her more tenderly than he ever has before. Gives more than he takes. Promises everything. Insists she stay wrapped in the duvet while he fetches her tea. Orders dinner; her favorite. Murmurs more apologies. Encourages her tentative feelings and urges her on when she says, "I was so scared you weren't going to come back." In a voice as low and gentle as hers, as if coaxing a scared animal back to him, he swears his loyalty. Promises to never leave. That every couple fights, but they are destined, and there is nothing more powerful than that. He tells her how intelligent he thinks she is. How different. How special. Each word followed by a kiss, a soft erasing of every ache that had settled on her body earlier that day.

She has never known a softness like it. Didn't think you could ever make a man this tender. Feels pleased that she has ended up with someone capable of such exquisite love. Somewhere, in a place inaccessible and far away, she wonders if a man can only ever be this soft once he's broken a woman. She wishes she could talk to Kees and Jenna about it, sure that they would have the answers that are currently just out of her reach.

BILQUIS

"Are you out of your fucking mind?" Addy stares at her.

She continues her story.

She tells him how her mother looked at her like she couldn't believe Kees had ever come out of her. How her father had cried and what the tears of a man you thought incapable of crying looked like. How the world had suddenly emptied out. Sure, there were still people in it, but not around her. She asks him if she could be a family all on her own and laughs without waiting for an answer. Of course not.

She tells him about the wedding and although he asks for the bridal details and what the embroidery looked like, she tells him of the small way Uncle Mahmoud had smiled at her with a grin that was reserved for uncles who still saw you as the chubby-legged baby wobbling to him for sweets. How that smile had become archived history, and who would know that she liked sherbet limes now?

She stops once the whole story is laid out between them. They're sitting in the members' club Addy insists on eating lunch in, and that she hates.

"So just to summarize," he says, an extra flick of the wrist because he got more theatrical the more annoyed he got, "you basically got banished from your house and broke your parents' hearts for the man you love, and then you came home and instead of falling dramatically into his arms, you broke up with him?"

She rolls her eyes, exasperated. "I didn't break up with him. I just didn't feel like wearing the ring today."

"Because you're thinking about breaking up with him, Kees," he hisses back at her. "It's a dress rehearsal. Don't you know how tortured love is supposed to work? Have you watched any of the movies? How would Romeo and Juliet have ended if Juliet decided halfway through that, actually, she wasn't that in love and she could take it or leave it?"

"Alive," she snaps. "She'd be alive and wouldn't have forfeited her life unnecessarily."

"Oh, Oprah have mercy on my soul and grant me patience," he moans, signaling the waitress over. He orders another gin and tonic and raises his eyebrows toward her.

"Just a coffee, please."

The waitress gives a half-smile before slinking off. She knows Kees isn't the type to leave five-hundred-pound tips like the traders do.

"You know something, you don't even deserve that ring."

"Addy!" She frowns.

"I'm serious," he continues. "Most women would be beside themselves to have a rock like that on their finger and a man who looks like—"

"Don't," she growls.

He holds up his hands. "Fine, but you get the gist. And here you are smashing jars around your flat, being a complete bitch to a man who has done nothing wrong, and then leaving your engagement ring at home. Which is why, I presume, you left it there; so he would find it and know that it wasn't on your hand?"

She starts to say something but is immediately stopped by him shaking a finger at her.

"Darling, don't even try it." He sips his gin and tonic, which the waitress has delivered, lightly touching his shoulder. With legs crossed more elegantly than she has ever managed, he leans an elbow on the chair next to him, perfect in his every movement. "And if I'm correct, which naturally I am because I'm always right, you're going to make sure you get home after him so that he comes back to an empty flat and the engagement ring, which he probably spent months agonizing over, subjecting all his friends and family to endless pictures that clogged up their camera rolls with diamonds they were never going to own, to find you gone and the ring there and he'll think that it's all over or that you are on the brink of ending things. And you'll want him to think that, won't you? And if it plays out the way you want it to, he'll sit down on the edge of the bed and put his head in his hands and cry. Big, pathetic sobs, and he might even call you to see where you are, but you won't answer the phone. And then, then, his stomach will sink, and he'll feel sick and he'll pace the apartment, wondering what he did and where it all went wrong. You won't answer any of his calls and then finally come home, super late, and of course, he'll still be up, looking like a haunted man. And you'll walk in and, knowing you, be a complete bitch to him and say something condescending about how you were at work and because you're brown you have to work four times as hard. And depending on how cruel you feel, you'll let this continue for days on end."

She is still. "You paint a vivid picture."

He shrugs. "I'm a lawyer. It's my job to sway the room."

"Even if that was all true," she says, "why would I want to do that to him?"

He puts his drink down and leans forward, hands clasped on the table, ready to deliver his final argument.

"Because you've just lost everything. And your heart is breaking. Your mother may never speak to you ever again. Your dad might start telling people he only has one daughter instead of two. And even though it was your decision, and even though Harry never pressured you, you did it all for him. You might not like to admit this, but the truth is, you want him to feel some of the pain you're feeling. You want him to break just a little bit because it's not fair that you had to be the sacrifice."

He leans back, picking up his drink, and says casually, "At least, that's what I would do."

By the time she pushes the front door open at 8:30 p.m., she has thought about Addy's hypothesis approximately 476 times. Kees has been described as cold. Overbearing. Blunt. Direct. Candid. Abrasive. Sharp. Sarcastic. Bossy. Bossy is the one she gets the most because she isn't afraid to let people know what should be done. She has never been described as cruel, but if Addy is right, what she is doing is cruel.

She knows instantly he isn't home but still calls his name and checks every room anyway. When she sees the roses lying next to her engagement ring, she knows he has seen it and that Addy was right. She wanted him to hurt. But this isn't part of the plan. He should be here. In the emptiness of the flat the idea settles in her stomach that she might lose him, and maybe she hadn't lost everything before. First Malak. Then her parents. Her siblings. Now Harry. All scattered to the wind, leaving behind the idea that she, Bilquis Saeed, who spends her life fighting for the oppressed, who at dinner parties puffs out her chest with pride when someone says she is an activist, is cruel.

She calls his phone three times and doesn't get an answer.

Wraps herself up in jeans, boots, and his winter ski jacket and goes for a walk, engagement ring firmly back on her finger. The idea of sitting in the flat waiting for him to return is unbearable. She has never been patient. She clicks her phone on every few minutes, just in case. She notices the cold and the people sitting on the street, digs into her pocket to find some loose coins, which she presses into a young woman's hand. Her cry of "God bless" follows her down the street like a blessing because it's the exact moment she realizes where Harry is.

Excitedly, she calls a taxi, fumbling with her phone and snapping in irritation at the driver who calls her three times to tell her that he can't see her. When finally they pull up at the church in Harry's parents' neighborhood, she jumps out and slams the door before he can finish telling her to take care, running up the steps just as the evening service begins.

She sees Harry in the same pew his family always sits in, mother on one side and father on the other side, heads bent in prayer, Nathaniel occasionally sneaking his phone out of his pocket to scroll through sports scores.

She tiptoes up to the pew and they all shuffle along in shock to make room for her, nervously glancing at each other in a way that tells Kees Harry has said something. Another twist of fear and she bends her head to join in with the prayer, talking to God for the first time in weeks, pleading, hoping that she hasn't lost everything.

"I hope you can hear me, God. I know I'm not in your usual house, but I figure you visit here just as much as anywhere else."

She feels guilty every time Father Bastian mentions that Jesus is the son of God and sends up her own prayer.

Finally, it's over. In her opinion it has, as always, taken far too long—if the Catholics spent as much time praying as they did making a fuss about the prayers, they'd be better off. This is a view she has, so far, refrained from sharing with Harry's family, although they did debate it in the early days of their relationship, Harry maintaining that people sometimes needed ceremony to appreciate the importance of something. They spill out into the street and Vivian turns to Kees and kisses her on both cheeks.

"Lovely to see you, darling, and so glad you could make it. I assume you're staying the night with Harry at our house?"

Kees almost runs back into the church to deliver another prayer, this time of thanks for Vivian's tact. She can tell by the way she smiled at her and the quick flick of her eyes down to her left hand, so quick anybody else would have missed it, that Harry has said something to her and she wishes white people didn't tell their parents every little thing.

She quickly glances at Harry, who looks tired, and replies, "I thought I would, if that's okay."

"Well, of course it is; Harry said you might still make it and lucky for us you did." She links her arm into Kees's and starts the ten-minute walk home, the lie hanging in the air over them.

Once they get home Nathaniel puts the fire on at his wife's request and Vivian bustles about making hot chocolate for everyone, apparently determined not to leave Harry and Kees alone. He doesn't suggest bed, despite the late hour, and so she sits in the living room with the family, sipping the drink she has always hated, for once not minding it that much.

She watches Vivian ask mundane questions about sofa coverings as she flicks through a copy of *Country Life*, pointing out different patterns to Harry, who doesn't care. Vivian doesn't want her son's opinion either, but she is adamant she will stay. Nathaniel tells some story from work that he has already told before. Harry sits sipping from his mug, looking drained.

This is a family protecting their own.

All Kees can think is that she doesn't have a family anymore. She is jealous of her fiancé, whose family is gathering around him like lions preparing to defend. She feels helpless. She watches Vivian lean on the sofa arm, resting one hand on Harry's back and pointing to something in the magazine, and feels the emptiness around her. It is only when Nathaniel says, "Kees, are you okay?" that she realizes she has started crying.

Everyone quickly stands and the room lurches into motion. Nathaniel hands her a tissue box and awkwardly pats her shoulder. Harry is at her side murmuring something, his hurt replaced by worry. He has seen Kees cry only a handful of times and it still feels like something is breaking when he sees it. Vivian kneels beside her and pushes her hair back off her forehead in the way mothers do and she cries harder. No one knows what to do or how to act now that the usually composed woman they know is sobbing hysterically on a three-thousand-pound chair that Vivian had shipped over from Paris.

In a brief lull, she blows her nose loudly, giving up the notion that she has to impress, and turns to Harry.

"I told my parents about you after Saba's wedding. That we're engaged."

"Oh fantastic. Maybe we can invite them over for dinner?" Nathaniel says, grinning down on the three of them until Vivian shakes her head gently.

Kees stares at Harry, who is gripping her hand, and as she opens her mouth to speak, she knows that the next sentence will change things for him. That she is now placing an unbearable weight on his shoulders and asking him to carry it. That he will feel the responsibility of being everything to a woman who has nothing because of him, and now he has to bear it.

"Mum told me that if I marry you, I can never go home. That I won't be allowed back." She sniffs again, somewhere in the back of her mind remembering that Vivian can't abide sniffing; she says it's common and ill-mannered. She pulls another tissue out of Nathaniel's outstretched hand. "I'm not allowed to contact Saba and Hakim either."

Harry looks angrier than she has ever seen him. "And what did you say?" he asks.

"That I love you and I'm going to marry you." She lets out a strangled laugh. "If you'll still have me."

"Oh, Kees, don't be stupid, of course I will. Why didn't you tell me?"

She shakes her head and says nothing, the second wave of tears falling. She puts her face into her hands and sobs, and when finally she lifts her head again, it is not Harry's arms she falls into, but Vivian's. Not because Vivian understands, but because the only thing Kees wants is a mother's embrace.

Downstairs in the Victorian townhouse, Vivian dries the mugs Nathaniel hands her and hisses, "What kind of mother does that to her own child?"

Nathaniel, who usually calms his wife down, has nothing to say. He hates seeing anyone upset and the way his son's girlfriend's shoulders had shaken tonight makes him acutely uncomfortable. Upstairs in the loft bedroom, Harry's T-shirt soaks through to his chest as he holds a shuddering woman who has not stopped crying for forty-five minutes. He doesn't say anything. She has gone to a place he cannot reach. He occasionally kisses her head before drawing her in a little closer. He thinks about writing Kees's mother a letter.

A few streets away—twelve, to be exact—Father Bastian gets ready for bed, contemplating how lovely it is that the

DuVaughns' soon-to-be daughter-in-law comes to church, and what a marvelous display of interfaith relations that family is. He scribbles down a note on the pad of paper next to his Bible on the bedside table to visit the Chelsea Muslim Community Mosque and invite the imam out for dinner, perhaps to one of the Indian restaurants, he'd like that. Next to the river, Abdel-Hadey locks up the mosque for the night, finally managing to usher the last man out of the building, thanking him once again for the food while thinking how much he hates Indian food. He gives it to a homeless man on his long walk home, grateful to be rid of it. Miles away, across hundreds of fields, Hakim types on his phone in the dark, quickly and before he loses his nerve, to ask the most beautiful girl in school to go out on a date with him. Temi replies in the same minute that she thought he'd never ask, and he falls asleep with a smile on his face. Downstairs his mother pops open a can of paint, deep Dior blue, and begins to add the second layer onto the kitchen cabinets. She has spent the last two days sanding and varnishing the wood to smooth perfection and today there are specks of paint all over her body like a second skin. In the sitting room next door, Itasham stares out of the window that looks onto the front gate and wonders if he sees someone coming. Every time he blinks, the path is clear, and he makes a mental note to call the optician in the morning. He has been meaning to get new glasses for over a year now. Across the other side of their town, Jenna sits in Mo's car as he drops her off at home and she thinks of Lewis. She wonders why everything has to end. She presents a couple of feeble arguments to Mo, but she is tired and he is persistent, so ultimately she shrugs and agrees. In her house, her parents sway in one another's arms as Roberta Flack floats out of the speakers. They whisper all the things they will do now that Nidal has a week off and talk about days by the coast. Hundreds of miles away, driving home from Liverpool, Lewis sees a message flash across his screen that makes him stare too long until the loud beeping of a truck driver jolts him back to the road and he swears, swerving back into his lane. He wonders why women insist on making everything more complicated. Not too far away Jacob sits in his attic room staring at his phone before eventually sending a message that will move him forward and away from the woman he had loved. Thousands of miles away, across oceans and clouds, Ali falls asleep while thinking about the woman he loves and how he'll spoil her this weekend. In the next room, Malak sits on the floor pulling clothes out of the wardrobe, sorting them into three piles. Keep. Throw. Alter. The third pile is the highest and she bags it up, placing it by the door ready to be taken to the tailor's where he will sew up splits and make plunging necklines disappear. The imam of Al-Azhar mosque slowly uncurls himself from sleep and heads to the washroom, easing himself down onto a marble stool; washing away the sweat of sleep from his brow, sighing with relief as he places his feet under the cold tap, watching the dust of Africa flow into the drain. He leaves wet footprints behind him, the one-eyed Bengal cat padding in them, eventually sitting down next to him, tail curled protectively around his feet, as he stands in position at the mihrab and flicks the microphone switch. He opens his throat and begins the call to morning prayer. A millisecond later the rest of Cairo's mosques ring out their own athen, each one adding to the city's symphony; "God is great! God is great! God is great! God is great!"

JENNA

Jenna spends a lot of time in the gym these days. There is always a new class to try, promising to change lives. First, it was spin classes, the idea that all you needed was a bike that didn't go anywhere to look like the people you scrolled past on your phone. Then it was yoga and Pilates, sold with the notion that your contentment was a few "Oms" away. Next came Zumba and dance, a chance to shake your way into a new life. Now everyone was obsessed with boot camps; grueling high-intensity sessions that tested your physical limits, as well as your patience, as some jacked-up Spartan look-alike screamed at you that pain lasted seconds, but regret lasted a lifetime.

She knows she's been spending too much time in the gym because her trousers have started to hang off her hips and the space between her breasts has gotten wider. She is slowly shrinking.

When she isn't in the gym she runs. Sometimes 10k in an evening, even though she isn't training for anything. She runs by the canals of the city, looping her way around the university and out onto the fields that wind into the countryside. She runs as far as she can but always comes back. She doesn't particularly enjoy running or working out. When she overhears people say things like, "It feels amazing when I'm running," or, "I love going to the gym, it's my favorite part of the day," she knows they're lying. The gym is no one's favorite part of the day and you have to be stupid to genuinely believe that. People are much more interested in the idea than the reality. They want to be able to flick their hair in conversation and in a cavalier manner say, "I went for a run this morning."

She has never claimed to love exercising. She does it because she loves the results, but mostly because in the gritted teeth of the last ten squats, the shaking arms of the final push-up, or the gasping for breath during the last mile, there is no room to think about anything else. It takes all her concentration just to finish the damn workout, and for once, her brain becomes a quiet place. No worries exist. Memories fade. The constant replay from that night, his smell, is magically absent. Her brain stops flickering like a light that doesn't work.

When she's not exercising or trying to become a doctor, the pull of how things used to be is too strong to resist and then she floats in a desperate nostalgia, longing for the impossible. All she wants is to go back.

Back to when Kees and Malak were firmly in her world, not just in pixelated form through her screen. She watches their lives with envy, not for what they have, but the way they smile. She misses Lewis, but the version of him before he had a girlfriend. She misses being sixteen. She misses flirting with strangers and giggling for no reason. Now there are no reasons to laugh. She is acutely aware that she misses performing but never allows herself to think about it; there is no point walking down a road with a dead end.

The engagement happens differently from every other proposal she has ever watched in her favorite movies. Mo doesn't get down on one knee. They haven't flown off on a romantic weekend away. They're not lying in bed. It isn't raining.

They just talk about it over textbooks and while shopping in the supermarket. When should his dad call her dad? Can his mother call hers? Maybe they should all meet? Perhaps next week.

It is logistical and practical. Ticked boxes and organized schedules.

She doesn't know when she decided to marry him, or if he asked per se, but she knows where this road ends. That if you're dating a Muslim man, things move quickly and parents are involved. That is how it always is. There is no such thing as a long engagement. So it comes as no surprise when her parents tell her that they've spoken to his parents and does she want to go ahead?

Of course, she had agreed because what else was the point of everything they were doing and her parents seemed exceptionally pleased with his family, so half the work was already done. Once the families like each other the momentum takes on a life of its own.

They came round for tea one Saturday afternoon and her mother made an assortment of sweets and snacks they all spent the next week eating because there were so many of them. Diamonds shone from Mo's mother's wrist and fingers, the biggest nestled on her wedding finger, proudly drawing the eye. She was a woman who was aware of how to dress and how to carry herself. His father had a face that always seemed ready to break into laughter and who knows what kind of man he would have been without his wife? Her touch was on all her sons, especially Mo, and as the Khalayleh family sat in their huge drawing room, Mo's mother flanked by her husband on one side and three sons on the other, each one manicured, well groomed, and excellently dressed, you could almost taste the pride emanating from around the woman at the heart of these men.

Jenna stayed silent for most of it but looked beautiful, and that was enough for everyone. She smiled and made a joke when Mo handed her a bouquet of long-stemmed roses so heavy she had to accept it with both hands and the Khalayleh family later spoke about how appropriate she was as they drove home that night.

Jenna was happy to watch her life spread out. These meetings are not for the lovers, they're for the families. While watching her father and her soon-to-be father-in-law laugh together, she had the thought that maybe Romeo and Juliet's family should have done this from the start and things would have ended very differently.

The weeks roll by and she watches things happen but does very little. Watches the mothers talk about flower arrangements and dresses. Watches the fathers talk about venue hire and catering. Watches Mo shake hands with friends at their engagement party. Kees can't get out of court in time and Malak is across an ocean and they're the only two people she cares about him meeting. He is attentive and occasionally rests a hand on her shoulder, looks deep into her eyes, and asks if she's okay. She always pauses for a minute, walks a knife edge before squeezing his hand and telling him she's just so happy. She wants to give more but doesn't know how to.

In the final thrust of their medical exams, it is agreed that the bride and groom are too busy and shouldn't be bothered with questions about color palettes and favors. They are surrounded by family and family are here to help.

One of the few things she does is finally upload a picture of her manicured hand with the gleaming engagement ring on it, with the caption: "The one where we got engaged." It's easier to borrow a line from a sitcom than to write her own. She puts her phone down and goes out for a run and by the time she gets back her battery is almost dead, worn away by a string of notifications from people she hasn't spoken to in years, friends who haven't messaged, and the capital-lettered congratulations of people over the Internet.

The only messages she opens are from Kees and Malak, who both separately message her.

Kees comments on the ring and sends a picture of her own, having forgotten to send it after Saba's wedding. They discuss diamond color and cuts but the conversation is brief. Kees is in the middle of defending a young man who didn't do anything; his need is greater.

Malak replies with a strangled-voice note that brings Jenna to tears, congratulating her and gushing over how happy she is.

It slices an opening between them and the conversation lasts all night and, at some point, they both cry. Talk about how much they miss each other. How long it has been.

They talk all that week, not bothering to say goodnight or good morning; the conversation is continuous. By the weekend she feels better than she has in a long time, skips the gym on Saturday, and by Monday morning, she has decided to visit Malak in Cairo as a treat for finishing her exams.

The final exams are easier to get through now that Malak is waiting on the other side of them.

"I think it's a great idea," says Mo, when she tells him.

"You do?" she replies, confused by his enthusiasm. She laughs then. "Are you trying to get rid of me?"

They're in the car park of the library after a late-night McDonald's drive-through run, all in the name of study breaks.

He reaches across the seat and strokes her cheek, and she closes her eyes and leans in. They rarely touch. He is always appropriate and proper, and she prefers it this way, but her body hasn't been touched in many months and it has turned into a physical ache across her skin.

"You've been super stressed and not yourself lately. And you work so hard, Jenna. Which is admirable, but you don't know how to stop and take a break. In fact, I'm putting my foot down; you're going on holiday, whether you like it or not."

He laughs as he says it and she leans further into his hand.

He smiles so softly at her and his eyes are so full of safety that her fingers twitch, and as she is about to reach up and pull his mouth to hers, he takes his hand from her face, squeezes her own, and says, "We'd better get back to the books," and so everything stays the same.

Her parents are full of enthusiasm about her trip and they too tell her she's been working so hard and she should have some fun before the wedding and married life starts.

Her dad booms, "Exactly, exactly," and she looks up at her mother, exchanging a silent look with her. She wonders what happens on the other side of married life that she needs to rest before it begins, but her usual flippancy is subdued lately.

Her father kisses her on the forehead and tells her he'll book her ticket himself, while Mo is adamant that he will be the one to drop her off at the airport.

Her mother stares at her across the dinner table the next night, a look Jenna doesn't recognize on her face, but when Jenna asks her what's wrong, her mother replies, slowly, "Nothing."

She walks out of the arrivals hall followed by a man pushing her cart who has assured her he wants to help, nervously looking around for Malak. Suddenly, she is painfully aware that she hasn't seen Malak in over a year. That although they have spoken sporadically, they haven't really talked. She fixes her headscarf. Pulls her jacket straight. Looks left and right.

The minute she sees Malak barrelling toward her she has a second to laugh before she is engulfed in the familiar smell of her friend and the worry that it would be awkward disappears. When they pull apart, tears in their eyes are threatening to spill over, and it makes them laugh again.

"Oh my God, you look incredible, Malak," Jenna exclaims, holding her at arm's length and finding no sign of the woman who had left England. By Jenna's estimation, Malak must have lost fifteen pounds since she saw her last. Her normally frizzy black hair is curled elegantly down her back in gentle waves, her skin is toned to a baked golden hue that any bottle of suntan lotion would be jealous of, her nails are long and manicured where previously they have never been, and a gold-chain hand-bag hangs delicately over one shoulder.

"Are you even wearing makeup?" she squeals. "Since when did you start wearing makeup and carrying handbags?"

Malak laughs at her shock.

"You don't think I look good? I thought you'd approve."

"I absolutely do; you look amazing," Jenna replies. "Although I am a bit jealous that, despite all my efforts at makeup and getting you out of those grungy hoodies you always wore, someone else has finally had some influence over you and made you into this coiffured fashionista."

"Let's not get carried away," Malak laughs, before grabbing her once more into another embrace. "I'm so glad you're here, Jenna."

"Me too!"

"Come on, Ali is waiting in the car outside, I can't wait for you to meet him."

Jenna initially thinks Ali is arrogant, but over her week with Malak, she sees the way he looks at her—like he's suddenly found all the good things in this life—and that's when she decides to like him. After all, Arab men had a weakness for arrogance and you just had to work a little harder to love them.

Jenna loves Cairo. The constant noise of seventeen million people trying to move around one another is oddly soothing.

As she sits with Malak in the gardens of the Sofitel hotel, perfectly positioned on the curve of the Nile to give its patrons a breathtaking view of the city, they watch two men whose boats almost collide shout at each other in a way that convinces Jenna that they're about to jump into the river, swim to one another, and begin physically fighting. It doesn't happen and eventually, once the waiter has run down to the railing and shouted at them for disturbing his guests, they continue sailing past.

She turns to Malak in glee and asks, "What were they saying?"

"I don't understand all of it, my Arabic isn't that good, but basically something about his mother being a donkey and how there is space across the whole Nile and why does he have to sail so close."

Jenna throws her head back and laughs.

"If two people are shouting at each other in Cairo, it's safe to assume that someone's mother has been mentioned," continues Malak.

Jenna laughs. "Such drama. I love it."

"I thought you might," Malak says, grinning. "This city is very you."

Jenna nods and murmurs her agreement. "Maybe I should leave off everything back home and run away to come and live with you here."

Malak laughs and agrees. "Ready and waiting, babes."

Jenna pulls her sunglasses off and looks at Malak. She still can't comprehend how much she has changed. "Well, this city looks good on you. You're practically glowing."

Malak laughs and squeezes her hand in thanks.

"I'm serious. You look phenomenal. But tell me everything now that the boy, who, by the way, is great, isn't here. It's time for some real talk. Give me all the relationship details. What's he like in bed? Are you happy with him? Do you think he'll propose? Will you live here forever? Do you ever hear from Jacob, by the way?"

Malak leans forward and puts her hands on Jenna's arms. "Slow down, that's so many questions. I was about to ask you the same thing. You're bloody engaged, Jenna. Engaged! And I know nothing about this man. I need to know what he's like. Has there been any haram behavior or have you kept it halal? Are you excited about the wedding? What's your dress going to be like? You're going to be the most beautiful bride the world has ever seen, but we always knew this."

They both laugh, hands still placed on arms and each other, finally on the same side of the ocean and with a mountain of questions to each get through beneath a hot Cairo sky.

"Hang on, let me just order us some dessert," says Malak, waving a waiter over. Jenna notices how she does it casually as if used to being obeyed, delivering their order in Arabic to a smiling waiter who asks where they're from originally. He can hear in Malak's accent that she didn't grow up here and she laughs and tells him they are both from England. He finishes writing their order down and then, with a hand over his heart, says, "*Nawarto Masr.* You have lit up Egypt with your presence."

Malak smiles back at him graciously and Jenna notices how much she has changed in small ways. How she seems more confident. More sure of herself.

"Now," says Malak, turning to Jenna, "let's dive in. Where shall we start?"

And this is where they begin to lie to each other.

Never big lies but a stream of steady white lies and hidden truths that, when pulled together, tell a completely different story.

Malak tells her all about Ali and how they met. The story is as great as any rom-com and Jenna listens with her chin in her hands, sighing in all the right places. Malak tells her that although she doesn't love her job, she loves life here. That she spends her mornings teaching, her afternoons in the pool or sunbathing. She details her favorite restaurants and how she's taking Jenna to some of the best ones this week. She doesn't tell Jenna that her job makes her feel useless. That the thing about teaching is you're not influencing anyone and if you're lucky, a handful of kids might remember your name when they're older. She doesn't bother talking about the traffic and how it's impossible to get more than one thing done a day in this city and sometimes that drives her to the point of insanity until she wants to scream from the top of her building. She doesn't tell her how her family, the ones she was longing to connect with, are mostly busy with work and life and because of the traffic, you can never really pop over quickly. Or how some nights she's so tired that she doesn't bother with the best restaurants and the great dessert spots, just orders a KFC on the sofa instead. She doesn't tell Jenna that Ali slept in the spare room for a whole week after he had sworn that Malak had said Jacob's name in her sleep, even though she was positive she didn't. She leaves out the part where being with him sometimes makes her feel like she has withered and died, but then on his good days, no one has made her feel more alive. Or how the weather here is so hot, and because you always have to be in clothes that cover your body, she feels like she's walking through hell sometimes. Instead, she tells Jenna that everywhere has air conditioning. That although the city exists in chaos most of the time, the living is good. She talks about praying with Ali, sharing a mat and a faith, and how having someone to practice with makes her feel closer to God. That her mother was right and building a life with someone on shared principles really is so important. That his faith brings her closer to hers, that they are always closer to God when they are together.

Jenna nods throughout. She understands. That this is what she has been saying all along. Sure, Jacob is lovely, but faith matters.

Malak emphatically agrees but leans over and says, "Obviously, I don't need to tell you this, but don't mention Jacob around Ali."

The very thought that Jenna might makes Malak almost bring up her breakfast. "I mean, he knows about him, of course, but you know what Arab men are like," she says, rolling her eyes as if the idea that you couldn't mention your past around your current boyfriend is more a gentle nuisance as opposed to something that could make you lose everything.

It is the one moment in the conversation when a pressure valve is released somewhere. You can almost hear the pop and the gentle hiss as Jenna lets out a breath. "Oh my God, I know. Mo is exactly the same."

Thankful that she isn't the only one and emboldened by this knowledge, Malak stresses, "Right! They're so ridiculous about it."

"I had to stop hanging out with Lewis because Mo found out we used to kiss when we were kids," says Jenna, no longer nervous about sharing this information.

"Oh, I bet," replies Malak. "If Ali ever found out I was talking to an ex or someone I had been with, he'd go mental." She shudders at a memory.

"Yeah, he wasn't happy. I could tell it was going to be an issue so I just made a decision. I think with some things you just have to compromise." Jenna shrugs.

"Absolutely," replies Malak firmly.

"And you know what," Jenna continues, "I get it."

"Me too." Malak nods.

"If he was hanging out with someone he had slept with or been with, I probably would be funny about it too."

"Totally," agrees Malak.

Neither of them point out that they are not jealous women. That it is not in their nature. Instead, they nod and agree, and egg one another on.

They laugh and stumble over each other in their haste to agree and share and convince themselves that being with jealous men makes them feel wanted instead of trapped.

Jenna says how she's now finished university, finally stepping over into work like Kees and Malak. How she will start her new training after the wedding, her father making the initial introduction. How happy she is to graduate and how proud she is of her work. She talks about her wedding dress—white silk with lace sleeves and a row of hand-sewn buttons down the back. She tells her about house hunting and how difficult it is. They're going to live with Jenna's parents for a bit, her mother is renovating the attic so they can have their own space because it's close to the hospital and her dad says buying a house right now is not a good idea. Bad time for the market. She talks about her plans and all the things that are about to happen.

She doesn't tell Malak that staying behind while her friends started new lives was the biggest heartbreak she's experienced so far. How she drank too much for months after everyone left and that it was her fault she wouldn't be a virgin on her wedding night. She doesn't talk about that night or how she's never touched another man since. How she hasn't let anyone touch her either. She wants to tell Malak that sometimes she feels sad that the last man to touch her didn't stop when she told him to and how the weight of him grunting on top of her made her feel ashamed. How she hasn't drunk since that night. She doesn't tell her that the past year has been the worst of her life. That she has been living a half-life and for a woman who squeezed life out of every corner, it feels like she may as well have died. That a half-life is not worth living at all because all she ever wants is to feel things, never in-between, and to throw her heart over every fence with abandon. But since that night when all the people left her, when she even left herself, she has been nothing but in-between, a long year of moderate middle ground that makes her cry most nights. She speaks only of future things. The wedding. The new job. How she'll decorate their home.

There is a pause in the conversation once Jenna has finished and Malak has the wild urge to reach over and place her hand on Jenna's cheek. Ask her why she's lost so much weight and where the light in her eyes has gone. Malak wants to confess that the man she loves is cruel and she doesn't know what to do about it.

In that same moment, Jenna sees Malak lurch forward but then grab her hands to sit on them. She looks nervous and un-certain and Jenna wants to reach out, thread her fingers through Malak's, and ask her what's wrong. Ask her why the haunted look on her face doesn't match the life she lives.

But the waiter arrives with their food and they smile up at him and the sky is so blue and the sun so hot on their heads and the music is drifting down from the hotel and the day is too bright and too perfect for such hard realities. It is too early in the day to be that heavy. So, they say nothing, and for now, they tell each other little lies to keep living a version of their truth.

BILQUIS

Kees's first big case is causing more late nights in the office than she thought was possible. There is a constant fear that she is going to fuck it up, and four young men with no previous criminal history are going to end up behind bars because she isn't smart enough to get them off.

When she'd discussed her worries with Addy, he had insisted it wasn't about being smart. "Dumb lawyers win cases all the time. It's about playing the system."

"But I don't want to play the system," she had groaned. "I want justice to prevail."

He had laughed for a long time then. "Get a grip, Kees. There is no justice in law, just smart lawyers who know how to play the judges and the jury."

She hasn't spoken to her family in over a month, but it hasn't stopped her from sending messages regularly anyway. She's texted Hakim to see how he was getting on with his GCSEs and if he needed any help with anything. She's messaged Saba and asked how married life was treating her. She's sent articles to her father that she thought he'd like, mainly about the Labor Party. She's asked her mother for recipes and has sent images of the dishes she's made. Every message always ended with a string of apologies. How she missed them. How she wished they could talk.

For every one of her messages, a wall of silence has greeted her back. Not even Hakim has anything to say. She suspects her mother has instructed everyone that silence is the new party policy. Harry asks her every night and she says, "Still nothing," and shakes her head sadly but still keeps her phone close all evening, just in case.

The months pass like this, her head buried in case files searching for answers or scrolling through Facebook, hoping to catch sight of her family. There is a new heaviness to the days, although time is moving quickly. She spends too much time in the office and Harry says nothing. *Smart man*, she thinks. He won't ask her to give anything else up; the weight of her lost family already rests heavily between his shoulder blades.

He never asks Kees to massage his neck the way he used to when he was stressed. She cannot know how hard his muscles are and the pain they give him.

He had written Kees's mum a letter but then didn't have her address. He had never needed to know where her family home was before, so he tore it up in the shredder at work. There is nothing he can do, so he just goes to the masseuse at lunch and says nothing about how long his fiancée spends at work.

Kees notices his silence and is glad. Every part of her energy is spent on trying to win her first case because she needs to feel like she's won something instead of lost everything. It also saves her from thinking about her family too much and so the shattering devastation is kept at bay a little longer, pacing on the sidelines, snapping at her heels.

It is the beginning of February when Harry tells her one night during dinner, the only time in ten days they've eaten a meal together, that the sale on the flat is complete and they can move in if she still wants to.

He says it quietly, afraid that he'll make her cry.

"Mum and Dad said they can rent it out for a while if we don't want to move in just yet," he says, squeezing her hand across the dhal that Kees has made over the weekend.

"Thanks, baby," she smiles at him, "but I'm already condemned by my family so we may as well get out of this cramped space."

He nods. "Whatever you want, love."

"But, Harry..."

"Yes?"

"I don't want to move in without being married," she replies, desperately. "I just can't do it."

He nods and murmurs that he understands, although, really, he doesn't. *God bless him for trying*, she thinks.

She doesn't tell him that if they live together, a new place with brand-new walls, without being married, then her mother will never visit it, but at least with vows behind them, it makes everything slightly less awful. But only slightly.

"You want to push the wedding forward?" he asks. Ever since he proposed, they have discussed a wedding in the summer.

"No, your mother is so excited about the wedding," she says.

"To hell with what my mother wants, this is our wedding, Kees," he says, exasperated.

"Don't be so white about it, Harry, have some respect for your mother. She's allowed to be excited about her son's wedding."

"She has had three other sons get married," points out Harry. "I think she's had her excitement."

"Don't be stupid," Kees says, shaking her head. "We're down on family members; let's not alienate any more of them."

Harry wants to tell her that he can't think of anything that would estrange his parents from him but wisely doesn't voice that thought. He understands that Kees is drawing as much family around her as she can.

"So, then, we just wait until the summer to move in; we can live here a little longer," he says and shrugs.

"There's no point in paying rent here and on your place, and all your stuff won't fit in here," she argues. "I don't want to do the whole big wedding that your mother has planned, but I'd like to do a nikah and be married Islamically before we move in. Then we can do the big one in the summer, although it won't be that big anymore, really, because none of my family will be there."

She struggles to keep the bitterness out of her voice.

Harry stands up and puts his arms around her. "Then that's what we'll do," he agrees.

"But super small, Harry. Maybe we could just do it in your parents' house? I'll invite my mum and dad, Hakim and Saba, although I know they won't come."

"Well, still, invite them anyway, baby. You never know."

Once they've decided to do the nikah, they go to Harry's parents the following weekend where Kees tries to delicately explain what a nikah is.

"So, you'll be married?" asks Vivian, chopping vegetables for the family dinner.

"No, Mum," says Harry, "at least not by British law."

"Think of it as an engagement," Kees says, enthusiastically.

Harry's eldest brother, Samuel, is leaning against the sink, his wife, Lottie, helping Vivian with the vegetables, and as he leans over to steal another slice of pepper from the chopping board, says, "But aren't you already engaged?"

"Yes," Harry and Kees reply together.

"So why do you have to do a whole ceremony to become engaged when you're already engaged?" he asks.

Harry sighs and Kees reaches out to stroke his leg. "What I'm trying to say is, we would be married by Islamic law only, which is not legally binding in this country, so technically, by British law we're not married."

"But by Islamic law, you will be, which, I assume, will make you more comfortable about living together?" asks Lottie, and Kees has the wild urge to hug her.

"Yes, exactly," she says, beaming and shooting Lottie a thankful look. Lottie winks back and keeps cutting peppers.

"But there's only one law or legal system. I don't understand," continues Samuel, who looks toward his father, who, until now, has been quietly marinating meat. "Dad, do you get it?"

Nathaniel looks up at his eldest son. "Samuel, this is what they want to do, there's nothing to get. What's the problem?"

"No, oh my God, no, absolutely no problem!" Samuel insists. "Kees, I hope you don't think I have a problem," he says, turning to her, hand on his chest in a gesture of shock. "I was just interested because it's so different from how we do things."

Kees feels, rather than sees, Lottie tense.

"But it is fascinating," he continues. "I'd love to learn more. There's a chap at work from India and I love chatting to him about his culture, you know. I hope you didn't think I was being rude. I just didn't understand."

Before Kees has a chance to say anything, Lottie interrupts.

"Exactly, darling, you don't, so perhaps let's leave them to it." She hands over the last tray of chopped vegetables to Vivian and unties the apron around her waist. "Shall we go and find our children and see what they're doing?"

"Yeah, I said I'd bring Livy some milk before she starts screaming the place down." He laughs and backs out of the room and while they walk into the living room, Lottie whispers, "Why do you always mention Indian people from work, for God's sake, Samuel? You don't even work with that many."

"What?" he hisses back. "I'm just trying to show her that we're cultured."

"Except you're not," snaps Lottie. "Kees is from Pakistan and you constantly mentioning India is probably insulting to her."

"Oh yeah, I always forget."

As they leave the room, Vivian shakes her head. "I don't know what's wrong with that boy, honestly," she says, smiling brightly.

"Sorry," says Harry.

"Don't be silly," Kees laughs brightly. "It is really confusing, sometimes it even gets me."

Without looking up Nathaniel says, "Don't make excuses for him, Kees, that boy is just an idiot, he's always been that way."

"Nathaniel!" exclaims Vivian, but Harry and Kees both laugh as he looks up and winks at them.

Kees gets up to start washing the dishes piled in the sink. "It's just something that would make me feel comfortable, that's all. You don't need to tell anyone we're married because then people might feel like they haven't been invited, which is not it. It only needs to be me, Harry, and you and Nathaniel if you wouldn't mind being the witnesses?"

"Of course not," says Vivian. "And if it makes you comfortable, then that's what we'll do."

For the next few weeks, Vivian is remarkably helpful about planning the nikah and sometimes Kees thinks it's because she's so relieved that Harry isn't converting to Islam. Other times she believes that she's doing it for Kees because she likes her.

Somewhere along the way Vivian calls her and explains that she's invited Harry's brothers, it wouldn't have been right not to, as well as Harry's grandmother, because she gets lonely and it's an opportunity for her to see the family. With three brothers, three wives, six children between them, the grandmother, Father Bastian, because he was so interested in the idea of an Islamic ceremony when Vivian had told him that he had asked to attend, and, of course, she couldn't say no to Father Bastian, Vivian's best friend Florietta and her husband, James, because they were, after all, Harry's godparents, it has turned into a bigger occasion than the hurried signing and family dinner Kees had imagined.

Vivian asks for her family's address as she'd like to send an invitation personally and Kees gives it to her, wondering if Vivian's lost all grip on reality. On her future mother-in-law's insistence, she invites Addy and Jenna, begrudgingly admitting that it might be nice to have someone in her corner. She tries not to think about Malak.

Harry and Kees argue about whether to invite Jacob and although she doesn't want to—it feels disloyal to a woman she no longer talks to—Harry reminds her that if it wasn't for Jacob they wouldn't even be engaged in the first place.

"Can't we just invite him to the actual wedding?" she complains.

"No, Kees. He deserves to be there. Plus, I'd like to have a friend there too," says Harry.

She snorts sardonically. "You have three brothers and your whole family, soon to be the whole neighborhood, if someone doesn't stop your mother. I think you'll be fine without having a mate hanging around."

He shakes his head. "I'm inviting him."

It is only a formality. A nikah is not a wedding. Rather, a ticking of boxes. Kees has never dreamed of weddings anyway. She is not losing out on anything; you cannot long for something you never wanted. This is a small affair. A tiny gathering. A practicality, just in case her mother ever decides to visit her home in the future. Her mother wouldn't step over the threshold if they weren't married and although there is nothing but silence from the woman who gave her life, Kees likes to be prepared. The day will go by quickly. It will be over before it's begun. It's not worth telling anyone about. It's just one of those things.

These are the things she tells herself as she sits alone by the east-facing window as the morning sun throws light across the room, reflecting off the sequins on her sari that is hanging on the back of the door, making the white material luminous in the light. The day is cold but clear and the family home is humming with warmth and the fragrance of the flowers Vivian has placed in vases throughout every room. She had insisted they stay the entire weekend, including the night before the nikah, declaring that Harry and Kees couldn't sleep in the same room as it wasn't good luck to see the bride before the wedding.

Kees had flushed with embarrassment and insisted that it wasn't really a wedding, but her arguments had been brushed aside. She could see how hard Vivian was trying to make this a nice experience for her; ordering too much food, cooking her best dishes, stringing floral decorations through the beams in the large living room where they'd decided to have the signing, ordering an excessive amount of champagne, including non-alcoholic champagne for her. She smiled through every question and hugged Vivian for an extra minute before going to bed, a way to say thank you, and from Vivian's satisfied glow, she had gotten the message. What she hadn't said was how all of Vivian's plans had made a sadness so sharp bloom in her chest that she didn't always speak for fear of what might come out. Sometimes she had the wild urge to wipe all the flower catalogs and recipe books off the table as Vivian was discussing a dish or showing her a bouquet and to shout at her for not knowing that this is not how they did things. That alcohol would never be at a nikah, not ever. That having it here felt like she was betraying everything she had ever believed in. That having alcohol at a nikah made her feel more like a shit Muslim than sleeping with the man she loved out of wedlock had ever made her feel. She wanted to say that the flowers were never put in vases but strung around the groom's neck and she was doing it wrong. That a salmon fillet for the main course was the same as serving a block of ice for dinner and her family knew how to give food flavor; their spices extending past salt and pepper. She wanted to tell Vivian that all her plans were wrong and the enthusiasm she was showing this nikah was making Kees want to fold into herself with embarrassment. That the real kindness here would have been to let her do this in relative quiet, Vivian and Nathaniel the only witnesses to her shame.

It had taken three weeks and all of Kees's research skills to find an imam who would agree to marry them. The only answer she would get before phone lines went dead was "mamnue," forbidden. If she managed to talk to an imam for longer than the two minutes it took for her to explain the situation, it was only so they could lecture her about fatwas and the sin of interfaith marriage. One of the imams had told her to ask both God and her father for forgiveness, and then submit to her father's punishment. She had hung the phone up on him on that occasion. Another one had asked her why, out of all the millions of Muslim men, she had picked a non-Muslim, especially when there were so many great men in the community. He had followed it up by saying if this man didn't treat her right, it would be because he wasn't Muslim, which had sparked her shouting a string of insults and swearing down the phone line. The insinuation that a family and a man who had shown her

nothing but care and love would be cruel and unkind just because they weren't Muslim was too much even for her tightly
reined patience. Harry had eventually wrestled the phone out
of her hand and hung it up, but she had continued to swear for
the rest of the evening.

"Why do they have to make everything so fucking difficult?
It doesn't have to be this hard," she had shouted.

Harry had been sitting on the sofa leaning over his laptop, a
spreadsheet of imams open in front of him, and in a dry tone
had said, "In fairness, the Catholics don't make it easy either."

Harry had had more luck, managing to speak to imams for
longer, but, eventually, they all asked if he was going to convert
and once he made it clear that he wasn't, they would quickly
bid goodbye and hang up. Eventually, after wondering if this was
God's way of telling her that she shouldn't be doing this, they
had found someone. Imam Abdel-Rakim, a man who had said
he couldn't make a decision without praying on it, eventually
calling them back to tell them his fee and that he could marry
them as it was better for them to be bound by marriage than
to live in sin. She didn't like him, and if she had a choice, she
wouldn't have picked him to marry her. She had dreamt that it
would be her dad reading the Quran in his soothing voice and
saying prayers, but since choice was out of the question, they
had reluctantly booked Abdel-Rakim.

Now that the morning was here she couldn't seem to make
her body move. She just stared out of the window, watching the
sunrise, tracing back to the moment she first met Harry in a bid
to understand how it had come to this.

She hears the house wake up around her but nobody disturbs
her and she is glad of it. The sun is still rising and she wants
to watch it. Eventually, Vivian knocks gently, pushing the door

open with a smile. "Your friend Jenna is here, and I've brought you some breakfast." She places a perfect tray on the sideboard, stacked with pancakes and orange juice, coffee the way she likes it, and a bowl of fruit. There is a single white rose on the tray and Vivian nods to it, "From Harry. Try to eat something, darling." She smiles with excitement, a woman who has been swept up in her plans for this day, excusing herself so she can go and get ready, although she already looks perfect. Vivian is always flawless.

She closes the door behind her, leaving Jenna standing in the middle of the room, a steel box with a handle under her arm, handbag in the other hand, and the two women staring at each other nervously.

"I never thought I'd live to see the day that Bilquis Saeed asks me for help with her makeup. Have I died and gone to heaven?"

The morning after she had told her family, she had sent Jenna a one-line message that her parents now knew about Harry, and since then she had adamantly ignored Jenna's requests to meet up. She couldn't bring herself to go into the details or see the look of sympathy that she knew would be on Jenna's face. Eventually, Jenna had stopped calling and checking in on her and she hadn't been entirely sure Jenna would accept the invitation.

The sight of Jenna is such a welcome one that Kees cannot breathe for a moment, floored by the overwhelming tide of belonging and security that hits her. That she is managing to drag something, some vestige of who she used to be, from the rubble of her old life and take it with her into this new reality, one in which she is orphaned and lonely, gives her the first glimmer of hope she has had since the night she stood in silence with her family, her revelation ricocheting off the walls.

They stand, holding each other in greeting. It is the longest embrace they have ever had.

"Thank you so much for coming, Jenna."

"Don't be ridiculous. I wouldn't miss it for the world. If not for the nikah, just to be able to get my hands on this face of yours. Do you know how long I've waited for this?"

Kees's face has gotten rounder than it used to be. Her hips have widened, and her trousers no longer fit. She's bought new ones instead of eating less. Her mother would finally be pleased she's put on weight after complaining for so many years that she's too skinny, but her mother is not here to see the sadness that is gathering around her body, as if trying to add layers of protection.

Jenna pulls out bottles of liquid and powder and Kees watches, for the first time letting her do what she likes to her face.

"It's not supposed to be like this," she says finally, looking up at Jenna, who is concentrating on her eyebrows.

Jenna stops, pulling back from her face, and nods. She doesn't laugh the way she normally would have, making a joke that Kees would find vulgar. They are far away from jokes now.

"No, it's not," she replies.

They say nothing more, Kees just lifting her face back up to Jenna, who continues powdering and painting. There is no music playing. No rounds of aunties sitting in the makeup chair. There is no one else to make up. There is just her.

Jenna sprays her face with something Kees has never heard of and for the first time she wonders if this really is necessary, but before she can say anything Jenna stands back, satisfied. "God, I'm good."

Kees rolls her eyes. "It's makeup, Jenna, not the Sistine Chapel."

When she turns around, however, she sees that Jenna has done an artist's work; giving her face sculpture when previously there was none, erasing her tired bags that are full of late nights and tears, giving her a glow that would fool anyone into thinking she'd just stepped off a beach.

"I should have let you do this sooner, huh?" She smiles.

"I did try telling you," Jenna laughs. "Hey, Kees," she continues, holding her gaze through the mirror.

"Yeah?"

"I'm sorry. That it's like this."

Kees sighs and turns around to face her. "To be fair, you were right all along, Jenna." She is unable to keep the bitterness from her tone. "I shouldn't have fallen in love with a white boy. I knew better."

"We all pushed the boundaries." Jenna shrugs.

"Not you," Kees disagrees. "You always knew where the line was."

Jenna stares at her for a long minute. "I lost that line a long time ago, Keesy. And I have done my fair share of wrong, even when I knew better. Especially when I knew better."

She takes a step toward Kees but then stops.

"I have spent years running around with a bunch of men, some whose names I don't even remember. I've looked love straight in the eye and walked away. I've gone home with men and never stayed the night. And you can call that toeing the line, if you like, but really, I'm just a coward. Not strong enough to love those I shouldn't. You stayed, Keesy. You have been brave beyond anything I have ever been capable of. You've lost your entire family and still, you've stayed. For love. It's the most romantic thing I've ever heard and there is no money in this world that I would have put on you being the most romantic one out of all of us. But then again, you've never been afraid, and you've always been ready for the fight. I've never told you how much I admire that in you. And here you are, on the day of your wedding or nikah, whatever you want to call it, it's still the day you say a vow in front of God and bind your life to the man you love, and you're doing it all alone. Without the people you thought would be here. You're the bravest woman I know, Keesy. I wish I had some of your courage."

Kees blinks back tears and for the first time notices how much Jenna has changed. That she seems calmer but in a subdued, blunt kind of way. As if something has been knocked out of place, slightly leaning at the wrong angle, but she can't figure out what it is.

She coughs, just managing to keep the tears at bay. "Well, it will be you soon. Being equally brave and getting married."

Jenna smiles sadly and shakes her head. "No, Kees. I will do it with my mother by my side. One day, maybe, I'll tell you how much of a coward I really am."

Kees frowns, but before she can say anything there is a knock on the door and Jenna shouts, "Come in."

Lottie and Adalyn walk in, both cooing at her and the sari hanging off the door. Adalyn is her favorite of all the wives, married to Max, who is the second oldest and closest to Harry. They have often spent nights together without the brothers, laughing about the peculiarities of the DuVaughn family.

"We thought we'd come to see if you need any help?" asks Lottie.

"Or if there's anything we can do to be useful," says Adalyn, walking up to Kees and hugging her. "I'm sorry we didn't get to see you last night. Vivian said you'd already gone to bed by the time we got here."

"I was tired, so I went to bed pretty early," Kees replies, squeezing Adalyn and feeling glad that they did make it in the end. Although she hadn't wanted Vivian to invite anybody, she's grateful for her presence.

"I'm just about to get dressed and then I'll be down."

They nod and talk about how beautiful she is, and how they'll leave her to it, and she feels sad that there are no jobs for her to give them. She knows they want to be useful in the middle of an event that makes no sense to them, unsure how to act in this wedding that is not a wedding.

They leave, taking Jenna with them, and she thinks that later, once this is all over, she must go to coffee with Jenna and ask her what she meant.

For now, she is left to wrap her white sari around herself, unfolding and folding the pleats three times before she gets it right. This is the part she always needs help with, but without fussing aunties and grandmas who always tell her she's done it wrong, no matter how perfectly she has wrapped the material around her, she's left to figure it out herself. Thinking of the aunties brings tears into her eyes and she looks up again to blink them back. Stupid. At this rate, she was going to spend most of this day looking up at the ceiling.

Once she has finished, finally taking the rose from the untouched breakfast tray and threading it into her hair, she stares at herself in the mirror, hoping to see what she saw in Saba on the morning of her wedding. A tap on the door is followed by Jenna's head appearing around the doorway, checking if she's dressed, before the door swings open fully and her father steps into the room, taking all the air out of it.

She stares at him. All of her words fail her. She is nervous, suddenly afraid in front of a man who has never raised his voice to her. The room feels too small and she doesn't know what to do with her body. Her arm, which she hadn't noticed before, suddenly hangs heavy by her side, awkward in its uselessness.

She lifts her hand and holds the other one but feels silly so drops her hands again. She fumbles with her sari for a moment but it doesn't need fixing. She remembers her duty to greet her elders and quickly blurts out, "*Assalamualaikum, Abaji.*"

She doesn't know if she can still use the word "Father."

"*Wa-Assalamualaikum, Beta.*"

His use of the word "Daughter" makes her feel weak at the knees.

"I didn't think you'd come," she says.

He shakes his head sadly. She notices that he looks older than when she saw him last. He moves more slowly. The curve in his spine the doctors say nothing can be done about is getting worse. He seems to be shrinking in front of her and later that night she will cry to Harry and insist that she is the reason her father is fading away. That she would rather her life be taken than her father's, and Harry will cry, "Hush," and rock her in his arms, repeating, "You must never say that," over and over again, hoping that when the big wedding comes, their wedding night is a happier place.

"Bilquis, I cannot stay."

Whatever hope had arrived with her father leaves as soon as he speaks.

"Your mother doesn't know I'm here. I came only to give you this."

He pulls a red velvet box out of his worn jacket and she notices the lining is ripped and frayed. He has been meaning to get a new jacket for months, but she imagines Saba's wedding has meant he has pushed it down his list of priorities.

He walks slowly toward her and she feels frozen to the ground.

He holds out the box and with shaking hands she takes it, snapping it open to see a single gold bangle nestled in the soft inner of the box. It has ornate goldwork on top of it, a pattern of leaves winding around it to meet a single gold flower that marks the top of the bangle. It is similar to the one that her mother gave Saba on the morning of her wedding, although the pattern is different. It is less ornate than Saba's, and Kees has always preferred more minimal designs, but the delicate goldwork makes it the most beautiful thing she's ever seen.

She looks up, a question in her eyes.

"Your mother and I bought these when you were children, one for each of you on your wedding days. We knew that we wouldn't have much to give you, but your mother maintained that no daughter of hers would get married without some family gold. Over the years we saved to buy these, and a third one when Hakim was born for the wife he will one day bring into our house, inshallah. I'm sorry it's not much, Beta, but alhamdulillah, it's something."

All of the tears she has done so well at holding back rain down her face and she does nothing to stop them. The idea that her father, the man whose spine is bending in front of her, is standing before her to apologize for having less brings all the grief up into her chest and out of her eyes. Self-disgust burns in her throat. She wants to leave, to take his hand and say it doesn't matter, none of it has ever mattered and this was just selfishness. She wants to run until she finds a way to run back through the years and choose a different path.

She tries to say something. To somehow let him know that he has given her everything. That apologies don't belong in his mouth.

The words stick and she chokes out a sound that is unrecognizable in English or Punjabi.

Itasham, who, like Nathaniel, has never been able to bear seeing anyone upset, takes the final step toward his firstborn and takes her in his arms where he feels a tide break against his chest and every painstaking brushstroke Jenna had previously made slides off his daughter's face and onto his freshly ironed white shirt, the old collarless one he has had for years because collars irritate his skin and they are hard to find.

He pats her back murmuring, "Beta, enough, enough," until Kees finally lifts her head and heaving chest off her father, taking the outstretched cotton handkerchief from him. She laughs into it.

"You must be the only person still using these, Abaji."

He shakes his head. "They're good for the environment and the tissues give me a rash."

He has said this same sentence to her a thousand times before, and she stands quietly, enjoying the comfort of his familiar words.

Eventually he gestures to the cream two-seater sofa by the window. "Can I sit?"

"Yes, of course, Abaji, sit, please." Her father asking her if he can sit is new. He's never asked before and she recognizes that something has changed here.

"Do you want some tea? I can go and make you some dudvali, the way you like."

He shakes his head.

"Come and sit with me for a second."

As she sits next to him, their knees almost touching, the white sari pooling around her feet, he says, "Bilquis, I cannot stay for this."

The tears rise once more.

"You know your mother does not approve of this match."

"And what about you, Abaji? What do you think?" she asks, unable to meet his eye.

"It is not what I think that matters. This is about what Allah Subhanahu Wa Ta'ala has told us is right. If he was prepared to become a Muslim, Bilquis, it might be different."

"But he has faith," she pleads. "And if someone asked me to change my religion I never would."

"Of *course* not," her father emphasizes.

"So why should it be different for him, Abaji? He goes to church every week. He believes in God. Is a good man. I could never ask him to give it all up when I believe we're praying to the same God. Aren't we?"

"Yes, Bilquis, we are," he nods, "there is only one God and Mohammed is the messenger. But they believe that Jesus was the son of God, not just a prophet. We know that God has no sons or daughters, no mother or father. The Quran is very clear about that."

He has taken on the voice he used to use when teaching his children something, or when debating an issue with Kees. It is filled with patience but has a firm, unyielding belief at the base of it.

"So how do you build a life together when you believe different things, Bilquis?"

She doesn't have any response for him. She just looks up at him helplessly, hoping that he has the answer.

"We believe in one God. The rest we'll figure out, Abaji, we will," she presses.

"This is why your mother and I cannot support this. It is not right."

Any hope that had flared in her chest is quickly gone. She feels angry. "So then why come and give me this?" she asks, gesturing to the box containing the bangle. It is the closest she has ever gotten to a raised voice with her father and his look of sadness makes her regret it immediately.

"Because even though we can't support it or be here to witness it, I am sure that your mother would have wanted you to have it on this day. That she is sad to think of you marrying without your family or anything you should have."

"Did Umee tell you that?" asks Kees, looking up at him.

"No, Beta. But I know my wife."

She says nothing. She just stares at the box and feels empty.

"Your mother is a good woman, Bilquis," insists her father. "She can be hard and stubborn, but she has had a difficult life, has fought for what little she has."

"But I'm her daughter, Abaji," she chokes. "How can she not want me?"

"Don't be stupid, Bilquis." His tone suddenly has an edge to it. "She doesn't know how to accept what you've done, and she is allowed to grieve. Your mother is proud of you. We both are. But you have taken many roads that she has been uncomfortable with, and now this is one she cannot follow you down. And I will not leave her to walk her truth alone, Bilquis. Your mother and I make our decisions together. Always." His voice softens and he lifts her chin. "But still, you deserve to have something from us on this day."

"Won't she be angry when she finds out you've taken this?"

"That is not your business, Bilquis," he replies.

A hurried knock on the door interrupts them and they both stand as Harry enters.

He doesn't look at Kees but walks straight up to her father, his hand outstretched.

"Assalamualaikum," he says.

"Wa-Assalamualaikum," Itasham replies, shaking Harry's hand.

"Abaji, this is Harry," she whispers.

"Yes," her father says, quietly.

They stand in a half-circle, the air thick around them, before Harry turns to her.

"The imam isn't coming."

"What?"

"He just called me. Apparently, he consulted his conscience and found he couldn't do it." Harry grimaces.

"But we paid him," she replies.

"I think that's the least of our worries," Harry says, and there is a part of her that feels ashamed that her father has heard him say that. Money has always been her father's biggest worry.

The door swings open once more and Vivian and Nathaniel enter.

"Hello, I'm Vivian, Harry's mother," she says, arm outstretched in a greeting, and Kees feels her stomach curl up. She wishes Vivian knew that men and women don't shake hands and offering hers to her father feels like asking him to step out of his beliefs.

To her surprise, he takes her hand and shakes it, clearly awkward in doing so but committed.

"I'm Itasham. Pleased to meet you," he replies.

"Won't you stay, at least for a little while? I know Kees would love it."

She almost wants to laugh at the notion that just because a child would like something the parent will oblige. It is not for her parents to oblige her, but rather the other way around.

"I'm sorry, I can't. I was just about to leave."

"Well, there might not even be anything to stay for anyway," Kees says bitterly. "The imam has canceled."

"The what?" Vivian asks, her face still lit up, trying to be helpful.

"The imam," sighs Harry. "I explained this to you. The man who will conduct the ceremony. An Islamic version of a priest."

She nods. "Of course, of course. Well, Father Bastian has just arrived; wouldn't he be able to do it?"

"No!" say Kees, her father, and Harry in unison, before shyly looking at one another, awkward in their strange unity.

Vivian trills, "Just trying to find solutions."

Nathaniel, who had previously been hovering by the door, steps in. "What can we do to help, Kees?"

"I don't know," she says, slumping back down onto the sofa.

Harry touches her arm and she flinches, aware of her father standing next to her. "I've got my laptop with me. It has the spreadsheet of names. Dad and I will start making some calls and see if we can get someone to come. It might be later in the day but we will do this nikah today, Kees, and with an imam, okay? I promise."

She nods as Nathaniel and Harry leave the room.

"I'll make some calls as well," her father says. "I have my address book with me."

"Abaji, you don't have to—" she starts before his hand cuts her off.

"I cannot stay, Bilquis, and I cannot get you to change your mind?"

She shakes her head slowly.

"Then I can at least make sure an imam does the nikah and reads the Quran over you."

Vivian, spurred on by the activity, resolves to make some tea and leaves the room, leaving them alone once more.

"Is she pagal? A priest?" her father asks and she can't help but laugh.

"She's a good woman. She just doesn't understand."

Her father takes a small address book tied in a blue plastic food bag out of his jacket pocket, and after untying the bag and taking it out begins to murmur as he looks over it.

The house vibrates around her, a new urgency added to the tempo. She paces between the window and the door, feeling useless. Jenna hurries in and out with tea for her father and reassuring glances for her. Adalyn pops her head in three times to ask if she's okay and she doesn't have an answer. Harry works his way through the spreadsheet, praying for some luck. Nathaniel calls the one Muslim man he works with to ask if he has any contacts or ideas. Father Bastian, who has been briefed by Vivian, calls the Chelsea Islamic Community Center to talk to Abdel-Hadey to ask if he can perform a "neeka." Samuel whispers furiously to his brothers that it's ridiculous that Father Bastian can't just do it. Lottie shakes her head at her husband, wondering how someone so intelligent can be so stupid. Gus, bored of his brother's moaning, tells him to shut up, pleased that someone in the family is going against social expectations and the whispers of the tennis club. He's jealous of Harry's courage in bringing someone different home. He wishes he was as brave and he flicks his phone open to message Drew, whom he wasn't brave enough to bring home when he had the chance. The children run laughing and screaming through the house, caring nothing about the adults. Some sixty miles away, Abida wonders what is taking her husband so long; he only went for duhr prayers. Not far from her house Evie Khatieb stands in her daughter's bedroom, hoping for a clue, something that will shed some light on what has happened to the daughter she used to know. Across the city Mohammed sits with his mother around their kitchen table talking about the woman he will soon marry and his mother smiles to see her son so happy. Eighteen streets away Lewis gets a call to tell him that he's got the job, and he whoops with joy, calling Zee to tell her that he's finally moving to Liverpool. Somewhere across the ocean a mug flies through the air, across the sitting room, and connects with the side of Malak's head. The Egyptian government declare a state of emergency. A revolution has begun.

In the end, it is her father who finds the imam that will marry his daughter, despite his wishes and reservations.

"He is on the way," he says, nodding to himself. "I know him from the mosque and, alhamdulillah, he has agreed, even though Harry is not Muslim."

She nods, unable to say anything else. Her face is bare. Most of the makeup is down her father's shirt and she washed the rest off while everyone made calls; it seemed the only useful thing left for her to do.

"I have to go, your mother will be wondering why I've been gone so long."

He doesn't step forward to place his hand on her head as he normally would have done, so she stays still, afraid to move and break whatever fragile alliance trembles between them.

He walks to the door and with one hand on the handle turns around to look at her. "Have you been keeping up your prayers?" he asks.

"Yes, Abaji, every day." The night she told her parents about Harry was the night her prayers came back to her.

"Alhamdulillah."

The door opens and he is gone.

Harry, who has been pacing outside the door to give them some privacy and time together, stops as he sees his soon-to-be estranged father-in-law and feels a pang of guilt. Itasham looks kind. Not the furious, raging man he had imagined all the years Kees had told him he wouldn't approve of their marriage. The guilt he feels is mainly for taking Kees away from her family and for so grossly misjudging them.

"I can't persuade you to stay?" he asks Itasham, who is zipping up his jacket.

"Thank you for your hospitality, but I must leave," he replies politely.

Harry nods. He wants to say something big and grand about how he'll look after his daughter, but it feels stupid and empty, a childish thing to do. Nervously he looks around, unsure what to say, and is saved by his father walking down the corridor toward them.

"Itasham, are you leaving? We can't persuade you to stay?"

Itasham smiles. "Thank you, but no."

Nathaniel nods, and Itasham remarks how like his father Harry is.

"Then let me walk you out at least," replies Nathaniel, arms open, gesturing for him to go in front.

Harry puts his hand out once more. "Assalamualaikum, Uncle." He has remembered how Kees had told him never to call her parents by their first name because she would die of embarrassment. "I'm deeply sorry for the pain and hurt I have caused your family. And if I have caused any offense, then please forgive me, it was not intended."

Itasham pauses before reaching out and shaking his hand in return.

"Wa-Assalamualaikum, Harry." He doesn't say anything else, just nods at Harry as he walks past him and follows Nathaniel through a house that is the biggest he has ever been in.

They don't pass anyone else. The news that the nikah is now happening again has sent everyone hurrying back to bedrooms to get ready, and Vivian to the kitchen to restart the preparations.

"Please let me call you a car, it will save you the train journey," says Nathaniel, pulling his phone out to make the call.

Itasham smiles and wonders what this man does to be able to afford such long taxi rides. "Thank you, but no. I like the train and will enjoy the walk to the station."

"Are you sure? It's still cold."

"Yes, yes, positive," replies Itasham, a hand on his chest in thanks.

They stand like this on the doorstep, unsure how to bridge the world between them, unwilling to cut it off.

They make comments about the weather and Nathaniel asks about cricket and whether he enjoys it.

A few more moments and then Itasham nods toward the road, mentions that he has to leave. He seems hesitant and as Nathaniel is about to ask him again if he wants to stay, he pulls out a brown envelope and hands it to Nathaniel.

The envelope is stuffed full of notes, about two thousand pounds is his estimation.

"For my daughter's wedding," Itasham says. "Thank you for organizing everything. I am sorry the burden has been yours alone."

Nathaniel doesn't try to decline the money or to give it back. He thinks for the first time he understands this man and the family Kees belongs to.

"There's absolutely no burden, rather a blessing. It's been our honor."

They shake hands and as Itasham begins to walk down the drive, Nathaniel calls after him.

"We'll take care of her, and you and your family are welcome here any time."

Itasham places his hand on his heart once more, nodding in thanks, before disappearing out of the gates and into the street.

Nathaniel watches him go. Later he tells Vivian how much respect he has for him.

Vivian hisses, "Why on earth did you take the money, Nathaniel? Did you see his jacket? It had tears in it and those shoes were in desperate need of replacing. I didn't realize her family was so poor, she always seems so well put together. They need that money more than we do, for God's sake."

Nathaniel shakes his head and draws his wife closer to him. "I know, but I understand his need to provide for his own children's weddings; I would be the same."

Vivian mutters about pride being one of the deadly sins. She feels irrationally upset about Itasham's jacket and doesn't stop thinking about it for weeks.

Outside in the street, Itasham walks around the corner and sits on the first bench he finds, despite the cold biting at his fingers and the ache in his spine being worse than it has for months. He stays there until the imam calls him two hours later to tell him it is done, that his daughter is married. Only then does he walk to the station and get on a train taking him out of the city and home to his wife.

She sits with Addy on the sofa, her head resting on his shoulder.

"Thank you for bringing so much ladoo, although God knows what we're going to do with it all."

"Well, someone had to represent," he laughs, "plus, you can't get married without ladoo."

The ceremony had gone perfectly, and the imam hadn't said anything about Harry not being Muslim or hellfire. She was worried he would slip in some sin, but he read the Quran and spoke about the blessings of marriage and she wondered if her father had briefed him or not.

Vivian's catering, although not her choice of food, was beautiful and the decorations she had hung around the house had transformed the place into a winter wonderland. Addy had also bought a flower buttonhole for Harry, who hadn't taken it off since Addy had put it in his suit.

"It's the small things," Addy had said, and he was right.

Vivian floats through the house, smiling at everyone, filling glasses, kissing a grandchild, insisting on second and third helpings, placing a cushion behind Nathaniel's mother, admiring an outfit. She is happiest like this, when all her children have come back to the nest, if only for the night or a few hours.

Addy kisses Kees on the forehead. "Right, I have to go. Come walk me out."

At the doorstep, she hands him his jacket. "Thank you so much, Addy. I don't know how to—"

"Oh, stop," he interrupts her. "No more tears. Enough."

"Surely the end is when we're all supposed to cry the most," she laughs.

"True. But you've done all your crying at the beginning. Still can't believe your dad turned up."

"Me neither," she replies.

"What a time to be alive," he sighs. "Okay, I'll see you on Monday morning, probably before everyone else gets in. Shall we have breakfast? Your desk or mine?"

"Mine."

"Done," he replies, slipping on black leather gloves. "By the way, did you know that your brother-in-law is gay?"

"What! No, he isn't. Which one?"

Addy raises an eyebrow. "Gus, obviously."

"He's married, Addy."

"So? That's never stopped anyone before."

"You're wrong," she whispers, afraid that suddenly he'll come into the entrance hall and hear.

"I'm never wrong, trust me, I know my own and Gus is one of mine. Anyway, it's cold, go back inside. See ya."

She closes the door and turns to see Jenna walking up to her.

"Hey, you," says Jenna, handing her a slice of the wedding cake Vivian had ordered on the insistence that the kids would like it. "I thought you might want some cake and a time out," continues Jenna, nodding toward the stairs.

"You hero, yes, please," Kees groans as they sit on the stairs, tucked out of the way.

"How are you holding up?" asks Jenna.

"I can't believe my dad came," she replies.

"I can't believe you rubbed all your makeup off on his shirt," laughs Jenna.

"I'm sorry, babes."

"I'll forgive you; just promise me I get to do your makeup again."

Kees nods. "For the actual wedding, it's all yours."

For a little while, they are both quiet, admiring the surroundings and eating the cake in the palms of their hands. Kees can feel something being tightly held back inside her, Jenna's too-loud munching the only sound in her ear. For the first time, she doesn't mind it.

"It's been a year and a half," says Jenna, breaking the silence, "since the night of your sister's engagement party."

Kees nods in acknowledgment. What they're really saying is, it's been exactly a year and a half since the three of them were in a room together. It has been exactly a year and a half since life made sense. It has been exactly a year and a half of the emptiness that comes when the women you love disappear.

"Everything is so different," Jenna continues. "I'm different. So are you, Kees."

"Am I?" she murmurs back. She can feel sadness emanating from Jenna and it is melting into her own, creating something heavy between them.

"Yes," Jenna nods, "you seem sadder."

"So do you," Kees replies.

Jenna doesn't reply, just rests her head on Kees's shoulder. Kees answers by resting her head back. They stay locked in this position, like jigsaw pieces that have finally found where they're supposed to be. At one point, Harry comes to find his new bride and, seeing them leaning on one another, he tiptoes away before he's seen.

He wishes he could have taken a picture of them like that. How they looked like soldiers on a battlefield once the fight is over, tired and weary and longing for rest.

MALAK

Certain moments in life crystallize, twisting from memory into something immortal.

The moment the first plate smashed off her elbow is one of those. She can remember what the light looked like pouring through the kitchen window and exactly what song was playing in the background: Snow Patrol, "Called Out in the Dark." She has never listened to that song again.

She remembers the soapy suds that were gathering like pearls around her wrist and how many dishes were dripping on the draining board. Two mugs. A bowl. Three plates. The big salad bowl she had bought from Khan Khalili: a navy-blue ceramic piece with curling bright orange patterns on the inside and pebbled design on the outside. If she closes her eyes for long enough, she can remember how many soap suds dripped down from the top of the bowl: three.

She can remember the air, how it felt tight around her ears, and although the oven was off, a heat burned behind her as Ali paced back and forth, back and forth, sixteen times in total, before he picked up one of the three plates on the draining board and cracked it across her elbow. The rest of the dishes didn't get washed that day.

Later he had said he didn't even realize it was in his hand; that he wasn't himself. She had nodded shyly, peered up at him through wet lashes, and let him kiss the long cut down her elbow, bandaging her as gently as if he was cradling a newborn. Once he had finished, he looked up at her, unblinking, holding her gaze for two long minutes before breaking the silence to tell her that she made him a better man. That being with her was a journey to greatness, and he couldn't do it alone.

That was the second moment immortalized. She has never forgotten how he looked at her, how the words formed across his lips, and how she had believed him. That what she did, the way she moved through the world, could make a difference to a man she sometimes thought was part devil. However, it was the moment she stayed that lives forever in her mind.

Not that she knew anything else. They never teach you how to leave. Women are taught to stay. To love unconditionally. To only pack suitcases for husbands but never for themselves. She has watched the aunties and uncles she knew since childhood stay exactly where they were, frozen like pieces on a chessboard.

Now she is on the board with nowhere to go. She may not know how to leave, but she has learned other things. How to shrink into a shadow on the days he is unhappy. How to put lightness in her voice so her words float unnoticed above him. How to stroke his shoulders just the way he likes so that he moans in pleasure, grabbing her hand to kiss it and say, "Hayati." She knows his favorite meals and his morning routine. She has learned how to talk to other men in a way that always borders on disinterested. Sometimes she is rude to other men because the thought that they may take her politeness as flirtation makes her blood turn to ice in her veins. She has a choice: friends of friends may think she's rude, or she can be called a whore later by the man she loves. She always chooses the former. Her friends have stopped introducing her to other friends now. She knows it is because the boys groan and ask them not to invite the "stuck-up rude one," and she is happy to be excluded from mixed gatherings. She has learned that female-only gatherings are unlimited. That when she's out with women he messages her things like, *I hope you're having a wonderful night with your friends, baby*, but when the gathering is mixed he will ask, *When are you coming home?* or, *Why aren't you answering your phone?* The only man she smiles at is her cousin Haytham, a man too close in family and too old to be a source of jealousy. She has learned that men can get jealous even when there are no other men around. That a bikini pulled too low on the beach is enough to transform him from man to beast and for the extra tan line, it's not worth it. She doesn't bother with the bikinis anymore; prefers a tankini and tells her friends it's because she hates her stomach right now. She has never been skinnier, but it is an excuse that women will accept. She always buys her swimwear in a size sixteen although she is a size eight. More room means more material, which means less cleavage and a happier time on the beach for them both. She agrees with him that cleavage is vulgar and common. Even she can't stop staring when she sees a woman's breasts pouring out of her dress and she doesn't want people looking at her like that. One night, while he's out with his friends, she goes through Facebook and deletes all her old pictures. Nights laughing, wrapped around Kees or Jenna in a top that with a belt and some high heels became a dress. She has always been proud of her breasts, but now she scrolls through the old pictures and feels a deep hatred for the woman she used to be. Her Facebook has become free of old lovers and boyfriends, incriminating photographs of drunken nights, and revealing pictures. The pictures of her laughing on holiday, surrounded by six men on the beach, are gone. The pictures of her being given a piggyback ride by male friends have disappeared. There is nothing here any longer that can incriminate or anger. There is nothing to suggest that her skin belongs to anyone but him. She does all this even though they're not friends on Facebook.

She once suggested they add each other but he had very reasonably gone through the argument of why they shouldn't, and she happened to agree. Thought that, actually, more people should think like that. The conversation had followed on from her signing up to Twitter and proudly showing him her first tweet—*popping my cherry*—and he had shaken his head uncomfortably, shrugging at her.

"I'm sorry, this is why I don't think we should follow each other or be connected online."

"But I'm just messing about, baby," she had laughed, "this is just my humor."

"I know, I just don't need to see it, you know?" he had replied.

She hadn't tweeted again. The timeline stayed empty, except that first tweet, which had three likes, all from bots.

After the first plate had shattered off her, more followed, but she didn't remember those in the same way. The memories are faded around the edges, frayed into a forgotten place. Sometimes she recalls a blurry dish spinning toward her. A vase crashing into her leg. The TV remote bouncing off her forehead. A bottle of cologne hitting her as she walked out of a room. It had smashed off the tiles after bouncing off her back and for the next two weeks they had to sleep in the spare bedroom because the smell of Davidoff Cool Water was so overpowering it gave them headaches. Their apartment is the best-smelling home in Cairo.

But these were few and far between; rare instances that always came at the end of an argument and in a lot of them she had shouted just as loudly as he had. Her voice had become a living thing, something that tore at them both, and while she never smashed plates, there was that one time she had shouted that he was insecure, and she had watched his ego smash across every surface in the house. She is still picking up those pieces, finding fragments unexpectedly in the most unlikely places; in a conversation, a weekend away, or down the pasta aisle in the supermarket.

They have learned how to tear at each other and the worst part about it is that it makes the loving better. The softness he shows her after something has crashed into her body is hedonistic, otherworldly, exhilarating. It is addictive. She has never seen a man crumble to his knees and plant apologies at her feet. To see him, her love, sink to the ground, kiss her knees, and swear that she is the reason he rises is the strongest drug she's ever taken.

Once, when sitting with her work friends, Delia, Reham, and Noha, during a break at school, Noha had asked how women could end up in abusive relationships.

"The minute a hand is raised or the first blow has fallen, I'd be out of there," she said, shaking her head over an article filled with domestic abuse statistics.

Noha is American and has the arrogance to match. Delia and Reham, who have spent their life in the same country, had shrugged and Noha had taken their silence for agreement.

Malak had continued cutting up her peach into slices, popping each freshly cut piece into her mouth, savoring the sweetness and freshness of fruit that hasn't been shipped.

It's easier than you think, she'd thought, and that is the third memory that lives with her for the rest of her life: the knowledge that she was in one and didn't have a single clue what to do about it. You can hardly share that kind of news over your lunch break, and although women always insist that you can talk to them about anything, how do you tell them something when you can barely admit it to yourself?

The 25th of January 2011 also stands out, but only because someone else's blood was spilled instead. It was also the beginning of Ali and Malak's greatest period, their love blooming and growing wild around them. The arrival of the revolution brought with it a bigger battle to fight, a common enemy, and they no longer needed to tear at one another. Ali was a consumed man, the realization of so many tweets finally unfolding out on the streets. He spent days and nights sitting in Tahrir Square, protesting against the government. She spent some weeks living back with her aunty and cousins because a revolution was no time to sleep alone. She would have gone back to her old apartment with Nylah and Rayan but their worried parents had shipped them home to England months ago. Ali and Malak had the opportunity to miss each other and when he came home to shower, sleep, or write articles that were sent off to editors in England, their love was all that is magical in the world.

School had stopped and she was glad of the break. The country was at a standstill. When the marches came, she joined them, protesting with Haytham and her cousins, or her aunties, who were tired of hard living. Sometimes it was with Ali and they screamed together, "*Ash-sha'b yurīd isqāṭ an-niẓām*" ("the people want to bring down the regime"). In those moments, surrounded by a million other Egyptians, she knew exactly who she was. Fighting for your country, either in war or protest, is the quickest way to be claimed. You cannot spill blood or risk your own for your motherland and not belong. She knew why she had come here and that everything leading up to this moment was worth it.

The revolution goes on. She learns to knit with her aunties while under curfew, long days spent threading wool through metal hooks. She cooks with her cousins and every day they make a new sweet or cake. The days are long and not every day is full of marches and protests. Some days the body count is too high and her aunties swear she won't leave the house, backed up by Ali, who refuses to let her step into the square for fear of losing her in a stampede. Too many men have died recently and women's bodies, whether dead, alive, or dragged through the streets, have become news stories and headlines. She talks to more friends back home as everyone suddenly reaches out to find out if she is still alive. Her mother and father call most days. Samir occasionally asks if she's okay but the revolution is a far-off thing to him and he has never been one to watch the news. She gives everyone the same answer: "It looks worse on the news than it is." She believes it too, until she's at a protest that should have been peaceful, and a man dies in her arms.

The bullets had been a few streets away and while she's fleeing the area she comes across a man doubled over on the curb, his blood draining into the gutter along with the dirty water of nearby washerwomen. Her body screams at her to run but she catches his eye and his own silent screams still her feet. She drags him into the shadow of a side street and in her broken Arabic tries to soothe him, but the only word she can remember is "okay," so she repeats it for ten minutes until the light goes out of him suddenly.

She can't remember who peeled him from her clutches but as she hazily makes her way back home she thinks, *perhaps it is as bad as the news is making it out to be.* When she arrives at their apartment, Ali has been angry; the revolution isn't going well and she was supposed to be home hours ago. Before she can explain that she was waiting for the dying man to heave his last breath, he begins shouting at her for being late. How she is selfish for making him worry so much. How she should have more respect for him. His anger covers every surface that night and she goes back to thinking about love, and how much it mattered when death came calling. Except every time she thinks about love, it is Jacob's face that swims into her mind, not Ali's, and as she watches him scorn her, not noticing her blood-soaked clothes, she thinks about death and all the things she's ever done wrong in her life.

Later that night she finds out about Kees's nikah and how Jenna was there, and although she is the one who got on a plane, she feels left behind. She can't stop thinking about the choices people make and how much everyone stands to lose.

In February and March, their life returns to normal, the country lumbering into movement once more now that Mubarak is a story of defeat and triumph the people tell around the dinner table. School is opened and she is back to daily battles with students as if they'd never stopped. She puts her feet back into high heels and clips through long air-conditioned corridors to teach the present participle to kids who didn't care before, but now, post-revolution, care even less. Their country is breaking into a new dawn and they have no time for the English teacher who didn't grow up here and who still doesn't understand the language. She is back to peach slices at break time and unvoiced thoughts. The smashed plates have started again; she is back to sweeping broken things off the floor. But the soft love has also returned.

She finds everything more difficult lately. She is less mo-tivated. She doesn't visit her aunties as much. She purposely misses Haytham's calls and later texts back apologies with no further conversation. She is tired all the time. The hardness of a city that houses seventeen million people is beginning to wear her down. The Muslim Brotherhood has been elected and a collective disappointment settles on the country. They talk about politics on the balcony after supper with less enthusiasm. The revolution is a faraway thing, a different time. They fight less and there are fewer broken things around the house, but she is finding everything harder to bear. For the first time, she pretends to be asleep when he comes at her with kisses and the worst thing about it is, he doesn't seem to mind. Somewhere she had hoped they would fight about it, that he would show some kind of sign that he wanted her, but when she gets up in the night to go to the bathroom, she finds him bent over his laptop, laughing over something she cannot understand, unbothered that his girlfriend was, for once, asleep instead of staying awake for sex. She can sense an irrational tide rising in her and does nothing to stop it. Just snaps at him for typing so loudly on his laptop and fumbles her way back to bed. Every day at 7:30 a.m. she stands at the back of assembly with Edlin, her closest friend despite the thirty years that separates them, desperately trying to wake herself up with a cup of tea while Edlin sips coffee and they both mumble the Egyptian anthem because neither of them knows all the words. Still. She asks around for other jobs but is only met with bemused smirks. The economy is destroyed. The country limping from the revolution. No one is hiring and international businesses that need her perfect English are not even looking toward Egypt or the Middle East where countries are toppling to revolution like dominos.

She slumps back into the staffroom to finish marking papers, wiping the sweat from her forehead.

"You look terrible," says Edlin in her slow southern drawl, looking up from her stack of grade-nine papers. It is the end of term and papers are due, the teachers caught up in marking and the students burrowed in exams.

"It's the third day I've been sick," Malak replies. "I think I ate a bad burrito because ever since Sunday night I've felt funny. It was in Amellios and someone else said they got sick from there."

"That place is dodgy," pipes up Andy from across the table. "I threw up four times after going there, never gone back."

"Are you going to butt into every conversation this morning?" asks Edlin, turning around to give him a piercing stare that women in their fifties can really get away with.

Malak shoots her a thankful look. "My back is killing me as well, but my period's due."

"Drink some peppermint tea, it will help with the nausea."

Malak nods back at Edlin and bends back over her marking, wondering if someone has turned the AC off because it's not as cold as it normally is.

Five minutes later, Edlin is standing over her chair, her handbag under her arm. "I'm driving to the gas station for some cigarettes. You wanna ride with me?"

"Thanks, but I'm going to finish this marking," Malak replies.

Edlin grabs her arm and pulls her to her feet. "They might have some peppermint tea," she says firmly, beginning to steer her out of the staffroom.

Malak tuts and frees her arm. "I don't know why you bother asking me if you're going to tell me."

"It sounds like you're pregnant," Edlin hisses in her ear and Malak stops and stares at her.

"Edlin, I'm on the pill," she whispers, shooting nervous glances over her shoulder. "It's probably just food poisoning."

Edlin shoots her a look. "I had Lucas on the pill." She keeps her voice low, stepping closer toward her.

"Are you serious?" Malak asks, holding on to the noticeboard to her right, suddenly feeling weak.

"Deadly," says Edlin firmly, stepping next to Malak and taking her arm. "Come on, we're going to the pharmacy for a pregnancy test and you're going to take it."

Half an hour later, they stand together in the ladies' bathroom, Edlin's back pressed against the door. Every time a child tries to enter, she snaps at them that this block is closed.

Malak stares at the positive pregnancy test in her hand, suddenly all her nausea gone from her body.

"Can you even get an abortion in Egypt?"

"Seeing as that's your first question, I guess that tells us what you want to do?"

"I can't have a baby, Edlin. I'm not even married," Malak breathes out, leaning back against the sink.

"You and Ali are planning to get married. If you want this baby, you could push the wedding up. You can do this, but only if you want to."

She nods, acknowledging Edlin's words but unable to find any of her own.

"When was your last period?" asks Edlin, all business and efficiency.

"I can't remember," she stammers.

"What do you mean, you can't remember?" asks Edlin, striving for patience.

"I've carried on my pill packet for the last three months because I didn't want to have a period."

"Jesus Christ." Edlin rubs her eyes. "I need some coffee. And you need to see a doctor. I'm going to make an appointment with mine; he'll see you after school. Can you tell Ali you're coming back with me and the kids for dinner?"

"Yeah, yeah. Let's do that." Malak suddenly feels like a wild animal. "Edlin," she whispers, looking up at the older woman.

"Don't worry, darling," Edlin says, for once softening and pulling Malak into her arms. "Everything will be just fine in the end. You'll see."

The bell shrieks them back to their jobs and Malak has to run through the campus to make it to her class on time.

For the rest of the day, she notices that the constant nausea has disappeared, replaced by a tight ball of worry and an entirely different kind of sickness. Later, when she sits opposite the doctor and he tells her that she's three months pregnant, everything in her body quiets down, even her heartbeat. The panic she felt in the toilets earlier has gone. The nervousness has fled. She has come settling down into herself, calm and empty, floating on an idea. A wish. An impossible thing. Another moment immortalized.

JENNA. BILQUIS. MALAK.

4:15 in the morning and Jenna's eyes have just opened. She is in the split second between a dream and all that is true; a foot in both worlds. The same dream has been visiting her sporadically for months but, lately, it comes more often. It's full of fuzzy details and nameless people but the one thing she knows is that she's killed someone. She can hear the sirens coming for her as she tries to hide the body and she always wakes just before she is caught, the clatter of her heart beating too fast against her chest the only sound in the house.

She lies staring at the ceiling, her body still trembling slightly, safe in a king-sized bed with too much space around it and nobody to roll over to. The light coming through the open windows tells her that it is too early to start the day. She tries to fall back asleep but her eyes keep popping open, her body wrestling with itself between the sheets. She considers going for a run but it is still too early; running at 4 a.m. makes you a crazy person. Running at 5 a.m. means you're dedicated, and she has forty-five minutes before her actions are seen as inspirational rather than deranged.

She can't bear the glare of a screen so doesn't pick up her phone or put a movie on, just lies in bed watching the light change through the open window. At 4:57 a.m. she rolls out of bed and pulls on her leggings, wrapping a white cotton scarf around her head, covering her hair. She leaves a note for her parents in the kitchen and quietly leaves the house, breathing a sigh of relief that her body can now move.

For an hour, she runs, only stopping on three occasions and never to catch her breath. She pushes her body to its limits and then asks a little more of it. By the time she circles back home and pushes the front door open, the house is awake and loud and she's completed 15 kilometers.

"*Sabah el keer, habibti*," shouts her dad across the breakfast table, gesturing to the food piled in front of him. "Your mother has cooked a feast. Yalla, come join me."

"Good morning, Baba," Jenna replies, unable to resist smiling back in the face of his joy, which is even more delightful for having no apparent reason. "I'm going to shower and then I'll be down. Morning, Mama."

"Good morning, my darling," her mother shouts back over her shoulder, concentrating on cracking six eggs into the shakshuka, which is filling the kitchen with the scent of roasted tomatoes and cumin.

She smiles at them both and remembers a time when there was nothing she wanted more than to be in the heart of her parents' happiness. She gets in the shower and cries. She doesn't know why. Now that daylight has arrived, she can see the boxes piled up around her room. A stack of papers, booklets, HR documents, and staff guidelines are piled on her desk, the welcome papers of her new job that will start in three weeks. Her wedding dress is hanging in the guest room. She is glad she doesn't have to look at it. What started as an inability to focus on wedding plans due to exams has turned into "You decide, I trust you." Her mother looks at her strangely when she says this and then Jenna knows to comment how much she loves

Mo, and her mother smiles and squeezes her hand, the worry clouding her eyes dissipating. Everything feels far away and out of reach to Jenna; a chain of beautiful things happening but she is unable to feel them.

A few weeks ago, Mo had taken her out for a drive to the coast. "I know it's not the same as the beach in Egypt that your friend took you to, but you keep talking about how great it was to be by the sea, so I thought I'd bring you here," he had said, looking at her with so much love in his eyes she felt horrible for being distant.

She then did something she had never done with him, stepping up to him, putting her hands on both sides of his face, and pulling him into her to kiss him. She had put everything she had learned from kissing men and women over the years into that kiss and by the time she was finished he looked at her, blinking in shock. For a moment she thought that maybe she had done the wrong thing. For the entirety of their relationship, she had only kissed him back when he reached for her, which he rarely did. There were lines not crossed and Mo was a man who always did the right thing. He was a man raised by a woman who talks more to God than to her husband and who has raised four sons to hold open doors and hold themselves back from women unless that woman is your wife. Jenna has never asked, but she would bet her father's fortune that all the women Mo has been with are white and not Muslim. She knows this because all the men she has been with are not Muslim and there is an unspoken agreement that if you're going to break the rules, don't do it with one of your own. People talk.

So Mo doesn't ask for Jenna's body and she never gives it. Their kisses are gentle and tentative and even when he does pull her into him, she makes sure her body doesn't react. But that day she had pressed her body against his, searched for his tongue with hers, and had let him know that she was a woman who wanted things. He, in turn, had looked like a man shell-shocked by the intensity of who Jenna might be. Just when she thought he was going to tell her off, quote the Quran, call off the wedding, or even walk away, he had pulled her back into him and they were once more locked in a kiss that was neither polite nor chaste and definitely not respectable.

That day had been their best yet. They had taken their shoes and socks off and run through the surf. Reached for each other. Stroked hands and foreheads. Constantly found their way to one another's lips, their tongues hungry and wanting. In front of the wild sea Jenna felt some of herself return. She has always believed the ocean to be magic. Has always felt the most power-ful when she stands beside it. As Mo laughed with her and ran alongside her, the beach empty because it was still too cold, she had glimpsed a man capable of more than medicine, expensive restaurants, and the lines of Quran he quoted on an annoyingly regular basis. And while she loved her faith and the melody of the Quran, she did wonder if it didn't get in the way sometimes and, sure, chastity was all well and good, but sometimes you really needed to feel a man's tongue in your mouth to know what he was made of.

4:15 in the morning and the rearranging of documents has been the only sound to break the silence around the table. Kees rubs her temples and curses whoever fitted this conference room with bright lights and no dimmer. Her headache has been beating a steady rhythm all night and it is about to reach its peak, despite the painkillers she's been swallowing every four hours.

Opposite her Nina stands up, gathering her papers into a pile in front of her. "I'm going home. We're due in court at 11 a.m.

I'll see you outside at nine-thirty and we can go through the defense a final time, okay?"

Kees nods. "I'm just going to go through the witness statements one more time before I leave."

Nina shakes her head while pulling her bag off the table. "I know first cases are scary. I was shitting it for mine, not that I can remember much of it, it was so damn long ago, but you're ready, Kees. There is such a thing as over-preparing."

"I know, I'll call my taxi shortly."

Nina nods, seemingly reassured. Just before she leaves the room, she turns to face her. "You know, in my thirty-five years of being a lawyer, I've learned that people stay late at work for one of two reasons. Either they're hungry and ambitious and determined to get to the top as quickly as possible, or they don't want to go home to whatever is waiting for them."

Kees opens her mouth but before she can say anything Nina waves her quiet.

"You are ambitious, Kees, and you want to change the world today, not tomorrow. But the hours you've been spending here are far beyond unreasonable ambition. Go home. Whatever it is, fix it. Whether you realize it or not, it will affect the kind of lawyer you become."

Kees stares incredulously at the door Nina closes behind her. Fix it. Fix it. She's too annoyed to continue working so closes her papers and calls her taxi. London is living between the late nighters and the early risers; the streets empty of even the workers who keep the capital off its knees. She still hasn't got used to her new address, or that it was gifted to her. She creeps in the front door and, as usual, feels like there's too much space around her. The rooms are mostly empty because they don't have enough things to fill them with or enough family to gift them housewarming presents. When Nathaniel and Vivian had tried to buy them something, she had told Harry that if he didn't ask his parents not to, she would. The flat was the present. She couldn't take the shame of them adding to the list of things they had already provided for her.

She puts her bag down by the front door and walks into the sitting room; a room with big bay windows and high Victorian ceilings, the only furniture an old brown leather pouf she'd had since her university days and a cheap IKEA coffee table from Harry's old flat. On the windowsill is a peace lily she'd bought on the spur of the moment a couple of weeks ago, and whose leaves were now browning into decay because neither of them had been home to water it. She picks it up and walks with it into the kitchen, holding it under the tap for a minute, before returning it to the windowsill. She should go to sleep. Three hours, if she goes now. Instead, she sits on the leather pouf, stroking its faded patterns. Nina is right; she has been avoiding coming home. At work, there are problems she can solve. Here there is nothing but an empty flat that reminds her of her missing family. She had sent pictures of the nikah in the mail to her mother but was haunted by the idea that she probably just burned them in the sink, the same way she had her letter. She sent images to Saba, who still hadn't returned any of her texts, and she had messaged Hakim, for the twentieth time, to see how he was doing. The same empty silence radiated back at her, not even a read receipt from her siblings. Her messages lay on their phones, unopened, gathering dust. Harry tells her to stop but, like an addict, she returns home every week, begging at the door once more to be let in. She hasn't told Harry that she feels like this new house isn't blessed and never will be. That her mother stepping over the threshold is all the blessing she needs.

Every roof Kees has lived under, her mother has been under also. In her university accommodation, her mother came to fill the freezer, complain about the dirt, and attempt to persuade Kees back to the family home. In her small studio flat, once she got the job, her mother had appeared again to fill the freezer, suggest where the furniture should go, and help her paint one of the walls. But here in this new place, there are no signs of her mother anywhere. It's as if she has died. In her angriest moments, Kees thinks it would have been better if she had and then immediately feels wretched for wishing her mother away when she's never wanted her more.

Occasionally, Harry suggests they go to IKEA or furniture shopping somewhere. He'll send images of sofas he likes and frames they should buy. She had momentarily been excited over the prospect of a bookshelf but the next day felt uninterested again.

It is unfair to him. He wants to make a home with her, and she does too; she just doesn't know how. And so she has spent all her hours in the office, poring over the case. She has given this all her energy, determined to save at least one family, even though it's not hers.

Now she is standing in a big old flat that she refuses to decorate because she doesn't know who she is anymore, so how is she expected to know what she likes? And anyway, how do you hold on to who you are without your family around to remind you?

4:15 in the morning and Malak can still hear Cairo beyond the windows; a dog whimpering, a baby crying, and the occasional shout of a beggar. She lies awake listening to his breathing, one hand on her stomach, the other resting behind her head as the clock on the dressing table flashes that it is too early to get up. She slides out of bed anyway, careful not to disturb Ali, and tiptoes to the sitting room. She flicks the kitchen light on and boils the kettle just in case he wakes and she needs an alibi, and then sits on the sofa with her laptop, blinking as the screen jumps into life. Just like she does every night, she types questions into the search bar and looks for answers. So far, she has searched how quickly they can get married in Egypt and what license they need to get. She's looked into the cost of nurseries and schools here. How much money she'll need for strollers and cribs. She's searched baby names extensively, both for a boy and a girl, as well as making a list of rare names that could be either. She's even searched "how to tell your boyfriend you're pregnant," and all the ways to surprise a man with great news. She researches how many weeks pregnancy is and how small a premature baby is. She counts dates on her fingers and wonders if she can fool her parents. Probably not, but once a ring is on her finger and a baby in the cradle, who will care really?

She lets her hand rest on her stomach more now, although she has to remember not to do it around other people. Her back aches every day and she thinks how strange that is because the baby is only the size of a bean.

She also researches whether abortion is legal in Egypt and finds out it's not. She spends hours scrolling through forums looking for women who know women who can help. Some look so unsafe she doesn't even follow a lead, and others she sends messages out to, asking for guidance. She looks up flights to go back home and researches the abortion process in the UK and how long it takes to get an appointment. She finds the one local to her family home and puts her name on the waiting list even though she doesn't have a ticket to go home. She also searches stories of women who have had babies with angry men but doesn't find any answers. The results are always filled with beatings and bruised faces and that has never been her, so they are unhelpful.

Every night, before she climbs back into bed with Ali, she deletes her search history, erasing the evidence of a woman caught between a man's jaws and a mother's instinct.

Last year they had spoken about baby names during one of their trips to the desert, arguing over whether the boy would be called Ismail or Adam.

"Of course, it has to be Ismail," Ali had argued. "It's such an Islamic name and everyone will know he's Muslim. I want the world to know my kids are Muslim, that's important to me."

She had thought it was one of the most beautiful sentiments at the time. Whenever she had conversations with Jacob about whether he believed in God, he would always comment on the improbability of it, as opposed to the miracle of it all. Malak and Ali had had sex under the stars that night, drunk on the idea of children and a life that was waiting for them.

Now it was here, growing in her belly, against all the odds and all the pills, and she couldn't stop careening between life and death.

When she was researching, she would occasionally look up to glance at the hole in the wall Ali's phone had made during their first big fight and wonder what that might mean to a child. But then she always remembered that Ali had never actually hit her with his own hands and wouldn't touch their child. He was great with children, better than her. She always loved watching him with his nephews or the latest baby in his family cradled in his arm as he discussed politics with his cousins and it was the same feeling she got when he melted into softness after a fight; as if she was momentarily looking through a window at the man he could become and the potential that lived inside him.

Potential, she had discovered, was a powerful drug and this creature uncurling itself in her womb had such great potential.

After so much research and so many questions, the decision eventually came to her all at once when Ali arrived home from a late night at work.

She has one minute to send this message and is unsure if the number is still the same, so she opens her inbox and writes a hurried email instead—*Can you come? It's urgent*—before closing the laptop, a second before Ali takes her hand and leads her into the bedroom.

He is topless and kissing her, hurriedly lifting her dress and then spinning her around so she is bent over in front of him, arms resting on the window ledge. "My bad, bad girl," he pants, already sliding himself in and out of her, the only time he is happy for her to be bad.

"Do you like that? Do you like that?" he asks, and she replies, "Yes, God yes." He doesn't see the way she stares out across the city, her well-placed moans meeting the cries of other Egyptians, all struggling and groaning, desperately working toward a better life.

BILQUIS

Ambition is an addict's game. Nothing is ever enough. Once you've fulfilled one goal or dream, you're already looking for the next hit. The high is so brief it's a wonder anyone strives for it at all.

Kees has been a slave to ambition for years. She has a quote about striving for greatness on the lock screen of her phone. She has spent too many childhood days with her father talking about the rise of poor people in politics and leadership when she should have been running in the garden. But now as she sits outside the courtroom hours after convincing a jury that another brown boy didn't need to be locked up for a crime he didn't commit, she feels none of the high that should come with winning.

"And against the odds! What a first case to have under your belt, congratulations," Nina had said, hugging her tightly at the end once the judge had receded to chambers. "Your hard work paid off. Drinks in the Pleasance to celebrate, everyone will be there."

"I'll be over shortly. I just need to finish some filing," she'd replied.

Nina had laughed. "Still working. Never stops, eh?"

"You tell me?" she asked.

Nina just shook her head, smiling. "Never. Not once. Welcome to the law, it's relentless."

Kees had smiled and waved her away, promising to follow, but that was two hours ago. Since then she'd sat on the bench outside the courtroom watching the final session of the day start, wishing that someone had told her that ambition wouldn't fill her, but rather empty her. No one had said that the hustle and the grind directly translated as sacrificing every inch of your happiness, sanity, and probably your personal relationships. She has barely seen Harry since the nikah, and sex has become a thing of the past. They're living in an empty house and she avoids talking about it. The energy she once put into her relationship has been diverted to her work and it's paid off. She won. Reunited a mother with her son. Kept a family together. And it hasn't made her feel better. At least, it doesn't feel like she thought it would: jubilant and on top of the world. She wants to call her father and tell him that, finally, after so many years of them discussing her dreams of becoming a lawyer, she has won her very first case. The emptiness in her chest is heavy and she is unable to move, rooted to the bench wondering if love is really enough, and can one man ever take the place of four other family members and an entire community?

The daylight is fading when her phone vibrates and she pulls it out to find Malak's email across her screen, so short it fits in the preview: *Can you come? It's urgent.*

She stares at it for twenty minutes. They haven't spoken in a year and a half. Why would she email that? What could have happened? Has a family member died? She would come back for that, not ask her to go to Egypt.

It says nothing but Kees realizes she doesn't need it to say more. Some things cannot be erased and, despite their recent silence, the years still count for something. She knows this woman, knows this message was desperately sent, and in an instant Kees knows that Malak is asking her to fly across the ocean and help her.

Fuck.

She pulls her laptop out of her bag and books the last flight from Gatwick that night, drawing the £600 from her savings account. She has been putting money aside every month, trying to work out how she can get her parents to accept it. Her father's torn jacket appears in her mind at least fourteen times a day.

She runs down the steps of the courtroom and turns toward the tube station, simultaneously cursing Malak while feeling slightly panicked.

Jenna, pick up, pick up.

"You'd better not be calling to tell me you're not coming to my wedding, Keesy," answers Jenna.

"Is this how you always pick up the phone, with threats?" Kees sounds like her mother and while the association at present feels comforting, it doesn't stop her from shuddering.

"Well?" asks Jenna again.

"Malak emailed me."

There is a sharp intake of breath. "What did she say?"

"'Can you come? It's urgent.'"

"Is that it?" asks Jenna. "What does that mean?"

"I was hoping you'd have an idea, Jenna," says Kees, exasperated. How Jenna always seemed to wind her up immediately never fails to astound her.

"Why didn't she message me?" asks Jenna, sounding hurt.

"What?"

"Well, why didn't she ask me to come too?"

"For God's sake, Jenna," says Kees, impatiently. "That's not important right now. Our friend clearly needs help and I'm asking if you know anything."

"You guys haven't even talked for a year," says Jenna, quietly. Kees can hear the rejection in her voice and softens.

"It's been a year and a half, actually."

Jenna is quiet. Kees knows she shouldn't have said that.

She tries to put some empathy in her voice. "Babes, you were with her in Cairo not that long ago. Was there anything she said? Any ideas you might have about what's going on?"

"It was three months ago, Kees," replies Jenna. She's still hurt. "A lot can happen."

"Clearly!"

"What are you going to do?" Jenna asks.

"I've booked a ticket, my flight is later tonight."

She can hear Jenna sit up with excitement. "Shall I come? I can book the same flight as you."

"Jenna, it's Wednesday."

"So?"

"Your wedding is on Saturday," she says, patiently. "That's probably why she didn't ask you to come."

"Oh yeah, I forgot about that," Jenna replies glumly, and Kees *knows* something is wrong with Jenna.

Then, in the next second, all the brightness of the Jenna she recognizes pulses down the phone line.

"Okay, go and help our friend. Send updates. If you need any money, just shout."

"Jenna," sighs Kees.

"Don't argue, babes," Jenna chirps, dismissively. "You're an ethical lawyer holding on to your morals, which means you're broke as fuck. And if even after marriage you're holding on to some stupid idea about not taking money off Harry, then you'll need some cash flow. Taking money from a guy is one thing, but from your best friend who's practically your sister, that's different."

Kees doesn't say anything.

"Hey," says Jenna softly. "I know we haven't talked much this last year, but that changes nothing."

"I know," mumbles Kees. "I'm sorry, Jenna, for not being around."

"No apologies. I've been gone too. Just go sort out Malak, she needs you. Don't forget, call me if you need cash; I can transfer you some."

"I will, thank you."

They both know she never will. If there's one thing Kees can't ask for, it is money. She hangs up and finally goes underground, rushing to get home, already making a list of the things she needs to pack. On the train she emails HR and her line manager saying she needs a few days off, family emergency. She knows they'll give it to her. The lists are forming in her head, the adrenaline is back. She tries to ignore how exhilarating it is to be wanted, no, needed, by someone who has known you since childhood and therefore comes so tantalizingly close to family. By the time she rushes back above ground, taking the stairs two at a time, Jenna has texted her to say she's booked a car to pick her up in a few hours and drive her to the airport, taking costs out of Kees's hands where she can.

It's one of the few times Kees has been on a plane and if she wasn't so panicked, gulping down the fear in her stomach along with three cans of Coke, she would be excited.

When she had called Harry to tell him that she was getting on a plane, the first question he had asked when he picked up the phone was "Did you win?"

She had already forgotten about the court case after being consumed by it for months and she kicked herself for forgetting to message him.

"Oh yeah, we did, sorry. I forgot to tell you."

Harry was silent then and she realized for the second time that day that she should hold her tongue sometimes.

"Oh. Okay, then," he replied, flat and suddenly faraway.

When she had told him that she was home packing to then get on a flight in a few hours, he was silent again.

"She needs me," Kees had said quietly. "She's one of my best friends."

"You haven't talked in a year and a half."

That had annoyed her, far more than when Jenna had said it. Why did men always assume that just because women didn't talk to one another they weren't friends? The simplicity of male relationships and the transactional manner with which they were conducted was an entirely stupid basis for friendship, as far as she was concerned.

"That doesn't mean we're not friends or that she doesn't need my help, Harry," she had replied, tersely.

His heavy sigh down the phone line was his only response to that.

"Do you need me to come and drive you to the airport?"

"No, thank you. Jenna has already ordered a car and I think she wants to help, so I'd best let her."

"Of course, the three of you have it all sorted, as per usual."

"Harry!" she exclaimed, surprised at his sharpness.

"I have to get back to work, Kees. Just because we're not all getting marginalized youths out of prison doesn't mean my work isn't important. I'll see you whenever you decide to stop saving other people and give yourself the same privilege."

He had hung up and Kees had stared at her phone in shock. His snarky comment was long overdue. He had borne the last few months with a humbling patience that she probably didn't acknowledge because she felt ashamed that she didn't possess the same.

Kees is about to start composing an apology message to Harry when tiredness rolls up around her, the last thought she has before she falls asleep is that she only had two and a half hours' sleep last night and barely any that week.

She only wakes up again once the plane hits the tarmac, punching her out of a sleep so deep she is surprised she managed it in such a cramped space.

As she waits for her bags, she is nervous for the first time, a fluttering around the edges of her stomach reminding her that she will shortly walk out and search for the face of a woman she hasn't spoken to in nearly two years. The only reply she has given to Malak's email is a screenshot of her flight details.

In return, Malak replied that she will be waiting at the airport to pick her up. One sentence, that had been it. It didn't even constitute a conversation. Despite her nerves, it has never occurred to Kees that she shouldn't have come. While she waits, she writes Harry a message to say she's landed, and that she's sorry for the last few months. That she will make it up to him when she gets back home. His reply is brief, an indication of how upset he's been.

The minute she walks out through the arrival doors she is hit with a noisy crowd but then sees Malak, craning her neck to look for her. In the few seconds before Malak notices her, Kees stares at her friend, surprised to see the changes that Jenna had briefly told her about. She said Malak looked well but that seemed like a gross understatement. Even in a baggy maxi dress that hangs to her ankles and covers her figure, Kees can see how much weight Malak has lost. Her skin is four shades darker than it ever has been and seems to radiate a glow that she imagines comes from living under an African sun for the last year and a half. She looks more than well; she looks incredible.

Kees is suddenly aware that for months she has barely seen natural light, let alone sunlight, and quickly she pulls her sweater further down over the weight she knows she's put on her stomach, just as Malak catches sight of her and waves.

As she steps up to her, there is a moment when they stare at each other before quickly pulling one another into an awkward embrace. Had she been a better friend at that moment, or less suddenly conscious of the heaviness of her own body, Kees might have held Malak more tightly, squeezing her reassuringly, but she quickly lets her go as soon as it is acceptable.

"Thank you for coming," Malak says, taking her suitcase and wheeling it behind her.

Kees follows her, trying to take the suitcase back, but Malak just waves her away. "Are you going to tell me what's going on?" she asks.

Malak nods. "Yes. But not here. We're driving out of the city, staying in the desert for the night. It's a long drive, I hope you don't mind."

"Sounds ominous." Kees shrugs.

Malak smiles then. "It's not. It's just so beautiful out there and it's one of my favorite places. I wanted to show you a little bit of this place. Plus, we won't be disturbed out there and the city is too noisy."

The drive is five hours and despite wanting to stay awake, Kees sleeps some more. More than she has slept in months.

The next time she wakes it is to Malak's hand on her shoulder, gently shaking her awake. She wipes her mouth with the back of her hand.

"We're here, babe," says Malak.

"Oh God, I'm so sorry, I can't believe I slept through all of that. I don't know what happened, I just suddenly felt so tired."

She stumbles out of the car into the afternoon sun, gasping as she looks around her.

There is nothing around them but Malak's car and three white tents. Other than that, the only structure is six or seven sand-colored rock formations. Everywhere she looks is rolling white sand that rises and falls as the landscape dips up and down.

"It's beautiful, isn't it?" Malak is looking at her shocked face.

"It's unbelievable. No wonder you haven't come back to England yet. I spend my days crowded in with millions of other Londoners and God knows why when you're out here with all this space."

Malak laughs and shakes her head. "Trust me, Cairo is way more crowded than London. You can't breathe there, which is why we need the desert, to get some respite every now and then."

She nods toward the closest tent. "That one is ours, I'm afraid we're sharing, the big one is for eating and relaxing in, and the other tent is for the workers."

"Workers?" Kees asks.

She hadn't even noticed that someone had taken her bags and already set them in the tent, and now a woman wearing a black headscarf loosely around her head and a long red skirt approaches them with a tray, two glasses of what looks like orange juice balancing in its center.

She replies, "Assalamualaikum," in response to her greeting, taking a glass, surprised to find it is mango juice.

Malak stares at her while she drinks, looks around nervously, is about to say something, but a bright smile flashes across her face instead.

"Okay, it's almost the hottest part of the day so I'm going to take a nap, and I think you could use the sleep as well," says

Malak, gesturing for her to follow her into the tent, which is surprisingly more spacious than the outside suggests.

"Honestly, Malak, I'm fine. Are you going to tell me what the hell is going on?"

Malak looks deflated for a second but then her shoulders straighten. "Of course I am, but I've just driven five hours and I'm exhausted, and you've traveled all night in a car and on an airplane. The guide will take you, if you want to go for a walk, but I need a nap."

Malak is already yawning, lying back against the thin mattress that is spread out across a thickly woven rug in the center of the tent.

The heat of the day seems to pull Kees down next to her and the last thing she hears before falling asleep is Malak saying it is good to see her.

She hopes she replied.

Malak's phone hasn't stopped lighting up since she pressed send on the message to Ali this afternoon: a single text to tell him that she is pregnant, and going to stay the night in the desert with a friend, and then she had stared at the phone in fear as he called, texted, called again, left voicemails and a string of voice notes, all of which she hadn't listened to or opened. She had purposely switched off the preview on her phone so that she wouldn't even be able to read the first few sentences. She didn't want to know.

She had sent it while Kees was sleeping next to her as she waited for the benzina to fill up the tank, just before they hit the desert road. Texting her boyfriend to tell him that she was pregnant and then ignoring his calls was not what any of the articles she had read advised. Most of them involved her cooking an elaborate dinner that was laid out among candles for his return home, and then handing him some corny homemade cake (that she would, of course, have baked) with the message, "You're going to be a daddy" scrawled somewhere on it. She had laughed when she'd seen that. Why should he get such a beautiful reveal when she had to find out panicked at school because she couldn't stop throwing up over the toilet bowl? So although her fingers had trembled when she had typed her single-sentence message, she continued driving, keeping the phone on her leg, watching it light up constantly, unable to peel her eyes from it like a horror film she had to see the end of, until the battery died. She'd then plugged it into the car charger and watched it light up once more as Ali's calls continued.

Kees sleeping in the passenger seat made everything feel better and worse at the same time. It was like stepping back in time to the comfort of her best friend and a small corner of her stomach felt calmer to have her here. On the other hand, she had dragged her friend here for a reason, and it wasn't a girls' trip, it was to help her ruin her life so, really, her presence wasn't that comforting.

By the time they had reached the tents the signal was gone, which was one of the reasons she had wanted to come out here. She wanted him to know that she was unreachable. She wanted him to stare at one tick not two. She also wanted to have as much space between them as she could muster, at least for now. She still compulsively picked up her phone every few minutes to see if anything had come through.

She brushes her wet hair and feels Kees stir behind her. She was shocked when she saw her and how rough she looked. Kees had always been slim, but somewhere in the last year and a half she has ballooned outward, her face slightly puffy, her skin ashy and unkept, the bags under her eyes dragging her whole face down. It hasn't taken away her looks. Malak has always marveled at how Kees's beauty needs very little upkeep, and it isn't the extra pounds that surprised her, but rather the way her shoulders drooped and how sadness seemed etched into new lines on her face.

Kees was not like Jenna. She had never laughed in the same easy way and had always been more serious than both of them, but she used to be happy and confident. Now Malak couldn't see any of that in her. Something had left and, in its place, was tiredness, worry, and heartbreak. She wants to hold on to Kees's shoulders and pull the truth out of her but fretting with worry over Kees was never the way to get results. She feels frustrated that Jenna hadn't mentioned anything and makes a mental note to reprimand her about it.

"Oh God, how long have I been asleep?" Kees asks, groaning.

"It's fine." Malak smiles. "I only just woke up twenty minutes ago." She had resisted the urge to crawl up behind Kees's body the way they used to, and sleep for the rest of the night.

"There's a shower here?" Kees asks hopefully, taking in Malak's wet hair and towel.

"No way," Malak laughs. "But there is a bucket of water, if you're determined?"

Kees rubs the sleep from her eyes. "Can you imagine telling Jenna to shower in a bucket?"

They both laugh at the thought, nervously looking at each other, and life suddenly rotates a little smoother on its axis.

By the time Kees joins her in the food tent she looks much better than when she had stepped off the plane, but she still isn't the woman Malak knows. However, she is on borrowed time and doesn't have the chance to ask Kees why she looks so devastated. She swallows the lump that seems to have taken permanent residency in her throat, bites her nails quickly before snapping her fingers out of her mouth, and as Kees is about to sit down, she quickly blurts out, "I'm pregnant, Kees, and I'm not keeping it and I think I need to leave my boyfriend."

Kees lands with an ungraceful thud next to her, curling her feet beneath her, cross-legged, and is about to open her mouth before Malak holds up her hand. She might as well get it all over with in one quick burst.

"He's not very nice. He doesn't hit me, but he throws things at me. He can be cruel. I love him, Kees. I think we could work it out, but I don't think that's the right thing. I've got an appointment booked for Saturday afternoon back home. For the abortion, that is. I need to get back in time. I need your help, Kees, and I know it's been a year and a half since we spoke and if I'm honest, I don't know why we didn't because none of that petty shit seems important anymore, although it must have felt important at the time but I didn't know who else to call. Jenna is getting married on Saturday." She laughs at this last point, not because anything is funny, but because she has somehow made the terrible things coming out of her mouth sound casual, unimportant, random; otherwise, she might not find the strength she needs for what comes next. She might prefer to crumble under the weight of it all.

Kees's mouth hangs open. The breeze that had previously blown through the tent has disappeared. Mohammed, the toothless old chef, pokes his head around the corner and says something about the sunset, beckoning the two of them out.

"Come," she says, holding out her hand to Kees, "the sunset here is spectacular, you can't come all this way and miss it."

And so she leads a speechless Kees, who still hasn't managed to say anything, out of the tent and up the short walk to the top of the sand dune and they watch the sun blaze into a ball of fire, throwing pink and orange jets across the sky, all the more brilliant because there is nothing but the dunes reflecting the light and the wide-open space creating an endless canvas of possible art.

"Look," she points up at the sky, and Kees wordlessly turns her face toward the light, wrapping one arm around Malak's waist as she does, pulling her in close. They stand like this for the entire sunset, saying nothing, just watching the sun sink into the other side of the world, the three of them wrapped around one another: Malak, Kees, and the child she's not going to have, until eventually there is nothing left but purple dusk.

BILQUIS

What she eats that night she'll never be able to fully describe. It looks incredible; small bowls with navy-blue and white patterns winding around them filled to the brim with hummus and salad, fried eggplant, and perfectly wrapped waraainab. At the center is a platter of fish, surrounded by lemons and served on a bed of zucchini and peppers, a steaming pan of rice next to it. The smell of the dishes fills the tent and although she keeps putting the different flavors in her mouth that Malak passes her, she can't remember the taste.

At one point, as Malak laughs over a joke the chef must have made and calmly hands her another dish, urging her to try it because it was "to die for and the best kibbah in Egypt," Kees wants to shake her and ask how she can act so calm and collected after everything she had just revealed.

Get yourself together, woman, she thinks. *Malak needs you and dissolving into Jenna-like behavior is not what she needs.*

She waits for Mohammed to leave the tent and then takes a deep breath. "Okay, tell me everything, from the very beginning."

She says nothing while she listens as Malak launches into the story about how she met Ali and their life together here, as if reading from a textbook; deadpan and without much emotion.

When Malak tells her about their first big fight, she seems to crumple into herself, the first glimmer of emotion clouding her face as she turns her head away in embarrassment when she says the word "whore" and how Ali had screamed it so loudly she was afraid the neighbors would hear. She then tells her about the first plate and how it smashed off her elbow leaving a scar running up her right arm with a calm detachment as if reciting a shopping list and she doesn't shudder or blink, even though Kees feels nauseous at the thought of it.

It's when Malak describes the way her boyfriend whispers that she's dirty and slutty that her shoulders sink and her eyes lower so she can't look directly at Kees, shuddering slightly. Malak then lists one terrible thing after the other, slowly at first, like a dam beginning to burst, and then suddenly and quickly all at once: how he told her that he couldn't marry a whore because the woman who raised his children would have to be beyond reproach; how he had sat, cup of tea in hand, and watched her pack her suitcase for their holiday in Dahab, agreeing and veto-ing each outfit as she tried them on for his approval before it got packed; how he sometimes slept in the guest bedroom because he said she disgusted him; how he would make her shower after sex before coming to bed because she was dirty; how he wouldn't let her touch him when she was on her period, unless it was to give him a blow job and then he didn't mind; how sometimes she gave him a blow job just to feel close to him; how he had told her off on the beach for pulling her bikini down a little and how he had hissed that she was lucky he even let her wear one in the first place; how he had seen her place a kiss at the end of a text message to a male friend and screamed at her in the middle of the street and how she had pleaded and said whatever she could to make him stop because she thought she might die of the shame; how he would often smile at her and sympathetically tell her she just didn't know as much as he did and that was okay; how he would stare at her while she dressed, often telling her that she needed to be careful or go to the gym a couple more times this week; how he would send her pictures of models or actresses and ask that she copy their style; how sometimes he called her secondhand because she had lost her virginity to Jacob; how she spent every moment of her day tentatively feeling out what kind of mood he was in and the ways in which she'd have to bend herself to make him happy. How sometimes, before she'd even opened her eyes, she would know he was in a bad mood and then she would wake to the devil beside her; how he had kicked the table so hard because he was angry at her that he broke three of his toes; how the punch mark on the wall made her shiver and how he had bought four new phones during their relationship because in a rage he had smashed them all, off the wall, the cupboards, and, once, her head. As she says this, she lifts the right side of her part to show a faint white scar running along her scalp, so thin it was almost invisible. Almost, but not quite.

All of this Malak delivers with her eyes averted, but when she tells Kees that Ali screamed at her for loving Jacob, Kees sees her first tears fall.

"He asked me how I could have done it. Given myself away to someone like that, especially since he wasn't Muslim, and do you know what the worst part about it was?" asks Malak.

Kees shakes her head.

"I apologized," says Malak. She laughs but the tears are falling faster now. "I apologized for losing my virginity to the man I loved more than anything else. Begged for his forgiveness as if he was God. And I meant it. I wished I'd never met Jacob and thought about how nice it would have been to have come untouched to Ali. So he could have been the first and I could marry him with my number only ever being one. I thought it was romantic. And every night I'd give myself to him in the hope that it could make him forget. That if I tried hard enough, I might forget too."

"And did he?" Kees asks, passing Malak a napkin.

"Never," Malak replies. "At some point, it would come back up. Sometimes he'd shove me awake and tell me I was saying Jacob's name in my sleep. He never lets me forget that I've been with someone before him."

Of all the books Kees has read, and all the lectures she has attended, no one has ever taught her how you react when your childhood friend tells you she's been living in a war zone. She feels angry at everyone for not preparing her adequately but mostly she hates herself for only ever watching Malak online instead of messaging her. The question she wants to ask is "Why did you stay?" but that feels like blame and if she is going to go down that road, then she, in her blind stubbornness, must accept her fair share.

"So why now?" she asks instead. "What's made you decide to leave him finally? Being pregnant?"

Malak shakes her head. "Partly, but it's not the thing that made me decide to leave or have the abortion. And none of the things I've told you did it either. Funny, isn't it?" She laughs.

Kees has never found anything less funny in her life.

"There was one night," Malak continues, "the night that I emailed you. He had messaged to say he was working late, some emergency, and I had waited. When finally he came home, he kissed me and I tasted Disaronno on his mouth and knew he'd been out drinking."

"Okay?" replies Kees, confused.

"He told me he's never drunk," Malak emphasizes. "And I, of course, didn't want to seem like a total heathen, so I told him I had never drunk either and then worked my ass off to hide it. I went through Facebook and deleted all the pictures I'd ever had of me with alcohol or looking drunk."

"That's a lot of pictures," muses Kees.

"Exactly!" says Malak, standing to pace around the tent. "I told Nylah and Rayan, my friends I was living with at the time, to never let on. The minute I had that conversation I gave it up anyway. He seemed to have a real problem with it. He even hated seeing drunk people in the street. Once, I found a bottle of whiskey in the cupboard at the back of the kitchen and I asked him why it was there and he went on this huge rant about how his dad drank and how it always upset him. He poured the bottle down the sink and talked about his father all night. *All night*, Kees."

She raises her eyebrow. "I can believe it."

"And then something just clicked in me when I tasted it on his mouth," says Malak, stopping to pick up the bowl of olives, popping them into her mouth, one after the other, almost talking to the distance. "I don't know how I knew, I just did. That he drank, always had, and there I was like a fucking idiot going through thirty-three thousand, five hundred and sixty-seven pictures on Facebook to get rid of any incriminating ones of me with alcohol or even a red cup, so he'd never find it and think I was bad. And you know what?" Malak asks.

"What?"

"We're not even friends on Facebook," says Malak, bitterly. "But that's what did it. The idea that I had been deleting pictures of me holding cups or glasses, even when I knew there was no alcohol in them, just in case he ever found them and thought I was a bad Muslim. I felt like such an idiot, Kees."

"Hey," she snaps, "you are not an idiot. Don't ever say that. You've done nothing wrong."

"Oh, I've done plenty wrong," replies Malak. "I've done my fair share of shouting and screaming; he's just been worse."

That her friend thinks that any wrongdoing can be attributed to her in this is perhaps the thing that makes Kees saddest of all, and though she's never been the tactile one in the group, she stands up and sits behind Malak, wrapping her whole body around her in the hope that it might say something she can't currently find the words for.

At some point, the plates are cleared, and a campfire has been lit outside. They drink mint tea and eat konafa by the fire, a constellation above them, unlike anything Kees has ever seen. She has noticed that in the middle of the stories Malak tells her, there is a constant thread of blame woven throughout, directed at herself as if she should have known the man she trusted would turn her inside out.

As the embers glow and the last of the flames flick away, Malak leans up on her elbows and looks across at her and says, "But what about you? Because I hate to say it, but you look like shit. What's been going on?"

Kees stares at her for a moment before bursting into laughter. "THANK YOU!" she exclaims. "I've been saying that, but everyone keeps telling me I look great. Thank you for just saying it."

"No, babe, they're lying to you. Your skin practically looks sallow, like you've got jaundice or something. You're not ill, are you?"

"No," Kees laughs in reply. "I've just not been taking care of myself."

"Why?" asks Malak, and so Kees, in turn, tells her everything. About her mother and the night she told her parents about Harry and how it had felt like having a front-row ticket to her own apocalypse. About the nikah with all Harry's white family and how the imam had canceled but, oddly enough, her father had saved the day, yet how it had still been the worst day of her life. How their flat was gifted to them and it makes her feel like she's an imposter in her own home. How she doesn't know if love is enough, and how she can feel herself pulling away from him. About how she often feels irrationally angry toward him because he still has his family and maybe they were too different, and it can never work.

As she says this, Malak sits up, throwing one of the cushions off her head.

"Hey. Don't you dare," she says, pointing across the fire pit at her.

"Ow! What's wrong with you?"

"Don't you dare break up with him," she repeats.

Kees sighs. "I'm not going to, Malak, but I just don't know how to be happy about it when it's the one thing that has ruined my family."

"Do you know why I was so angry with you that night? The night we had that fight?" asks Malak, twisting the tassels from the cushion she was leaning against around her fingers.

Kees shakes her head, tentatively looking at Malak.

"You made me believe that if I wanted to, I could have had it all. I could have stayed with Jacob after all, but that I just wasn't brave enough to do it."

"Malak, I didn't mean that—"

"No, don't," interrupts Malak. "You were right. I wasn't brave enough. I didn't have your courage. And it could have been done. Sure, my parents would have been gutted, but have you ever known my father to be mad at anyone past sixty seconds? They would have come round. It was everyone else I couldn't stand up to. The Aunty Naseemas and Um Munthers. The Noras and Zaynebs who were married already to perfect Muslim boys.

I couldn't stand to not be one of them. And then I met Ali and finally I had it, was living the dream, and the night he smashed the plate off my arm I wondered, where were they? All the aunties that told me I had to be with a good Muslim boy who ended up using my body like target practice, and I compared it to Jacob, who couldn't even spank me during sex because he said any violence against women made him so uncomfortable, and it made me so angry at them, but also at you."

"At me?" Kees yelps.

"Yes. Because you knew. You knew all along."

"Oh, Malak," she sighs. "I didn't know this. I didn't know you would fall for someone who would treat you like that."

Malak smiles at her. "Maybe not. But somehow you knew that it was all fake. That it wasn't worth giving up love for. And I was still fighting for that perfect dream, the good Muslim life, and I would have given anything to have it. I did. I gave Jacob. And then myself. And look at me now." She shakes her head repeatedly. It reminds Kees of when they were ten and had trashed the school kitchen out of sheer boredom to make it look like there had been a robbery, an idea that Malak had come up with, and as they had sat with their legs dangling from chairs outside the headmaster's office, she had kept shaking her head back and forth in despair saying, "What have I done?" over and over again. Watching the same tiny gesture, Kees feels her heart crack. She wants to hold her still and shout that she has done nothing.

"I was winning the game and thought I had proved you wrong," continues Malak. "And then it started to fall apart and I didn't know how to call and say that you were right all along. I didn't even know how to admit it to myself. And now I have a baby growing in my belly that I can never have, not with him, and I just wish I had called you sooner."

Kees stands and pulls Malak to her feet, hugging her, before holding her at arm's length in front of her.

"No, I'm sorry. I felt like you'd abandoned me, and I was angry and proud. You know I've never been good at saying sorry."

"You're actually the worst person in the world when it comes to apologies," sniffs Malak.

"Fine, I'm terrible at saying sorry. But I should have. To you. Ages ago. And for what it's worth now, I'm so sorry, Malak. For failing you."

"Come on, you didn't—"

"Yes, I did," she interrupts firmly. "I absolutely did. And had I not been so proud I would have been around and maybe I could have done something before it got to this stage. Forgive me."

"If you'll forgive me," replies Malak, drawing her back to her chest.

They stay like this for twenty minutes, maybe more, locked in all the embraces they hadn't had over the last year and a half. They lie down in the sand and stare at the stars, little fingers intertwined the way they used to when they were girls. They talk about Jenna and send her kisses on the stars. Sometimes they cry and other times they're caught in laughter that borders on hysterical. How the balance of the universe can tip so completely in the wrong direction. The sky lightens and they climb the dune once more, this time to watch the sunrise. They rest heads against each other, a full circle, from sundown to sunup, complete. Only then do they fall exhausted into their tent. The last thing Kees says is "I'm going to sort everything out, Malak, I promise," and in response, Malak whispers, "I know."

Before Kees falls asleep, she does that thing women do when they hear about the wreckage another woman has survived at the hands of a man. She drafts a message to Harry, telling him how grateful she is for him. That she is thankful she chose him and reminds herself that their love is enough. That love like theirs is a one-time thing. That most men are cruel or thoughtless or careless or just plain mean. That a lot of men want to watch things burn, including women. That he may think too much and not say enough, but he is always thinking of her, and that he is kind, and a kind man is no small thing. And that, in every lifetime, she'd choose him.

Whatever magic got them through the night is gone when they wake. Malak is nervous, worried about going back.

Kees has gone into lawyer mode by the time they're back in the car and on the road, asking Malak a string of questions, trying to compile as much information as she can.

"Does he know you're pregnant?"

"Yes, but he doesn't know I'm not having it. I have to be back for that appointment, Kees. It's the last one I can get before it's too late to do the procedure."

"Don't you worry, I'll get you there."

"What about Jenna's wedding?" she asks, nervously.

"I think she'll understand," she replies.

Malak nods.

"Will he be at home?" Kees asks.

"Depends on what time we get back. It's the weekend, so he might be at juma, but if not, he'll be home."

Kees sends Harry a string of text messages roughly explaining the situation but not going into detail.

She sends Jenna another string of messages explaining the situation a little more and asks for her financial help, for the first time not feeling ashamed about it. She'd do anything to get Malak safe and back home. She tells Jenna to book them two tickets tonight on the last flight out.

By the time they hit the edges of the city, Jenna has sent her flight confirmation, 10:30 p.m. tonight, first class.

God bless that girl and her father's money, she thinks.

Harry has replied with a long message declaring his love and something firmly slots into place in her stomach: the re-assurance that she is loved by the person she loves most in the world.

She sends Harry their flight details for Saturday morning and he promises to be there to pick them up and reminds her to be safe today.

She nods to herself, the tears of the previous night dried and washed away.

By the time Malak pulls up outside the flat, she hates herself. She has spent the hours on the road internally berating herself for acting too rashly, for calling Kees when she shouldn't have. The city envelops her with its friendly noise, the familiar smell of jasmine floating above her, and she remembers that you can love the messy and the chaotic. That Ali's love is some of the softest she's ever known and who is she to think herself above the labor and toil of relationships? "They are hard work" is what everyone says. A wave of sickness hits her and, instinctively, she places her hand on her stomach and everything shifts again. She remembers not to hate herself.

She had called Haytham on the way because he's the one family member she can't bear to leave without saying goodbye.

As she pushes the door open, she instinctively knows the flat is empty.

"He's not here," she whispers.

"Okay," Kees nods, "let's pack your stuff."

She still creeps through the apartment and checks every room, just in case, the familiar scents of home greeting her.

She hears his key in the lock as they're midway through emptying her wardrobe, packing essential and favorite clothes into the suitcase, the rest into a bin bag for rubbish, and she walks to the door to greet him because that's what she's always done.

He stares at her without seeing Kees, who has followed behind, too nervous to let Malak out of her sight.

"Are you okay?" he asks, frowning in worry.

She nods because her throat is suddenly dry.

"Hayati, why didn't you tell me about the baby?"

She shrugs and feels adrift because of the softness of his voice. Something in her shoulders droops as he crosses the final distance and takes her in his arms murmuring gently above the top of her head. She indulges in the moment, allows doubt to swim through her one more time.

He sees Kees then and steps back in alarm.

"This is Kees," says Malak quickly, gesturing for her to come forward. She says nothing, just nods at him.

"Hi, I've heard so much about you. I didn't realize you were visiting."

"Neither did I," she replies coolly.

Ali looks at Malak, confused, and once more she feels like a ship without an anchor.

"Can you give us a minute, Keesy?" she asks, nodding back toward the bedroom.

"Is that a good idea?" she replies pointedly.

Malak sighs, wondering if she should have asked Jenna to come. Everything is less confrontational with Jenna and standing opposite Ali makes her want to fold instead of fight. "Yes, it is."

"Okay, but I'll just be right over here if you need me."

As Kees walks back toward the bedroom, Ali looks at her again, confusion flashing across his face.

"I have to go back home," she says, in a voice that is too uncertain, too afraid to hold steady. The tremble is audible to them both.

"What's wrong, Kookie? Is your family okay? Has something happened?" He steps back toward her, picking up her hands.

All the words seem to have stopped somewhere in her throat and she looks at him searchingly, wondering how he doesn't know that she can't stay, that nothing is right. It makes her feel unhinged, as if all the problems and the smashed crockery have either been a figment of her imagination or just a normal byproduct of relationships that she is lazily opting out of. There is always more work that can be done and perhaps she could sweat more and work harder.

He is still talking and as she tunes back in to what he's saying, she realizes he's smiling and discussing baby names, and something in his grin makes her feel sick, so she takes a step back.

"I'm not keeping the baby, Ali." The words fall out of her mouth like small bombs.

He stares at her dumbly. "What do you mean, not keeping it?"

"I don't want to raise a baby by myself."

"Why would you be raising the baby by yourself?" he asks, and she wants to scream at him for making this harder, for being so intelligent but not understanding anything.

"Because I'm leaving. You. This. Whatever we're doing here. It's done."

It is his turn to take a step back. "What we're doing here is a relationship, Malak," he replies, coldly.

"People don't lie in relationships, Ali. You're not supposed to lie to the person you're with."

"What are you talking about? I would never lie to you."

Before he can say anything else, she interrupts him. "You drink, don't you?"

By the look on his face, it's clear it's the last thing he expected her to say.

She continues. "I told you the truth about how many people I had slept with because honesty is important. And you punished me for it. Over and over again. But you drink." She laughs now and it's the first time she's felt truly reckless in front of him. "I'm an idiot for even telling you the truth when you've been lying all along."

"Malak, these are not things you end a relationship over," he replies, in exasperation. It is the same patronizing tone he uses when he's talking about politics or anything he believes he knows more about and it makes her want to scream.

"You're not always nice to me," she replies, and he laughs.

"I look after you. Protect you. You are my only concern." He is looking at her like she's mad and she thinks for a split-second that maybe she is.

"Sometimes you—"

But he cuts her off. Like he knows what she's going to say.

He takes her face in his hands, his thumb stroking her cheek, and she remembers the first time he did that and how it had felt like coming home. "When I lose my temper and throw things, it's normal, habibti. All men feel these things. They don't matter. They're just small things. What matters is how I look after you. Don't I look after you, Kookie?"

She nods, looking down, pressing her face into his hand further, unable to meet his eyes. He's right, he does always pick her up from places, makes sure she has everything she needs, and she wants for nothing. She has the fleeting thought that they have moved on so quickly from his lies about drinking and how he admitted nothing.

Haytham knocks on the half-open door, which Ali hasn't had the chance to close yet, stepping into the flat, "*Zayokum ya gama*," he says, smiling happily. Ali turns and shakes Haytham's hand and suddenly everything happens at once.

Kees walks back into the room and sharply says, "We have to get going, Malak, we'll miss the flight."

At the same time, Haytham smiles and asks if she's traveling while Ali waves Kees off dismissively and says, "She's fine, she's not leaving."

Malak doesn't see Kees pick up the ornate plate his grandfather gave his grandmother on their wedding day, but she sees it fly across the room, narrowly missing Ali's head and shattering on the wall. She doesn't see Ali move but sees Haytham step in front of him, his hands pressed against Ali's chest to keep him at bay. She doesn't see the look on Kees's face, but she can feel the anger filling the room. Everyone's voices rise, everyone talking over each other all at once, Kees screaming about pressing charges. All Malak hears is the silence that met her when she asked Ali if he drank and how it feels like the biggest betrayal of them all.

She leaves the room and walks back to the bedroom, once more dividing her life into a suitcase.

"Are you okay?" Kees asks, rushing into the room.

"He didn't deny that he drinks," she replies, feeling dazed.

"That's because he's a piece of shit. We have to go, Malak."

She shrugs. "I don't know what to pack," she says, looking helplessly at Kees.

"Don't worry, I'll do it all." Kees's voice has turned soft as she gently pulls the dress from Malak's hand.

Malak sits on the edge of the bed trying to understand how she went from the ecstasy of a brand-new life to the broken possibilities strewn around her. She thinks about how she ended it with Jacob and now Ali and, for years, she will believe that she's incapable of staying when love arrives. She hears Ali's voice shout throughout the flat, complaining to Haytham about overemotional women. Kees keeps glancing worriedly at the door and Malak refuses to look, instead staring fixedly as Kees packs up her life like it's someone else's and has nothing to do with her. She doesn't want to see Ali burst through the door and she's afraid that he won't so her eyes flick from wardrobe to suitcase, wardrobe to suitcase.

She hadn't admitted to herself how bad things had become between her and Ali until she saw Kees's expression as she told the story. Although Kees had tried to keep her face still, Malak saw the horror flick over it and heard the slight, barely audible gasps that had escaped from her mouth. Perhaps that's why you're supposed to tell your girlfriends everything: so they can assess it with you and collectively decide if it's acceptable behavior because women can't be trusted not to give their whole selves away to the men opposite them.

She notices the talking in the living room has quieted and walks down the corridor in a daze.

Haytham is standing in the doorway, his frame, although slight, acting as a divide between her and Ali, who she can see pacing the living room, eyes wolf-like and frantic.

Kees walks up behind her, dragging two suitcases, and Haytham jumps to help her. In the gap Malak steps into the room.

"I'm going," she says, and Ali looks at her like a man who has finally found a puzzle he cannot solve.

"You're pregnant with my child" is his only response.

Haytham's head snaps around in shock and Kees quickly suggests they take the bags down to the car. Malak knew she was right to call Kees.

She nods and says nothing. He doesn't say anything either. He looks suddenly forlorn.

Instead, she says, "You do drink, don't you?"

Still he says nothing. Asks his own question instead.

"Are you really going to leave me?"

Later, she will look back on this moment and think if he had only answered the question, she truly might have stayed. If only he had acknowledged what she was so pissed off about, then maybe they would have talked about baby names.

She places her key on the table. No one says anything.

JENNA

Everything happens to her that day and she watches it like one of her favorite rom coms. She hears the movie score in her head as she steps into the wedding dress that two mothers from different families have picked. She sees the smiles on everyone's faces as they fuss around her, adding blush, another layer of lipstick, handing her a glass of water, fanning her face so the setting spray holds everything in place. She gently touches the necklace her mother clips around her neck; a diamond collar that had arrived on the doorstep that morning with a bunch of flowers, a wedding present from Mo. The note had read, "I can't wait to marry you," and she had wondered why. Was it the prospect of sex that night, the idea of a wife, or the company he longed for? Mo had sent the gift not because he saw the necklace and thought his bride might like it, but because that's what the kind of man he wanted to be would do. In truth, it wasn't really her style and she never would have picked it, but how was he supposed to know that? And so she gently touched it and smiled as it was fastened around her neck; because that's what the kind of woman she wanted to be would do.

Her parents' house has been festooned with decorations and flowers; bouquets arriving all week to congratulate her and her parents on the wedding of their daughter, their only child.

Her father knocks on the door gently and the makeup artist, hairstylist, and dress designer, who is frantically adjusting a seam on the dress with her assistant, leave the room to give them some privacy.

Her father pulls out a velvet box with a diamond bracelet inside, the date of her wedding carved along the clasp. "A gift from me to you, habibti, on your wedding day."

She wonders if this is where Mo got the idea from and holds out her wrist for her father to put it on. She hears him say beautiful things: about how proud he is of her, how excited he is for her to start her job in the hospital, and how she has always been a good daughter to them, that she is, and always has been, a credit to the family. She laughs and says, "Baba, stop, you'll make me cry and ruin my makeup," even though she doesn't feel like crying at all. He flusters and apologizes, calls the women back into the room to continue getting her ready, the only time a father is ever worried about his daughter's makeup instead of wanting to wash it off.

Once everyone has finished making up their perfect bride, her mother enters, a box beautifully wrapped under her arm. She, like her father, says things that on any other day would have made her weep, but as she is watching it happen rather than feeling it happen to her, she stays dry-eyed, reaching out to clutch her mother's hand; she had already started crying the minute she saw Jenna.

She unties the ribbon around the box to find a white silk nightgown, an intricate lace back and a train that floats behind it.

"I thought this would be nice for tonight." Her mother smiles. It is the closest they will ever come to talking about sex.

She smiles back at her. "It's beautiful. Thank you, Mama."

Her mother dries her own eyes again and wants to hug her or kiss her, but, too afraid to mess up her makeup, she pats her on the arm instead before leaving the room. Jenna is alone, staring at the transformation in front of her.

For so many months now, a feeling of nothingness has floated through her so she doesn't expect to feel anything today. She flicks open the flight tracker on her phone and watches as the plane carrying her two best friends hovers tantalizingly close to London. Against her wildest dreams, the two women she has longed for this past year are closer than ever, and yet neither of them will turn up to be with her on the biggest day of her life. If the wedding could happen without her, she would take Malak to the clinic with Kees instead. She should be there. But, instead, she will be where everyone wants her to be, dancing in the arms of the man soon to be her husband. She will soon win the game.

"Is that Lewis?" Kees asks, squinting into the distance where Harry is standing at the arrival gate.

"As in Jenna's Lewis?" asks Malak.

"Yes, Jenna's Lewis. What other Lewis do we know?"

The crowd parts and when Kees sees Harry, although he is just in a hoodie, she doesn't think he's ever looked so good. She hurls herself at him and he catches her, all the worry that he might have had enough of her melting away when she feels how tightly he holds her.

"Welcome home, baby," he whispers in her ear.

"I'm sorry I've been such a cow lately."

He laughs and they forget Malak and Lewis are beside them.

He smiles and kisses her again. "I'm glad you're back. You must be exhausted."

"As much as I hate to interrupt this lover's moment, can you two please stop doing that," interrupts Lewis, looking irritated.

Kees turns to him and grins, "Hello, Lewis. Long time no see. What are you doing here?"

"I thought you moved to Liverpool," interjects Malak, still looking confused.

"I did. I drove down last night because I need to talk to you two."

Kees knows Lewis mostly through Jenna's stories and the odd birthday party where they would inevitably get into a debate about religion, and while neither of them has ever managed to change the other's mind, a begrudging respect has bloomed between them.

Malak and Jenna have both agreed that the two get along so well only because they can argue and debate to their hearts content while everyone else eventually gives in or gives up.

"How did you even know we were here?" Kees asks him.

"Well, I tried messaging you both on Facebook, but you didn't answer."

"My notifications are off," says Malak.

"Are we even connected on Facebook?" puzzles Kees. "I never go on there."

"Yeah, I know, check it every once in a while, Kees."

She's taken aback by his irritation but before she can say anything he continues.

"I messaged Harry in the end and he told me you were out of the country and arriving today, so I thought the quickest way to talk to you was to turn up here."

"So, what's the emergency?" asks Malak, frowning at him.

"Jenna can't get married," he blurts out, shoving his hands in his pockets before taking them out and crossing his arms defensively.

"Oh, for fuck's sake," snaps Kees, a nascent theory coming to her in a rush.

"What do you mean?" Malak places a soothing hand on Kees's arm.

Harry says nothing and she guesses he's already heard this story.

Lewis just shrugs. "It's the truth."

"Yes, but why?" stresses Malak, trying to roll her suitcase out of the way of a family with too many carts.

"I'll tell you why," says Kees, interrupting him. "Because he's going to come out with some completely ridiculous statement about how he loves Jenna and despite having about seven fucking years to arrive at this conclusion, he's just realized it now and wants our help to stop the wedding because she is, in fact, the love of his life."

She has often asked Jenna about Lewis, but Jenna has always maintained they were just friends. Now she knows she was right. She continues, stepping threateningly close to him. "I won't have you barging into Jenna's wedding day to fuck it up for her when you had your chance years ago."

"Oh, NOW you're looking out for your friend? Where the fuck have you been the last year, Kees? Malak wasn't in the country but you live forty-five minutes from Jenna and you still didn't manage to look after her, so don't try now."

"Lewis, mate," says Harry, stepping forward.

Kees is about to say something but Lewis talks over her.

"Save it, Kees. I didn't come here to have a friendly debate, this is serious. Jenna doesn't want to marry this man, and she's doing it for all the wrong reasons."

"What are you talking about?" The irritation at not under-standing something is rising in her chest.

Lewis stares at her for a minute, before he opens his mouth again and says quietly, "She was raped. About six months ago.

That same night she messaged this Mo guy and said she wanted to be with him. She doesn't love him; I think she's just scared."

No one says anything, the three of them clutching on to the suitcases as if it could stop their stomachs from falling into the ground.

He doesn't wait for them to ask questions, just offers up the answers he knows they're searching for.

"She was on a date with some piece of shit, whose name she won't give me, and they ended up back at his. She told him to stop. Three times. But he did it anyway. I had to go with her the next day to get the morning-after pill."

Kees now understands why he looks sick.

"I told her to report it to the police but she wouldn't. She won't even call it rape. Said it was her fault for being drunk, for going back to his. I brought it up every chance I could, but you know how stubborn she is. Once she gets it into her head about something you may as well talk to the fucking wall. And then she said we couldn't be friends anymore and so I didn't even have the chance to bring it up," he finishes.

"What?" asks Kees, frowning.

"She sent me a big, long message about how this idiot she's marrying doesn't like that I'm her friend. Something about finding out how we kissed when we were younger, like that juvenile stuff even matters, but clearly because he's a sack of shit, he asked her to end the friendship."

"Jenna wouldn't do that," replies Kees, defensively, looking at Malak for confirmation, but Malak is nodding her head in horror.

"She did it," she whispers. "She told me when she was in Cairo."

Lewis nods. "She did. Some bullshit line about how she had to concentrate and prioritize her relationship. But I know her.

You have to believe me when I tell you she's fucking miserable. I don't even need to be living around the corner to know that, I can feel it. It's like someone has reached inside her and turned off all the lights."

"That's it," gasps Malak. "I was struggling to put my finger on it when she visited me in Cairo. Something had changed but I couldn't tell what and, to be fair, I was too miserable to see it, but that's the perfect description. Someone has turned off all the lights."

"Exactly," says Lewis. "Trust me when I say she does not want to marry this man. She's just being an idiot as fucking usual."

"Why would she do it if she didn't want to?" asks Harry, confused.

"Once Jenna has an idea, she sees it through, whether it's good or not. Somewhere she'll have come to the conclusion that this man is the answer. I told you, she's an idiot," Lewis groans. "You two have to help her, you know she doesn't listen to anyone else."

"We have to go to her," says Malak, turning to Kees.

"Your appointment, babe," she replies.

"It's okay, we've got time."

"Fine, okay, let's go," says Kees. "I'll ride with Harry, I have the address. Lewis, you follow in the car with Malak."

"I'm not coming," he replies, and they all turn to stare at him.

"We haven't talked in months. She sent me a message saying the friendship was over. I can't just waltz into her wedding, for fuck's sake. Plus, if that idiot sees me there it could backfire for Jenna. I came to tell you guys so you could do something about it. She needs *you*."

"Are you done?" Malak asks him with a raised eyebrow.

He nods.

"Good, then shut up and get in the car," says Kees.

As they drive to the hotel, her hand clasped in Harry's, he says mildly, "You know, I do pity the men that get caught between you three," and although she wants to smile, she thinks about Ali's face and the way he had looked at Malak, the same way some people look at homeless people in the street, and she replies, "I don't."

JENNA

Many years later, Jenna will look back at a picture of herself on her wedding day and not recognize the woman staring back at her.

For once, she isn't wearing her headscarf in front of her family because the unspoken rule exists that if you do wear hijab, you are given one free pass in the whole of your life, and that is on your wedding day. Everyone acts like it's completely normal for the woman who hasn't shown her hair since she was sixteen to now show everyone. Her caramel hair falls loosely around her face and then gathers at the base of her neck in a delicately wound bun that, when you look closer, has tiny pearls woven throughout it. Although she's lost too much weight, she knows she looks beautiful. Not just from the gasps of different family members who sneak into the room to give her a quick cuddle or to blow kisses before the ceremony starts, but from her reflection. She's always known she was beautiful. When the world always reacts to you in that way, you become used to the sound of their collective appreciation, their approval that your beauty has met a standard they can either relate or aspire to.

She can hear everyone rush to take their seats as the wedding planner announces that the ceremony will start in five minutes and she pauses for the butterflies to float across her stomach but sighs in disappointment when she feels nothing.

Her mother slips into the room just in time to catch the sigh and another frown passes over her face, the uncomfortable sensation that she cannot put her finger on a problem settles across her chest.

"Habibti," she says, joining Jenna at the big bay windows that look out onto the rose garden and sprawling lawn where the ceremony will take place.

Jenna doesn't turn, her gaze locked into the distance beyond the imam and celebrant, who are walking together to the front.

"Hey, Mama," she murmurs.

They both look out across the immaculately landscaped grounds and the backs of the guests who have traveled from all over the world to be here. She thinks she should comment on how beautiful it all looks but she doesn't have the energy, so she thinks it instead and hopes her mother picks up on it somehow.

"Jenna," says her mother, casually.

"Hmmm?"

"Are you happy?"

"So happy, Mama," she replies, softly. She ignores the sudden flick of her wrist that wants to reach out for her mother's hand.

They stand still, both lost in the wedding that is beginning to unfold before them, and in that moment the two women slightly tilt their heads to the left and admire their impeccable taste.

The quiet breaks as the door bangs open and mother and daughter jump, turning to see Malak and Kees spill through the door.

"What the f—" she starts before they all start talking over each other.

"You can't marry him," shouts Kees.

"Lewis told us everything," says Malak.

"What on earth?" asks her mother.

"Assalamualaikum, Aunty," say Kees and Malak in unison, turning to nod at her before turning back to Jenna.

There is a brief pause, Jenna's jaw hangs loose, before they talk over each other once more.

"Do you even love him?" asks Malak.

"You don't marry someone because of what happened," insists Kees.

"What happened?" says her mother, turning to Jenna.

Seeing all the people she has longed for suddenly, and unexpectedly, in the same room, strangles the breath from her throat. Her mother's question hangs in the air and nothing moves.

The tears she was supposed to weep this morning suddenly arrive and make a river out of her face. She feels her chest heaving itself up and down. It feels like the moment in the dream; everything is about to be found out and she stumbles backward, trying to put distance between them until the cold wall on her back is all she can feel, the room swimming through a glaze of tears and she doesn't know who is walking toward her and it is only when she feels Kees on one side of her and Malak on the other that she sinks to her knees because there is nowhere else to go. As they lower themselves down to the ground with her, she feels surrounded and finally loses the last remnant of control and she folds in half, face buried in her wedding dress.

Standing outside the room Harry and Lewis hear Jenna's cry and they think it sounds like the howl of a caged animal. They look at each other, both paling as it runs up their spine. Lewis clenches his fists, the feeling of panic that had left him once he had got to Malak and Kees now rushing back through his body, making him want to run or kick something. He looks around maniacally as if looking for someone who wants to fight but, instead, he feels Harry's arm around his shoulders.

Harry put his arm around Lewis because he needed something to hold on to, an anchor. He whispers a prayer of thanks in his head but he's not entirely sure what he's saying thank you for.

A waiter walking past the room with a tray of champagne flutes, which suddenly wobble when he hears the noise, wishes the glasses were full of alcohol instead of sparkling elderflower. A baby in the very back row of chairs suddenly starts crying. Uncle Omar, a long-time friend of the family who never arrives on time, hears the noise as he is hurrying past the window and it makes him think of his wife, who died sixteen years ago. Evie hears the sound from a few feet away as she watches her daughter crumple into the floorboards and she gets a lurch in her stomach, the kind mothers get when they watch their children break a bone. Kees hears the sound in her dreams later. Malak clutches her chest and thinks she understands whatever language Jenna is speaking.

The sound doesn't last long, just long enough to pull out the saddest parts from the muscle memory of everyone who hears it. Between Jenna's last cry and her next heaving breath, there is a pause, and then everything happens quickly and at once.

The wedding planner cheerily pokes her head around and asks if Jenna is ready to walk down the aisle. The makeup artist strides arrogantly in to touch up her bride one last time. Mo's mother walks through the door and stares horrified at the bride's tear-streaked face. Kees and Malak throw panicked glances at each other and Evie claps her hands so that everyone stares at her.

"We need a few more moments, we're not quite ready," she says, smiling collectively at the room, her voice as calm as if she was announcing dinner.

Aida Khalayleh, who doesn't possess the same level of calm and has never been committed to such a notion, tears her eyes from Jenna and asks, "What's happened, is she okay?"

Evie smiles as if they are discussing the weather and laughs gently. "Of course she's okay, she just needs a touch-up. Why don't we leave them to it and let's check on the kitchens and make sure the canapés are ready." She says this while smoothly guiding Aida out of the room, her left hand taking the wedding planner with her.

The makeup artist has lost her arrogance in the lost cause of Jenna's face, but like the professional she is, starts scrambling in her box to see what can be salvaged.

"We're going to need a minute," says Malak, gently looking toward the door.

"Well, we don't have that much time if she wants to look good in her wedding pictures," the makeup artist snaps. "I can't re-create two hours of work in five minutes."

"Would you please just get out and give us a goddamn minute?" barks Kees, and the woman jumps and scurries from the room muttering something no one hears.

Everything is still again. The sounds of the wedding fade away once the door clicks shut and all that's left is Jenna's smeared face, stained and creased dress, and the two women on either side of her, each looking from one to the other.

"You've looked better, if I'm honest," quips Kees, finally breaking the stunned silence.

"I thought you'd make a bit more effort on your wedding day," agrees Malak.

Jenna stares at them, shock etched on her face, but then a half-laugh, half-sob escapes from her throat before she pulls them both into her.

"How are you here?" she asks, finally letting go once Kees mutters that she can't breathe.

"Lewis met us at the airport," says Kees. "He told us what happened. That night."

"Why didn't you tell us, my darling?" asks Malak, reaching out to push the curls back behind Jenna's ears.

Jenna looks down at her hands wishing everything would disappear, including her.

"It's not really the kind of thing you drop into a text message."

Kees opens her mouth to argue.

"I couldn't," Jenna whispers.

Kees closes her mouth and for once lets the argument die on her lips.

"I don't know how to say it out loud," she says and she feels them nod.

"What about Mo?" asks Kees, instead. "Is he good to you? Has he ever touched you? Raised a hand to you? Smashed anything off you?"

Jenna sees her throw an apologetic look at Malak.

"No, God, no," she gasps, finally looking up at them. "He's a little obsessive about my clothes and other men, but just standard Arab-man stuff."

She sees both their disbelieving faces mirroring each other.

"Honestly," she insists. "He's done nothing wrong. He's a good man. Great man, in fact. He's lovely."

"Fine," says Kees, "he's lovely. But do you *love* him, and do you want to marry him and spend the rest of your life with him? Because Lewis says you don't and while I'm loath to agree with that man about anything, I think he might have a point. Is he right?"

Jenna looks miserable.

"Why go along with this wedding if it isn't what you want, Jenna?" asks Malak softly. "I thought you were happy with him."

"I thought you were happy with Ali," replies Jenna, wiping stray tears from her face.

Malak winces. "Point taken."

Jenna hiccups a sob and grabs Malak's hand. "I don't mean it like that," she insists. "I just mean, you think it's what you want and you go along with it and then suddenly it's too late to say anything. And it was what I wanted. Sometimes. Maybe. I don't know, everything has been so awful, and no one was around."

She sees the apologies begin to form in her friends' mouths and waves them away before they can start.

"You both had things you needed to do, and rightly so," she insists, "but I was lonely and then that night happened and Mo was safe and reliable, and he was there."

She looks helplessly at Malak and Kees.

"There's a lot to be said for safety," says Malak.

Jenna squeezes her hand again.

The room pauses once more, and nothing is said but everything somehow passes between them.

"All right." Kees finally nods. "Let's get you out of here." She pulls Jenna and Malak up off the ground with her as she stands.

They stare at each other for a moment, the sounds of violins floating through the windows. Jenna takes a deep breath and smooths her dress down, though it doesn't repair the damage.

"Okay," she says, and she smiles at her two friends. It is the first real smile she has felt break across her face all year.

"Okay," she repeats.

Malak nods.

"Okay," replies Kees.

The makeup artist walks in to find the three women smiling and nodding at each other before they all snap at her to leave again. She will later tell this story when she moans about difficult brides.

"I need you to find my mum, please," says Jenna, turning to Kees. "Do you mind?"

"Of course not," Kees replies, "whatever you need."

"I want to stay," interrupts Malak, "but if I don't get to this appointment it's going to be too late, I have to go. I'm so sorry." She turns to Jenna apologetically.

"Don't be stupid," Jenna says, pulling her into her and hugging her hard. "Go, go, go. I can't believe you're still here."

As Malak turns to walk out of the room, Jenna grabs her arm and pulls her back to her side. "Are you sure you want to do this?"

They stare at each other and eventually Malak nods.

"Okay." Jenna nods. She turns to Kees. "You have to go with her, I'll figure this out."

"No!" Malak's voice is firm. "No, Kees, stay here. Jenna needs you. I'll be fine. Plus, I've already dragged you across an ocean to help me, the rest I can do alone. Please stay here and make sure she doesn't accidentally marry this guy."

Kees nods. "Fine. But you're taking Harry. He can drive you and sit with you. You're not going alone."

"For God's sake, Kees, I'm fine to go alone," hisses Malak.

"Take Harry or take Lewis; your choice," Kees snaps back.

Malak raises her eyebrow. "Why would I take Lewis?"

"Well, then, Harry it is." Kees smiles.

"You're so annoying," Malak mutters.

"Can you please go?" interrupts Jenna. "And Kees, go get my mum, for God's sake."

As they turn to leave, Jenna calls them back.

"All four of your parents are here, by the way."

Two stricken faces stare back at her.

"Don't look at me like that," replies Jenna with a shrug. "You knew my mother would invite them. You know how this works. Just stay alert and maybe away from the windows. And get me a tissue. And a drink; I can barely talk, my throat is so dry."

Kees rolls her eyes. "And yet somehow you still manage to."

Malak grins.

BILQUIS

In her leggings and an oversized sweater, Kees is aware that even the waiters are more dressed up than she is. The corridors have suddenly taken on an edge, a fluttering of people who have realized that things are not going according to plan, and the wedding planner is beginning to live out her worst nightmare: the bride refusing to emerge.

Kees feels the panic radiate through everyone and steps softly down the corridor, tentatively peering around doors to see if she can find Aunty Evie, praying that her mother is, as usual, in the front of the rows because she never likes to miss a wedding.

Kees is about to return the way she came when Hakim walks down one corridor and steps into the rotunda she's standing in, both of them seeing each other in the same second and stopping suddenly.

"Hakim!" she calls out on the breath she hadn't realized she was holding.

"Kees."

They stand there looking at each other, bound by their years under the same roof and their shared blood but unsure how sibling bonds work when the ties of family are frayed. He's taller than when she last saw him. His shoulders broader, his face stretching into manhood. By the looks of it, he's started shaving.

Adulthood has crept over him somewhere and she doesn't see her kid brother anymore. This means he's old enough to make better choices and she is suddenly more angry than sad.

"Why the fuck haven't you replied to any of my messages?" she asks.

He raises his eyebrow at her, and she thinks it must be a family trait from her mother, passed to every one of her children.

"I had to hear Umee spend every night crying after you'd gone and she asked me not to," hisses Hakim. "What was I supposed to do?"

"You were supposed to message and tell me that. Something. Anything."

"You didn't see her, Kees," he says, stuffing his hands in his pockets and looking down at his shoes. "She's been a mess."

Kees barks out a laugh. "And what about me?"

Hakim gives a worried shrug.

He might be growing into adulthood but he's not there yet and he doesn't have the answers. She feels suddenly deflated; there's no point in being angry with him.

"How's Dad?" she asks.

"Yeah, good. Seems a bit sad too, but not as bad as Mum."

"Saba?"

"Pregnant," he replies with another shrug.

She smiles. "Of course she is. Mum must be thrilled."

"She's started painting patterns on a crib she's redoing."

"Hakim, Beta," a voice calls, and their heads turn to look at their mother, who steps into the rotunda with them.

She takes in the huge Greek urn in the center filled with lilies and then looks to either side at each of her children, her eldest and her youngest.

"Assalamualaikum, Umee," says Kees.

She has never thought of herself as particularly brave but as she stands with legs that don't shake and knees that keep her standing straight, she wonders if perhaps she is braver than she gives herself credit for.

Her mother says nothing, just takes Kees in from head to toe. Hakim looks nervously from right to left, watching the two women. After a minute has passed and her greeting still hangs in the air, Kees shrugs and turns to leave.

"Bilquis," calls her mother, and Kees turns around to face her. "Why are you here?" she asks.

"It is my best friend's wedding," Kees sighs.

"Your friend is marrying a Muslim."

"Actually, she's not," she snaps. "The wedding isn't happening. She doesn't love him, and unlike you, we happen to think love matters when you're picking the person to spend your life with."

Her mother puts her hand on her chest, taken aback by the venom that Kees has never, not once, directed toward either of her parents.

"And I'm here to get her out of the wedding, so now you can hate me for ruining her as well as myself. Maybe you can continue to not talk to me for another six months. Did you even get any of my letters or messages?"

Her mother says nothing, staring wide-eyed at her daughter, whose frizzy hair is standing up of its own volition, face smeared with a pain and an anger in her eyes that Abida has never seen before.

"Well, DID YOU?" she shouts.

Her mother jumps and Kees knows she is being cruel. She can see the sadness etched behind her mother's eyes and the idea that she is the cause of it is more than her shoulders will bear so she chooses anger instead. It is easier. She can survive this way.

"You haven't replied to a single one of my messages," Kees continues. "I just wanted to talk to you. Was that too much?"

"Yes, Beta," says her mother, not taking her eyes off her daughter. "You asked too much of us. What you did was wrong, and you asked us to support it. He's not Muslim."

"I DON'T CARE," Kees yells.

Her mother pales, hand still locked across her chest as if it could keep her heart from jumping out and spilling itself across the floor.

Kees feels wild.

"This isn't Islam. Ignoring me. Turning my siblings from me. I'm going to be an aunty, Umee. Saba is pregnant and I wouldn't have known."

The tears that Kees has been unable to cry in front of her mother now begin their slow descent down her face. She shakes her head and rubs her nose on the back of her sweater sleeve, laughing maniacally.

"This isn't the Islam you and Abaji taught us. This isn't what the Quran says, or what the Prophet preached. So don't tell me it's because he's not Muslim and then tell me it's about God when my uncle brought home a baby boy and refused to marry the mother and you still talk to him. I came back with a ring on my finger and a man who loves me. Who will spend his whole life standing by my side, which is more than I can say for my own family. And you want to talk to me about what's right and wrong? So what's it really about? Why won't you talk to me, Umee?"

No one says anything and she demands loudly, "WHY?"

Hakim jumps. Her mother doesn't flinch.

"Bilquis!"

Her head jerks around to see Harry walking up behind her. He doesn't shout, but she has never heard him say her name like that and he never calls her by her full name. Like a whip, it snaps through the air and pulls her back. He walks up to her and wraps his hand around her arm.

"Don't talk to your mother like that. Not ever. And never on my behalf."

Kees is too shocked to say anything.

"Assalamualaikum, Aunty," Harry says, turning and, with a hand over his heart, he bends his head toward her, an almost imperceptible bow; an acknowledgment of respect. "Hakim," he says, nodding at him, who nods back, confused by what's unfolded before him, dazed at this sudden stranger knowing his name.

Harry's hand tightens on her arm. "Come on, walk away, you're done here."

The last thing she sees is a look of surprise on her mother's face.

JENNA

She stands alone in the room filled with flowers, nervously biting her nails waiting for Kees to return. This was where they were supposed to have their first pictures taken after the ceremony. It's a beautiful room filled with light from the floor-to-ceiling windows, the perfectly curated gardens rolling behind them. They would have opened the French doors and stepped into those gardens for more pictures, with Cambridge sitting beautifully in the background, barely visible except for the twisting spires of its ancient buildings.

Thinking about the wedding photos she should be in makes Jenna wonder if she's doing the right thing. Whether she's foolishly just being swept up in another moment.

The door opens and Kees steps in with her mother.

"Mama," mummers Jenna nervously and Evie hears the tremble in her daughter's voice and is reminded that she is still needed.

As Evie wraps her arms around her daughter, who has begun to cry again, Malak puts her head around the door to grab Kees and tell her she's leaving with Harry.

Jenna doesn't notice them leave.

She hears only the soothing sounds of her mother's voice.

Eventually, Evie lifts her daughter's head off her chest.

"Jenna, I'm going to ask you a question and I want you to be very honest with me."

Jenna swallows the bile in her mouth and nods.

"Do you want to get married to Mohammed?"

She can hear the shuffling of guests in the distance, the clink of glasses, and the wedding planner announcing that canapés will be served in the meantime.

She slowly shakes her head. "No, Mama. I'm so sorry."

Her mother surprises her by breathing a sigh of relief. "Thank God."

Jenna feels her own eyes widen in shock.

"You didn't want me to marry him?" she asks.

"Habibti," murmurs her mother, taking a tissue out of her sleeve and handing it to Jenna, "I want you to marry someone that you love and who makes you happy, but you haven't been happy for such a long time. I knew you weren't, and that you didn't really want this, and I should have said something instead of going along with it. Forgive me."

"Mama, no," Jenna chokes. "I'm sorry. For going through with it. For putting you both to so much trouble. Baba has spent so much."

Her mother waves a hand. "That is not important, Jenna." She leads her over to the bay windows and sits her down.

"Now tell me, what happened?"

"What happened?" she asks.

"Yes, Jenna, what happened?" her mother says, calmly. "How is Lewis involved in this? Do you love him?"

Jenna laughs at the last question. "No, Mama, I don't love him. Not like that."

"Well…?" Evie folds one hand over her daughter's, waiting patiently, sounds of the wedding swirling around them as everyone waits for the bride.

There is a time for lies and even though Jenna is very good at them, she knows the time isn't now. So, she tells her mother about *that night* and in a voice that hovers just above a whisper, says the word rape for the first time and cracks her mother's world in half.

Evie takes a deep breath and closes her eyes, making sure to not react; instead, she just squeezes her daughter's hand and rubs her arm, the way she always liked when she was a baby.

Jenna says nothing of the details, only that it did happen, purposefully making it vague and cloudy. You can't tell a mother too many terrible things at once. It isn't fair. So she tells little bits. How she said no three times. How there was no one around. How it happened late one night on the way home. How she had left her car at home so had to wait for a taxi. How she had called Lewis that night for help because she didn't know who else to call. How Lewis had taken her home and how his mum had looked after her. She cannot tell her that she had to get the morning-after pill, just that she took the correct procedures. That she sorted everything out, but she couldn't go to the police. How she had started seeing Mo around that time because he was nice to her and, at the time, that seemed like a good enough reason to be with someone. How she didn't care about anything in those days afterward and she thought if she started seeing him it would help her care, but one thing just led to another.

"That night. Was it in November?" her mother finally asks.

"Yes. How did you know?" she asks, startled.

"Because that was the same time you disappeared," replies her mother. "Why didn't you tell me, Jenna?"

Jenna looks down at her rumpled wedding dress, squeezing the material into a ball in her hand once more. "Because then everyone would know," she whispers.

"Would know what?"

"That I wasn't a virgin, and who would marry me then?" She looks up at her mother, her eyes filled with tears again.

"Oh, my girl. That's what you were worried about?" Evie says, brushing her forehead and the stray hairs away.

"I thought if I didn't tell anyone it wouldn't be real. That I could still be a virgin on my wedding night."

"Jenna, Jenna," soothes her mother. "I wasn't a virgin on my wedding night to your father," she says.

"Yes, but you weren't Muslim at the time, it's not the same."

Her mother shoots her a glance before saying, "Your father wasn't either, my love."

"What? He said you were the only woman he's ever been with."

"Your father is a storyteller," says her mother. "He cannot resist a good performance and he won't let the truth get in the way. Most people aren't virgins on their wedding nights."

"But you said—"

"It's just a game we all play, sweetheart. We all pretend, but it's not real. And your situation is not the same, and I wouldn't have you marry anyone who doesn't understand that." She wipes her daughter's tears away while Jenna gapes at her in shock. The realization that even the elders don't believe in the game sits like a lump in her throat that she will still be trying to dissolve four years later.

Before she can say anything, her mother calls Lewis's name.

"Lewis! I know you're skulking outside that door, please come in here for a moment. Kees, you too."

The door creaks open and Lewis slips in, a guilty look on his face. She can tell he thinks he's in trouble from the way he's standing.

Instead, her mother stands up and strides up to him, and taking his hands in hers, she plants two kisses on each of his palms.

"Thank you for looking after my daughter when I didn't. It should have been me."

Lewis looks horrified. He has spent a lifetime trying not to get in trouble with Jenna's parents and this show of respect makes him more uncomfortable than he's ever been in his life.

"I'm sorry for causing so much trouble."

"No. You don't apologize to this family. We owe you our gratitude."

Lewis turns to Jenna finally. "Hello."

"Hello, you," she replies.

"Does this mean we can be friends again?" He grins.

She stands and hurls herself at him, throwing her arms around his neck.

"You're a real dickhead," he whispers in her ear.

"I know," she replies.

Her mother claps her hands, commanding attention once more.

"Kees, can you please take my daughter out of here. Lewis, you can drive them, I presume?"

"Of course, Aunty," he replies.

"She can stay the night with you, Kees?"

"Yes, Aunty, no question."

"Good," Evie replies. "I think that's for the best. We have too much family staying at our home and there will be no peace and I don't think she wants to stay in her bridal suite. Look after my daughter."

Lewis and Kees nod.

"But, Mama, what about Baba? And the wedding. The guests."

"Leave that to me."

"Mo…" says Jenna. "Should I talk to him?"

Her mother looks at her for a moment. "Do you want to?"

Jenna shrugs. "Not really. At least not right now."

Evie nods. "Maybe tomorrow."

"Yeah," agrees Jenna, "maybe tomorrow."

She steps up to her mother and throws her arms around her and they stand like this, uninterrupted, for what feels longer than the few seconds they hold on to each other for.

MALAK

"We're going to be late," Malak says nervously, biting her nails and staring at the traffic around them.

"We're not, I promise. I'll get you there."

She smiles at him. "Thank you for doing this, Harry."

"Of course," he responds. "Don't think I don't know that Kees calls me a shared resource for you guys."

She laughs. "I'm afraid that's the deal with being with one of us."

"I figured." He nods.

By the time they arrive and park on the street, Malak is five minutes late for the appointment and she runs into the building. They only allow a ten-minute window. There are too many women in line waiting to change the course of their life, so there is no room for any delays.

"I'm here," she breathes over the receptionist who looks up at her unsympathetically.

"And who are you?" she asks.

"Malak Abdel-Aziz. I have an appointment at twelve."

"It's five past twelve."

"I know that but I'm only five minutes late."

"Take a seat."

"I'm good? I can still make my appointment?"

"Apparently," grunted the receptionist, pointing again toward the waiting room, already talking to the woman behind her.

Malak sits and tears the skin around her nails until three of her fingers are bleeding. She doesn't bother picking up the frayed magazines, all stuffed full of beauty regimes and top tips to make women more attractive to men.

Harry walks in, nervously looking for her, and she waves him over. There really isn't much to say and he is a fan of brevity so he picks up one of the magazines, flicking through it trying to look like a man who is here from goodness instead of bad behavior.

A couple opposite her clutches hands, small tears occasionally escaping from both of them. The woman is wearing a brown scarf with yellow patterns and Malak stares at it for a long time. She wonders why they can't have the baby because, judging by the sadness radiating off them, they both want it badly. A red-haired teenager sits with her mother, angrily scrolling through her phone while her mother rubs her back, stopping every now and then to shake her head. Malak feels sick at the thought of her mother being there and wonders what world these people come from where you casually bring your mum to the abortion clinic with you like you were taking her to the nail salon. A woman is sitting by herself in the corner, her suit perfectly tailored as she taps away on a laptop. She looks busy. Malak has the fleeting thought that yesterday she was in Cairo with a boyfriend and an entire life, and now she is in England with her friend's fiancé, single. It hasn't occurred to her that she is no longer bound to someone else. Untethered in the world after long years of belonging to another human.

At 1:10 p.m. she returns to the receptionist and asks why everything is delayed but she is only met with a shrug. She wants to say more but is aware that the woman behind this tall desk and glass partition could make life difficult for her, so she smiles and says thank you before sitting back down.

At 2:05 p.m., she picks up a magazine and throws it back down again. "I'm sorry this is taking so long, Harry."

He looks up from his phone, throws a glance over his shoulder before standing, seemingly just hearing her for the first time. "Sorry, what's that?"

"I'm just saying I know this is taking ages and I'm sure you'd rather be doing a hundred other things."

He runs his hands through his hair and gestures emphatically, the way he always does when he feels like he has hurt someone's feelings or offended someone by what he says. He does it a lot.

"No, no, not at all. I'm just worried about Kees."

"So go to her, Harry," says Malak. "Kees shouldn't have made you even come with me, she's being over-protective. And so bloody commanding. As usual."

Harry laughs. "She's incredibly commanding, but she's also right. I wouldn't have let you come by yourself, even if she hadn't said anything."

Malak smiles and is glad that her friend is with the right person.

"I am going to go, actually, but only because my replacement has arrived," says Harry, picking his jacket up off the back of the chair and turning toward the door.

"Replacement?"

"I just thought there was someone better suited for this job. Someone you'd rather have with you."

Malak finally follows his eyeline to see Jacob standing on the edge of the waiting room, a hand raised in greeting.

She barely feels Harry squeeze her arm as a goodbye and watches him walk up to Jacob. They hug briefly, quick slaps on the back, before Harry disappears out the door and she is left staring at the man she used to love, the one she hasn't seen since she switched off his bedroom light and said goodnight.

For a reason she cannot understand her hand flies to her belly and rests gently over her stomach. Her breasts ache. She feels something stir and later will swear it was the baby.

Jacob walks across the room, through the maze of fraught women to the one woman he has been desperate to see. They say nothing. Malak stares and he stares back, the silence between them thick and heavy.

She feels another movement and as Jacob finally opens his mouth to talk, the nurse steps into the waiting room and calls out.

"Malak Abdel-Aziz."

They wait. Everyone stares at the nurse.

"Malak Abdel-Aziz." More urgent this time. Heads start turning. People search across the rows of chairs. The teenager has the wild thought that she could say it's her and this could all be over sooner.

"Malak," says Jacob, finally.

Malak turns toward the nurse and follows her through the door.

MALAK. BILQUIS. JENNA.

Nowhere in Malak's research did she learn that the nurse would be legally obligated to ask if she wanted to see the ultrasound of the baby. She didn't realize this would be an option. She hadn't thought about having an ultrasound at all because she wasn't keeping it, so why did they need to see, but as the nurse points out, they need to know what they're taking out, just in case it's twins, and then a different instrument, a wider one, will have to be used. It makes perfect sense when you put it like that.

She nods because she does want to see. She is curious to know what the ache in her back looks like.

"Is that its heartbeat?" she asks, pointing at the screen.

The nurse is a lot kinder than the receptionist. She is a Jamaican woman in her fifties who instantly makes her feel calm with her warmth, her name badge flashing *Imelda*.

"Yes, dearie. But we call it a heart tube. It's not big enough to form into a whole heart, just a little tube at this stage."

Malak stares at it for a bit longer. She wants to ask if she can have a picture but recognizes how strange that is and even though Imelda makes her feel calm, she doesn't feel brave enough to ask for that.

"Do you have any questions, lovie?" Imelda snaps her gloves off and clicks the machine back to sleep.

Malak shakes her head but then asks, "What happens to it? Once it's done?"

"We dispose of it, unless you'd like to take it home and do it yourself."

She shakes her head quickly. "But how do you do it?"

"It's burned, dearie. Any other questions?"

She shakes her head but can't stop thinking that cremation is haram in Islam and how she doesn't want it to leave the world like this, but she doesn't know how to make sense of that. Not wanting to burn the remains of a baby you should never have had in your belly is stupid, so she says nothing.

The nurse pats her hand and leads her up a set of stairs, dropping her off in the care of another nurse, younger.

She directs her to the gown and where to leave her clothes and Malak smiles and says thank you a lot. She doesn't want to seem rude.

When it happens, as her stomach contracts, desperately making a final bid to hold on to what is leaving, she lets out a long scream. The people in the waiting room hold each other a little more tightly. Jacob throws up in a wastepaper basket. The receptionist remembers she must get a new job, one that is far away from the screams of women who are losing babies they never asked for. Even when the screams stop and she has left her job for the day, she can still hear them. Even when they don't scream at all, she can still hear them. A woman has a way of screaming with her whole body that only other women can hear.

Harry pulls into his car parking space as Lewis pulls up with Kees and Jenna. He waves him into a spot in front of him and then the boys pull suitcases out of the car while Kees wraps her arm around Jenna and steers her into the house.

As Kees pushes open the front door, it is the first time the house has felt like home.

"Come on, let's get you cleaned up and into some pajamas," she says to Jenna.

"Kees," calls Harry as she starts walking up the stairs behind Jenna, her arms full of her wedding dress so Jenna doesn't trip. Kees turns to look at him.

"I'm going to drive to the supermarket with Lewis and get some duvets and maybe an airbed, if they have it. We have nothing for everyone to sleep on and I figured everyone would be staying."

She loves him all over again in that moment and nods. "Good thinking."

"Lewis, will you stay the night?" calls Jenna down the stairs.

"Yeah, of course, if you want me to," he replies.

"I do."

Kees steers Jenna into the bathroom and sits her down on the toilet, beginning the task of finding every pin that is keeping her veil and hair in place, pulling them out one by one, and placing them on the windowsill. She works quietly, not knowing what to say to a woman who's just walked out on her wedding day.

"It wasn't supposed to be like this," says Jenna, staring out of the window across the London rooftops.

Kees laughs wryly, remembering when Jenna had said that to her on her own wedding day. "I know, babe, I know."

Slowly she unravels Jenna; putting jewelry safely aside, painstakingly undoing each tiny silk button down her back to help her step out of the dress, putting the pearls from her hair into a tiny food bag, helping her slip her silk stockings off, eventually taking a wipe to rub off the makeup that is left smeared across Jenna's face.

Kees gets the comfiest pajamas she can find, although they are too hot for this time of year; she wants to wrap Jenna in something soft in the hope that it will take the forlorn look off her face.

Jacob texts to say they're on the way home and can she draw a bath? Malak wants one.

The boys are back with duvets and pizza and so she steers Jenna down to the sitting room, leaving her under Lewis's arm as she goes back up the stairs to prepare the bath.

Harry puts his head around the door. "How you holding up, soldier?"

Kees just shakes her head and he walks over to kiss her. "I know."

"Hey, I figured we might want to give Malak and Jacob our bed for tonight and we can sleep in the living room with Lewis and Jenna. I think Malak probably needs the bed out of all of us."

"Yeah, she does, thank you."

"Okay, I'm going to go and put fresh sheets on it."

"Thank you so much."

"Kees…"

"Yes?"

"Stop thanking me. Aren't these girls your family?"

"Of course."

"Then they're mine, too."

Malak can feel her body trembling as Jacob leads her up the steps to Kees's flat, but she can't stop the shaking. She has the impression from the worried look on Jacob's face that she's walking very slowly, although it feels normal to her.

They have barely said anything to one another since she was guided out of the patient-only area and back to the waiting room where Jacob was nervously standing.

She feels herself push her body through the motions. She comments on how beautiful Kees's home is. Smiles at Lewis. Rejects the pizza. Feels Jenna, then Kees, hug her as they ask if she wants anything. She repeats she just wants a bath and looks to Jacob, who nods that he'll help her.

As she sinks into the hot water, she doesn't try to cover her body or hide from him. In the back of her mind, she remembers Jenna telling her all those months ago in Cairo that he had a girlfriend now. She registers that you're not supposed to show your naked body to a man who has a girlfriend, but these are not sexy times and the rules don't apply.

Jacob pulls off his sweater and rolls up his shirt sleeves, sinking to his knees and taking the sponge Kees has left out. He squeezes soap onto it before dipping it into the water and making gentle circles on her back.

"You didn't have to come," she whispers.

Jacob doesn't stop sponging her back. "Maybe not," he replies. "But I never would have not come, Malak."

She says nothing, just rests her head on her knees and concentrates on the pain passing through her stomach. She didn't think it would be this bad.

"Harry told me what happened."

She smiles. "I see you're still friends, then?"

He gives a small laugh. "I told you we were." He pauses for a moment and then says, "Malak, I'm so sorry. I thought you were having an amazing time in Cairo."

"I was," she sighed. "Until I wasn't."

He dips the sponge back into the bath and slowly leans her back, soaping down her arms and chest. He looks at her before he brings the sponge across her stomach, waiting for her small nod. He is even more gentle when he draws the sponge slowly over her belly and down her legs.

He has always been delicate with her body, but now he touches her so softly it's barely a whisper across her skin.

Eventually, he lifts her out of the tub, wrapping her in a towel and carrying her into the bedroom to sit her on the bed. Kees has left out pajamas and underwear and Malak watches him peel off one of the sanitary pads the nurse has given her and stick it to the underwear, before slipping her feet in them and pulling them up over her hips. She rests her hands on his shoulders as he pulls up the pajama bottoms and lifts her arms to slip the top over her head.

He repeatedly asks her if she wants anything and the answer is always no until she wants a glass of water and then it's back to nothing. He tells her to eat but the thought of anything, even the ice cream she had desperately wanted before, makes her feel more wretched than she already does. All she wants to do is to slip into an unconscious state.

"I'm just so tired," she says and Jacob nods.

He lifts the duvet and swings her legs up onto the bed.

"Will you stay with me?" she asks and he nods again.

He climbs into bed, gently placing himself around her the way he used to do, their bodies maintaining a muscle memory of how to slot next to each other, easily falling into the curves like old friends.

He holds her tightly to his chest and she feels one of his tears on her shoulder and she squeezes his hand, which is laced through hers, even more tightly.

"Does your girlfriend know you're here?" she asks. It is easier to ask this now they are in the dark, her back to him.

"Yes, of course," he replies.

"What's her name?"

"Grace."

"She didn't mind?"

"She understood."

"Do you love her?"

There is a pause and the darkness seems even heavier around them, the night suddenly blacker than it was before.

"Yes, I do," sighs Jacob reluctantly, remembering a conversation he had with Kees in a pub one night, in what feels like another life.

Malak nods. "Are you happy?"

"Yes. It took a really long time to get there, Malak; you broke my heart."

"I know," she whispers. "I'm sorry." She lifts his hand to her lips and kisses it. "I'm so sorry."

"I know," he replies. "Me too." After a pause, "You'd like her, actually."

The most depressing thing Malak thinks just before she falls asleep is that he's probably right; Jacob has always been a good judge of character.

Jacob feels her body go limp in his arms and her breathing slow and he tries to pace his racing heart to hers. He doesn't sleep much that night, wanting to be awake in case she needs anything.

Downstairs, Jenna curls into Lewis's chest and sobs into his T-shirt, tripping over her apologies for what she did to their friendship.

In the kitchen, Harry stops Kees from putting dishes away and pulls her into his arms; with her friends safe, she lets her own tears spill, repeatedly asking Harry if there is any chance that her mother will ever talk to her now that she's screamed at her, and he doesn't have an answer. He just remembers the cold look in Abida's eyes and how much it had hurt him to see it and doesn't know how Kees is bearing it. The woman who had cried more in the past few months than he had ever known her to in four and a half years.

Forty-five minutes away, Hakim messages his sister Saba and says he thinks they should visit Kees in London. He didn't like the way she had looked at him and, seeing his betrayal on her face, he didn't like what he had done. Downstairs, Abida and Itasham rest their foreheads against each other and worry about all of their children. Abida eventually says, "I think this Harry boy might be a good man, you know," and her husband agrees that even though he's not Muslim, he seems good. Fourteen streets away, Evie sits her husband down in their bedroom and gently explains what happened to their daughter, and then thinks she may as well have not bothered, since her husband spends the next four hours shouting and pacing back and forth. Four streets away, Malak's mother sits on the sofa in her house, on the phone with her friend murmuring about what a shame it was that the wedding didn't happen and how she hopes her own daughter will be safely married soon. At the venue, Mohammed helps his mother pack items from the wedding that didn't happen into the car, even though everyone said he didn't have to help.

Eventually, the last dog barks, the babies stop crying, and London enters its only quiet period somewhere between the hours of 4 and 5:30 a.m. The final tear that night has fallen and bodies reach for each other all across the city.

WHEN THE DUST SETTLES

The day breaks across the house and they wake, two by two, stretching out of each other's arms.

"Do you remember the first time we slept next to each other?" asks Jenna, rolling to sit up, detangling her legs from Lewis's.

"David Grate's house party when we were sixteen," he laughs.

"You stole that flimsy blanket off what's-her-name. The one that always got really drunk and passed out?"

"Natasha Birtch," he says and she laughs. "You can never say I'm not a gentleman," Lewis adds and smiles.

"At least we had more bedding this time," she says, pulling the duvet off her.

"But still in the corner of a sitting room with other people," remarks Lewis, nodding to Kees and Harry, who are yawning themselves awake.

"Jenna, why do you always feel the need to talk so much in the morning?" groans Kees.

Upstairs, Malak sits on the edge of the bed watching as Jacob pulls his clothes on.

She has slept heavily and feels calm despite the bomb that went off in her belly yesterday. Her insides still feel like rubble toppling to the ground, the smoke from the fire still drifting up, but at least her body has stopped trembling. She had forgotten what it felt like to sleep next to someone who wouldn't put you on trial in the morning for what happened in your dreams.

"Do you have to go?" she asks, putting a world of want into the question.

He nods. "Grace is on the way to pick me up. We've got a friend's wedding to go to."

He has become a "we" with friends she knows nothing about, a couple who is obligated to turn up at weddings together, and she feels bereft.

Over the last year, Malak has become a woman who has learned how to be deliriously happy and devastated all at the same time and she recognizes the feeling now as she stares at him, locked in his gaze. She thinks life is full of impossible things.

Jacob's phone eventually breaks their gaze, ringing loudly twice before stopping. He looks down at it, then back to Malak.

"She's outside."

In the time it takes to breathe in and out she wants to become a woman who throws caution to the wind. Close the distance between them and pledge fealty. Loyalty. Forever. Whatever he needs to hear to understand that it is, has always been, will always be, him. Stamp her name upon his lips. Kiss him long enough to make him forget that she left. Build something out of the wreckage.

She exhales.

"Okay. Let's go."

He follows her down the stairs and they both walk into the living room where camping mats and duvets are sprawled everywhere, a pot of tea and a canister of coffee balanced on the only piece of furniture in the middle of the room.

"Morning, gang." Malak smiles, and in the chorus of greetings and the faces that turn toward her she thinks that maybe she will survive this after all.

"Hey, mate." Jacob nods to Harry, who nods back in turn.

Kees and Malak exchange a smile, sharing a joke about how the boys became friends only when the women left. A moment passes.

"Well, I'd better go," says Jacob and they all stand, looking at each other. The thought, *remember the last time we were all together*, flashes in all of their minds and they each recall something different from that day: the blossom across the blue sky, the sun on golden-brown skin, the sound of laughter.

Malak wants to freeze this moment, to hold them all here. Because right now they are together and the last time that happened they didn't know it would be the last time, but now they know better.

Jenna breaks the silence by holding out her arms and dramatically shouting out, "Come on, guys, bring it in. Come on, group hug."

Kees looks at Malak and groans, a half grin fighting its way across her face. "Why does she always do this?"

Malak laughs. "You know what she's like."

And so they reach out arms to pull each other close to one another, the five of them slotting into each other's bodies, Lewis hanging back by the wall, not wanting to be part of something he has no right to, until Jenna says, "Don't be stupid," and pulls him in and, like Kees, he complains about organized affection but still wraps his arms around whoever he can hold on to at that moment, hiding a small smile.

Jacob leaves and they are five again, standing in the bare living room, the three women looking at each other.

Lewis suddenly feels out of place. "What do we do now?" he asks Harry.

"Nothing. Our bit is done. We just leave them to it."

★

Once the boys leave, Kees organizes breakfast, ordering Malak to sit down, but she insists on helping to make toast anyway, and commanding Jenna to make fresh tea.

"Why does it always sound like an order when it comes out of her mouth?" Jenna asks Malak, who laughs and wraps an arm sympathetically around her.

"Well, that's because it is. Don't ever get it twisted."

Eventually, they are standing in the kitchen, a tray of tea, toast, and crumpets ready, Jenna cradling two jars of jam in her hands, a box of chocolates under her arm.

"I see you found my chocolate stash," says Kees.

"Obviously. Your house may be barren, but I knew there would be chocolate somewhere. Where shall we have breakfast?"

"I just want to get back into bed," says Malak, cradling the hot-water bottle Kees has given her for her stomach.

"Bed it is." Kees nods and they follow her up the stairs, each one carrying either the carton of milk, mugs, or extra pillows from the living-room floor.

Kees and Malak climb in, fluffing pillows behind them, and Jenna still manages to take up the most space, sprawling on her stomach at the foot of the bed, knocking both Malak's and Kees's feet out of her way, the breakfast tray between them all.

"So," Jenna smiles, glowing from ear to ear, "what's new?"

Malak laughs and Kees raises her eyebrow. "Jenna Khatieb, did you stage a fake wedding just to get us all together?"

"If that was my plan, I would have done it sooner," she snorts, holding out her plate to Kees, who puts two crumpets on it without having to ask what she wants.

Slowly, over breakfast, and then chocolate, and eventually kebab boxes and chip cartons, they unfold the last year and a half, never leaving the bed, just moving around it into different positions, sometimes resting on each other, sometimes on their own arms or with faces propped into palms. They sprawl easily over one another, bodies touching, the warmth of each other's skin reflecting the light bouncing through the window.

At one point, Jenna reaches over to her phone and sees a list of missed calls and messages from Mo, but nervously stuffs it beneath a pillow out of sight.

Malak sees it and with raised eyebrows asks, "Are you not going to talk to him?"

"I will at some point," whispers Jenna, "just not now."

The sun changes position in the sky and they debate whether Aunty Abida will ever talk to her daughter again.

"You know, it already doesn't feel as bad with you guys back," says Kees, smiling. "Not that I'm saying my mother ostracizing me from my family and refusing to talk to me isn't entirely fucking heart-breaking, because it is."

They murmur in agreement, silently glad that their mothers still answer the phone when they call.

"I'm just saying it feels like at least now I have some of my family back," and Kees reaches out to both of them when she says this.

Eventually, Jenna asks Malak the question Kees has been too afraid to ask.

"Did you want it? The baby."

Malak can't say the words. She just nods.

"Oh, Malak," says Kees, sitting up. "Why did you do it, then? I know doing it alone would have been hard, but would it have been harder than this right now?"

"No. Probably not," she answers. "You know, I think it would have been the easier choice, despite my mother's broken heart. She's never been able to resist a baby and, eventually, she would have come around. But I think if I had gone through with it, it would have been the selfish choice. It took less than a year to become a new person entirely, and I didn't even notice it happening. I became anything he wanted just to get his approval. Imagine what our child would have become to please its father. It sounds morbid, but I understand why animals eat their young. Isn't that what I've done? Destroyed something because it wasn't safe. It's funny, you know, because at the clinic they ask you loads of difficult and horrible questions. Like, do you want to see the baby's heartbeat? Are you doing this by your own volition? Do you absolutely want to terminate this pregnancy? If it's twins, would you like to know?

"It feels like everything they ask is designed to break you, to get you to change your mind. What they should ask instead is, is the father a piece of shit? Will this baby be better off in heaven than in the father's arms? Will you be able to live a better life? Are you saving yourself by doing this? Are you saving this child a lifetime of misery and therapy? That's what they should ask. Yes, I did want it. The only thing I wanted more was to protect it, and so I did."

The thing that Malak cannot say is that maybe part of the reason she did it was because she knew it would hurt him, and it was the cruelest thing she could do to him after his long days of cruelty toward her. But she will never say this out loud to anyone.

The day moves again, the sun hangs lower in the sky.

They lie back, somehow all of them touching in one way or another. An arm resting on a leg. A foot touching someone's hip. In these gentle movements of their connection, they feel a circle join back together.

On the other side of London, Harry asks his parents if he can join them in church and, leaning on a hard wooden pew, he throws thanks up to the sky with all his strength that the woman he loves has come back to him with the help of the women she loves, and he asks God to bless all three of them. Vivian steals a glance at her son, whose face is turned up to God, and wonders what he is so thankful for. Two hundred and sixty miles away, Lewis steps through his front door, finally back home, and feels Zee jump on him in greeting and, although he doesn't believe that anything exists above them, he believes in the woman wrapped around him and thinks how grateful he is, sending it into the universe anyway, maybe to the stars. Back in Cambridge, Abida is cleaning out her chest of drawers, ready to take it into the kitchen to decorate; she is thinking of painting small orange flowers along the sides when she notices that the bracelet for Bilquis's wedding day is gone. She runs her fingers over the space it used to be in and smiles slowly, remembering the day her husband came home far later than he should have. She is glad she married that man. She quickly wraps her dupatta over her head and bends down into two ruku, thanking God for sending him to her. Downstairs, Itasham bends his body in half, placing his forehead on the prayer mat, throwing his thanks up as high as he can, grateful that although they were words of anger, some words have been exchanged between mother and daughter and that is enough for today. In his bedroom, Hakim smiles as Saba messages him back agreeing, *Yes, let's visit her soon, before the baby is born.*

Fourteen streets away, Evie and Nidal sway slowly in one another's arms, the house finally empty of guests and family, and they whisper thankful prayers together, glad their daughter is safe now, "Alhamdulillah, alhamdulillah," passed back and forth between them like kisses. Sixteen streets away, Malak's parents sit on different levels in the house, suddenly glad that although they haven't always been happy, they have each other and no one had left anyone standing at the top of an aisle. On the other side of the city, Mohammed scrolls through the messages he's saved from Jenna, the ones that had made him excited about life, and decides that he no longer wants any distractions. He is a man focused only on his career. He never tells anyone that on what was supposed to be his wedding night, he stayed in the marital suite they had booked because it was too late to cancel and had cried until dawn cracked its way through the window. He doesn't even tell the woman he eventually marries ten years later.

Sixty-four miles away, London enters its only quiet period, between 4 and 5:30 in the morning, and at 4:15 a.m. exactly, Kees's phone softly calls them awake and the three women in one bed, each one slotted into one another, stir.

"It's time for Fajar," whispers Kees. "Go back to sleep, I'm just going to pray."

"Can I pray with you?" asks Jenna for the first time and a surprised Kees agrees.

"Can you do it in here so I can listen?" asks Malak, and Kees and Jenna both nod.

Back in Cairo, the imam of Al-Azhar mosque uncurls his old bones, the way he does every morning, and after washing the dreams from his eyes, heads over to the mihrab, flicking the same switch he has been pressing for forty-seven years, and placing his hands on either side of his face, fingertips resting over his ears, he leans his head back and begins the morning call, the cat curled up at his feet. Across the world, wherever the dawn is beginning to break at that moment in time, phones light up, clocks flash, imams face Mecca, microphones click on, people creep out of bed, some stand shoulder to shoulder and others just listen while the call rings out in houses and across cities, vibrating above them all in a perfect symphony: "God is great! God is great! God is great! God is great!"

Acknowledgments

I believe the world is split into two types of people: those who don't read the acknowledgments, and those who will devour every single word on every single page of a book. If you are the latter and you have stayed until the credits have rolled, my first thank you is to *you*. You're my kind of kindred spirit.

I have never considered a book finished until I've read the acknowledgments and the About the Author section, and, just in case, turned over every one of those blank pages at the end of a book that are in there for reasons I have yet to understand.

I have also been known to roll my eyes at some acknowledgments while wondering if it was strictly necessary for the author to thank everyone they'd ever met in their life…but then I wrote a book and realized that yes, yes it was. Because writing a book is a terrible, back-breaking, sweat-inducing, glorious, awful thing to do, and without the help of the people around you, it can really break your heart.

So, let me begin by thanking my agent, Florence Rees, for sending that first email and starting what I know I will describe in later years as one of the most important relationships of my life. Thank you for believing in my story, and for believing me when I told you I had "basically written it" even though there were only three chapters in the bank. Thank you for your tireless reading of drafts and for your sharp observations. For not batting an eyelid when I firmly laid out my life plans to you and asked if you wanted to be a part of them. I owe you the biggest thanks.

Thank you to my editors Sam Eades, Seema Mahanian, and Zoe Yang. It's been a dream to be surrounded by your love, care, diligence, and enthusiasm for this book. Seema, Zoe, I know I fought you on a lot of the edits, but you made this book so much better. Thank you for always talking me round.

To the entire team at Orion, I could just kiss you. Thank you to Cait Davies and Leanne Oliver for your marketing and publicity genius and your willingness to go along with my grand plans. When I said we should have party bags at the book launch, just like the kind you used to get at kid's birthday parties, you just shrugged and said, "Yeah why not," and I have a lot of respect for that. Thank you to Georgia Goodall for understanding my hatred of dashes and for talking me down off the entirely irrational but hysterical ledge I was sitting on.

A big thank you to the publicity team at Grand Central for your work and dedication, and for making my day over and over again. I want to sit down and feed you all cake.

Thank you also to everyone else across Trapeze, Orion, and Grand Central; it truly takes a village to publish a book and I'm honored to have you in mine.

This book exists around the world today because strangers who I'd never met before loved it, gushed about it, and then sold it internationally. So a thousand thanks to Alexandra McNicoll, Prema Raj, and the foreign rights team at AM Heath. Not that I want to go all Jackie Wilson on you, but your love for my book truly lifted me higher and higher.

I owe a huge debt of gratitude to Richard Scriven for reading the earliest versions of this book, and despite the fact that it was truly terrible, continuing to encourage me to write it. You lied about how good it was, Richard, but those lies kept me going and allowed me to write something far better; thank you. Since we met over a campfire in Iceland some decades ago, your friendship has been a constant and beautiful presence in my life.

Thank you to my darling friend Linda Mackessy for believing in me as a writer and in this book so wholeheartedly. While you unfailingly take the piss out of me (and admittedly your impressions of me are hilarious), thank you for never joking about the one thing that's so important to me: my writing.

Thank you to Linda Ayoola for your belief in me. It was so unwavering that even when I doubted myself, I took great courage from your belief and the knowledge that you're always right about these things.

And lastly, but no less importantly, thank you to Lewis for picking up the phone that night.

Reading Group Guide

Discussion Questions

1. Malak, Kees, and Jenna's deep friendship is one of unshakable love and honesty. Discuss why you believe Kees and Malak's differing views about chasing tradition, family, and community approval was the reason for their fracture.

2. These three women are working to hold on to the different parts of themselves—which sometimes contradict one another—to create an authentic life. Discuss your own experiences in having to negotiate and reconcile conflicting parts of your own identity.

3. Discuss Kees and her sister Saba's differing views on marriage, love, and relationships.

4. How do Jenna's views on love and sex stand in contrast to Kees and Malak's? How do you think Jenna's mother's revelation toward the end of the novel would have influenced her behavior had they had these conversations earlier?

5. Describe the ways in which Malak and her life change once she moves to Cairo. Why do you think this change had such an impact, and how does the city affect her sense of self?

6. What did the author mean by the line, "It never fails to amaze her that the real C-word for white people is culture and once it's mentioned people compete to show their respect for it or their knowledge of it"? Discuss whether that resonates with you and your experiences.

7. What were Jacob's motives when he went to Kees and told her the news of Harry's eventual proposal. How do you feel about his involvement in this moment?

8. By the novel's end, all three women have gone through a difficult situation or traumatic event independently. In what ways do you see that being alone impacted their decisions in these situations?

9. Discuss the scene between Kees and her father before the nikah and how that affects Kees's feelings about proceeding to marry Harry? How do you think this impacted your appreciation of her parents' relationship—the sometimes silent but resounding support for each other?

10. Discuss the way the novel's depiction of friendship resonated with you. What does Malak, Kees, and Jenna's relationship say about the bonds of female friendship, as well as regrets, forgiveness, and chosen family?

Author Q&A

1. What inspired you to write *These Impossible Things*?

I did my master's thesis on the representation of Muslims across Western literature and the conclusion just irritated me so much I had to write this book. After studying literature from the UK, the U.S., and Australia for twelve months, I couldn't find me and my friends anywhere. Muslim women didn't exist outside of the narrative of honor killings and terrorism and I couldn't relate to any of the characters I read about. I wanted to see myself and my friends. I wanted to see characters who just happened to be Muslim instead of it being the sole focus of the work.

2. Jenna, Malak, and Kees have very different personalities. What drew you to these particular characterizations and how they work together for the story you were trying to tell?

I don't know if it's a northern thing, but me and my friends all grew up teasing each other. My girlfriends are whip-smart, sharp, and hilarious, and I wanted to put all of that into the characters in the book. I wanted to convey that sense of deeply rooted bonds, the kind that allows you to really laugh at your friends while loving them entirely, which is where lots of their traits come from.

3. Who are some of your favorite writers, and did they influence the way you wrote *These Impossible Things*?

Hanya Yanagihara and Lisa Taddeo are the queens of my heart. I would walk to the ends of this earth to read what they write. I wish I could say they influenced my writing, but I wouldn't be so presumptuous. When I'm writing I have a strict rule of not reading anyone else's work because I specifically don't want to be influenced by their work or my longing to write as well as the people I'm reading.

4. What were some of the harder moments to write in *These Impossible Things*? What moments were easier to get down on the page?

The hardest moments are the mundane details that have to be included to let the reader know the facts. What month it is, the weather, the logistical information that gets a character from A to B. I find them dull and uninspiring. It's a little bit like doing the laundry, a boring task that just needs to be done.

The easiest parts were the saddest parts. Writing out pain and heartbreak and fear comes worryingly easy to me. I have always joked about my wasted heart, but perhaps it came in handy here.

5. These scenes where Malak is in Cairo are immersive and lush with description. What is your connection to this city, and what made you want to write Malak there?

Well, I was born in Cairo and have a lot of family there, so it's home. I also lived there for a few years after university and it was some of the best and worst days of my life. Cairo is a place that can drive you mad if you let it, but if you don't fight her, and if you give in to the chaos, she'll make you feel more alive than you ever have been. That's Cairo for me.

Malak goes through such a transformative period in the novel and I wanted that transformation to happen far away from home and everything familiar, because I think you can't grow into yourself fully when tied to old things and old places.

6. *These Impossible Things* is an honest exploration of the inter-sectionality of women of color. What drew you to writing the two main love interests as white men?

Ha, that's a story for another book. However, the short answer is I grew up watching friend after friend fall for men who were white non-Muslims, and it always ended in heartbreak. I wanted to tell that story, but also the story of what happens when you decide to break all the rules and stay with that man. What life could have been like for many Muslim women if they'd stayed with the men they loved, and perhaps it wouldn't have been the catastrophe we'd all been raised to believe it would be.

7. This novel is a love letter to friendship. How do you feel about the way female friendship is portrayed in media today and what did you want this novel to achieve in the way it represented Jenna, Malak, and Kees's bond?

We're getting better at portraying female friendships but we're still a long way off. Growing up the residing stereotype was still that women are catty and competitive with one another, when in truth, women save each other every day. I would still be on a bathroom floor somewhere crying if it hadn't been for the women in my life. I owe them so much of who I am and what I've been able to achieve. It was crucial that the heartbeat of the novel was those friendships and how when their ties dissolve, life can begin to unravel. Every woman needs her girlfriends, more than she needs men and her family. And that's what I wanted to convey.

8. Did you learn something new about yourself in the process of writing *These Impossible Things*?

That I can write a novel a lot quicker than I thought I could and, really, I should get on with writing lots more.

VISIT **GCPClubCar.com** to sign up for the **GCP Club Car** newsletter, featuring exclusive promotions, info on other **Club Car** titles, and more.

About the Author

Salma El-Wardany is a writer, poet, and BBC broadcaster. As a half-Egyptian, half-Irish woman, her work focuses on telling the stories of women, especially women of color, that have for so long been ignored. She has contributed to the anthology *It's Not About the Burqa*, and her writing has also appeared in *Huffington Post* and *Metro* and she has given two TedxTalks.